College life 101;

Freshman Orientation

J.B. Vample

Book One

The College life series

COLLEGE LIFE 101-FRESHMAN ORIENTATION

Printed in the United States of America

First Printing, 2015

ISBN-10:   0996981713 (eBook edition)
ISBN-13:   978-0-9969817-1-2 (eBook edition)

ISBN-10:   0996981705 (Paperback edition)
ISBN-13:   978-0-9969817-0-5 (Paperback edition

For information contact; email: JBVample@yahoo.com

Book cover design by: Najla Qamber Designs

Dedicated to my sister Jawhara—my first and most loyal reader—Thanks for staying on my back about these "documents".

Chapter 1

"Hey honey, do you need any help with anything?" Mrs. Howard asked. She stood for a moment, watching her youngest child and only daughter pack.

"No Mama. I'm fine," Sidra replied, satisfied as she placed the last of her meticulously folded and expensive blouses into an oversized suitcase. Sidra liked wearing the best brands, and – thanks to her family's upper-middle class status – she indulged quite often. The pretty brown skinned eighteen-year-old was considered the epitome of class and style: elegant, ladylike, well-mannered, but never hesitating to curse a person out if she had to.

"I'm very proud of you, you know," Sidra's mother gushed. Their close relationship wasn't hard to work at; being the only two women in the house, it came naturally.

"I know that Mama. You've told me about a hundred times already," Sidra responded, a trace of frustration in her voice.

"Well. I *am*," Mrs. Howard reiterated with a big smile as she sat down on her daughter's perfectly made bed. Sidra had always been a bit of a neat freak, a trait that she had picked up from her mother. "And maybe it's my hearing, but do I detect a bit of frustration in your voice?"

Sidra sighed and sat down next to her mother. "I'm sorry Mama. It's just that I'm so nervous about going away to college. Virginia seems so far away from Wilmington. I'm not saying that I don't *want* to go, but still…"

"Sweetie, I know how you feel. That's how *I* felt when *I* went away for the first time. But despite how you feel, it'll be a great experience. You'll learn new things, you'll make great friends, and you might even meet your future husband there," she replied. Sidra smiled at the thought of meeting the love of her life. "But Princess, you better finish school first before you get married and have children, do you hear me?" She continued sternly.

"Mama, calm down. I don't even have a boyfriend yet, and you're already talking about *marriage*. Can I get to the school first?" Sidra said with a laugh.

"I'm not playing with you Princess," Mrs. Howard continued.

Sidra kept laughing as she put her arm around her mother and hugged her.

"I hear you," she replied, putting her head on her mother's shoulder.

"Sidra I'm serious – don't come home with any babies," her mother warned sternly.

Sidra's head popped up "Mama!"

"I can't wait until you're out of my house for good." Brenda Parker sneered, making no attempt to mask her hostility.

"That makes *two* of us," Chasity mumbled angrily.

Arguments were nothing new in the Parker household. Eighteen-year-old Chasity had never gotten along with her mother; she was always told that she was never liked and never wanted. Whenever she could, she escaped to her aunt Patrisha in Florida or her grandmother in Pennsylvania. Now she was packing up the remainder of her things. She knew that she wasn't going to be returning home to Tucson any time soon. She was leaving for Pennsylvania the next morning and from there she would drive to Paradise Valley University. Chasity would be taking everything she owned, one bad attitude, and a very bad temper.

"What? I didn't hear you, smart ass. What did you say?" her mother questioned angrily.

Chasity tossed her bag on the bed, turned, and looked at her mother. "I said that makes two of us," she spat. "I can't stand you and your screwed-up attitude."

"My attitude? *My* attitude?!" Brenda Parker screamed in outrage.

"Who else am I talking to?" Chasity retorted smartly.

"Please, bitch; *you're* the one with the damn attitude. Walking around here like everyone owes you everything."

"*Bitch*? See, that's the stuff I'm talking about. What mother stands there and calls her daughter a bitch?" Chasity countered, folding her arms. "*I'll* tell you what kind, Brenda. The kind who's a miserable, lazy, pathetic, life-wasting drunk. You've treated me like a mistake my whole life, and you wonder why I have such a bad attitude. Screw you."

"Oh, spare me the sad story, Chasity." Chasity rolled her eyes at her mother's nasty tone. "You have everything any girl could want – good looks, nice clothes, money. You're just an ungrateful, spoiled brat."

"Yeah? And not *one* of those things that you just mentioned was given to me by *you*."

Chasity looked her mother up and down. She was right; the money and all of her possessions had been given to her not by her parents, but by her aunt Patrisha. Chasity didn't even look much like her mother – more like her aunt. Brenda and her aunt were both tall, but Chasity had Patrisha's long black hair, light-brown skin, delicate features and slender frame. It was no wonder that Chasity was wanted by guys and hated by girls. She didn't care.

"Just shut the hell up and get out my house now!" Brenda screamed.

"You yelling at me isn't gonna make me move any damn faster," Chasity spat. "I'll leave when I'm done; now get out of my face."

Brenda grabbed her daughter's arm and gave her a cold look. Chasity returned it in kind, one of the few traits they shared.

"If you don't take your hand off my arm, I *will* hurt you," Chasity threatened in a low tone.

"You try it, and I'll break your arm, right here and now."

"What? Is that supposed to scare me?" Chasity asked, casually glancing up and down her mother's tall, solid frame. "You can't beat me anymore; now let go," she demanded, not blinking once.

Her mother dropped her arm and stood there as Chasity pushed past her and walked out of the room.

In a large single-family house in Baltimore, Malajia Simmons danced around her bedroom, singing along at the top of her lungs to the music blasting from the radio. Excitement overwhelmed her as the day had finally arrived. She was packing, getting ready to leave for college. To celebrate, she'd dyed her naturally brown hair a deep wine color, and had it cut into a short, trendy bob. She was hoping the style would make her look more sophisticated.

Malajia's older sister Geri stomped into the room and turned off the radio just as Malajia was in mid-scream. "God girl. You so cannot sing," Geri said with a laugh.

"Girl please, it sounds better than *your* singing," Malajia shot back playfully. Of her six sisters, Malajia was closet with Geri.

"You can hear that music half way down the block," Geri replied as she flopped down on the bed.

"NO!" Malajia screamed, causing Geri to jump up quickly.

"What!"

"You sat on my brand new dress," she complained, before rescuing the short, sexy, burgundy strapless dress from any harm.

"I take it that Dad hasn't seen your new wardrobe," Geri said.

"Are you crazy? He would kill me if he saw my new clothes. Either that, or he would take away my rights to his credit card, which would be *like* killing me," she replied. Their father was very protective of his daughters. If he only knew that he had good reason to worry. In high school, Malajia would hide her skimpy wardrobe in her book bag and change at school; she would call boys while she spent a night a friend's house, and she would sneak out to the mall alone in order to meet up with her guy friends, or buy the clothes that she wanted.

With six sisters, Malajia craved attention growing up. She didn't care what anyone thought of her, as long as they *thought* of her. She carefully selected her wardrobe to show off her figure in ways her parents would never in a million years consider appropriate—short miniskirts, bustiers, crop tops, plunging necklines, and backless halters. If a story or event was lame to her, a little exaggeration never hurt. Friends and family never quite knew whether her stories were accurate, or enhanced.

Geri shook her head and smiled. "The new hair color looks good on you."

Malajia spun around and struck a pose. "I know right?" she boasted. "Doesn't it complement my complexion?"

Geri narrowed her eyes at her sister. Sure the color complemented Malajia's brown skin tone and brought out her big brown eyes. But the girl never could take a complement without adding her vain comments. "Never mind, I take it back."

Malajia giggled at Geri's nasty tone. "Too late, you already said it," she teased.

"So are you finished packing yet?"

"Nope. Oh yeah, give me the hairdryer," Malajia said as she held her hand out.

Geri looked at her with confusion. "*What* hairdryer?"

"The white one."

"Heifer, that's *mine!*" Geri exclaimed.

"So what if it is. *You* don't need it, you have braids." Malajia argued

"So what, that's not the point. It's still mine, and when I take these things out, I would like to have my hairdryer around."

"Just give it to me, and hurry up; I need to run to the mall for some last minute accessories," Malajia prodded.

Geri looked at her for a second. "Fine, if I let you borrow it then...You have to let me try on your new dress." Geri snatched the burgundy dress off the bed and bolted out of the room.

"Noooo," Malajia whined, chasing after her sister. "You can't fit your big butt in it!"

"Jazmine, why do you always have to treat me so bad? I never do anything to you. Even though we share a room, I'm never in your way," Emily replied softly.

Emily Harris never got smart or raised her voice, this girl was too afraid to stand up for herself. She always worried that she might get her feelings hurt, or worse – get hit.

"Emily, whatever. I can't stand your whining. You act like a big-ass baby. You need to get it together and grow a damn backbone; you make me sick. Hurry up and get out," Jazmine said angrily.

"You—you know, you really h—hurt me when you talk to me that way," Emily struggled to say as her eyes started to tear up. Jazmine was right. She'd never had the backbone or confidence to stand up for herself in the family. It wasn't just Jazmine who picked on her; her brothers did too. Maybe, she thought, it was because she was the baby of the family, or maybe because they suspected that Emily was their mother's favorite.

"Aww, what's the matter Pasty face? You about to cry?" Jazmine taunted.

Emily looked down at her hands, she hated that nickname. Her sister called her that because of the simple fact that Emily's complexion was so much lighter than that of her brown skinned siblings. "Can—can you please not call me that?"

Jazmine frowned at Emily's soft voice. "Girl, just shut the—"

"What's going on in here?" Ms. Harris asked as she walked in the room, interrupting Jazmine.

"Oh nothing Mom, just helping my dear baby sister pack," Jazmine lied. Emily just looked at the floor.

"Jaz, get out."

Jazmine shrugged, but obeyed the command without any comment.

"What's wrong Emily?" Ms. Harris settled down on the bed next to her daughter.

"Nothing, I'm fine," Emily lied. How could she tell her mother that she was afraid of being on her own at college, with no one there to look out for her?

Ms. Harris pulled Emily close. Deep down, she wished that Emily didn't have to go. If it was up to her, Emily would be going to a college closer to home. *There are plenty of good schools right here in Jersey*, she thought. She was so worried about this shy, quiet child who always hid in long dresses, sweat pants, and baggy shirts. Not that they ever had much left over after paying the bills to splurge on fashion fads. Money was tight, but they did okay in the finance department.

"Your father called today," Ms. Harris said after a while.

"Really? What did he say?" Emily asked, a glimmer of hope slipping through her voice. Perhaps her dad could come and see her off after all. Even though he lived several states away, the man was still a big part of her life.

"He said that he's sorry that he can't see you off," Ms. Harris answered carefully. "But he promises to send you something in the mail," Emily smiled, but deep down she wanted to unpack everything and crawl into bed. She didn't want to be anywhere else but in her mother's arms.

The doorbell barely finished sounding when Alexandra Chisolm threw open the front door to her parents' small row house in West Philadelphia. Her two best friends had promised to drop by. In a few days, Alex would be leaving for Paradise Valley University, and they wanted to say goodbye.

Stacey and Victoria rushed in, talking immediately by way of traditional greeting.

"Alex, we just looked up the Paradise Valley campus online," Victoria said with a huge grin. "And we talked to some of the girls who go there, and they said that the campus is gorgeous, the dorms are big, and the guys down there are sexy."

"Going to college isn't just about the men, Vicki," Alex scolded, watching her friend set her bag on the couch.

"Um hmm. Coming from an old married woman," Stacey teased.

Alex laughed, "Paul and I haven't been together that long."

"Sure," Victoria commented sarcastically, "I mean it's *only* been three years."

"Oh, whatever," Alex replied with her trademark nonchalance.

"You *do* know that he's gonna start acting all weird and jealous right?" Stacey added. She looked at Alex and thought her friend was enough to catch any man's eye—tall and curvy, but toned, with a mane of shoulder-length wavy dark hair, and glowing dark skin. Paul might be justified if he started acting weird.

"Probably, but who cares," Alex responded as she twisted her thick hair into a bun. "If he had *graduated* on time, he could've been going to college too. So that's on him." The comment came as no surprise to Stacey or Victoria. Alex was bold, smart, and confident—and very opinionated. Sometimes her forthrightness got on their nerves, often because it turned out she was right.

"I'm really gonna miss you and that tell-it-like-it-is attitude, girl," Victoria confessed, "but I'm sure you'll put it to good use up at school." Stacey and Victoria often teased Alex about her maternal streak. The oldest of three children in a close-knit family, Alex slipped easily into the role of mother figure, protective and caring. And even though some thought that her protectiveness was sometimes overpowering, she made friends easily.

"I'm gonna miss you guys too, but you can always come down and visit," Alex said happily.

"Just let us know when, and we'll be there," Stacey said with a smile. "And now we are going to go and let you get back to packing."

"Okay, I'll call you two when I get settled," Alex grinned as she walked her friends to the door. "I love you both." Alex watched them leave with a broad smile on her face. She was *really* going to college.

It had been a close call.

Her family didn't have any money; Alex had always worked to help out and pay for her own things. Her wardrobe mostly consisted of jeans (preferably wide-legged or boot cut), and various tops. Although no one could call her shirts "trendy," she had flare and managed to develop her own personal style on a meager budget. Without the generous scholarship, she wouldn't be going to Paradise Valley. Student loans wouldn't have come close to covering all of her expenses. She'd still have to watch every nickel and dime, but it was going to be the greatest time of her life.

Chapter 2

Three days later, the entire freshman class, along with accompanying family members, descended on the Paradise Valley University campus. Fathers unloaded cars. Mothers asked for directions. Grandparents took pictures of everything from the gardens to the buildings. Siblings either annoyed or helped their relatives. The new freshmen checked out prospects and sized up competition as they made their way through campus—all except Chasity. She couldn't care less about what her fellow classmates were doing. She had come to college to get away from home. Chasity planned only on doing what she needed to do to graduate on time and move away permanently. She was in no mood to socialize or make any friends.

After leaving Tucson, Chasity had spent time with her grandmother in West Chester, Pennsylvania. Her aunt Patrisha had even flown up from Florida to join them. Patrisha had just bought a new house a few blocks from her grandmother. The trip gave her a chance to get the renovations started, and to take Chasity on a shopping spree that would make any of her new classmates jealous. Besides, she wanted to see Chasity's face when she gave her the keys to a brand-new black Lexus as a sending off present. It made

Patrisha happy to see Chasity get in the car for her drive to Virginia. Brenda would be so furious; the woman pigheadedly resented the close relationship that Patrisha and Chasity shared.

Although the new Lexus was easy to handle on the road and she enjoyed the alone time, she found the long drive very tiring. Chasity rubbed the weariness from her eyes as she made her way to her room in Torrence Hall, one of the newest dorms on campus.

Two others were in the process of being built, but construction could not be finished in time for this year's freshman class. With space tight and single rooms at a premium, Chasity had put in an early request. Her aunt's large donation was viewed now as extra insurance. She figured that she'd never shared a room before, and she wasn't going to start now. She had always been a loner; being the only child of a mother who hated her didn't make socializing easy.

When she was younger, Chasity had tried to make friends, despite what she was going through at home. But her peers never accepted her. Chasity learned that she didn't need people around her, and decided that she was better off alone. Even her aunt sometimes had to work to get through her tough exterior.

She went directly to her spacious room, relieved to find it equipped with a private bathroom, and dropped her bags by the door. But her relief was short lived. Her sense of ease gave way to a frown when she noticed someone sitting on the bed across the room.

Chasity snarled, "Who the hell are you and what are you doing here?"

The girl's nasty tone shocked Sidra, but she managed to keep her cool. "Well, my name is Sidra, and it appears that I am sitting on the bed," she answered evenly. She really didn't want to put up with this kind of attitude all semester.

"That's real cute," Chasity responded in a nasty tone. "Why are you in this room? I was supposed to have my own room. I *paid* for my own room and I *want* my own room."

"Um...Chasity right?" Sidra questioned as she glanced at the name listed on her room assignment. Chasity gave a slight smirk as she folded her arms. "Well Chasity, according to the office, they ran out of double rooms; and since there are so many new students this year, they decided to turn all of the single rooms into double rooms. At least until the new dorms are ready. So that means that we're roommates," Sidra continued with a forced smile. "Hello *roommate*."

Chasity shot a piercing look Sidra's way, turned on her heel, and walked out of the room without a word.

Sidra let out a long, frustrated sigh. "Seriously?" she groaned to herself.

Emily had been assigned to a triple in another dorm across campus. None of the rooms in this dorm had separate bathrooms; rather each floor was equipped with two communal bathrooms. The rooms were equally simple in furnishings. Emily looked around, trying to take it all in at once. There was one single bed, a set of bunk beds, a couple of dressers and three small desks. She was putting her things in a drawer when Alex walked in.

"Hello," she called out happily as she dragged her trunk into the spacious room.

"Hi," Emily responded with a smile.

"So I see that you've picked your side," Alex observed.

"Oh, do you want it? You can have it if you want it," Emily offered nervously.

"No, no. It's okay, I was just making conversation," Alex smiled and threw her hands up in a show of peace. "I mean no harm. I'm Alex," she said, placing her trunk against one of the dressers.

"I'm Emily." The shy response was soft and low.

"It's nice to meet you Emily."

"Same here," Emily said, pushing some of her mid-neck length, sandy brown hair behind her ears.

"Are you okay? You seem kind of sad." Alex asked, concerned.

"Oh, I'm fine, just a little nervous about starting college that's all," Emily answered, closing her drawer with her knee.

"Oh, I know what you mean," Alex commented with a wave of her hand. Before she could continue, Malajia walked in wearing sunglasses and carrying a large overnight bag. She had left the rest of her things in the car for her parents to bring up. She took off her sunglasses, and looked around.

"Three girls to a room? God this is just like being at home," she complained.

"Hello," Alex ran her fingers through her wavy hair and gave the newcomer a welcoming smile.

"Hi, I'm 'the fabulous' Malajia. Where do I sleep?" she asked with a wave of her hand.

Alex frowned slightly at the over the top introduction. "Okay, 'the fabulous' I'm Alex, her name is Emily and why in the *world* do you call yourself 'the fabulous' Malajia?" she asked, her voice brimming with laughter. Emily giggled.

Malajia rolled her eyes. "Isn't it obvious? *Look* at me," she responded striking a pose that had Alex shaking her head. "Anyway, where is my bed? And please don't tell me that those are bunk beds," Malajia protested.

"Okay, I won't," Alex shrugged and turned to grab some clothes out of her trunk.

"Oh, come on!" Malajia whined. "Can I at *least* have the bottom one?"

"No that's *mine*," Alex replied, mocking Malajia's whiny tone of voice. "You better climb that ladder 'the fabulous' because that is your bed."

Hands on her hips, Malajia looked from Alex to Emily. "Hey, Emma—"

Alex frowned. "*Emily*," she corrected on Emily's behalf.

"Oh what-ever. *Emma, Emily* they both start with the same damn letter," Malajia shot back.

"Oh? How would you like it if I started calling you Melon Ball or something other than *your* real name?" Alex argued.

"*Melon Ball?*" Malajia repeated with a frown. "*That* was corny. Anyway *Emily*, how about we trade beds?"

Emily looked down at her hands. "Well…"

"No!" Alex interrupted. She was getting very annoyed with *the fabulous* Malajia very fast. "Emily got here first and chose that bed. So shut your mouth, suck it up, and be fair."

"Who made *you* leader of the room?!" Malajia challenged, folding her arms over her chest.

"I'm *not* the leader, you just need to stop complaining, and like I said, be fair," Alex argued, holding a stubborn look on her face that dared Malajia to say something else.

"You know what? Screw that raggedy ass bed! With those ugly ass sheets. Just don't say anything to me for the rest of the day!" Malajia shouted as she stormed out of the room.

Alex looked at Emily and laughed. "We're going to have a problem with that one, Emily." Emily gave another one of her giggles.

Ms. Smith, Paradise Valley's freshman advisor and counselor, was in her office preparing for her first meeting of the day. She met with each freshman individually at the beginning of term to discuss any concerns or questions that they might have. She pulled the top file off of the pile on her desk and opened it. "Sidra Howard," she read. Looking over the comments, she thought, *at least I'm starting with an easy one*, as she asked her secretary to send in Sidra.

"Hello please take a seat," she said, indicating the chair across from her desk. Sidra walked over to the seat, smoothed her black pencil skirt with her hands, sat down and crossed her legs. "Now, Miss Howard, how are you settling in? I can give you an overview, but first I'd like to know if you have any questions or concerns."

"No Ms. Smith, I don't have any questions to ask really. I'm settling in fine," Sidra informed with a smile as she smoothed her bang out of her face.

"Are you sure? I know that attending college for the first time can be a little unnerving, so if you have anything that you want to discuss you can do it here," Ms. Smith prodded.

Sidra folded her hands over her knee and smiled brightly. "Everything is fine," she said.

"Miss Emily Harris right?" Ms. Smith quizzed.

"Yes," Emily responded. Her voice was so soft that Ms. Smith could barely hear her reply. More disturbing, she thought, the girl wouldn't look up.

"Okay. Um….." Ms. Smith searched for a look at the bowed head. "Emily, are you okay?"

"Yes," Emily repeated.

"Are you sure?"

"No."

"Okay, let's just forget about all that other stuff," Malajia forfeited, putting up a well-manicured hand. "Just tell me two things—when do the parties start and are there any cute guys?"

"Miss Simmons, that's not exactly what we're supposed to be talking about right now," Ms. Smith said in a frigid tone.

"Aww come on Betty—can I call you Betty?"

"No, you *can't*," Ms. Smith replied sternly.

"Thanks Betty," Malajia obviously had not been listening. "Now, I know that we're supposed to talk about classes and activities and stuff like that, but I'd much rather talk about the fun stuff."

Ms. Smith frowned in concern. "Miss Simmons...I am a little concerned at the fact that you have the opportunity to talk about anything here in regards to entering your first semester of college, and the only thing that you *choose* to talk about are boys and parties."

Malajia frowned in confusion. "Umm, yeah. That's what I want to talk about right now."

"Look, you already have my name on that paper, so why do I need to tell you what it is," Chasity complained without looking at Ms. Smith. "I've had a long day. I'm tired, I'm cranky and I *don't* want to be here," she continued as she examined her black and silver painted finger nails.

"My, you have quite the attitude, don't you Miss Parker?" Ms. Smith looked across the desk and folded her arms

Chasity looked up at her, frowning with frustration, gaze pointed in annoyance. "So I've been told," she replied smartly.

Ms. Smith didn't notice Alex when she came into the office. She had her head down, praying for the day to end.

"Ms. Smith, are you all right? Do you need some air?" Alex asked as she sat down across from her.

"No, no I'm fine," she said, quickly sitting up and straightening her blazer. Somehow she had lost control of the interview before it had even began.

"It's okay," Alex reassured, "If you need to talk, I'm a good listener."

"Miss Chisolm, I'm supposed to be helping *you*, not the other way around,"

"Why *not*? I mean, I don't really have any concerns or anything. Nothing that I can't handle. However, you seem to be having a hard time with some of my other classmates.

Maybe I can help," Alex prodded, sitting on the edge of her seat.

Ms. Smith pushed her glasses up on her nose. "Miss Chisolm, nothing that I have discussed with any of the other students can be discussed with *you*. So while I appreciate your need to be helpful, we really need to get this session started, All right?"

"Okay, I understand," Alex replied.

"Well I'm the youngest child, and I've never been on my own before. I don't actually *want* to be out on my own just yet," Emily confessed, fidgeting nervously with her hands.

"Well you have a lot of things to look forward to. There's independence, freedom to make your own choices—it's a big world out there. There's a lot to explore and learn about," Ms. Smith assured with a smile. "You can take it slowly."

Emily just sat there, a worried look still on her face.

"Miss Howard, you don't have *any* concerns? No questions about your major? No worries about campus life? Nothing?" Ms. Smith asked.

"No." Sidra held her smile and polite tone, even though she was growing tired of the constant questions.

"So everything is fine?"

Sidra chuckled, "With all due respect Ms. Smith, why does it seem like you find that hard to believe?"

"Miss Howard, my intention is not to insult you by making it seem like I don't believe what you're saying. However, it seems to me like you're putting on a façade— this prim and proper façade."

"I'm sorry, what do you mean by *façade* exactly?" Sidra questioned as she gave a slight frown. "Are you implying that I'm being fake?"

"No, Miss Howard, I'm not calling you fake. I am just saying that it seems like you could have a different personality underneath of what you're presenting."

"Okay, yes. When faced with stressful situations I have a tendency to show a different side of my personality. However I'm not, nor have I *ever* been, fake." Sidra resented the fact that because she carried herself in a certain manner, that people assumed that she was being phony.

"Now, can you look at this sexy outfit and tell me if it will attract guys?"

Malajia stood up and proceeded to model her outfit for a visibly annoyed Ms. Smith.

"Miss Simmons please, we have to—"

"And check out my new walk," Malajia persisted, cutting off Ms. Smith and strolling across the room in long sexy strides.

"Miss Simmons, I suggest that you re-think your priorities."

Malajia stopped walking. "I don't follow." The girl looked perplexed. She didn't understand why she had to be so serious at this moment.

"You are more concerned with being seen, rather than thinking about what's actually important; such as your major, or your classes. You're coming off as very shallow."

So you're judging me, Malajia thought. She had to deal with people judging her due to how she dressed and acted every day of her life. It started with her parents; they always assumed the worst of her. They always tried to tell her how she should or shouldn't act, but Malajia refused to be placed in a neat little box. She didn't feel the need to take everything so seriously; if she wanted to spend her day talking about guys and parties, she was going to do just that.

"I'm far from shallow Ms. Smith, I just don't feel the need to be so serious. Granted, this is college, and it's about studying and passing classes. But it's also about having fun, meeting new people, and trying new things. I, for one, plan on taking advantage of my *entire* college experience."

"And you *should* take advantage of the entire college experience. But, the way that you've chosen to start out might not lead you into the direction you want to go."

"Okay…That's your opinion, and you are entitled to it. However, I am not going to stop being me, no matter *how* I come off."

Chasity let out a frustrated sigh. She had grown tired of this meeting.

"Yes, I know that I have an anger problem. It's nothing new to me."

"I really feel that you may benefit from some anger management sessions," Ms. Smith suggested.

"No, I think I manage my anger quite well actually," she hissed.

"The fact that you are comfortable with being so angry doesn't concern you, Miss Parker?"

"Nope."

"Really? Not even a little bit?" Ms. Smith persisted.

"Nope," Chasity repeated defiantly.

Ms. Smith rubbed the bridge of her nose with her fingers. This girl was making her job very difficult. She'd never had to encounter a student with so much attitude.

"Miss Parker, you come off as being very abrasive. But it makes me wonder if this is just a defense mechanism. I find it hard to believe that there isn't an ounce of softness underneath all of that anger."

Chasity narrowed her eyes slightly. She didn't need anyone to try to figure her out. She just wanted to be left alone.

"Are we done?" she asked, trying hard to keep calm. It was in her nature to fly off the handle at the drop of a dime; it didn't matter who or where it was. However she figured that this wasn't the time or the place for her to let her temper flare. It wouldn't be smart to wind up kicked out of school on her first day.

"Miss Parker, I wouldn't be doing my job if I didn't suggest that we try to explore where all of this hostility is coming from. I find it hard to believe that you were born this way. Would you be willing to explore this?"

"Nope." Chasity smirked, relishing the fact that she was annoying Ms. Smith for her efforts.

"Alexandra, let's just finish the meeting," Ms. Smith suggested.

"I have a small favor to ask, please don't call me that. Call me Alex, I can't stand the name Alexandra, and I don't know what my parents were thinking when they named me *that*," Alex said with a laugh, and rocked back in her chair. "Aside from that, things are fine with me. I mean I've only been here for a few hours so there isn't much to be concerned about," she paused as if she meant to finish, but finally the words came tumbling out. "Well, the only thing is, I think that one of my roommates may be an issue."

"How so?"

"Well, first off, she came in there like she was walking in a fashion show. Then she tried to persuade our other roommate to give up her bed and I had to tell her to back off and be fair. "

"Did your other roommate tell her that she couldn't have her bed? Or did you put yourself into their confrontation?"

"Well…I jumped in it only because my other roommate wasn't saying anything. And I didn't want the girl's bed to be taken just because she was too nervous to object. That wouldn't have been fair, would it?"

Alex squirmed in her seat as Ms. Smith jotted down some notes on to her notepad. She became uneasy after she hadn't heard a response from her for a few seconds. "Is something wrong?"

"No Alex, nothing is wrong. I'm just making an observation."

"And what have you observed exactly?"

"Well, to be honest, you seem to be kind of intrusive."

Alex was shocked by her response, and it showed on her face. "I'm sorry, but did you say intrusive? As in *pushy*?" she asked. "I don't think that I'm pushy."

"Maybe I used the wrong word," Ms. Smith amended. "I should have said that you seem to be the type of person who inserts herself in other people's issues. Like you *have* to be the one to fix the problem. For example, instead of letting your roommates hash out their issue, you felt the need to step in and resolve it for them."

Alex pondered Ms. Smith's words. "Well I admit that I do tend to feel the need to fix everyone's issues. I don't like to see people hurt or angry. I'm the oldest child in my family so I'm just used to taking on that motherly role when it comes to people. Is that a bad thing?"

"No, I don't think it's a bad thing. I do suggest that you watch who you try to force that role on. Not everyone will be receptive of that. Not everyone needs another mother figure or needs someone to fix their problem for them."

"I just feel that if someone is important to me, it's my duty to make sure that they are okay. I can't change that part of me."

Emily started to cry, "I want to go home."

"But you just got here!" Ms. Smith exclaimed alarmed at the scene.

"I don't care. Please call my Mom. She can come get me."

"Emily, while I understand that you're scared, I don't think that running away will solve your problem."

"I just don't think I'll fit in here," Emily sniffled, wiping her eyes.

"Well how will you know for sure if you don't make an effort to get out there and explore this world?"

"I'm just...scared."

Chapter 3

Sidra spotted a row of five seats in the crowded auditorium. Talking and laughter from eager freshmen radiated off of the beautifully renovated walls and ceilings. Housed in Brandywine Hall, the former theater also housed several classrooms for the Arts. Relieved that she hadn't stalled after leaving her meeting with Ms. Smith, she made a beeline for them. Standing through freshman orientation would have been a nuisance. She settled into one of the cushy seats and spotted two classmates heading her way, obviously intent on grabbing the empty seats in Sidra's row.

"Wow, what a turnout," Alex said, setting her book bag down on the floor. The girl in the seat next to her was fixing her ponytail with her hands, which already looked pretty good to Alex. "Hello, I'm Alex."

Sidra dropped her hands and looked over. "Hi, Alex; it's nice to meet you. I'm Sidra," she replied cheerfully. She leaned forward and smiled at the girl with Alex. "Hello," she acknowledged with a wave.

"Hi, my name is Emily."

"So Sidra, what do you think so far? Do you like it here?" Alex fanned herself with a notepad. There were so many bodies; the auditorium was starting to heat up.

"Yeah, I do actually. The campus is pretty, the people are nice...well, my roommate's a bitch, but I can't do anything about *that*," Sidra said. "What about *you*? How are you making out?"

"I love it so far. One of my roommates is a character, but it's nothing that I can't handle," Alex replied with a little laugh.

Malajia and Chasity arrived at the same time with the other last-minute stragglers. Without acknowledging each other; they walked over and claimed the empty seats next to Sidra.

"Hello, roommate," Sidra greeted, drawing out the syllables with delight. She knew full well that Chasity didn't want anything to do with her. Chasity shot her a lethal glare, sharp with attitude. Sidra, suppressing a smirk, just shook her head.

"So, 'the fabulous,' how has your day been so far?" Alex asked with feigned innocence.

"Very damn funny, heifer," Malajia barked, sitting back in her seat. "You can stop making fun of my name, too."

"I'm sorry, but *you* were the one who introduced yourself as 'the fabulous Malajia.' What am I supposed to do? You left yourself wide open; I couldn't resist," Alex explained, a hint of laughter in her voice.

"Shut up," Malajia ordered, adjusting the strap on her shirt. "I'm in no mood for your crap. I've already had to deal with that annoying freshman counselor."

"Yeah, I had to see her, too," Alex replied.

"She tried to catch an attitude with me and I said to her 'look Betty—'"

Alex looked at her. "Who?" she asked, puzzled.

"Betty," Malajia replied.

"Who is Betty?" Alex questioned with confusion.

"The counselor."

Alex thought for a second before exclaiming, "Girl, her name is Mary!"

Malajia stared at Alex for a few seconds before comprehension set in. "Soooo, her name isn't Betty?"

"Girl, you're crazy," Alex said flatly, and dissolved into a fit of laughter.

Sidra, curious to discover what Alex found so funny, bent forward and noticed the girl sitting so stiffly next to Alex, the girl Alex called "Malajia." *I know that name*, she thought. Surprise flashed across her face as she made the connection.

"Oh, my, god!" Sidra exclaimed. "Malajia I'm-as-easy-as-I-look Simmons?"

Malajia let her glance roam over Sidra; taking in the perfect posture, her perfectly styled ponytail, the elegant, royal blue sleeveless silk shirt, the immaculate manicure. *Who the hell wears silk to a freshman orientation in a damn auditorium?* she thought. "Well, well; if it isn't Sidra I-have-a-stick-up-my-ass Howard," she ground out.

Sidra sucked her teeth. *Seriously?* she thought, *of all the colleges in this country, we had to pick the same one.* She had known Malajia for years. Right up until their second year of high school, they had been friends. Then the arguments started, and they drifted apart. They didn't have anything in common anymore; their new personalities and interests clashed. It was a relief when Malajia and her family moved to Baltimore.

"So I take it that you two know each other," Alex concluded.

Sidra rolled her eyes, "Unfortunately, yes."

"You act like knowing *you* is a joy," Malajia snapped.

Sidra huffed, "Still loud and extra."

"And *you* still overdress," Malajia shot back.

"Ah, here we go with the comments about my damn clothes." Sidra dismissed her negative comments by elegantly tossing her hands in the air. All through high school she had been the butt of snide remarks. She ignored them and never attempted to dress down.

"So? You started it, you snobby, prissy, freak," Malajia shot back, pointing at her.

Emily hated it when people argued, and petty arguments simply annoyed Chasity. Both girls, so unalike in personalities, reacted in a similar fashion. They turned away, trying to pretend that Sidra and Malajia were not sitting a couple of feet away.

"Come on you two, that's enough," Alex interrupted, her patience exhausted. Malajia and Sidra startled, stopped arguing, and sat back like two children whose mother had told them to be quiet. "We're in college now," Alex reminded. "Whatever happened between you two in the past needs to *stay* there."

"Whatever Alexandra," Malajia responded acerbically. "Save that nonsense for this girl over here," she advised, pointing to Chasity. "She looks like she needs a good talking to."

"Bitch, I'll beat that fake ass hair color off your head," Chasity threatened, gesturing to Malajia's burgundy locks.

"I'd pay to see *that*." Sidra cracked up laughing.

Malajia rolled her eyes at Sidra, then focused on Chasity. "Was that really necessary?"

"You shouldn't have said anything to me. That was *your* mistake," Chasity pointed out.

Alex decided to diffuse the situation. She leaned over and introduced herself to the sullen girl. "Hey, I'm Alex. What's your name?"

"Why are you talking to me?" Chasity snarled with a cold bluntness that took Alex aback. Chasity had insulted Malajia, but Alex figured it was payback for saying something smart to her first. She didn't think that she would snap over a simple introduction.

"Alex, this ball of sunshine is my roommate Chasity," Sidra interjected in a not-so-enthused tone.

"You won't be my roommate for long," Chasity threatened.

"What are you going to do? Kill me? Because that's the *only* way that you're going to get me out of that room," Sidra shot back.

"Don't tempt me Princess," Chasity warned.

"Will you two stop it?" Alex butted in sternly, her patience worn out. "Can we all just start over? I think that if we can do that, then we're all gonna end up being the best of friends."

The four girls stared at her, dumbfounded at the insane suggestion.

Alex shrugged, "We *could*," she maintained.

Chapter 4

After orientation, each girl went back to her dorm room. Sidra was sitting in her room, talking on the phone to her mother, when Chasity walked in.

"Okay, I'll talk to you later Mama...I know, I'll try to talk to her...Yeah...Bye."

Hanging up the phone, she looked over at Chasity; she was sitting on her bed looking at her class schedule. *I really need to find something to say to her*, she thought. Sidra hated awkward silences.

Chasity looked up, catching Sidra's stare. "What the fuck are you looking at?" she hissed. She couldn't stand being stared at. It always rubbed her the wrong way and Chasity never hesitated to retaliate.

"Oh my god! Why are you so damn hostile? I was just about to say something to you," Sidra explained, putting her hand up.

"What the hell was taking you so damn long?" Chasity asked, anger still lacing her words.

"Your damn attitude is what took me so long. Do you treat everyone you come in contact with like this?"

"Pretty much," Chasity admitted.

Sidra took a deep breath. "Look, Chasity, we're going to be living together for a whole year." She struggled to remain calm. "Can we please at least *try* to be civil towards each other?"

"No," Chasity answered bluntly, then stood up and walked to the bathroom.

"Be that way then!" Sidra shouted after her.

"Oh, don't worry I will," Chasity punctuated her response with a sharp slam of the bathroom door.

Frustrated, Sidra flopped down on her bed, and began punching her pillow.

Later that evening, just around ten, Alex and Malajia were getting ready to go to a campus party.

"Em, do you want to go?" Alex asked, slipping a shirt over her head.

"Uh sweetie, what's up with your shirt?" Malajia looked at her with disgust.

Alex had on a cute pair of jeans, but the shirt? She liked the way it hung off of one shoulder, but the color. Not at all.

"What's wrong with my shirt?" Alex asked, puzzled. The shirt, one of her few new purchases, was a favorite.

"Come on Alex, the shirt is cute, but *brown*? Eww girl, brown is so dull," Malajia commented with her nose turned up.

"No it's not. Your skin color is brown, are you saying that *you're* dull?" Alex demanded.

"Never will I *ever* be dull, fine as I am," Malajia boasted, running her hands down the sides of her short, red skater skirt.

"Girl please," Alex protested. "Anyway Emily, are you sure you don't want to go with us?"

"No thanks, I'm just gonna stay here and finish putting up my things. But you two have fun," Emily replied, sitting on her bed.

"Wait a minute. Are you telling me that you're willing to pass up a college party, where you can meet plenty of cute guys, to stay here and unpack your crap?" Malajia questioned, unconvinced.

"Well, I..." Emily couldn't get the words out; she was too embarrassed. Here she was in college, and she was going to hide in her room like a middle-school child.

"Leave her alone Malajia. She doesn't have to go if she doesn't want to," Alex jumped in.

"Can you keep your mouth shut and let the girl speak for herself?" Malajia argued.

Alex narrowed her eyes for a second. "Let's just go," she said sternly; one hand pointed at the door.

"Fine Alexandra, let's be out," Malajia agreed, leading the way.

"Don't call me that," Alex complained with a laugh before waving goodbye to Emily.

Already in the hallway, neither girl heard Emily's soft sigh as the door closed behind them.

About an hour later, the campus gym was packed. Music blared from the speakers at both ends. The high tempo hip-hop track was great and tempted almost everyone onto the floor, even without partners. Sidra didn't have that problem. No sooner had she finished dancing with one guy then another, intent on a dance, popped up behind her.

"No I'm fine, thanks. Maybe later," she said walking off the floor. She needed a breather. It was getting a little too hot for her.

Malajia had paired off with a tall, dark guy; the way her arms were locked around his neck, it was safe to say she was having a good time—until, that is, Alex accidentally-on-purpose bumped her. Malajia stopped dead, extricated herself from her handsome partner, and stormed after Alex.

"What the hell was *that* for?" she asked angrily, moving some of her hair out of her face with her hand.

"Sorry, I didn't see you," Alex lied.

"Sorry? Do you see that guy over there? Do you see how sexy he is? He was just about to ask me out." Malajia fumed, pointing to the guy.

"Ask you out? Oh, I don't think so sweetie," Alex stated flatly.

"Are you kidding? Do you see me? Do you see how gorgeous I am?" Malajia retorted, her vanity surfacing with its customary regularity. "He'd be *crazy not* to ask me out."

"Malajia, *I'm* not looking at you, so shut up." When Malajia turned to walk away, Alex grabbed her arm. "Don't go back over there with him," Alex cautioned. "Seriously sis. He has a girlfriend. A *big* girlfriend, who seems to be *very* jealous of anyone with better looks. Leave him alone, okay?"

"Please, I'll beat the fat off her," she said confidently. Then she spotted the guy, leaning against the gym wall with a girl standing next to him. Malajia's mouth dropped open. She locked eyes with Alex.

"*Her?*" she whispered. "She's freakin huge."

"Oh yeah," Alex nodded.

"Shit, what the hell does she *eat?*" Malajia wondered, shocked at the odd pairing. "To hell with that, she can have him. He better stop dancing with other girls before she eats *him.*"

The parking lot next to Chasity's dorm was full. She circled round and round, trying to find a convenient spot. Nothing turned up any closer than the gym parking lot. *This is some straight bullshit*, she thought. A long hike back to the dorm was not on her preferred agenda.

Suddenly, a guy came out of nowhere, right in front of her bumper. Luckily the gym parking lot was not conducive to speeding; Chasity was able to slam on the brakes with room to spare. In a flash she was out of the Lexus, slamming the door.

"Watch where the fuck you're going, you blind son of a bitch!" she screamed.

"Calm down, you don't need to scream at me; I didn't see you," he replied calmly, then gave a slight laugh. "You cuss like a sailor."

"You know what, I should get back in my car and run you the hell over."

"No," he replied, unruffled. "Not a good idea. You're too pretty to go to jail for vehicular manslaughter." Without another word, he turned and walked towards the gym. Chasity followed his progress, confused; then let out a frustrated sigh and got back in the car.

The guy walked in, scanned the gym, and headed for Sidra; the girl was standing alone and fanning herself.

"Hot enough for ya?" he asked with a smile. Recognizing the voice, she turned around and jumped up and down with excitement.

"Josh! How are you sweetie? I haven't seen you all summer," she exclaimed, giving him a big hug. Josh and Sidra had been friends since pre-school; they were as close as brother and sister.

"I went to stay with my Mom for the summer. I had a good time, it was really good seeing her every day again," he responded. She studied him closely.

"You're shaking. What's the matter?" she asked with a frown.

"Oh, it's no big deal. I accidentally ran out in front of some girl's car and she almost hit me. It's cool though, I'm okay," he answered with a shrug.

"Are you serious? People should look at what they're doing when they're driving."

"Well, it was *my* fault for running out in the middle of the parking lot like that," he shrugged. "But the crazy thing is, she threatened to get back in the car and run me over," he said with a chuckle.

Sidra's eyes became wide. "Run you over? Who could say something like that?—" then she paused.

"What's wrong?" he asked her. Sidra's expression had gone from concern to anger.

"Would you mind describing her to me?" she requested. She had an inkling of who the driver might be.

"I don't really remember...Um, she was about your height, light skinned; she had long black hair. She was wearing some jeans and a black short-sleeved top. She was really pretty, but she looked mean as hell. Her car was black. I think it was some sort of luxury car, a Lexus maybe," he said.

"Oh you don't remember huh?" Sidra stared at him. "You reeled off a pretty comprehensive description."

"What? She was cute; I guess I remember cute girls...and nice cars," he said with a shrug.

"I'll be right back," she tossed over her shoulder. She wanted to have a look around the parking lot. She scanned the entire lot until she saw what she was looking for—her roommate's car.

Chasity shoved some papers into her glove compartment. She was just about to get out of the car, when Sidra walked up to her window. As Chasity opened the door, Sidra pushed it shut. Startled, she turned around with a piercing look in her eyes.

"Are you crazy?!" Chasity blurted out.

"No, but obviously *you* are," Sidra shot back.

"Sidra, *what* the hell are you talking about?" Chasity frowned in confusion. "And get your damn hand off my window."

"Little girl, I will smear my damn fingerprints *all over* your car window," Sidra threatened. "It hasn't even been a whole day yet, and I'm *already* fed up with your bullshit."

Chasity's head was pounding. She was in no mood to have this argument. "Sidra, I have a headache. I'm not going to argue with you over dumb shit. So just move out the way so I can go."

"I *don't* like you!" Sidra shouted, stomping her foot on the ground.

"And I *don't* care!" Chasity shouted back.

"Did you know that you almost hit my friend with your car?"

"You mean that idiot that ran out in front of my car?" Chasity frowned. "Yeah, I almost hit him. What's your point?"

Sidra angrily put her hands on her hips. "He could have gotten hurt. And you didn't even show any remorse. He said that you threatened to run him over."

"*He's* the one who ran out in front of *my* car and *I'm* supposed to show remorse?" Chasity questioned, confusion written on her face. "You're making no sense whatsoever, and I am in no mood to hear this shit right now."

"Oh, you're *going to* hear what the hell I'm going to say to you."

Chasity stepped out of the car and stood in Sidra's face, staring her down. "You are really trying my fuckin' patience."

"I am not afraid of you or your little nasty-ass attitude," Sidra hissed. "Don't let these dress pants, and this blouse fool you, I will tear you up."

"Trust me when I say, you don't want to go there with me," Chasity stated calmly. "Once I start beating your uppity ass, I won't stop."

"Yeah, whatever," Sidra shot back.

"Whatever then, bitch," Chasity deliberately bumped Sidra, then walked away without another word, leaving Sidra seething.

"I...hate...that...girl," Sidra snarled to herself between deep breaths. Her hands were clenched into fists.

Chapter 5

The walk back to the gym did little to temper Sidra's frustration. She wanted to scream—or vent to someone. She slammed the heavy door behind her, and immediately regretted coming back inside. It was so hot.

Glancing around, she saw Malajia and Alex, leaning against the tile wall, fanning themselves and watching people work up a sweat on the dance floor.

"Hey, Alex," she greeted, joining them.

"Hey, girl." Alex replied.

"What? You can't say 'hi' to me?" Malajia objected. She couldn't stand being ignored, and certainly not by Sidra.

"Not really," Sidra put in, absently.

"Sidra, something the matter?" Alex asked, noticing the frown and distraction.

"It's Chasity," she responded.

"Your roommate? Again?"

"Yes. She is just so damn evil. I can't talk to her without her snapping at me," Sidra complained. "She doesn't care about anything or any*one*. I can't deal with her attitude for a whole year. I just *won't*."

"Well, what are you gonna do? I mean it's only been a day," Alex shrugged.

"Yeah, my point exactly. It's been *one* day and it has been terrible so far." Sidra pushed her long ponytail over her shoulder with a vicious flick. "I can't believe I'm stuck with her."

"Shit, *I'd* move if I were you," Malajia commented, studying her bangle bracelets on her arm.

"Girl, please. Give up that big room and that private bathroom? Ha, not *this* lady." Sidra waved aside the whole idea as too stupid to contemplate. "But I just don't have the patience to deal with that attitude all day every day."

"Well, there *must* be a reason why she acts the way she does. Why don't you try to have a heart-to-heart with her?" Alex suggested.

"Oh sure, *that's* a good idea. You two are just full of bright ideas tonight," Sidra looked from one girl to the other. "Not happening."

Malajia sighed loudly. "Okay, listen. I'm sick of Sidra whining about her evil ass roommate, and it's been one damn day. Are we gonna have to hear this shit all year?" she interjected. "Just fight the bitch, or move out. If you're not gonna do *either*, then shut the hell up and deal with it."

"Alex, tell your damn roommate to slither her ass somewhere else before I smack her," Sidra instructed, glaring at Malajia.

"You ain't gonna do nothin', Princess," Malajia taunted.

"Will you two stop it? I have never seen so many hostile young ladies in my entire life," Alex interrupted. "Come on now, we're sisters. We have to stick together."

"If your last name ain't Simmons, then you're no sister of *mine*," Malajia argued.

"You know what I mean, smart ass," Alex said, facing down Malajia.

"You see? She's always starting stuff," Sidra complained. "I wish someone could just staple her damn mouth shut." Unable to fire off an instant retort, Malajia just stared daggers at Sidra. "And don't look at me like that!"

"You're lucky anyone is looking at you at *all*, you uptight heifer," Malajia declared, pointing at her.

"Who are you calling uptight?" Sidra's eyes narrowed. "More *importantly*, who are you calling a heifer?"

"What are you gonna do, smack me with your ponytail?" Malajia taunted, hands on her hips.

"Okay that's it. You two need to stay separated." Alex gave Malajia a little push. "You, go over there and finish dancing. Sidra, you go find your friend." *Just plain ridiculous*, Alex thought, stealing a glance at her watch. Thank goodness. Her first college party was almost over. Maybe, just maybe, they'd make it through with no bodily harm committed.

Alex got her wish, but she was among the last to leave. Malajia refused to miss out on even a minute of dance time. Alex had to admit, the girl *could* dance.

"How was it? Did you girls have fun?" Emily asked, putting down the book she was reading.

"It was all right," Malajia shrugged, "Too many damn freshman boys. I need the upperclassmen to get here."

Emily forced back a smile. After only a day, she realized that Malajia was definitely boy crazy. "There are a couple of messages on the machine."

"Thanks, Em." Kicking off her shoes, Alex hit the "play" button.

"Malajia, honey, it's your mother calling." Malajia rolled her eyes. She'd recognize that scolding tone anywhere. *"You should give me a call back. I mean, I know that you're going wild out there without me and your father, but at least do us the common courtesy of giving us a call. After all, we are paying for you to be there. Thank you, my darling."*

"Oh Please," Malajia sneered, removing the high-heeled sandals from her feet. "What am I? Twelve? I'm not returning that call. She can forget that."

Alex giggled. "You seem pretty angry," she teased.

"Emily, it's Mommy. It's a bit late for you to be out sweetie. Call me back."

"Oh, shut up!" Malajia hollered at the machine. "What is with all of these nosey-ass mothers?"

"Alex, it's Paul. You know...your boyfriend." Alex made a face at the snarky tone. *"Anyway, I was calling to talk to you because that's what people in a relationship do. But, of course, you're probably out with all of your little college friends. Don't bother calling back. I'm gonna go out with some of my friends, too."*

"Damn," Malajia said at the sound of the phone clicking on the machine. "Girl, somebody's mad at *you.*"

"That fool has some damn nerve." Alex stood with her bare feet planted and an angry look on her face. "What does he expect me to do? Stay in the room and wait for his call? He's trippin'."

"Why is he so mad?" Malajia asked, taking her earrings off.

"He got held back and he's pissed because I didn't put off college for a year and wait for him." Alex twisted her hair back into a ponytail with an angry jerk. "You know what? I'm gonna call his bluff and call him."

She grabbed the phone from Emily's nightstand, punched in a number, and tapped her nails on the stand as she waiting for someone to pick up. "Hello?" a male voice answered after three rings.

"Hey, Bruce. This is Alex. Is Paul home?"

"Naw, Alex. He went out a while ago. He seemed pretty mad when he left."

"Yeah, so what else is new?" Alex muttered. "Listen, you tell your brother that the next time he feels the need to leave sarcastic messages on my answering machine, he'd better think twice."

"Okay. See ya."

"Bye," she said. Alex hung up the phone and rubbed the back of her neck.

"You okay?" Malajia asked, surprised to see Alex jolted out of her usual calm.

"Oh, girl. I'm fine. He can be miserable all he wants," Alex took off her shirt and tossed it into the laundry basket. "He's not gonna ruin my night."

Chapter 6

"This campus is so beautiful I could stay outside all day long," Alex sighed, basking in the beauty of perfect weather, beautiful architecture, and gorgeous landscaping.

"I know," Sidra nodded in agreement. "But then you'd never get to class."

"We could have jogged over, you know?" Alex put in, taking a sip from her water bottle.

"Yes, but I like this walk, this path has the prettiest flowers." Sidra shifted the gym bag on her shoulder as she gazed at the rows of blue hydrangea.

Alex looked at her with amusement. "Girl, why do you carry a gym bag? All you have is a towel and a water bottle in there."

Sidra smiled. She and Alex had begun to go to the fitness center every day or so. It gave Sidra a chance to work off some excess frustration. Since rooming with Chasity, she'd become especially fond of the punching bag. Even five minutes of imaginary sparring did wonders.

"I honestly don't know. I guess I just *have* to have my things in a bag." Sidra shrugged, then paused. "You hear that?"

"Yeah. Somebody sounds pretty mad," Alex said, pausing on the walkway as the sounds of an argument drowned out the birds' chatter.

"And one of those somebody's sounds real familiar. I bet you my evil roommate is involved. She must have found somebody on campus to pick a fight with," Sidra declared.

Alex shot her a sympathetic glance. "You two *still* not getting along?"

"No. Every time I try talking to her, she jumps down my throat," Sidra replied dramatically.

"You feel like being nosey?" Alex asked, grinning.

"Sure do," Sidra said. "Let's find out who the latest victim is."

They walked along the path in search of their quarry. They rounded a corner. Sure enough, there was Chasity, fists clenched and arguing with another girl. Alex and Sidra were silent as they sized up both Chasity, and the girl. Both were around the same height, but their complexions were a contrast. She was several shades darker than Chasity, and although her figure was slim like Chasity's, she wasn't nearly as toned.

"Look bitch, I don't know who the hell you think you are, but I will stomp your ass if you keep on talking that shit!" the girl warned and took a step closer to Chasity.

"Yeah? I *highly* doubt that," Chasity shot back, full of confidence.

"Ain't nobody scared of you!"

"You *should* be." Chasity was no stranger to fights; she'd been in plenty of them growing up. Win, lose, or draw – she was not one to back down.

"Keep talking!" the girl shouted. "I already told you what I'm gonna do."

"You've got five seconds to get out of my damn face," Chasity warned, staring the girl down.

"What are ya gonna do, huh?" the girl taunted.

"Stay here for four more seconds, and I'll show you," Chasity threatened.

"I think Chasity really will hit that girl," Alex whispered on the sidelines.

"Oh, I'm sure she will," Sidra replied.

"This isn't good. She can get in trouble."

"Alex, the five seconds are almost up." Sidra nudged Alex. Alex hopped over the hedge and grabbed Chasity's arm.

"What the hell are you doing?" Chasity shouted, whipping around.

"Stopping you from making a big mistake," Alex responded.

"Please, that bitch better be glad for the interruption," the girl taunted. "She don't want none of this."

Chasity made a lunge toward her, but Alex held her back. "You'd better leave," Alex advised.

"Until next time, bitch," the girl promised, locking eyes with Chasity before flipping her long braids over her shoulder, and leisurely walking away.

"Are you crazy?" Chasity broke free of Alex and shoved her away. "What the hell were you doing?"

"Like I said, I was keeping you from making a big mistake," Alex replied, setting her bag down as she put her hands up cautiously. "If you fight on campus, you'll get kicked out."

"Why should you care? I don't even know who the hell you are," Chasity hissed.

"Sure you do. I'm Alex; I met you at the orientation a few days ago. I hang out with your roommate," Alex reminded.

"And I would know that *how* exactly?"

"Look, I was just trying to help the situation," Alex explained, voice laced with frustration. *Geez, this girl is so mean*, Alex thought.

"Nobody asked you for your damn help," Chasity shot back. "You and your little friend Sidra, who I see playing watcher over there, can just leave me the hell alone." The girl stomped off without another word, fortunately in the opposite direction of her opponent.

"That went well," Sidra commented, walking over after Chasity stormed off. "You just had to come to the rescue huh?"

"Hardly. I just wanted to stop her from doing something stupid," Alex protested, picking her bag up from the ground.

"You aren't fooling anybody," Sidra began, regarding Alex skeptically. "You see her as a project. You think you can *reach* her, don't you?"

"Honestly?" Alex thought for a moment. "Yeah, I do. There's nobody I can't reach."

"Well, good luck. You're certainly going to need it," Sidra concluded. "Clearly that one doesn't do friendship."

"We'll see." Alex picked up her gym bag. "Come on, let's go before all the good machines are taken"

"You can have the machines; I need to hit that bag."

The beautifully landscaped grounds, bright sun, and gentle breeze did little to calm Chasity down after her encounter. She wasn't just upset at the fact that she had the argument with that random girl in the first place, but also at the fact that Alex had the nerve to butt in her business.

Who the hell does that nosey bitch think she is? she thought. If there was one thing Chasity couldn't stand, it was a nosey person.

She reached her dorm within minutes but knowing that her temper was still high, Chasity decided to keep walking in hopes that she could calm down.

Her walk took her to the large football field near the gym. As she slowed her pace to check out the grounds, she happened to see the football team practicing some plays a few feet away from her. She watched them for all of one minute when she noticed that one of the players had spotted her and began staring.

Why the hell is he staring at me like he's never seen a damn girl before? She rolled her eyes as he smiled and managed a slight wave to her. She had no intention of returning his smile or his wave. Instead, she tilted her head slightly, taking in his light-brown complexion, muscular body, and handsome face. *He's cute,* she mused before continuing on her way.

The upperclassmen arrived on campus over the weekend. What began as a trickle turned into a flood, much to Malajia's delight. Intent on checking out the new arrivals before class, she managed to make breakfast in the cafeteria for the first time. Sidra was already there with Emily and Alex, sprinkling granola on her fruit and yogurt parfait.

"Eww, you eating that nasty mess?" Malajia sneered. "Not surprised. You wear those prissy ass clothes. Hell, why *wouldn't* you eat prissy food?"

"Well, I wouldn't judge *your* food by *your* clothing Malajia," Sidra ground out. "If I did, you'd be eating nothing."

Craning her neck every which way, afraid she might miss a choice male specimen, Malajia let the comment slide.

Suddenly, Sidra half rose in her seat and waved. Josh was queued up in the cafeteria line with two of his friends. Sidra had been friends with all three guys since childhood. She'd always been amazed at their closeness; even though they were so different in personality. Josh, the sweet introvert; Mark, the popular jokester; and David, the reserved brainiac.

"Hey, Sidra," Josh greeted, pulling up a chair and setting down his tray. "Mark and David will be over in a sec. You going to Intro to Psych?"

"Uh huh," she smiled. "This is Emily. She's in that class too. Did you already meet Alex?"

"I don't think so," Josh admitted, opening his carton of milk.

"Oh, I'm sorry. I could have sworn I introduced you two at that party." Sidra placed her spoon back into her bowl. "Alex, this is Josh Hampton." Josh and Alex smiled and waved at one another.

Emily mumbled a hello, then reached for a packet of sugar to avoid having to make conversation. That was one of the reasons she'd camped out in her room all weekend, even though the weather had been so beautiful.

"Damn, I can't escape *nobody* from Delaware huh?" drawled Malajia. As if four years of middle school and two years in high school weren't enough, now she had to deal with Josh and his friends in college too.

Josh was okay, she guessed, if you liked them tall, brown-skinned and timid. Mark, on the other hand, was a total write-off in her opinion. She couldn't stand the loud-mouthed jerk with his stupid jokes and dumb pranks, even if he *was* six-foot-three, dark skinned, and handsome. David, with his silver-framed glasses, she considered a nerd and avoided in the past. His brown complexion, height and athletic build made him attractive and all, but what do you say to a guy who gets straight A's?

"What's up baby girl?" Mark inquired with the volume on high.

"Do you always have to be so damn loud?" complained Josh. "I'm sure they heard you across campus."

"Yes, he does, *always*," David quipped, spreading butter on his toast.

"Boys, this isn't high school. You'd better behave yourself," Sidra warned, laughing. "Josh, where did you go after the party the other day?"

"Back to my room," Josh said. "Because Mark and David left me."

"Tell her *why* though," Mark ordered, a glint in his eyes.

Josh frowned slightly. "What?"

"Tell her why we left you," Mark repeated.

"Whatever, man," Josh mumbled defensively. "You could've waited five more minutes."

"What's with all of the secrecy? What were you doing, Josh?" Sidra prompted, intrigued.

"He was looking for *you*," David interjected.

Alex, enjoying the play by play, became a quiet spectator. Then she saw the embarrassment flash across Josh's face, the quick swallow. *So*, she thought, *he has a crush on Sidra, and she doesn't have a clue.*

"Sidra, introduce me." Alex decided it was time to short-circuit the awkwardness and intervened.

"Oh, where are my manners? Sorry, Alex. These guys are my other old friends from high school, Mark Johnson and David Summers."

"So, who do you room with?" David asked after pleasantries were exchanged.

"Emily, and *this* one over here." Alex pointed to Malajia before taking a bite of her cream cheese covered bagel.

"And I'm the best roommate ever. She's so lucky to have me." Malajia chimed in. "Hey David. Hey Josh."

"What's up Malajia? Long time no see. How have you been?" Josh asked, picking up his cup to take a sip of his orange juice.

"Great. Since I left Delaware, that is," Malajia corrected, then groaned as she caught Mark making weird faces at her. "Oh God."

"Damn it! You're still alive?" he shouted. The dislike Malajia felt was mutual. Mark thought she was a loud, ditzy, attention-seeking whore.

"You shut the hell up. I'm surprised that you even got into college. Or know how to *spell* it," Malajia shot back. She was racking her brains for another insult when Mark let out a loud, phony laugh. Heads turned, and Malajia felt as if everyone in the cafeteria was staring at them. Not all attention, Malajia discovered, was welcome.

"Do you *have* to do stupid shit like that?" she spat out.

"I wouldn't be me if I didn't," he replied coolly, picking up his book bag, and pointedly turning his attention to Emily.

"You going to class?" Mark asked, "I'll walk you over. You're cute, how about you give me your number?"

Flustered, Emily stared down at the oatmeal congealing in the bowl in front of her. Sidra grabbed the back of Mark's shirt. "Back off, boy. We can all go together."

"Don't nobody feel like sitting through no damn psychology class," Malajia complained, tugging up her strapless top. "It's too nice outside."

"Girl, just hush," Alex shot back. She then stood from her seat. "Time to get a move on. First day of class, we don't want to be late."

On the way to return their trays, Mark waved a piece of paper in front of Alex. Slamming her tray on the used stack, she grabbed the sheet. Crude stick figures kissed above an inscription in equally crude printing: *"This could be you and me."* Alex crumpled the paper into a ball and tossed it at Mark.

"Come on now," he laughed. "You have to admit that was original."

"Yeah, originally *stupid*," Alex returned. Suddenly Mark let out another of his piercing phony laughs right near her face. "Oh my god! My ears," she groaned.

"Can somebody just shoot him, *please*?" Malajia pleaded.

Chapter 7

The group filed into the crowded lecture hall. Most of the freshman class were there. Emily summoned up the courage to suggest they sit in front; she wanted to be sure that she was able to catch all of the lecture notes. Mark was quick with a veto, pointing to seats in a row at the back.

"God," crooned Malajia after the hour was up. "I could watch him teach all day, he's so sexy. But does he really expect us to do all that reading? On the first day though?"

"He may be cute," Alex laughed, "but Professor Watson has a reputation for being very demanding."

"I don't give a damn," Malajia replied. "I'm not reading all that."

Alex shook her head. "Do you guys wanna go to lunch?"

"What time?" Malajia asked, as she looked at her watch.

"Um, now?" Alex chuckled.

"Sure," Emily put in cheerfully.

"Wow, she speaks," Malajia teased.

"Leave her alone, Mel," Alex warned. "Can I call you Mel?"

"Um, no," Malajia replied, shaking her head. "My name is just fine without you shortening it."

"Well, Mel," Alex continued, ignoring her objection. "It's not nice to make fun of Emily."

"It's also not nice to go out in public with a shirt like *that* on," Malajia retaliated, pointing to Alex's mustard yellow, flowy tank top.

"There's nothing wrong with my shirt," Alex protested. "At least I don't have to keep tugging on it to keep my breasts from popping out."

"Say what you want about mine, but *yours* is still ugly," Malajia retorted. Emily just giggled.

After a quick lunch, the three parted ways. Alex headed off to the bookstore. She wanted to get a head start on their psych reading. With so many in the class, she was afraid the books she needed might be gone if she waited around. Not worried by the prospect, Malajia opted to go watch a movie in the dorm lounge with some other students, and Emily headed back to the room to relax while waiting for her next class.

Head down, preoccupied, Chasity was making her way to the science building. Her thoughts were a million miles away, she wasn't paying attention and walked straight into someone on the narrow walkway.

"Um, my fault," she mumbled and took a long stride away.

"Hey, wait a minute," the guy said, blocking her path.

She looked up, startled. It was that football player who was staring at her from the field the other day. She'd forgotten how handsome he was. "What do you want?" her voice was traced with frustration.

"What's the matter with *you*?" he asked with a little laugh.

"I just wanna know what it is that you want. I bumped into you, and I apologized. What else could you possibly want?" she replied impatiently.

"You know, you're too beautiful to be acting so mean." He returned her glare with a smile. He'd wondered how long it would take for him to track her down. He had to admit, she was pretty hard to miss—or to forget. In a swift glance, he took in the slanted hazel eyes flashing at him, the long black hair, smooth light-brown skin, and slim shapely figure. *She's the most gorgeous thing I've ever seen,* he thought, *and straight mean.* Odd, but he even found her hair-trigger temper appealing. He was determined to get to know her.

"Boy, please," she sneered, rolling her eyes.

"Okay, I'm sorry," he said quickly, catching her by the arm to halt her departure. "I just want to know your name."

"Why?" she snapped impatiently. "What purpose would that serve?"

"You're someone that I would like to get to know, and I'd a least like to know your name."

She frowned at him. "Who says that I want you to get to know me?"

"I can see that this isn't going to be easy, but I love a challenge," he said, running a hand over his short curly hair.

"Well, then you have your work cut out for you," she promised.

"I'm cool with that; I'm Jason Adams by the way."

"I'm Chasity Parker. Happy now?"

"Extremely," he responded. "Now when I see you around campus, I'll have a name to go with that beautiful face."

"Flattery will get you nowhere, *Jason.* I already know that I look good."

"And you *should*," he said, still smiling.

"You're wasting my time. I have to go."

As Jason watched her saunter off, one of his teammates walked up. "Jason, we have to meet with the coach now."

"Okay, let's go," he said absently.

His eyes were still tracking Chasity's progress, but he couldn't afford to miss his session with the coach. He'd come to Paradise Valley University on a football scholarship. He'd had scouts watching him play long before he graduated high school, and before his tall, lanky frame filled out. He was that good.

"Who was that girl?" his teammate asked, curious.

"My future wife," Jason replied in quiet confidence.

By Saturday afternoon, they had made it through the first week of classes. To celebrate, Sidra invited Alex, Malajia and Emily to go to the mall to meet up with the guys. "I'm glad that you came, Emily," Sidra said, boarding the bus for the twenty-minute ride to the mall. "It's good that you're getting out more."

"Yeah. I'm slowly but surely coming along," Emily replied, taking a seat.

"*Extremely* slow," Malajia mumbled.

"I heard that," Alex said as she playfully backhanded Malajia on her arm.

"Hit me again, and I'll smack your hair straight," Malajia threatened, waving a hand in the direction of Alex's wavy hair.

Within a week, the pair had fallen into the habit of verbal jousting. Alex still thought that Malajia talked too much and let her know it, and Malajia got tired of Alex trying to mother her and Emily, but they were cool with each other. Emily liked being around them, but still she would hang back, still shy and timid. Alex and Malajia were determined to bring her out of her shell. The three were not the best of friends yet, but they were friends nonetheless and were drawing Sidra into their circle. Helped along by Alex's prodding, Sidra was even starting to rekindle her old friendship with Malajia.

"Anyway, Sidra, how have you and Chasity been getting along?" Alex asked, hoping to hear a bit of progress on that front.

"We *haven't*." Sidra thought for a moment. "Well, it's not like we haven't been speaking. Actually, we haven't even been *seeing* each other at all. She's going when I'm coming."

"It'll get better," Emily said, trying to be optimistic.

"I hope so, it's getting frustrating," Sidra admitted. She wasn't satisfied with the situation. She wanted things to be cool. She really wished that they could be friends; it would make her life so much easier. "At least with our schedules, we're not arguing anymore. We don't have the chance to."

"Look, *I* for one don't like her. And I don't see how you people can even consider being friends with her," Malajia huffed.

"I'm sure she doesn't like you either," Sidra replied, glancing out of the window.

"Here's our stop; get the hell up and let's go. I need to go to the bathroom," Malajia ordered after several more minutes of riding.

"Don't rush us. Nobody told you to drink that big jug of juice before we left campus," Sidra scolded as she stepped off of the bus.

"Less bitching, more walking," Malajia countered.

"So, Sidra, where are your friends?" Alex asked, looking around once they made their way inside the crowded mall.

"I don't know, probably going crazy over some new game system," she said, keeping an eye out. "Ah, there they are."

"What's up, people?" Josh greeted Sidra with a kiss on the cheek and nodded to the others.

"Nothing much. Glad the first week's over," Alex smiled. Josh was always so sweet with his greeting.

"Where's that damn Malajia?" Mark inquired, looking around. "I know she's slithering her ass around here somewhere."

"Wow, such hostility," Alex put in.

"She gets on my damn nerves," he complained, scratching his head.

"As *if* you don't get on *mine* jackass," Malajia blurted out. She couldn't help but hear his comment halfway back from the bathroom. Hell, the whole mall could have heard.

"You make me sick," he retorted

"And you look like an ass," she shot back.

"You two need to cut it out. I mean, can't you at least *try* to be civil?" Alex asked, shaking her head at the juvenile pair.

"People, can we make moves?" Josh requested. He didn't want to spend his Saturday standing around listening to Mark and Malajia bicker like children.

"Sure, let's go," Sidra shrugged. The mall was huge—and elegant. Skylights lit up the marble interior and fountain gurgling at the center. The group ambled along, window shopping and checking out the stores.

"So Sidra, where's that bitchy roommate of yours? Shopping for a new broom?" Malajia asked.

"Mel, hush. That's not right," Alex rebuked.

"Malajia, you have no right to talk about *anybody* with *your* dumb ass," Mark pointed out.

"I'm not dumb, you ugly-ass jerk!" she hollered back, hitting him on the arm.

"OUCH!" he shouted at the top of his lungs.

"Oh my god, do you have to be that loud?" Alex protested, putting her hand to her ear.

"YES!" he shouted close to her ear.

"You know what?" Alex began, and moved away from him.

"You're such an asshole," Malajia ground out, putting her hand in his face. He smacked her hand away and she responded with a sharp punch.

"Stop hitting me!" he shouted, clutching his arm.

"Will you shut up? You're just loud for no damn reason," Malajia paused. "You make me sick."

"I don't give a shit about how you feel, you fuckin' fool," Mark shot back. "Anyway, I'm hungry."

"Well, genius. The mall has a food court. Knock yourself out," Malajia said, her tone dripping with sarcasm.

"You make me wanna squeeze your head until it pops off," Mark glared at her.

"Why don't you squeeze your own head?" Malajia shot back "I'm pretty sure you're good at *that*."

Josh and David cracked up. "Damn," Josh laughed. "You should see your face Mark."

Malajia smirked at their reaction to her remark. Alex and Sidra were studiously avoiding eye contact. Mark, on the other hand, was regarding her with a salty look on his face.

"Let's just get something to eat," Sidra suggested. Maybe their sour dispositions would improve with some food.

"Hey, Sidra," Alex broke in, noticing a familiar figure in the distance. "There's your roommate. Should we ask her to join us?"

"Are you crazy?" Malajia grunted. "Hell no."

"Maybe she would like to sit with us," Alex countered.

"So?" Malajia objected.

"Call her over here and see what she says," Sidra encouraged.

"Girl, you better not call that she-devil over here," Malajia warned.

"Wait," Alex raised an eyebrow, "did you just say that I *better* not call her over here?"

Malajia narrowed her eyes at Alex. "You heard what I said."

"*I'd* smack her," Mark offered.

Alex looked at Malajia, her expression bored as she fiddled with the curls on her hair. Then she called out, "Oh Miss Chasity, could you come here for a minute?"

"Seriously?" Malajia huffed.

Chasity crossed the marble floor, resignation in every step. "What?" she answered. She thought about ignoring

Alex, but Chasity had a feeling that if she did, Alex would only shout her name louder.

"We're about to go to the food court," Alex explained. "We were wondering if you would like to get something to eat with us."

"No, *we* weren't," Malajia slid in smartly.

Chasity shot Malajia an angry glare. "Nobody wants to sit with your stank ass anyway," she snapped. The comment and sudden retaliation had Malajia's jaw dropping; Emily's eyes widened in shock.

"Whoa," Josh commented. Not many people got the last word in with Malajia around.

"Wow," Sidra echoed, a laugh bubbling up.

"Did you hear what she said to me?" Malajia demanded.

"Uh, yeah," Alex said.

"Well, defend me, damn it."

"You'd better defend your*self* on that one," Alex responded. Noticing that Chasity was about to slip away, she motioned to her. "Hold on a second."

"I wasn't planning on staying anyway," Chasity said, anxious to be away from all of them. She was going to buy something expensive, something very expensive. Maybe it would make her feel better. "I have things to do."

"Chasity, come on. Stop being so stubborn. Shut your mouth and chill with us for a bit," Alex commanded.

Alex's boldness caught Chasity off guard, and it showed on her face. Most people were too afraid to talk to her like that, or so put off by her attitude that they didn't bother, which was just the way she wanted it.

"Will you stop talking to me if I go? Because hearing your voice is making my fuckin' face hurt," Chasity sneered.

"Oh, sure," Alex lied without a qualm.

Chasity shook her head. "Freakin' liar." Not having the energy to argue, she followed Sidra's lead into the food court.

"Yeah, I lied," Alex admitted. "It's not in my nature to not speak to people." Chasity took a seat as far away from

Alex and Sidra as possible. Across the table, Mark was staring at her hard.

"What the hell are you staring at?" Chasity hissed.

"You see that stick over there?" Mark pointed to a mop handle sticking out of the bucket, just outside the restroom entrance. "Somebody needs to beat you with it. You need a damn attitude adjustment."

"Why don't you beat *your own* stick?" Chasity snapped back. "I'm pretty sure you're an expert at *that*."

Mark turned his palms up in surrender, annoyed to hear the laughter breaking out around the table.

"Oh my god, I *just* said that!" Malajia exclaimed.

"Nobody asked your hype ass what you said, Malajia," Mark hissed. *Will that damn girl ever shut up?* he wondered. Now starving, he ordered a large supreme pizza to himself, while the others ate wraps, salads, burgers, and fries. Finally, they finished. He balled up his napkin and tossed it onto Sidra's plate.

"Man, that food was good," Josh mused, patting his stomach.

"Let's get out of here. I want to play some ball." Mark looked at his watch. "There's a bus we can catch in ten minutes."

Malajia let out a groan. She had major window shopping on her agenda, and it certainly had not been checked off yet.

"Okay, I'm over this," Chasity remarked, getting to her feet. "I'm leaving."

Alex observed Chasity's hurried departure closely. If she didn't know better, she'd say the girl was embarrassed or feeling uncomfortable.

"Mark, you guys go ahead. I want to stick around a bit," Sidra put in. "There's a boutique here I've always wanted to checkout that we don't have at home."

Alex nodded. She wasn't much of a fashionista; fancy brands and labels didn't appeal to her. But she was happy to tag along to the store to see what all the fuss was about.

Malajia sucked her teeth. "Boutique," she jeered. "Just say *store*...with your uppity ass." Sidra flagged her as she continued her walk.

An hour later, spirits were fading and every shop with any importance had been visited. With relief, Alex spotted Chasity, carrying several shopping bags sporting impressive labels. She cut her off at the main entrance.

"You about to leave?" she asked. "Can you give us a ride back?"

Chasity ignored her and headed for the parking lot. Alex signaled to the other girls, and they followed Chasity to her car.

Shifting all of her bags to one arm, Chasity rummaged through her purse and came up with the keys. She hit the button to unlock the doors. By the time she'd stowed her things in the trunk, Alex and Malajia were sitting in the back seat and gesturing to Sidra and Emily to jump in. Chasity was too tired to scream or fight, so she slid into the driver's seat without a word.

By the time they made it back to Torrence Hall and Chasity parked the car, she was too exhausted to climb the stairs to her room. She collapsed on the couch.

"Did you see Mark's face when he slipped and fell in the food court?" Malajia gloated, sitting on the couch. "Then his dumb self had the nerve to run, like nobody saw his ass fall."

"We shouldn't laugh," Sidra said, but giggled anyway. "He could've been hurt."

"Who cares? It made *my* day," Malajia replied with a shrug, "And *you're* laughing too."

"No, I *giggled*." Sidra put her finger up. "There's a difference."

Malajia made no comment, for once, and looked over at Chasity, who was now dead to the world. She nudged her hard.

"Wake your ass up," she insisted, nudging Chasity again.

Chasity snapped out of her sleep, grabbing the hand that Malajia used to nudge her in a firm grip. "Don't make me break it," she threatened.

"Lighten the hell up." Malajia condemned, snatching her hand away.

"Get away from me," Chasity hissed, sitting up and rubbing her eyes.

"No, I'm comfortable right here next to you," Malajia taunted as she sat down next to her and leaned against the couch pillows.

"Forget her, Chaz—can I call you Chaz?" Alex said.

"Hell no," Chasity sneered, still trying to focus.

"What's with you always trying to shorten people's names?" Malajia demanded. "Just because you don't like *your* full name, doesn't mean you need to mess with anyone else's."

"Malajia, nobody was talking to you. I was talking to Chasity," Alex shot back.

"Why *are* you talking to me?" Chasity asked.

"I'm just trying to be friendly," Alex replied.

"Oh my god," Chasity groaned. She was so completely tired of Alex talking and pushing at her.

"Can we *please* find something to do?" Malajia complained. "I mean, come on. It's a Saturday night." She wasn't about to spend a weekend night at college sitting around listening to Alex's nagging.

Chasity pulled herself up off the couch and started for the stairway.

"Where are you going?" Malajia demanded. She got no verbal response. Chasity, without turning around, simply gave her the finger.

"You *can't* go. We need your car!" Malajia shouted after her.

"You know she's not paying you any mind," Sidra cautioned, standing with her arms folded.

"Oh, so what," Malajia huffed and stretched out onto the now vacant couch.

"All right, Sid." Alex yawned and stretched as she rose to her feet. "I'll see you tomorrow."

"Really? Now you shorten *Sidra's* name?" Malajia scoffed.

"Sure did, good night."

"Wait for me, Alex," Emily called out, jumping to her feet to follow her out of the door. "Night, ladies," she called out over her shoulder as she shut the door behind her.

Sidra stared at Malajia, willing her to follow her roommates. But she just sat there, twirling a strand of her hair, oblivious. Sidra cleared her throat, then cleared it again, louder this time.

"Do you need some water or something?" Malajia asked. "Why are you looking at me like that?"

"Time for you to go back to your dorm, Malajia."

"What?" Malajia said, standing.

"Get out," Sidra demanded.

"I don't want to," Malajia replied. "Alex is just gonna be studying and Emily is gonna be talking to her damn Mommy all night. I'm bored."

"Not my problem," Sidra commiserated. Patience exhausted, she let out a frustrated sigh and started for the stairway.

"You just gonna leave me here?"

"Yep," Sidra replied.

"Go on then, you hag!" she shouted, her feelings a little hurt.

"Get out," Sidra repeated from the bottom step.

Malajia picked up her purse and walked out only to find Alex and Emily standing on the dorm stoop, waiting for her.

"I thought that you two had left," Malajia said.

"We knew that it was only a matter of time before you were kicked out," Alex joked.

When Sidra opened her room door, she found Chasity lying down not in her bed, but with her face buried in the plump pillows on the small white loveseat near the window.

"Shouldn't you be in bed?" she asked.

"As you can see, I didn't make it past the couch," Chasity mumbled. Her voice was muffled by the pillows.

"Wow, you *actually* spoke to me in a civilized manner," Sidra observed with a laugh. "You must be sick or something."

"No, I'm just too tired to be a bitch right now." Chasity sat up and rubbed her neck.

"That couch is going to be hell on your back."

"Sidra, shut up," she replied, running her hand through her hair.

"Ugh, you're tired and you *still* can't be nice," Sidra pointed out. At the risk of being swung at, she grabbed Chasity's arm and pulled her off the couch.

"Why are you bothering me?" Chasity demanded. "Leave me alone."

"Oh, shut up. I'm just trying to be a good roommate, unlike you," Sidra answered and prodded Chasity over to her bed. "Look, there's a flag football game tomorrow. Alex, Malajia, Emily and I are all going...Why don't you join us?" Hands on her hips, she waited for an answer.

Silence.

"Chasity," she snapped after a moment or two.

"Oh my god, can I get to sleep *some*time this year?" Chasity complained, lifting her head up.

"Not until you accept my invitation." Sidra folded her arms and didn't budge.

"*What* invitation? What the hell are you talking about?"

"Just tell me that you'll go."

"Sidra, I'm not going anywhere with you," she protested and laid her head back down.

"Well then, I'll just have to jump up and down on your bed until you say yes." Sidra grinned, making long strides over to Chasity's bed.

Chasity quickly sat up and put her hands up in surrender. "Okay, okay. I'll go. Just leave me alone and let me sleep before I pass out."

"That's all you had to say in the first place," Sidra said. She flicked her long ponytail off her shoulder and let out a big smile. She was proud of herself; she was making an effort and maybe her roommate was too. She picked up her nightgown, and then looked over at Chasity. Her roommate had not even bothered to get undressed.

"You know, you should really put on your pajamas. It's not a good idea—"

Chasity didn't give her a chance to finish. She jumped out of the bed, grabbed her pajamas and stormed toward the bathroom. "That's it, I'm sleeping in the tub," she announced and slammed the door.

Sidra stepped out of her grey pencil skirt, took off her black sleeveless blouse, and folded them neatly before slipping the nightgown over her head. Climbing into bed, she relished that slammed door, laughter bubbling up before she drifted off.

Sunday afternoon brought at least half the campus to the football field. Regular season wasn't scheduled to start for another week, but the coach suggested a flag game, with his players divided into blue and red teams. Only a couple of minutes into the first quarter, Sidra noticed that, in between plays, one of the players from the blue team kept looking at Chasity.

"Chasity, that guy is checking you out," she nudged, pointing to the player near the sideline.

"So?" Chasity cocked her head. "Am I supposed to jump for joy?"

"Girl, do you know who that *is*?" Malajia interjected, craning her neck to get a better view.

"I don't know his name, but I've seen him around campus a few times," Sidra added, adjusting the silver bracelets on her slender wrist. "He's a cutie."

"His name is Jason," Chasity drawled, enjoying a moment of private amusement at Malajia's expense. "I met him about a week ago."

"How come *I* never met him?" Malajia exclaimed. "And I've met damn near everyone on that football team."

"Yeah, I'm sure your fast ass *has*," Chasity sneered. Malajia's hyperactive nature was really bugging Chasity. The girl never stopped moving or talking. The high-pitched voice Malajia made every time she became excited was just another reason to keep her distance.

"You don't have to be so sarcastic, bitch," Malajia hissed.

"*You* don't have to be that fuckin' hyper all the damn time," Chasity shot back.

"I'm *not* hyper."

"You wanna bet?" Alex interjected, popping a cheese curl into her mouth.

"I didn't ask you for your input, fat ass," Malajia snarled.

"I'm not fat." Alex dismissed the comment with a wave of her hand. "I'm curvy, there is a difference."

"Whatever," Malajia conceded, anxious to pick up the earlier conversation. "That guy is *beyond* sexy. Look at that face, those legs, and those muscles. Don't you just love the tight football uniforms?"

"No, not really Malajia," Alex interjected, but her curiosity was piqued. Chasity seldom talked to anyone much less remembered a name. "How did *you* meet him Chaz?"

"So you're just gonna shorten my damn name anyway?"

Sidra chuckled as Alex shrugged at Chasity's observation.

"More importantly, why would he waste his time talking to someone like *her*?" Malajia interrupted.

"What's the matter? You jealous?" Chasity taunted.

"*Me*, jealous? Girl, please; I have no reason to be jealous. Anyone can see how fine I am," Malajia boasted.

"Ladies, this argument is stupid," Alex chimed in. "You both are beautiful."

"Alex, mind your business," Malajia advised, completely overlooking the compliment. "Your voice is distracting me. I need to focus my attention on that sexy man down there. He's gonna be my love slave."

"Oh god," Sidra groaned. "Here we go."

"Excuse me," Malajia hissed. "What the hell is *that* supposed to mean?"

"Malajia, you're always talking about making some guy your 'love slave', and you always end up looking stupid in the end," Sidra replied, softening the rebuke with a smile.

"What's a love slave?" Emily asked as she shook the popcorn kernels around in her little bag.

Malajia and Chasity looked at her in amazement.

"You need to keep questions like that to yourself," Chasity commented, playing with her cell phone. She could care less about the rest of this game.

"Emily you don't know what a love slave is?" Malajia queried.

Emily looked up from taking a sip of her soda. "Um...no." She didn't understand why her question was being criticized. *Why do I even say anything?* she wondered.

"Oh my god. My poor, poor sheltered roommate."

"Malajia, leave her alone. Your ass don't know anything about that *either* from what you told me," Alex retorted.

"You don't know my damn business," Malajia argued, pointing an unopened candy bar at Alex.

"That's a shame, you run your mouth so much that you don't even remember all of the stuff you told me," Alex shot back. "We had a whole conversation last night over popcorn in the dorm lobby."

"I don't remember that shit," Malajia sneered, adjusting the top on her black sleeveless romper.

"Guess she *told you,* Mel," Sidra teased.

"Sidra, fix your bangs, and leave me alone," Malajia spat.

Alex shook her head as Sidra, unaware if Malajia was just being smart or if there really was something wrong with her hair, quickly reached for her pocket mirror. "Okay enough, let's watch this game," Alex ordered.

In the last seconds of the game, Jason scored the winning touchdown for the blue team. Amid all of the commotion, he managed to wave at Chasity. "Did you see that?" Malajia exclaimed, holding her hand over her heart. "He waved to me."

"No, he did *not*," Sidra contradicted. "He waved at my roommate."

"Does it matter?" Chasity asked, bored with the silly discussion.

"Oh please," Malajia argued. "Why would he wave to her, when for some crazy reason she's obviously not interested?"

Malajia took out her little pocket mirror and began applying a fresh coat of her burgundy lipstick.

"You better hurry up and finish your touchup," Alex advised. "He's on his way over here."

"Oh man. He's coming over." Malajia gave herself one final glance into her mirror, fixing one wayward curl. "He's coming to see me."

"Malajia, don't embarrass yourself," Sidra cautioned. "You've never met him."

"Whatever Sidra. Malajia Lakeshia Simmons does not get embarrassed."

"Was it *necessary* to use your full name?" Alex teased. "We got the point"

"Very funny," Malajia said, then broke off. Jason was only one row away, his helmet tucked under his arm. She was about to say something to him when he kneeled down and whispered to Chasity.

"Hello again," he said softly, but within earshot of Malajia, Mark, Josh and David, who were sitting in the row behind her. "Remember me?"

Malajia's smile faded and she stood up, a stupid look on her face.

"I *told* you," Sidra put in, but was soon drowned out by Mark.

"That's what the hell you get Malajia!" Mark shouted, laughing.

"Where the hell did *you* come from?!" Malajia spun around to face him.

Chasity shook her head. She wished she hadn't come.

"Did you hear what I asked?" Jason repeated.

"I heard you. I'm just trying to ignore you," she responded with an attitude.

"Come on, Chasity. You shouldn't act so nasty."

"Who are *you* to tell me what I *should* or *shouldn't* do?" she threw back.

"It's a good thing I knew that you'd give me attitude, or my feelings would've been hurt," he replied.

"Ask me if I care."

Jason leaned in closer and she shot him a warning look. "What you're doing has no effect," he whispered.

"What are you talking about?" she asked, her temper rising.

"You think if you keep talking to me as if I'm garbage that I'm gonna run away like a scared puppy."

"What's your point, Jason?" She blinked in surprise. He'd read her like a book.

"My point *is* that I was raised to go for what I want—always. I'm very determined."

"I'm not going to be one of your fast-ass girlfriends. So get out of my face."

"I don't *have* a girlfriend," he clarified.

"I promise I don't care," she snarled.

"Oh my god, you bitch!" Malajia exclaimed.

Chasity rolled her eyes at the loud interruption.

Jason shuffled on his cleats, cursing his timing. "Listen, I really would like to get to know you better. How about you come to my place?"

"What?" Chasity snapped. "You've got a lot of damn nerve saying that shit to me."

"For a *party*, babe," he said with a laugh. "You know, a social gathering."

"Funny." She scowled at him.

"Some of my teammates are throwing a party at my dorm. I really want you to come. You'll have a good time. I'll see to that."

"You can't be serious."

"As a heart-attack," he responded.

"You better say yes!" Malajia intervened, leaning forward in her seat.

Chasity spun around to face the meddling Malajia. "Scream in my ear *one* more fuckin' time," she threatened, "and I swear I'm gonna smack the bullshit outta you."

"Bitch, I wish you *would*," Malajia shot back.

"Will I see you later?" Jason asked quickly, sensing that Chasity was fed up with the whole scene.

"Hell no," she sneered, frowning at him.

Definitely fed up, he thought; then Sidra came to his rescue. "She'll be there."

"Good, it's going to be at Thompson Hall." Jason winked at Sidra. "Bring your friends."

Chapter 8

The four girls arrived when the party was already in full swing; none of them were surprised when Emily elected to stay in the dorm, and it was a close call with Chasity. Sidra practically had to drag her out of Torrence Hall. She wasn't keen on another confrontation with Jason. He was great to look at, she admitted, but she couldn't stand his cocky attitude.

"You don't want him to know he gets under your skin," Sidra pointed out. The offhand comment sealed the deal, and a reluctant Chasity tagged along.

Malajia looked around, eyes bright with excitement. If there was anything she adored, it was a party, especially one with a bunch of good looking men, music blaring, and plenty of liquor.

"Where is he?" she wondered, assuming a provocative pose. "My soon to be boyfriend?"

"In hell with the other goblins," Sidra suggested. Malajia's bravado was wearing thin.

"*You're* a goblin, jerk," Malajia retorted.

"I'm over this," Chasity said to Sidra. "I'm about to go."

"Why? You just got here," Sidra replied, voice laced with surprise.

"Give it a chance," Alex chimed in. "You might actually have a good time."

"Just let the witch go," Malajia urged with a wave of her hand. "She'll just get in my way anyways."

"Shut your dumb ass up," Chasity spat. "Not everyone is desperate for dick *anyways*." Alex put her hand over her face to conceal a laugh.

"Ha!" Sidra taunted. She loved the fact that someone was quick witted enough to go toe to toe with Malajia.

"I'm leaving," Chasity concluded before sauntering away.

"I hate that bitch," Malajia said, pointing her finger at the retreating figure.

"Oh, Malajia, please. You're just mad because Jason ignored you," Alex offered, voice filled with amusement.

"I wasn't *ignored*. I was blindsided by the devil," Malajia retorted, folding her arms.

"No, you were ignored," Sidra put in. "Just admit it."

"Whatever. Men love me. I'm their freakin' dream."

"Yeah, right," Sidra slid in, "more like a nightmare."

A lot of bodies were crammed into the room. Chasity dodged and weaved, making her way to the door. She froze anyone who tried to stop her with a single look. She had made it out of the door and almost escaped down the path when Jason stopped her.

"Where are you going, beautiful?" he asked.

"Home," she answered abruptly. *Did the guy ever stop smiling?* she wondered.

"Why do you always have such an attitude?" he asked.

"Because dumb asses like *you* won't leave me alone."

"You have a mouth on you, don't you?" he observed. "You're too hostile. You need someone to calm you down."

"Oh really? And who would that be?" she challenged, already knowing what he was about to say.

"Why *me*, of course," he responded as if on cue.

"You think so, huh?"

"Mmm hmm. Why don't you come up to my room and find out," he joked. Usually his teasing banter was a hit, but it missed its mark with Chasity. The coldness in her eyes sliced into him.

"Screw you, jackass," she snapped.

"Hold on a second." Realizing his mistake, he grabbed Chasity's arm, halting her hasty departure. He didn't want her to leave again before he could explain.

"Get your goddamn hands off me," she hissed. "Now."

"No, don't leave yet." Jason didn't mean to, but as she tried to yank away, his grip tightened on her arm. After only two brief encounters, he knew enough to expect her to be difficult, but he underestimated exactly how difficult she actually was.

Chasity, realizing that he had no intention of letting her go, yanked him close and kneed him in the groin. He dropped to the floor like a stone and she hurried off.

Jason doubled over. When he finally caught his breath, he rose cautiously to his feet, his mouth twisted in an ironic smile. He thought his usual approach would be enough. He'd have to change tactics. *Be a shame to risk our future children.*

A couple of minutes later, and Jason was back inside Thompson Hall in search of Sidra.

"Oh, hi Jason," she said, moving some hair away from her face. "Did you see Chasity?"

"Uh huh. She left, I'm guessing she went back to the dorm. You might want to check on her."

"And why is that?" Sidra inquired, eying him suspiciously.

"Look, I messed up. She's upset." Jason ran a nervous hand over his hair.

Sidra took a good look at him. *What the hell did you do?* she thought.

"I'll go find her. I'll take Alex with me. Malajia will never leave a party early."

"Thanks."

Alex, feeling a little down, didn't need any persuading. She wanted to call Paul; she hadn't spoken to him in two days.

The two hurried up the stairs at Torrence hall, but stopped abruptly in the hall outside Sidra's room.

"What's going on?" A loud crash startled Alex. "Should we call security?"

"Not just yet," Sidra said. Knowing Alex's penchant for meddling, she'd deliberately kept her in the dark about her conversation with Jason.

Cautiously, Sidra unlocked the door and pushed it open.

They were greeted by a mess on Chasity's side of the room. Chair toppled over, her desk swept clean, its contents littering the floor.

Temper spent, Chasity sat on the loveseat. "What the hell are you doing back so early?" she demanded.

"Jason sent me," Sidra stated, carefully stepping over the mess.

"Sent you for *what*?" Chasity snapped. "Whatever he said, I don't want to hear it."

"What happened?" Alex questioned, sensing Chasity's frustration at the mention of his name.

"He's a jackass and I kicked him in his dick."

Alex and Sidra gave a collective gasp. "Um, wow," Sidra replied calmly. "He neglected to mention that."

"Not surprised," Chasity sneered.

"Well Chasity, he seems like he's a nice guy...at least that's how he comes across to *me*," Sidra put in quietly. "He seemed genuinely concerned about you."

Chasity looked away. Absently, she rubbed her arm. "Hey," Alex pounced. The bruise was just beginning to show. "Or, maybe, he got what he deserved. Did he hurt you?"

"No," Chasity sighed. "He *did* grab my arm to stop me from walking away, but it didn't hurt. I just bruise easy." She didn't really want to go into any detail with the girls about her confrontation with Jason. She was used to keeping her business to herself. However, she didn't want them to think that he had intended to physically harm her. She may have been angry at his approach, but she didn't want a rumor like that to spread.

"He should have kept his damn hands to himself anyway," Alex concluded. "So in my opinion you were justified in what you did."

"Alex, I think she may have overreacted. It's not like he was trying to hurt her," Sidra debated.

"Sidra, you may have very well done the same thing," Alex argued turning her attention from Sidra to Chasity, "You agree, right Chaz?"

"I react how I need to," Chasity admitted, pushing herself up from the couch. Her reaction may have shocked the girls, but it was nothing new to her. She'd dealt with her short temper for a long time, but had yet to learn how to constructively handle it.

"So, what happened to our room?"

"I couldn't calm myself down, so I fucked up my stuff," she confessed, examining the mess. "It was either *that* or punch a wall...or fuck up *your* stuff."

"Your temper tantrum do any good?" Sidra asked, curiously as she folded her arms. She'd never been tempted to throw anything.

"A little. Now I'm just tired."

"Well, sleep it off," Sidra ordered. "While I hide my breakable things."

"I agree with her," Alex added. "It's been a long night. You can clean up this mess in the morning."

Chapter 9

Pointer in hand, the professor paced back and forth across the stage of the darkened lecture hall. Slides of microscopic images flashed across the huge screen behind him. Biology was a tough course, and all around Chasity and Alex were students bent over their notebooks, diligently taking notes.

Chasity thought, *that Advance Placement class I had in high school barely prepared me for this crap. And I wish this idiot behind me would shut the hell up.* She was distracted and getting more and more annoyed. Jason, sitting directly behind her, kept pestering her.

"Leave me the hell alone," she hissed, swinging around in her seat to confront him. "You haven't learned your lesson from the other night?"

"Oh, that's real cute," Jason shot back, eyes narrowed.

The professor laid his pointer on the lectern and looked up. "Miss Parker, Mr. Adams, we are discussing the structure and function of cells," he reminded dryly. "You might be surprised, but some of your fellow classmates are actually interested. No more distractions, please."

"Leave her alone, Jason," Alex warned. "You'll get her kicked out of class."

"I can't believe she couldn't take a damn joke," he muttered.

"Some joke," Alex whispered, "suggesting she come to your room. That was disrespectful." Jason rolled his eyes as he shifted in his seat.

The professor banged the pointer against the lectern. "That's enough. All three of you, out. You obviously have more important matters to discuss."

"Damn it," Jason complained, slamming his textbook closed.

"Fine, I'm over this shit anyway," Chasity fumed, grabbing her bag and standing up.

"Well, that's just great," Alex spat, shoving her pen and notebook into her book bag. "You happy now, Jason?"

Alex was still fuming when she got back to her room. She needed to get her swipe card to use at the cafeteria. Barely in the door, she dropped her book bag and made a dash for the loudly ringing telephone. "Hello?"

"Alex, I called to see what you were up to."

Alex grimaced at the sound of Paul's voice. That's all she needed for the morning to go downhill even faster. She really didn't want to talk to him. They'd been together so long, she was beginning to wonder if they stuck together out force of habit.

"Um, I'm on my way to meet my friends for lunch."

"Oh, really? Do you have to meet them *now*?" Paul asked, obviously frustrated.

"Well, yeah. The cafeteria stops serving lunch after a certain time. You know I can't afford to do a bunch of extra food shopping or eat out."

"Fine, Alex. Go on then."

"Paul, I'll be back and I'll call you later," she said, trying to reassure him.

"Whatever!"

Alex stared at the phone, listening to the dial tone. Then she angrily punched the redial button.

"How dare you hang up on me? What the hell is your problem?" she demanded, "You've been giving me attitude for the past couple weeks. What's wrong with you?"

"What's wrong with *me*? Alex, I'm not stupid. I know that you're cheating on me," he spat out.

"Are you crazy?" Her jaw dropped. "I would *never* cheat in a relationship. I can't believe you would accuse me of something like that!"

"So what am I supposed to think when you're up there with all those college guys, huh?"

"What do you want me to do? Come home and sit with you?" she yelled.

"Yes. Yes, Alex, I want you to come home!"

"You would love that, wouldn't you? For me to give up my dreams, come home, and sit there doing nothing with *you*."

"You know, I don't need this from you. There are plenty of girls right here who wouldn't mind being with me," he threatened.

"What? You mean those smutty girls with their tits and asses hanging out of their clothes? You know what? If you'd rather be with someone like *that,* then by all means go for it. I don't want to talk to you anymore." She slammed the phone down and ran her hands over her face. She wasn't about to be disrespected. Nor was she going to sit there and sulk.

She made it to the cafeteria before the kitchen shut down. The hurried walk over cooled her temper. It was simply too beautiful a day to mope over Paul and his stupid threats. The entrees of the day were lasagna and meatloaf with mashed potatoes; she concluded that neither one looked that appealing to her and headed for the salad bar. She filled a large plastic bowl with romaine lettuce, red onions, some croutons, green peppers, and a couple pieces of grilled chicken.

She squeezed in next to Emily at the table in the corner. Acknowledging Malajia and Sidra, she speared a piece of lettuce with her fork.

"Jason managed to get me and Chasity kicked out of Biology class," she said between crunches.

"Really? Did Jason get kicked out too?" Emily asked.

"Yep"

"Chasity probably started with him first. That's so typical," Malajia put in.

"What do you mean *typical?*" Alex asked, shooting her a glance. "You don't know her well enough to know what's typical of her."

"Alex, please. That girl is evil," Malajia replied, waving her spoon in Alex's face. "You can play Captain Save-a-Bitch if you want, but don't get an attitude with *me* because I don't like her."

"It wasn't *her* fault," Alex maintained.

"You've got to be kidding me." Malajia tossed her fruit cup in the trash. "I don't want this shit. I'm going back to the dorm. Y'all coming or not? I don't have all day."

"I'm going to need for you to check that tone," Sidra put in, stirring the soup in her bowl.

"Check that bun in your hair," Malajia shot back, gesturing to Sidra's tightly wrapped bun pulled off to the side of her head.

Sidra, holding a phony smile moved her bang out of her face using her middle finger.

Good one, Malajia thought, smirking.

"Stop it you two. Come on, let's go," Alex interjected, glancing at her watch. "Chasity's probably there already waiting at our dorm. I have David's notes from his earlier Bio class; I told her she can come over and copy them too."

Malajia let out an audible groan, but for once kept her mouth shut. Any comment was sure to provoke another one of Alex's lectures, and she was sick of them.

They found Chasity standing in the hallway outside Alex's room, propped against the wall, eyes closed, resting her head against the wall. She wasn't going to come because, frankly, the girls annoyed her. But she knew that those notes held details about an important assignment that was due soon. She may be annoyed, but she wasn't stupid.

"That's great, the whole damn crew," she moaned as they tromped up.

"So happy to see us," Sidra laughed. Not bothering to reply, Chasity pressed her hand against her forehead. Unsteady, she continued to lean against the wall while Alex unlocked the door.

"Are you okay?" Emily asked.

"No, I have a headache, and I know y'all are just gonna make it worse," she muttered.

"Aww, she's mad cause her head hurts," Malajia teased as she stood next to Chasity.

"Somebody get her away from me," Chasity seethed. The offhand comment caused Malajia to chuckle.

"Why don't you take some aspirin or something?" Emily suggested, setting her book bag on the floor once she and the others walked into the room.

"If I *had* some, I would have *taken* them already." Chasity sighed. What a stupid question. Her head throbbing, it was all she could do to keep from snapping at Emily.

"That's no problem," Emily offered. "Malajia has some, next to her vitamins, over there on the dresser. Can Chasity take a couple?"

"Yeah. Anything to keep her from being a bigger bitch than she already is." Malajia flopped down on the chair and dug around in her book bag for a pack of candy. She waved a piece in Alex's direction. "But I'm not moving. You're closest. Toss her the bottle."

"Malajia this is a mess. How do you find anything?" Alex commented idly as she rummaged through the jumble of bracelets, makeup, and nail polish littering Malajia's dresser top. "Ha, found them…" she broke off and frowned. Tossing the bottle to Chasity, she confronted Malajia. "What are you doing with these?" she asked.

Everyone in the room, except Emily, recognized the familiar pills. "What is she doing with them? That's a dumb question, Alex," Chasity interjected, removing a bottle of water from her book bag. "I'm figuring that she doesn't want any babies, *that's* why."

"Why am I not surprised that you would have them all out in the open," Sidra commented. "Some guy can walk in here and see them and think it's open season."

Malajia frowned. "Open season for *what* Sidra? Huh?"

"For your legs, sweetie," she shot back.

"Heifer, you know what…"

"Malajia, is that what they're for?" Emily wailed, her eyes widening in shock, interrupting Malajia's rant.

"Not at all Emily," Alex interrupted. "Malajia's never had sex. Isn't that right Malajia?"

Sidra's mouth dropped open with shock.

"Say what now?" Chasity questioned, nearly choking on the pills. She didn't know what to make of Malajia, the loud, skimpy dressing, party girl—a virgin?

"Yes…and Malajia go ahead; lie and say that we never had that conversation," Alex said, pointing the birth control pills in Malajia's direction.

"I don't care that people know that I'm a virgin, Alex," Malajia shot back, arms folded.

"Why are you taking them?" Alex quizzed.

"Look, it's not a big deal," Malajia blurted out defensively. "So what if I want to be prepared? I could meet my first at any time."

"You really that pressed for some dick?" Chasity asked smartly.

"Were you *born* ignorant?" Malajia scowled.

"Nope," Chasity smirked.

"Wait a minute, hold on," Sidra interrupted, putting her hand up. "Malajia you're really a virgin? Seriously?"

Malajia rolled her eyes. "Is it that much of a shock?" she questioned.

"Yes. All this time I thought that you slept around," Sidra admitted.

"I don't understand," Emily put in shyly.

"Of *course* you don't," Malajia bit out, throwing up her hands in frustration. "God you act so clueless Emily, I just haven't found anyone—"

"Nobody gives a shit," Chasity interjected, tired of hearing Malajia talk.

"Oh, *I* do, and that explanation is straight bull," Alex put in, pointing at Malajia.

"Geez, Alex. Who died and made you mother of the group?" Sidra joked.

"I'm *not* Sidra, but *she* needs to stop telling lies...Malajia," Alex pressed.

"All right fine," she growled. "I've been having irregular periods. My doctor prescribed them. He thought they'd help."

"Well, that makes more sense," Sidra said. "Why didn't you just say that in the first place, instead of feeding us that other crap? You made yourself look desperate."

Chasity was confused, and it showed on her face in the form of a frown. "Wait, did you really just sit here and come up with that dumbass lie?"

"What? Ya'll mad because I'd rather say that I have the pills to prepare for my first, rather than tell y'all that they're for my irregular period?" Malajia shot back.

Chasity narrowed her eyes at Malajia "Okay, repeat that question and tell me if that makes as much sense to you as it does to me." She didn't understand why Malajia would just lie about something so simple.

"Exactly," Alex chimed in. Malajia flagged them, and proceeded to eat her candy.

Two or three minutes ticked by before Malajia finally broke the silence. "Well, now that the discussion about my virginity and my period are over, let's go out somewhere."

"What do you have in mind?" Sidra asked, tossing a big red pillow at her.

"I don't know," Malajia said, tossing the pillow back.

Sidra ducked, "Wow, good plan."

"It should have hit your smart self," Malajia mused. "I just thought I could add some joy to your worthless, boring lives, okay?"

"Malajia, nobody wants your damn joy," Chasity declared, sipping her water.

"Damn it Chasity, will you chill with the smart ass comments?" Malajia let out a frustrated sigh. "Just angry for no damn reason."

Sidra chuckled to herself. *Mad because you're not the only one making the smart comments huh, Malajia?*

"We could go for a ride," Alex broke in. "You know, do some sightseeing."

"You have a car?" Chasity asked Alex, even though she already knew the answer.

"No, but *you* do," Alex replied.

"I'm not taking y'all no-damn-where," Chasity stated.

"Yes, you are. Come on, grab your keys." Alex stood up, taking a few steps toward Chasity.

"Alex, I have a damn headache, not to mention that I can't stand you."

"Those pills that you took will kick in soon." Alex shoved Chasity's purse and keys at her. "You know that we're growing on you"

"Growing on my last damn nerve," Chasity retorted, walking out the door. It was clear Alex wasn't going to back down. Maybe some fresh air would clear her head.

"Come on, before she changes her mind," Malajia called, skipping out the door.

"Hurry up, Emily," Sidra instructed. "You know her mean self will drive off without us."

"Can I drive?" Malajia pleaded, prancing alongside Chasity as they walked to the car.

"Fuck no," Chasity retorted "Don't ask me another stupid question."

"Oh, she will," Alex put in, climbing into the backseat. "Stupid questions and answers are her specialty."

Sidra opened the door on the passenger's side, but Malajia scooted around her. "I wanna sit in front," she complained, trying to nudge Sidra out of the way with her hips.

"Hell no; get your ass in the back, or you don't go," Chasity commanded.

"How come *she* gets to ride in the front?" she complained, pointing at Sidra who just stood there with her perfectly manicured hand on her hip.

"Because I'm the roommate, so HA!" Sidra shot back.

Resigned, Malajia climbed into the back next to Alex. "Move over," she ordered, "that orange shirt you got on is making me hot." Malajia leaned forward, craning her neck so she could fix her hair in the rearview mirror. With a smirk, Chasity immediately adjusted the mirror.

"You are so *ignorant*," Malajia declared. She was beginning to get a handle on Chasity. Her nastiness, the rude comments, were like those electric fences people used to keep stray dogs out. Zap and off they'd run tails between their legs. *Not this girl, she doesn't intimidate me,* Malajia thought. She knew all about the masks people used to hide behind.

"Stop messing around and move over, Malajia," Alex said. "Emily still needs to get in."

"Um." Emily hesitated on the parking lot pavement, shifting from one foot to the other. "I can't leave. I'm...Um..."

"That's it. Close the door. I'm pulling off," Chasity warned, voice full of frustration.

"No. Wait a minute," Alex protested, straightening up in her seat.

"Look, I'm sorry, okay?" Emily stammered.

"Are we going to go through this *every time* we want to go somewhere?" Malajia asked. "Don't you guys remember how long it took to persuade her to come with us to the mall a few weeks ago? I don't feel like it today."

"Leave her alone," Sidra said, fastening her seatbelt.

"I wanna go," Malajia whined, slamming her hand on the back of the passenger seat.

"Girl, will you shut up," Chasity interjected, tired of hearing the sound of Malajia's voice.

"Emily, why don't you want to go?" Alex asked.

Emily shrugged. "My Mom is going to call in a few minutes. If I'm not in the room, she'll flip out," she said.

"Oh my god," Chasity mumbled. *Is this girl serious?*

"Seriously? Girl, tell your mother that you're grown and get in this car," Malajia commanded, fluffing her hair with her hand.

"Listen Emily, you don't have to do anything that you don't want to do, okay?" Alex assured her roommate.

"Are you sure that you don't want to go?" Sidra asked.

"She's sure, let's go," Malajia said quickly. "Nothing against you honey, but we want to get going."

"Okay. I'll see you all later," Emily said in a small voice.

"*Now* can I pull off?" Chasity asked, glancing at Alex through her rearview mirror.

"Sure can," Alex replied, sitting back in her seat.

Emily watched the sleek black car until it disappeared around the corner. Then she turned and walked slowly back to her room.

Chapter 10

A week later, the weather took one of those sudden turns that signaled fall was on its way, even in Virginia. The brisk wind sent leaves scuttling across the path. Walking to English class, Chasity kept her head down. She folded her arms to her chest, wishing she had put on her leather jacket over the lightweight long-sleeved top.

The weather suited her mood. She was sure she had just failed that pop quiz in Math, coming on the heels of the Dean's warning. He wasn't amused that one of his professors had to kick three students out of class.

"Seriously?" she sputtered when Jason bumped into her. "Watch where you're going!"

"My fault, Chasity. It was an accident," he apologized.

"Whatever," she grunted. "Just get out of my way, Jason."

"At least you remember my name," he pointed out.

"I never said that I *didn't*," she replied, voice not masking her irritation.

"I know," he said casually, "I just wanted to get a rise out of you."

"Move," she ordered. "I need to go to class."

"Not just yet. I want to talk to you," he protested, stepping in her way to halt her departure.

"Talk?" she ground out, "Oh, now you wanna talk?"

"Chasity—"

"No. *Talking* wasn't your main priority last week now, was it?" she scolded.

"Listen, I really *did* want to talk to you. I honestly didn't want to sleep with you that night. I mean, I *did*, but—"

"Fuck you," she hissed.

"Hey, I'm just kidding, don't get upset," he urged, swallowing a laugh.

She shot him a cold look. "Do you think you're funny?" she asked.

"Sometimes. But honestly, I was just joking with you," he said. "I won't disrespect you again, I swear. My parents raised me better than that."

"Are you finished?" she finally asked after staring at him for a long moment.

"Almost...Look, I sometimes have a rude sense of humor," he admitted. "Sue me. It won't stop me from pursuing you."

"Get out my face," she enunciated slowly.

"Listen, can't we just start over?" he asked.

"No." Chasity's reply was instantaneous.

"Damn. Can you at least *think* about it?" he asked playfully.

She glared at him, and his smile quickly faded. She looked at her expensive silver and diamond watch and tapped the face. "You've just made me late for my class."

"Oh, I'm sorry," he replied, then smiled. "Again."

"That's funny?" she questioned.

"No, of course not," he muttered, his smile fading.

"You're an asshole."

"And *you're* difficult, but that won't keep me away," he advised.

Chasity rolled her eyes. "I hate you," she hissed, turning to walk away.

"I know that you don't mean that," he called after her. "My team is having a party next Saturday, and I would love for you and your friends to come!"

"How many damn parties are you gonna throw?" she yelled back

"As many as it takes for you to have a good time," he guaranteed.

"Chaz are you going to Jason's party?" Sidra whispered. Chasity made a face that Sidra had grown accustomed to. It was her way of saying 'hell no' without actually saying the words.

"He's got some nerve," Alex whispered They'd gone to the library to cram for their Psychology quiz, but huddled over their books, Chasity mentioned to Sidra and Alex about her conversation with Jason earlier that day. "To ask us to a party. After he got us tossed out of class and hauled in front of the Dean?"

"What? A party?" Malajia asked loudly from the other side of the library table.

"Shhhh," Sidra admonished. "You don't have to be so loud. In case you hadn't noticed, this is a library."

"What time is the party?" Malajia persevered. A party was far more interesting than the psych chapter she had been reading.

"Malajia, I don't know and I don't care," Chasity ground out, annoyed that Malajia had been eavesdropping. "So drop it and leave me alone."

"Look you—"

"Shhhhhh," Sidra repeated, nervously looking around. *She's always so damn loud.*

"I will *not* leave you alone. How could you accept an invitation to a party, and not find out what *time* it is?" Malajia asked, exasperated.

"First of all, I never *accepted* his invitation," Chasity tossed her notebook down on the table. "Secondly, I don't give a shit about this party because I'm not going."

"Ugh, are you out of your mind?" Malajia asked.

"No stupid, I'm *not*," Chasity responded slowly, shaking her head.

"This is *Jason Adams* that we're talking about here," Malajia continued.

"No, we should be talking about Psychology here," Alex said, tapping her book with her pen.

"That can wait," Malajia protested.

"No, it *can't*, Malajia," Sidra chimed in. "We have a quiz tomorrow."

"Fine." Malajia picked up her notebook and leaned back in her chair. "I wonder what I'm gonna wear."

"Malajia," Sidra called, prompting Malajia to look up at her. "Shut. Up."

Alex looked over at Chasity. "Did you take notes in History class?" she asked.

"Yeah, why?" Chasity asked, curious. Alex had been sitting right next to her during class.

"I need to borrow them. Mine are a mess. I wasn't paying attention," Alex explained.

"Yeah. Go ahead," Chasity replied as she pointed to her notebook.

"You seem preoccupied." Sidra took a long look at Alex. "You okay?"

"Yeah, I'm fine, I just have something on my mind," she replied, skirting the truth. She hadn't had a civilized conversation with Paul in over a week, not since he'd hung up on her. Not quite sure why, she'd kept her problems private, not sharing them with anyone.

"Forget Alex," Malajia exclaimed, grabbing the girls' attention. "Did Chasity just do something *nice*?"

"What?" Chasity frowned. "You hype because I gave Alex my notes?"

"Uh, *yeah*," Malajia replied, "Since you're in such a generous mood, can—"

"No," Chasity supplied before Malajia could continue.

"You don't even know what I was going to ask," Malajia complained.

"Doesn't matter, the answer is 'no' no matter *what* you ask," Chasity responded. Malajia sucked her teeth as Sidra giggled.

Alex threw her books on the table. "Hey, Emily," she greeted. "Girl, I'm glad that Psych quiz is over. I think I aced it."

"Hi," Emily said softly. "That's good news. Alex, can I ask you a question?"

"Sure, sweetie. You can ask me anything," she answered, flopping down on the bed next to Emily "What's on your mind?"

"Uh," Emily faltered, not sure she actually wanted to know the answer. "Do you guys mind me hanging out with you?"

"What? No, of course we don't mind," Alex stammered. "Why would you even ask that?"

"I don't know. I mean, I do," she said, fiddling with her hands. "I just get the feeling that you guys let me stick around because you feel sorry for me."

"That's *not* why we hang out with you," Alex protested. "You're a good person, sweetie. I mean, come on; you've seen how the rest of us act. We have to have *someone* nice in the group."

"You mean, a naive little girl who can't stick up for herself," Emily amended, "but a *nice* addition to the group."

"We like you. You just need to loosen up a little. You're in college. It's okay to go out and it's okay to miss your mother's call every now and then, and if someone says something to you that you don't like, it's okay to *tell* them.

How are we supposed to know that we are upsetting you if you don't say anything?"

"It's not that you guys upset me," Emily fumbled for an explanation. "I'm just so used to my mother standing up for me that I've never had to do it for myself. Now I'm paying the price I guess. I'm going to try, but it's hard, and I don't want you guys to stop hanging out with me because of it."

"Emily, honey, you don't have to worry," Alex assured. "Malajia and Chasity can be a couple of jerks sometimes, but they're harmless. Just be yourself okay, you don't have to worry about trying to please us."

"Okay," Emily sniffed. "Thanks...Thanks for talking to me about this."

"Anytime sweetie," Alex smiled, and threw her arms around Emily.

Chasity and Alex were in the gym working out, while Malajia watched the guys work out.

"Damn he's fine," Malajia sighed and pointed at the tall, light-skinned guy lifting weights.

"Look at all those muscles. You better lift those weights, you sexy thing."

"I'll bet twenty dollars you're thinking about sex," Chasity challenged.

"Girl why would I take that bet?" Malajia laughed back. "You think I'm dumb? I'd lose. And I *need* my money."

When Sidra walked in wearing sweats with her gym bag over her shoulder, Malajia's mouth dropped to the floor.

"Miss Sidra? No dress slacks, no silk blouse?" she gaped. "What have you done with my friend?"

"Funny," Sidra fired back with an equally phony smile. "At least I actually *wear* clothes."

"Ooh, you shouldn't hate honey." Malajia cautioned, fiddling with the strap of her red sports bra. "Jealousy doesn't look good on you."

"Give it a rest, Malajia," Alex interjected. "Nobody is jealous of you, and you know that."

"Alex, I wasn't even talking to you," Malajia complained. "Can you at least *try* to mind your business?"

"I'll mind my own business when you start wearing clothes that have more than two strings of fabric to them," Alex retorted, picking up her water bottle.

"You're just mad because you're fat," Malajia huffed and walked away.

"Hey, I'm not fat!" Alex yelled after her. She turned her focus to Sidra "Since when is being curvy, fat?"

"She doesn't think you're fat really; she's just being a jackass," Sidra assured her, knowing her childhood friend all too well.

"What's up, ladies?" Josh greeted, ambling toward the group with Mark and David in tow.

"Where are my hugs, ladies?" Mark demanded.

"In the trash!" Malajia shouted from a few feet away.

"I wasn't including *you!*" Mark yelled back.

"Being around the two of them is gonna make me go deaf," Sidra predicted and rubbed her ears.

Alex watched as Mark walked up to Malajia and started swatting her with his towel while he screamed like a fool. "Seriously? You play too much!" Malajia hollered while he walked away laughing.

"Sidra, Mark is an idiot," Alex commented.

"Every day," Sidra giggled.

"Hey, Jason," Josh called out. "Want to play some ball? We're having a pickup game."

"Be there is a sec," Jason replied, setting the barbell he was using back on its rack. He picked up his towel and wiped the sweat off his forehead and arms. After wrapping the damp towel around his neck, he took a deep breath, and walked over to the elliptical machine. Chasity was putting the machine through its paces.

"Hello, beautiful," he whispered and rested his arms on the control console. Chasity checked her stride for an instant, then resumed her punishing pace.

"Go away," she groaned.

"Can't you just say *hello* or *hi?*" he asked, cocking his head at her. She looked great, so toned, glistening, and disheveled.

"Nope," she shot back and tightened her grip on the machine's handle bars. "Go away."

"Not until I find out if you're coming to my party."

"*I'll* be there Jason," Malajia interrupted. She'd scurried over as soon as she saw Jason corner Chasity. "Just tell me when."

"Uh, hello...um...." Jason stuttered, searching for a name.

"Malajia Lakeshia Simmons," she put in enthusiastically.

"Please," Chasity muttered, rolling her eyes at Malajia's eagerness.

"Any chance you might persuade your friend here to come too?" he asked with a conspiratorial wink.

Chasity turned her lip up. "*Friend?*" she scoffed.

"I don't like *her*," Malajia sneered, pointing to Chasity. "Besides, there's no chance that she can be persuaded." She knew Chasity well enough now to guess that persuasion wouldn't work. Just for spite, the girl wouldn't go, and would tear through anybody who tried to make her.

"Y'all want to stop talking about me like I'm not here?" Chasity sighed, irritated that her workout was being disrupted.

"If you would stop ignoring us, we wouldn't *have* to," Jason stated, grabbing his towel with both hands.

Malajia tapped Jason's arm, smiling slyly "Jason, she's just extra. She's too afraid to come to your party. Don't even waste your time."

Chasity snapped her head towards them. "Afraid? Of what? *Him?*" she blurted out, halting her stride.

Malajia shrugged. "Obviously it's *something*, if you don't want to go to this party." Jason suppressed a smirk as he watched how easy it was for Malajia to work Chasity into a frenzy.

"Don't play yourself; I'm not afraid of a goddamn thing." Chasity hopped off of the elliptical machine. "Y'all make me sick."

"Oh, she'll definitely go now," Malajia murmured to herself as she watched Chasity grab her gym bag. "You just have to know what buttons to push." Jason gave her the thumbs up sign, before walking off to play basketball with the guys. Malajia let out a long sigh of pure pleasure. Now she had a whole week to think about the men that would be at the party, and more importantly, her wardrobe.

Chapter 11

Saturday afternoon, Malajia was electric with excitement, counting the hours until the party. "What do you ladies think I should wear?" she asked. Bits of color that masqueraded as dresses covered Sidra's bedspread. She picked up a short one-shoulder red cocktail dress, but after some consideration tossed it back on the bed.

"How many times are you going to ask us that damn question?" Chasity complained, her voice rising with each word.

"As many times as it takes to get a freakin' answer out of you assholes," Malajia shot back.

"Why do we have to be assholes?" Sidra questioned. "And why did you feel the need to bring your whole damn wardrobe over here to show us? Take that back to *your* room."

"Look here, Ponytail—" Sidra couldn't help but chuckle at that comment. "I already told you earlier that I was coming over here to ask y'all opinion," Malajia explained, tossing a black dress back on the bed.

"I know that, and I asked you *then* why you were going to do that?" Sidra reminded. "We could have come over to your room."

"Because that one over there was bitchin' about not wanting to come over," Malajia shot back, pointing to Chasity.

"And I was hoping you would take the hint that I didn't want to see you. Obviously, I gave your simple ass too much credit," Chasity retorted with an even tone.

Malajia sucked her teeth. "I don't need this kind of treatment. I deserve you people's respect."

"Who told you that lie?" Sidra put in.

"Whatever, with your overdressed self," Malajia pointed out, slowly surveying Sidra's dark-blue pencil skirt and white silk blouse. "And," she added, "Emily—what the hell do *you* have on?"

Malajia turned her nose up. She couldn't believe that Emily actually intended to show up to a college party in a frumpy, shapeless maxi dress, paired with a cardigan. To make matters worse, she had tied her sandy brown, mid length hair into two ponytails.

"Emily, we're going to a *party*," she grumbled, "not to church. You look crazy; you better go pick out something else to wear. And *please*, take those damn ponytails down."

"Malajia, the party is like eight hours from now," Alex objected. "Will you chill out?"

"What's wrong with this dress?" Emily asked, grabbing some of the fabric "My mother picked it out."

"Should you take this? Or should *I*?" Malajia asked Chasity.

"Let me," Chasity replied. "Emily, sweetie—that dress is ugly."

"It is?" Emily asked as she looked down at her dress.

"Yeah, girl, Chasity's right," Malajia agreed. "That dress is quite ugly...*extremely* ugly."

"Stop it you two," Alex interjected. "Emily, your dress is *not* ugly."

"Oh, like you're gonna take fashion advice from *Alex*?" Malajia laughed. "Emily, have you seen her shirts?"

"Why do you always have to talk about somebody's clothes?" Alex slapped her hand down on the loveseat. "Why can't you accept that we all have our own sense of style?"

"I respect that and all." Malajia moved a stray hair out of her eyes. "But if you have on something ugly, I'm gonna tell you. That's just who I am."

"How would you like it if we started picking on *your* clothes?" Alex questioned.

"Oh, there's nothing that you can say about *my* wardrobe," Malajia returned confidently.

Alex looked at Sidra. "Should you take this? Or should *I*?" she posed.

"Allow me," Sidra replied.

"Oh, what are you gonna say Sid? What?" Malajia taunted. "That my clothes are too tight, too short? Come on, help me out here."

"You look like a whore," Chasity interjected, nonchalantly examining her nails. On hearing a loud huff from Sidra, she glanced up. "What? You were taking too long."

"I don't give a damn what you say, I still look good, screw y'all," Malajia maintained, unfazed.

"Malajia," Emily protested, "I like this dress. I'm comfortable in it."

"Girl, when it comes to fashion, comfort has nothing to do with it," Malajia instructed. "It's all about style."

"Sorry, Malajia," Sidra objected, "but comfort rules in any case."

"Playing Princess Dress Up every day can*not* be that comfortable," Malajia fired back.

"Neither is playing Come Fuck Me Dress Up," Chasity commented dryly, prompting a laugh from Alex.

Malajia's head snapped in Chasity's direction. "Bitch!" she snapped.

"Too easy," Chasity chuckled.

"That was mean, but you leave yourself wide open for her comments Malajia," Alex commiserated.

"Whatever." Malajia dismissed Alex's intrusive sympathy with a wave of the hand. "Let's get off me, and back to Emily. She's needs to change that dress." Malajia grabbed the unsuspecting Emily by the hand, and marched her toward Chasity's closet.

"What the hell do you think *you're* doing?" Chasity demanded, following her progress.

"Emily doesn't have anything in her closet that isn't *Mommy* approved," Malajia stated patiently, "so I'm gonna take her shopping. In your closet, Chasity."

"Whoa." Chasity shot Malajia a dangerous look. "Nobody's body goes in my clothes but mine."

"Listen—"

"Hell no!"

"No, listen..." Malajia pleaded. "Emily doesn't have the guts to pull off *my* wardrobe, Sidra is too damn dressy, and Alex wears ugly colors."

"Hey, dark green is bangin', girl," Alex inserted, amused at the summary. "Don't knock it."

"You're not going into my closet, you freak," Chasity warned, earning a snicker from Sidra.

"What she said wasn't even funny!" Malajia yelled at Sidra. "You always laughing at dumb shit."

"Who the hell do you think you're talking to like that?" Sidra shot back.

"Whatever." Malajia refused to be distracted. On a mission, she threw open the door to Chasity's closet, and began closely examining its contents.

"I told her ass no," Chasity gritted her teeth. At the sound of hangers clanking, she jumped up from the couch. "Are you fuckin' stupid?" she charged, yanking Malajia away from her closet. "I said no."

"I'm not stupid," Malajia jeered, pulling the top of her shirt back into place. "But you're being stingy. You have enough clothes in this closet to dress half the school."

"Malajia, it's no big deal. I'll just wear *this*," Emily put in. She hated all the fuss.

"Will you lighten up, Chasity?" Malajia appealed. "Look at her. Isn't she too nice to say 'no' to?"

"No, not really," Chasity answered, shaking her head.

"Okay, I am begging you. *Please* don't make me be seen in public with her wearing that dress, *please*," Malajia bleated out. "She's gonna embarrass me."

"I don't give two shits about you *or* her," Chasity barked, folding her arms.

"Listen, it's just one outfit." Malajia reasoned. "You won't even miss it. Hell, you probably don't remember you had it."

"That's not the damn point," Chasity argued. "Now, skip your happy ass away from my closet."

"So, you're *really* gonna be like that?" Malajia pestered

"Get away from me!" Chasity snapped, prompting a laugh from Sidra.

"Man," Malajia whined with frustration.

"Calm down," Sidra advised. "*I* have an outfit that Emily can wear."

"Nobody wants those damn dress suits," Malajia groaned. "This ain't gonna be no better."

Ten minutes rolled by. Malajia sat on the bed, beating out a nervous rhythm on the side rail with her nails. *What the hell is taking so long?* she wondered. She was itching to get to her room. She figured it would take about three hours to perfect her look.

"Ooh, I found it!" Sidra finally exclaimed.

Malajia shifted on the bed and propped herself up on one elbow. "About time."

"Malajia, I'm gonna hit you in a minute." Sidra threw the outfit at her. It missed its target and slid off the bed. Malajia bent over and examined it.

"Not bad," she concluded after checking out the baby-blue skirt and white sleeveless top.

"You don't have to say it like that," Sidra muttered and rolled her eyes. "I have more than suits in my closet, smart ass."

"That's so cute, Sidra," Alex raved, "Perfect for Emily. She will look—"

"Nobody asked you," Malajia pointed out. "You don't need to give any fashion advice." Malajia began taking the skirt and top off their hangers.

"Keep talking that smack, hear?" Alex warned, pointing a finger at her.

"Uhh, Sidra sweetie, these are clean, aren't they?" Malajia questioned, ignoring Alex.

"No, I keep dirty clothes in my closet," Sidra replied, her voice dripping with sarcasm.

"You *do*?" Malajia's mouth fell open in shock. "Eww, dirty ass."

"No," Sidra spat out. "The damn outfit is clean. I've never worn it."

"All right, geez," Malajia shrugged. "That's all you had to say. Can Emily try them on now?"

"No, wait." Sidra shook her head and ran back to her closet. "I have something else to complete the outfit."

"No, not one of your blazers," Malajia pleaded.

"Shut up," Sidra hissed and pulled a sheer, white, long-sleeved shirt off of a hanger.

"Oh, that'll work." Malajia nodded and handed it to Emily along with the skirt and top, while tossing the hangers on the floor. "Try these on."

"Thanks," Emily beamed, then looked at the floor. She hated getting undressed in front of anyone. "Um, can I use your bathroom?"

"Sure," Sidra said, eyeing Malajia sprawled out on her bed. *Ugh, she's annoying me,* she thought. A little push was all it took to dump Malajia on the floor. She landed on her butt with a thump and Sidra's lips curled up in a satisfied grin.

"Ouch!" Malajia yelped. "What the hell was *that* for?"

"Talking about my clothes," Sidra fussed, "and sitting on my bed."

"Play nice, you two," Alex cautioned as Malajia picked herself up from the floor.

"What's going on out here?" Emily inquired, stepping warily out of the bathroom.

"Our friends are crazy," Alex replied with asperity. "But you look nice Em."

"Mmm hmm," Malajia murmured, for once agreeing with Alex's opinion when it came to fashion. "That'll do, Emily. That's a hundred times better than that raggedy mess your mom picked out." She glanced at her watch and gasped. "Oh man, I have to go back to my room and start on my hair."

Malajia darted for the door, completely unaware of the hanger that was lying on the floor. "Mel, be careful—" Alex was too late, Malajia's stiletto heel had gotten caught, and she tripped and fell against the door. Loud laughter erupted from Chasity and Sidra; Emily covered her face with her hands, trying not to laugh out loud.

"God Mel, are you okay?" Alex asked between laughs.

Malajia jumped up from the floor embarrassed. "Really? Who left that damn hanger there?" she exclaimed.

"*You* did," Chasity declared. "You were all hype snatching the clothes off the hanger. That's what the hell you get." Chasity noticed the menacing stare that Malajia was giving her. "Don't get mad at *me* because you smacked your damn face on the door," she shot back, earning a louder laugh from Sidra.

"Was it that funny?" Malajia glared at Sidra.

"Did you see her face?" Sidra laughed, tears rolling down her cheeks. Annoyed, Malajia stormed out of the room.

"Ta da. I'm here," Malajia announced, striking a pose outside Jason's dorm. The short strapless dress in black and red left little to the imagination. Long sparkling silver earrings glittered, complementing her curly asymmetrical bob.

"Yes, we know. We walked over together remember?" Sidra muttered, rolling her eyes.

"I wasn't announcing that for *y'all*," Malajia shot back, tugging her dress up on her chest. "I was talking to those guys over there." Gesturing to a group of guys posted up by the wall. Noticing the eye roll that Chasity gave her, Malajia placed her hands on her hips. "What Chasity? What smart thing do you have to say?"

Chasity flicked her long curls over her shoulder. "I'm paying you no mind. Just like *they* aren't." She pointed to the aforementioned guys before walking inside Thompson Hall.

Noticing the taut look on Malajia's face, Alex chuckled. "Stop coming for her Mel, she'll grind you up every time."

"Shut up Alex, nobody says 'grind'," Malajia huffed, walking up the steps. *Maybe the five-inch peep-toe pumps weren't such a good idea,* she thought. They looked great, but being a recent purchase she hadn't had time to break them in; her feet were killing her already. The tiny dress kept slipping as she awkwardly navigated the steps.

"You look uncomfortable...and cold," Sidra teased. "Bet you could use one of my blazers now, huh?"

The door to the dorm was open, the sounds of music and laughter radiated through the lobby. Chasity surveyed the tangle of bodies crowded inside. "God, why do I keep coming to these hot ass parties?" she commented tersely.

Alex looked around. "Wow, this party has a bigger turn out than the last one. Hopefully it won't turn *out* like the last one." She looked at Chasity, "no kicking anyone in the groin tonight okay?"

"Can't make any promises," Chasity proclaimed before walking away.

Emily stared. Everyone seemed to be having a good time. But there were just so many of them—it was intimidating. She wasn't sure she wanted to stay, even if Sidra's outfit had given her a major boost.

"Come on Em, let's get something to drink before they run out," Sidra suggested, sensing Emily's reluctance. Alex moseyed behind them and joined the line at the drinks table.

"I don't drink," Emily stammered. "I'm only seventeen."

"No kidding," Sidra joked and assessed the supply. "They have water, cola and ginger ale."

Before Emily could make up her mind, a burly guy in a button-down shirt and jeans sidled up to Sidra. "Forget the drinks sexy," he slurred, "you gotta come dance with me."

"How about no," she tossed over her shoulder and immediately regretted it when she got a noseful of beer breath. "Eww! Get away from me. I don't dance with drunks."

"Forget you, bitch," he muttered and stumbled away.

"Wow," Emily whispered. "That was awkward."

"Wait. Did he just call me a bitch?" Sidra questioned after registering what she had just heard. "Because I wouldn't dance with him? How freakin' rude."

"Well, you certainly got rid of him," Emily murmured. "Weren't you even a little bit nervous?"

"Girl, no," Sidra denied, "he was so drunk, he could barely walk straight. He was harmless."

Alex reached for a bottle of water and turned to Emily. "A word of advice Em. Not all drunks are harmless. So be careful, alcohol has a way of turning some people into monsters."

"Well, thank you for that advice, Mother," Malajia mocked. She just heard what Alex had said as she approached them in line. Alex noticed that she took a sip from a red plastic cup.

"What are you drinking?" Alex queried. "There are no cups over on this table."

"That's because the corny drinks are over here. I have a real drink."

Alex went to grab for the cup. "Girl, have you lost your mind?" she chided as Malajia moved it out of her reach. "You're nineteen, you can't drink."

"I'm in *college* and I can do what I want," Malajia shot back. "Back off, you're not my damn mom."

Alex sighed. "Fine Mel. Did you at *least* keep an eye on your cup when the drink was being poured?" she asked.

"No. I poured it myself, I'm not stupid." Malajia took another sip and adjusted her dress.

"What's the matter?" Mark jeered into her ear. "Dress too tight for ya? You look like you can't breathe."

"Where the hell did you come from?" she hissed. "And my dress is just fine, fool. You know you like it and you like what's *in* it."

"No chance in hell," he fired back. "Now if the body went with a different face and a better damn attitude, then *maybe* I'd like it. Maybe."

"You're an asshole," Malajia retorted, nudging him away from her. Taking her drink from her, he laughed and ambled along. *Jackass, I didn't want that nasty drink anyway,* she thought.

The crowded room started to close in on Chasity. She rubbed her temples and knew she needed some fresh air, or she'd get another one of her tension headaches.

Chasity went outside and sat down on the dorm stoop, relieved to be away from the party noise. The night was clear with only a sliver of moon. Relishing the quiet, and the slight breeze, she let her mind wander.

"Leaving?" Jason asked from the doorway.

She jerked around, annoyed at the intrusion and the intruder. "So what if I *am*?"

"Well, I would be really disappointed," he replied with a deceptive calm. All evening he'd been trying to engineer a conversation, but she'd sidestepped every approach.

"That would make me want to leave even more," she muttered, standing and brushing off her black skinny jeans.

"Still with the smart mouth," he chuckled, walking to the bottom of the steps.

"Look, shouldn't you be getting back inside? I'm sure there's some stank thing in there just waiting to throw herself at you."

"If I wanted to be in there with *another woman*, then I would be in there. But I'm *not*. I'm out here with *you*."

"Awe, I'm so touched," she mocked.

"Really?" he said, ignoring the sarcasm. "When can we go out?"

"When hell freezes over twice," she fired back instantly.

"You're funny,"

"And *you're* a pain in the ass," she declared bluntly, "so go away."

"I'm sorry, I can't do that." He folded his arms across his chest and stared at her.

"You are determined to piss me off aren't you?" she hissed.

"No, not really," Jason admitted, "But it seems to be the only way that I can get any conversation out of you."

"You're wasting your time talking to me," she swore. "You make me sick and that'll never change."

Jason stared at her for a few seconds so intensely that she blinked and looked away. "We shall see."

A high-pitched shriek broke the tension building between them. Chasity frowned, recognizing the voice of her roommate. A moment later Sidra sprinted down the steps. At the bottom, she spun round and stood still, hands on her hips.

"Listen, you drunk bastard!" she yelled. "Get the hell away from me!"

"Quit playing hard to get, you know you want me baby," he mumbled, lurching forward.

"Enough of this bullshit," Chasity decided, catching the worried look on her roommate's face. "Jason, get him."

"Way ahead of you." Jason grabbed the guy off the stoop and threw him to the ground. Before Jason could haul him to his feet, he rolled over and moaned. Jason smoothed down his long sleeved shirt and, leaning down, grabbed the guy's shirt collar. "The lady said leave her alone. Back off, or I'll kick your ass. Got it?"

"Thanks, Jason," Sidra said, as they watched the guy stagger off. "I could have handled him, but I'm glad I didn't have to."

"Sure, sweetie. Anytime," Jason assured her with a wink. "If he bothers you again, let me know, okay?"

Sidra winked back, signaling a thumbs-up to Chasity when Jason wasn't looking. Chasity returned the gesture with the middle finger of her right hand.

Chasity glanced over at Jason. "I bet you feel like the big hero, don't you?"

"No, I was just helping the lady out," he responded. "Why? Does that sort of thing turn you on?" he joked.

She couldn't help but laugh. She was still laughing when she and Sidra turned to walk back inside the dorm. Jason followed their progress and smiled. At least he'd been able to make her laugh.

Sidra groaned when she looked at the clock. It was almost three. She'd had a great time at the party, drunken thugs notwithstanding. She'd actually discovered that her callous roommate had a funny side. The byplay between Chasity and Malajia had her and Alex cracking up laughing. Even Emily managed a giggle or two at their comments.

"So, Chasity, when did you and Jason become an item?" she inquired.

Chasity's head snapped around. "Look, just because you saw me outside with him, doesn't mean that we're going to start dating. I don't even *like* him."

"Sure you don't," Sidra retorted. "You were just having an unfriendly chat alone, outside, while a party was going on inside. His party."

"I *don't*!" Chasity protested defensively.

"I think you're protesting a little too much. That's a sign, sunshine," Sidra chimed back.

"Don't feed me that bullshit," Chasity spat.

Sidra giggled as she heard someone bang on their door like they were the police. "Damn, is that banging really necessary?" she complained.

Chasity snatched open the door it. "What?" she sneered. The girl from across the hall stood there. Her head was wrapped in a scarf, she was wearing baggy printed pajamas, and her face held a mutinous expression.

"Do you know what time it is?" she hissed. "Keep the noise down. Some people are trying to sleep."

Chasity frowned down her length. "If you don't take your fuckin' ugly ass—" Sidra softly backhanded Chasity, before she got her rhythm and the insults flowed.

"We're really sorry," Sidra apologized, barely able to smother a smirk. The girl huffed, threw Sidra a venomous look, and flounced back across the hall. When she slammed the door, Sidra doubled over with laughter. "Oh my god, Chasity. You are so ignorant."

"No, her *face* was ignorant," Chasity frowned. "With those ugly ass pajamas on."

Chapter 12

"C'mon, guys. Get it together." David was annoyed, more than annoyed. It was stupid to leave the lab experiment to the last minute. It was even dumber to piss off the lab assistant.

"Kenneth isn't going to give us another chance at this. He hung around all afternoon waiting for us, and he doesn't appreciate being blown off." They'd signed up for a late afternoon session at the lab, but Jason's football practice had run late. Unfortunately, football didn't rate high on Kenneth's list of excuses.

I hate group experiments, David decided, watching Jason, Josh, and Mark stroll into the lab as if they had all the time in the world and not just an hour to finish the experiment. *Why are they acting like this isn't important? At least the girls are here.*

Slamming his science notebook down on the lab station, he went over to Kenneth, who mixed up some chemicals in beakers and handed them over. "Nice of you to show up."

"Uh yeah, right," David mumbled and hustled over to the supply cabinet to get a Bunsen burner. "Okay, let's get started."

Malajia ignored him. She was too busy trying to open a jar of salsa that she had brought to go with a bag of tortilla chips. "Did they superglue this jar shut? I can't get this damn thing open."

"Hey, ugly, need any help?" Mark offered.

"No, fool. I need a *real* man to open this," she replied, then looked at Alex. "Alex, could you open it for me?"

Alex glared at her. "Funny, wench," she shot back, casting a quick glance over at Kenneth. "And you know that you're not supposed to eat or drink in the lab."

"So what? You're also not allowed to have *animals* in here, but you see *Mark* walking around and shittin' all over the place."

Mark glared at her. "Keep talking your shit, you triflin' sack of rat piss."

"Eww!" Emily complained.

"Will you two stop with the shit and the piss talk, it's really nauseating," Sidra put in, shooting Malajia a disgusted look.

Malajia frowned. "What the hell is your problem?" she questioned. Sidra's tone was a lot sharper than normal.

Sidra pinched the bridge of her nose with two fingers. "I've been suffering through these damn cramps all damn day, and now I'm supposed to sit here and listen to you idiots argue over nothing?"

"It's not *our* fault that you're on your damn period," Malajia fired back.

"You're skating on thin ice, heifer."

"Please, nobody else talk to her," Mark pleaded. "Last time somebody made her mad during this time of the month, she blacked their eye."

"Yeah, it took a long time to open your eye again, didn't it Mark?" Josh recalled with a laugh, prompting Mark to give him the finger.

Malajia, bored with their antics, gave the salsa jar a good twist and popped it open. Setting the jar on the lab counter, she picked up the chips and tugged at the top, sending chips flying.

"Nice going, stupid," Chasity commented, jotting down something in her notebook.

Malajia glared at her and started to sweep the chips into a pile.

Exasperated, David pulled the Bunsen burner forward and began to fiddle with it. "All right, enough," he interjected. "We have half an hour to get this experiment finished."

"Could you hurry up and set the stupid juice on fire. My insides feel like they're gonna fall out," Sidra complained, clutching her stomach.

"Okay. First of all, it's not juice. If you drink it, it'll probably kill you. Second of all, I'm not setting it on fire. I'm going to heat it up and find out what happens," David replied, setting the beaker full of liquid on the burner.

"Well, whatever you're doing, just do it," Sidra responded impatiently. David shook his head and fiddled some more with the burner, but it wouldn't light.

"What's the problem?" Alex asked, looking over his shoulder.

"It doesn't seem to be working," he replied. "Maybe I should get another."

"Oh, god," Sidra moaned, sitting down and cradling her head in her hands. "Are we ever going to get out of here?"

"Now listen," Alex put in, "I know that it's late, and we're all tired. But we *have* to get this done."

"David, just light it," Mark demanded. He didn't care about the stupid experiment; he just wanted to get it over with so he could go play basketball with some of his buddies from his dorm.

"Man, I told you that I can't," David said as he fixed his glasses on his nose.

"COME ON, MAN!" Mark snapped.

"Could you stop being so damn loud?" Alex asked angrily as she covered her ears.

"*I'll* take care of this," Mark said and took a lighter out of his pocket.

"What do you think you're doing?" David asked, grabbing Mark's arm.

Mark jerked his arm out of David's grasp. "I'm turning the gas on, and then I'm gonna light it. *Duh.*"

"Mark, don't do that," David warned. "It's not going to be pretty."

"Hey!" Kenneth shouted from across the room and jumped up, knocking his chair over.

"Man, I know what I'm doing," Mark replied, flicking his lighter.

"Mark, NO!" Alex shouted.

Mark jerked back at the sudden burst of flame. The beaker cracked, spilling fluid all over the lab counter. Within seconds, the surface was ablaze and set off the overhead sprinklers.

"See what you did!" Malajia shouted, dodging out of the way of the water streaming down on the lab.

"Don't start with me!" Mark shouted back.

Kenneth rushed over and began barking orders. "You," he pointed at Emily, "get the fire extinguisher."

"I found it!" Emily ran up with the fire extinguisher. Kenneth took it from her. He turned the nozzle and a thick white spray gushed out, sending bits of black ash flying until the fire sputtered out.

"This is bullshit," Malajia fumed and stomped her wet high heeled boot on the floor.

"Mark, you never listen," Josh barked. "What's wrong with you?"

Mark looked around with a stunned expression "Why is everyone coming down on *me*?"

"You're not *serious,* are you?" Chasity asked with a deceptive calm. She could have choked him right then and there.

"You set the damn project on fire, you dumbass!" Jason shouted at him.

"Man, that was *David's* fault. If he had lit the burner in the *first* place, then *I* wouldn't have had to use my lighter."

"And if you had bothered to read the experiment protocol," Kenneth interrupted, his voice dangerously quiet, "you would have known you were dealing with combustible substances. They can take slow heating, but no direct fire." His arctic gaze swept over the group. "Now, I suggest you clean up this mess. The utility closet is over there."

Chasity drew him aside. After a short exchange, he nodded, and walked back to his desk to supervise the cleanup. Sidra made no move to get up; she gripped the sides of the chair hard, her cramps were so bad she thought she would break down and cry.

"Your friend is an idiot," Chasity commented and crouched down next to her. "You look like you're dying over here. You want a ride back to the dorm?"

"Oh god, yes," she groaned, struggling to stand. "Thank you." Chasity grabbed her arm to help her up, then turned toward the door.

"Where do you think *you're* going?" Malajia hissed at them.

"Die please," Chasity shot over her shoulder as she and Sidra continued to walk out of the lab.

Alex ran her hands through her hair and let out a loud sigh. "Okay, we just failed this project, we almost set the building on fire…All in all today has been a really crappy day."

"I guess we better start cleaning this mess up," Jason said, bending to pick up some of the scorched papers off the floor.

Malajia was sitting on one of the tables surveying the damage to her boots. "I'm not cleaning up a *damn* thing."

"Oh yes, you are," Jason contradicted, "Last time I checked these were *your* chips all over the floor."

"Oh, what are you gonna do if I *don't*. You gonna hit me?" Malajia taunted.

Jason looked at her with his eyes narrowed. "First of all, I would *never* hit a female."

"But *I* would," Alex interrupted, thrusting a mop at Malajia. "Get to cleaning." They stared at each other for a long minute, then Malajia grabbed the mop.

Mark looked over and grinned. He had been picking up bits of shattered glass from the lab table. "You wanna switch? You can pick up this glass...or eat it, I don't really care."

For once refusing to be drawn into an argument, Malajia swore under her breath and gripped the unwieldy mop. "Punk," she muttered.

Malajia was still steaming the next afternoon. On her way back from Math, she saw Chasity coming out of another classroom and erupted.

"You stupid heifer," she bit out. "Leaving us to do all the damn dirty work."

"What the fuck is *your* problem?" Chasity asked, with a dismissive flick of the hand. "The damn lab guy didn't care, why should *you*? Sidra wasn't feeling good."

"I'm dead tired," Malajia groaned, tossing her head back. "We had to clean up the whole lab. There was black shit and water everywhere."

"You mean ash?" Chasity mocked.

"What-the-hell-ever. I didn't get to bed until three this morning. So right now, I am seriously hating you."

"You really have to stop thinking that I care about what's going on with you." Chasity shrugged. "My roommate was in pain; I thought she was going to pass out."

"Right," Malajia hissed. "I see right through your evil self. You used Sidra's cramps to get out of helping us clean up."

Chasity let a sneaky smile creep across her face, giving Malajia the answer that she already knew. "What? No, not at all," Chasity insisted, voice full of feigned innocence.

Malajia shook her head. "You make me sick," she declared.

Chasity let out a quick sigh. "Don't get mad at *me*. It's not my fault that your friend set fire to the project. It's not my fault that you spilled chips all over the floor. So back the fuck off."

Malajia's eyes turned to slits. "One of these days I'm gonna tear every damn strand of hair off your head, one by one."

"Real cute." Nodding, Chasity turned and walked away.

The student lounge was across campus. By the time Malajia walked in the building, her temper had cooled. She was too tired to waste any more energy. She glanced around the crowded room to see if she could find any of her friends. A laugh rang out, and Malajia jerked around. There was Sidra, chipper as ever, chatting away on a couch. Malajia narrowed her eyes as she made her way over.

"Looks like *you're* feeling better Sidra."

Sidra ignored the sarcasm dripping from Malajia's voice. "Well, I took some pain pills and had a good night's sleep."

"Yeah, I can't believe how tired I am," Mark yawned. "I hate cleaning."

"Hardly a news flash," David commented dryly. "Josh and I shared a cabin with you at camp, remember?" Mark gritted his teeth and stretched out on the couch.

Sidra stood up and grabbed her purse.

"Leaving, crampy?" Malajia inquired. "About to go wiggle your damn way out of something else?"

Sidra glared at her. *She's on my last nerve,* she thought. "That's great Malajia," Sidra said. "Make fun of another woman for having bad cramps. Such a prime example of a lady."

Noticing the disdain in Sidra's tone, Malajia made a face at her. "Boo hoo," she jeered. "I have bags under my eyes because we had to do extra damn cleaning last night."

"Look, Chasity and I didn't flake out on your guys. I could hardly stand up." Sidra drew in a long breath. "You guys had more than enough people to clean up last night. So stop complaining, and get out of my face."

"Look, the cleanup is done. No sense in playing the blame game," Alex put in as Malajia continued to stare daggers at Sidra's departing back. "But what are we going to do about the experiment? Do you think Kenneth will let us do a makeup?"

David's chuckle turned into a laugh.

"What's so damn funny?" Alex asked. "I bet you've never gotten a zero on a test or project in your life."

"Not going to happen," David said with a grin. "Talked to Kenneth this morning. Except for Mark, we are all going to write up the effects of direct heat."

"And Mark?"

"Oh, he's going to discuss the many dangers of not following experiment protocols—an essay, not a workbook write-up."

"That's great news! David, you're a life saver," Alex cried, clasping her hands together. "I can do without a zero at this point, believe me."

"We'll have to give Mark the news later," Josh advised, pointing to the couch where Mark was slouched, mouth open and sound asleep.

"Yeah, Malajia too," David added, pointing to a sleeping Malajia. "I didn't know she snored. It took us almost destroying the chem lab to get both of them to shut up."

Chapter 13

Malajia climbed down from the top bunk and threw open the curtains. Taking in the blue sky and leaves gently shifting in the wind, her lips curved in a huge smile. *Perfect,* she thought. A perfect day for a picnic and hanging out in the park.

"C'mon girl, get up," she called to Alex. "Time to pack up the cooler."

"God, what time is it?" Alex mumbled, the comforter over her head.

"Time to get the hell up and come on."

Malajia found the cooler in the bottom of the closet and dragged it out. She glanced over at the lower bunk, and saw no movement. In a flash, Malajia crossed the room and pulled Alex's comforter off.

"Okay, okay," Alex grumbled, struggling to sit up. "At least let me take a shower and get myself together."

"Hurry the hell up. You're fine not showering any *other* time," Malajia joked.

Alex pointed a finger at her. "Don't start your nonsense today."

Malajia giggled. "Fine. Just hurry up." Malajia started piling sodas and snacks in the cooler. "Emily's already getting ready."

"Can I help?" Emily approached, toothbrush in one hand and toiletry bag in the other.

Malajia shook her head. "Naw, we don't have much stuff to put in here," she replied. "Chasity and Sidra have all the good snacks in their room anyway." Malajia rubbed the back of her neck as she glanced up. Annoyed, Malajia smacked her palm against her forehead. Emily was wearing the most god-awful dress. The fabric fell almost down to her ankles, and was multi-colored at that. "Come *on*, Em!" Malajia exclaimed. "Don't you have anything besides those ugly ass dresses in your closet? We're going to the damn park for a picnic."

"Malajia, stop picking with her," Alex warned.

"I'm *not*. But even *you* have to admit that her dresses are ugly," Malajia argued pointing to Emily's ensemble. "She has a cute shape and needs to stop hiding behind those damn curtains."

Emily looked down at the floor. "Maybe I shouldn't go."

"Oh, you're *going*," Malajia warned, remembering the hour it took for them to convince Emily to come. She shoved aside the cooler and grabbed a lavender sundress, short and trendy, out of her closet. "Here, I never wore this. It's not really my color." Malajia shoved the dress at Emily. "Put this on—no arguments. Chasity's picking us up in like fifteen minutes and you *know* she'll leave if we're not ready."

They found a nice shady spot under a large tree, and spread the blanket out. After fiddling with the radio, Sidra found a good station and laid back, staring up at the light filtering through the leaves. Alex popped open a soda and took a long swallow.

"It's fall, why is it so hot?" Malajia complained, fanning herself with her hand. "I can't take it."

"You were just complaining that it was chilly a few days ago. Quit your damn whining," Sidra ordered. "It's lovely out here. Besides, I don't know how you're hot. That skirt barely covers your behind."

"Bite me, you prissy heifer," Malajia retorted, adjusting the straps of her red and black designer tank.

"No, thank you," Sidra shot back.

Alex leaned over. "Chaz, can you pass me a bag of chips, please?"

Chasity propped up on her elbows and stared off into space, oblivious. Alex repeated her request, but louder.

"Uh Chaz?...Cha-si-ty!"

Chasity snapped out of her trance. "What!"

"I asked if you can pass me a bag of chips," Alex chuckled. Chasity rolled her eyes as she tossed Alex the small foil bag. "What's with you? What were you staring at?" Alex asked, fishing a chip out of the bag.

"Nothing."

"Um hmm. That's nothing playing football in a sexy black T-shirt," Malajia clarified, pointing to Jason.

Chasity narrowed her eyes at her. "Didn't I ask you to die not too long ago?"

Malajia sucked her teeth but had no chance for a smart retort.

"Heads up!" Josh called out as a football came flying toward her and bounced onto the blanket.

"Watch what the hell you're doing!" Malajia barked, smoothing her black skirt down with her hands.

"Shut up!" Mark shouted.

Jason jogged over and picked up the football. "Sorry about that."

"Nice pass," Chasity jeered. "I thought that you were the star football player."

Jason chuckled and blew her a kiss. "My aim got me to come over here and see you didn't it?"

"Why don't you girls come and play with us?" David suggested.

"What? And ruin my skirt? Uh, no." Malajia grimaced.

"Forget her, *I'll* play," Alex agreed, standing up and brushing off her dark jeans.

"Me too," Sidra put in, scrambling to her feet.

"What? Miss Lady is gonna play, with her perfectly pressed pants and her crisp new blouse?" Malajia teased.

Sidra glared at her. "You're not even worth my time."

"I'm not playing a damn thing," Chasity protested, stretching her legs out on the blanket.

Jason couldn't help but stare. The form-fitting black short-sleeved shirt and the jeans showed off her shape perfectly. "Nice outfit."

Chasity stopped stretching and looked at him. "Boy, go play football, and stop staring like a creep."

Emily jumped up. "Come on, Malajia, let's play."

"But I might mess up my hair," she whined. "Do you know how long it takes me to style it?"

"Why? It's not but *so* long anyway," Chasity asked.

"Hey, my hair is short by *choice*, weavie," Malajia shot back.

"Sorry sweetie, this is not a weave; it's all mine." Chasity replied, wrapping a lock around one finger.

"All yours, huh? It's amazing how you style it to keep your horns from showing," Malajia retorted. Chasity made a face at her while flipping her off.

"Listen," Alex broke in. "Everyone shut up with the arguing, and get up. Lord knows we all need the exercise."

"Speak for yourself," Malajia, Sidra, and Chasity replied in unison.

"I'm sexy, slender, and gorgeous. I don't need no damn exercise," Malajia continued as she hopped off of the blanket. "But I'll play if the devil plays."

"Oh my god, how many damn devil jokes are you gonna make?" Chasity exclaimed, moving a stray hair off her face.

"As many as it takes to keep you mad," Malajia shot back.

"You two really need to stop it," Alex cut in.

As everyone got into position to play the game, Malajia held up her hand. "Look, no tackles, and no hard throws. I just got my nails done."

"Stop being so damn conceited. You're not even cute," Mark complained, turning to Jason. "Just throw the ball, please."

Jason tossed the ball to Sidra. Seeing both Mark and David running toward her, she passed if off to Chasity, who caught it with ease.

"Run, Chasity!" Emily shouted, jumping up and down.

Mark chased Chasity. Bumping in to her with intended force, he sent her sprawling to the ground.

"Hey boy, this is touch football, damn it. Don't break my roommate!" Sidra shouted.

"Mark, that was too rough!" Jason hollered, running over to help Chasity off the ground.

"Too damn bad," Mark muttered, dusting himself off.

Chasity snatched away from Jason. "That hurt," she said to Mark, her eyes flashing.

"Man up, Princess. This game is all about pain," he sneered.

"No, it's *not*," Jason cut in.

"Yeah?" Chasity seethed, "let's see how *you* like pain." Jason didn't even see her move. The quick punch to Mark's stomach had him gasping for air, sending him to his knees.

"Time out, man, time out. I can't breathe," Mark grumbled, voice trembling.

"Dude, are you crying?" David asked, voice filled with laughter.

"Chasity, that was unnecessary roughness," Mark moaned, rolling over on his side. "You ain't have to do that."

"Man up, *Princess*," Chasity spat before sauntering off.

"Nice one," Jason said to Chasity's back, before kneeling down next to Mark. "That's what you get. *This* time *she* hit you; next time you hurt her, *I'm* gonna hit you."

"Shut up, you're not her man," Mark retorted, trying to hide his embarrassment.

"I'm working on it."

"Yo, be careful man. She punches like damn a boxer," Mark warned. "Don't make her mad."

"Duly noted," Jason muttered to himself.

"Okay guys, let's finish the game, no more unnecessary roughness," Emily said with a laugh. Once they were all back in position, Jason picked up the ball and started to run.

"Get him!" Malajia screamed. But before Chasity and Sidra could grab Jason, he threw the ball. "Oh, I got it! I got it!" Malajia shouted, intent on grabbing the ball. She didn't see Mark, who was also reaching for the ball. She collided with him; the two went down in a heap, landing on the cooler. Sodas, ice cubes, and snacks spilled out. Malajia and Mark jerked apart. Once Mark managed to hoist himself upright, he plucked a sliver of ice off of his shirt.

Alex had her head in her hands, shaking with laughter. "You two are beyond embarrassing."

"I can't breathe," Sidra moaned. "Please, please, I can't take it." She was laughing so hard tears started running down her cheeks.

Surrounded by cans and ice cubes, Mark and Malajia sat there looking stupid. "I'm all wet and shit," Malajia fumed. "I hate this stupid ass game!"

"Why are you *always* in the goddamn way?" Mark shouted, throwing a soggy potato chip at her. "That's why I hate you."

Malajia grabbed an opened can and flung the remaining soda at him. "Nobody told you to come over here. I had the damn ball," she hissed.

Mark pointed at her, preparing to fire off another insult. But then, a flash of red caught his eye. "Nice underwear."

Malajia looked down and saw that her skirt had hiked up almost to her waist, giving him a good look at her red panties. "Pervert!"

Emily began to chase down the soda cans and put them back in the cooler. Reaching for one by the tree trunk, she tripped over a root. Losing her balance, she fell heavily, skinning an elbow and both knees.

"Em, are you okay?" Alex asked.

Emily examined the damage and nodded, mortified at her clumsiness.

"Let me see," Alex persisted. "You need to get something for those scrapes. Chasity, do you have a first-aid kit in your car?"

"I don't know."

The careless reply annoyed Alex. "Will you stop being so damn mean and help me find something for Emily's cuts?"

Chasity sighed and got to her feet. "Fine. I'm ready to go anyway."

Blood trickled down one of Emily's legs from the cuts on her knee, and her elbow stung. Once they got to the car, Chasity opened the glove compartment and a bunch of paper napkins fell out. "I'm sick of Malajia always stuffing extra freakin' napkins in here, with her napkin stealing ass."

"Girl, hand me a couple," Alex prompted. She crouched down and gently swabbed the dirt and blood off Emily's knees and wiped her elbow. "Does that feel better?" Glancing up, she caught the startled surprise in Emily's expression.

Emily wasn't paying attention to Alex's ministrations. Her eyes were riveted on the blue sedan that had pulled into the parking lot. "Ummm," she whispered. "I seem to have a visitor."

"You *do*? Who?" Alex asked, turning to see who Emily was referring to.

"Mom!" she shouted across the parking lot. "Over here."

Alex and Chasity exchanged glances that mixed confusion and dismay in equal parts. Chasity got out of the car, and shut the door. "How did her mother know that she was here?" she whispered to Alex.

"Well, she talked to her mother earlier today and told her that she would be at the City Park with us. I'm pretty sure it wasn't too hard to find it."

Chasity rolled her eyes in disgust and watched the mother-daughter reunion.

"Mom, what are you doing here? Did something happen?"

"Is that any way to greet me? Can't a mother visit her daughter without something being wrong?" Yolanda Harris rebuked.

"I'm sorry. I'm just surprised to see you." Emily confessed and gave her mother a hug. Ms. Harris quickly pulled away.

"Baby girl, why do you have grass in your hair? And what have you done to yourself?" She asked, pulling a strand of grass from her daughters' hair.

"I was playing football with my friends and—"

"You were doing *what*?" Ms. Harris exclaimed, appalled.

"Yes, Mommy I—"

"What have I told you about playing rough sports? You know how delicate you are," Ms. Harris scolded, then held Emily at arm's length. "And what in the world are you wearing?"

Ms. Harris's voice carried across the parking lot. Emily, certain that her friends could hear, shifted from one foot to the other in embarrassment. "Who do you think you are, wearing a dress that short?"

Sidra and Malajia finally made it to the car, carrying the blanket and the rest of their paraphernalia. "What's going on?" Sidra asked, setting the blanket on the top of Chasity's car.

"Meet Emily's mom," Alex whispered as Ms. Harris's ranting continued.

"Are you serious?" Malajia's eyes widened in disbelief.

Ms. Harris marched over to the car and planted her feet. "Excuse me, who gave my daughter this dress? It's certainly not one that I packed for her."

Alex, Chasity, and Sidra quickly pointed to Malajia, who in turn looked at them in disbelief. *Tattle tales*, she fumed.

"Well um…first off, hi, I'm Malajia," she smiled. Ms. Harris was not amused. "She liked the dress, and so I kinda let her borrow it. It looks really good on her."

"Listen girls, I don't know how *your* mothers let *you* dress, but *my* daughter isn't allowed to go around dressed like a common slut." Ms. Harris took a deep breath. "With your tight jeans and tight shirts and miniskirts, what type of image do you want to portray to this innocent child here?"

"With all due respect, Ms. Harris, Emily is not a child anymore," Alex objected.

"She is seventeen. She is a child to *me*, and who are you to comment on my daughter? Obviously you girls still need your mothers, so you can be taught to respect yourselves and others."

Chasity had had enough. "First of all, lady, don't come over here implying that I don't respect myself. You don't know me, so don't you *dare* judge me."

"Ooh, Chasity don't," Alex murmured and tried to pull Chasity away.

"No, hold on," Chasity fumed, jerking her arm out of Alex's grasp. "You think that you've done such a damn good job of parenting? Your own daughter can't even stand up for herself. And another damn thing—I don't need my damn drunk of a mother. I can take care of myself, and have been doing it well, so stick your judgments where the freakin' sun don't shine."

"Chasity, enough!" Alex broke in and grabbed Chasity's arm, pulling her off to the side.

"She's right, Alex," Malajia commented to Alex through clenched teeth.

"Emily, are these the kind of people that you hang around with? People who disrespect your mother?"

"Ms. Harris, *you* disrespected us first, implying that we're just a bunch of sluts who don't respect ourselves," Sidra retaliated.

"I didn't ask for your input," Ms. Harris said, ice in her voice.

Sidra fought the urge to give Ms. Harris a piece of her mind. Her mother didn't raise a punk, but Emily was embarrassed enough.

"O-kay," Malajia said as she turned her head.

"Come on, Emily. I don't want you associating with these disrespectful little whores."

"Mom," Emily cried out. "How can you say that to my friends?"

"These girls are *not* your friends. You are not to hang out with them again, do you hear me? If I catch you with them again, I'm pulling you out of this school!" Ms. Harris yelled, dragging Emily away from the group and back to her car.

"That woman just called us whores! Can you believe that shit?" Sidra exploded.

"Poor Emily," Alex said, shaking her head.

"Poor Emily? Poor *us*." Malajia pulled her skirt down. "I swear, that lady is so ignorant."

"She's far from a lady," Sidra adjusted the collar on her shirt. "That chick is going to make me call Vanessa Howard down here so she can straighten her ass out."

"No need to get *your* mom involved, Sidra," Alex slid in.

Sidra rolled her eyes. She was over the conversation. "Whatever. Let me go ask these guys to bring that cooler over."

"That damn girl needs to stand up for herself," Chasity declared, yanking open her car door.

"You got that right, Chaz," Malajia added.

"What time are we meeting the guys at the movies?" Alex asked. The last thing that she wanted to do was continue to talk about Emily when she wasn't there. "Mel, you need to change out of that skirt. It's all wet."

When the gang came back from the movies, they found Emily sitting on her bed, folding the laundry that her mother had washed for her.

"Hey, we brought you a slice of pizza," Alex announced. "Pepperoni and extra cheese."

"Thanks, I don't have much of an appetite. I had lunch with my mother."

"Was it bad?" Alex asked, voice laced with sympathy.

"Ummm, she kept going on about what happened earlier and threatening to pull me out of this school, so I could go to a school closer to home."

"Tough," Alex commiserated.

"Yeah, my mother always makes me feel guilty about not wanting to spend all of my free time with her."

"Then your crazy mother has a big-ass problem," Malajia muttered.

"So, did you guys have fun?" Emily asked, desperate to change the subject.

"No," Chasity lied.

"Yes, she did," Jason contradicted, sitting down next to Chasity.

"Speaking of what happened earlier," Alex began, removing her sneakers. "Emily, I'm sure Chasity is sorry for coming at your mother the way that she did," she said, unaware of the pain she was inflicting.

Chasity looked at Alex as if she had lost her mind. "What? I'm not apologizing for *shit*. I meant every word that I said."

"Chaz, you told the woman to stick her judgments where the sun don't shine," Alex recalled.

"And? I *wanted* to tell her to shove em' up her ass," Chasity spat out.

"I actually agree with what Chasity said," Sidra put in. "She called us whores, and that was totally out of line."

"I'm so sorry for what she said to you guys," Emily stammered, rising from her bed.

"You don't have to apologize for your mother, she's a grown woman," Malajia replied.

"Man, if my mom came up here talking that yang, I would—"

"Be scared out of your mind," Josh interrupted. "Mark's mom don't play games."

"True," Mark nodded. "My mom *is* crazy."

Alex chuckled at him, then turned her attention back to Emily. "Look, sooner or later, your mother is going to have to stop treating you like a little girl—packing your clothes, telling you who to hang out with. That's not healthy."

"I know, but she's my *mom*. She's always there for me, I can't hurt her feelings," Emily whined.

Chasity slammed her hand on the arm of the chair. "Are you fuckin' serious?" she snapped. "I can't believe that you're actually going to take that crap from her."

Alex's head snapped towards her. "Chasity, not everyone hates their mother. Not everyone tells their mother to go to hell. Leave her alone."

"She needs to stop being so damn sensitive," Chasity argued.

"Well, maybe *you* need to be a little bit *more* sensitive," Alex shot back.

"Don't tell me what I should be. You don't know me, and you don't know what I grew up with."

Alex jumped up. "Well, why don't you *tell* me, so that I can understand where all of your anger comes from?"

"And give you the satisfaction of getting in my business? I don't think so."

"God, Chasity, you really need therapy," Alex argued. "I've never in my life met anyone who has so much and who's still so damn bitter. You have plenty to be grateful for, and you walk around acting like such a bitch."

Chasity's eyes widened. She wasn't upset that Alex had called her a bitch. She'd gotten used to the label over the years. But Chasity was appalled that Alex could so easily assume that her life was great because she had money. She shook her head, got up, and walked out of the room without a word.

The door slammed shut and Jason asked, "Should I go after her?"

"Uh, no, sweetie. I think that at this point in time, she'll kill you," Malajia said, giving him a sympathetic pat on the arm.

Emily sighed. "I feel bad that you guys were arguing because of me."

"It's okay, it's not your fault," Alex offered in a comforting tone.

Nobody had anything to say, and the silence grew awkward until Mark shattered it.

"Anyone wanna play cards?"

"So stupid," Malajia commented, shaking her head.

"What?—"

Malajia flicked her hand in Mark's direction. "Don't say anything to me, just don't."

Chapter 14

In the weeks after her confrontation with Emily's mother, Chasity withdrew into her shell. Burying herself in her studies, she avoided Alex and the other girls. She couldn't stomach her overbearing, meddling, and patronizing comments; Malajia's mindless chatter and Emily's gutless passivity were almost as hard to swallow.

Skipping up steps to the dorm, she hoped Sidra wasn't in the room. She wanted peace and quiet. Crossing the entry hall, she checked her stride.

The woman standing at the front desk looked oddly familiar, sort of like her mother, but she brushed the possibility aside. *I must have moms on the brain,* she thought.

Relieved to find Sidra gone, she tossed her bag on the bed, and was heading for the bathroom when she heard a knock on the door.

Annoyed, she flung the door open and immediately wished she could slam it shut on the person standing in the threshold.

"Mom?"

Brenda Parker stared at her daughter, and all of the old resentment welled up. So beautiful and young was Chasity, such a constant reminder that Brenda would never be as pretty or as successful as her sister Patrisha. How she hated them both, with their looks and their attitudes.

"What are you doing here?" Chasity frowned, confused. She was certain that she would never receive a phone call from her mother, let alone a visit.

"Are you going to let me come in?"

"Do I *have* to?" Chasity replied, her hand still fixed to the doorknob.

With a disgruntled huff, Brenda pushed past her daughter, and looked around.

"What the hell are you doing here?" Chasity repeated, stepping away from the door.

"I've come to deliver some news," she replied with a tight, hard smile.

"This sounds like something that's going to piss me off."

"Good thinking. At least you're not *entirely* stupid."

This is what Chasity had to grow up with, constantly being put down and criticized. *And Alex thought I was lucky. How funny.*

"Hurry up and say what you have to say, and get out," Chasity spat out.

Sidra paused, wondering why the door was half open and who the hell Chasity was talking to. She wasn't talking to anyone these days, except her professors. Chasity had been so distant, Sidra almost wished for the old Chasity. She could deal with the hostile bitch, but not the Ice Queen. Well, judging from the sounds coming from inside, hostile Chasity was back, and this was one conversation Sidra was not about to interrupt. But she'd be damned if she wasn't going to eavesdrop.

"Chasity, I just want you to know that I don't want you to return to my house ever again. I'm putting you out," Brenda announced with less emotion than she used ordering takeout.

The flat statement, so coldly delivered, shocked Chasity. She wasn't planning on going back anyway, but to hear her mother declare her unwelcome at home hurt. Chasity was surprised to find that it actually hurt, that her mother could still inflict pain.

"You came *all* the way from Arizona to tell your only child that she's no longer welcome in your house again?" Chasity asked in a deadly tone. "What's wrong with you?"

"Well, your father has asked me for a divorce."

The answer confused Chasity—it explained nothing. "What the hell does that have to do with you coming here to my school?"

"After I got that phone call from the lawyer, I started thinking about our lives and what drove us to this place, to where he would want to leave me for good."

"I assume he got tired of your drunk ass passing out on the living room couch every night," Chasity sneered.

"My *drinking* started when you were born, you stupid bitch!" Brenda hollered. "This divorce is *your* fault."

"Oh, you're right. I shouldn't have poured that vodka down your throat. My fault," Chasity mocked.

"You watch your mouth, before you get slapped," she hissed, pointing at her.

"Yeah, whatever," Chasity shot back. "What was the point in coming all the way here? Why not just call me?"

"You have *always* been a burden. I wanted to see the look on your face when I told you that I no longer wanted you around me."

Chasity bit her lip hard. She hadn't cried in front of her mother in years, and she wasn't going to let her see tears today. "Why do you hate me? What did I *ever* do to you to make you hate me?"

"I could stand here and tell you everything that led up to you being a part of my life, but I choose to spare you," her mother said smugly.

The smug, sanctimonious reply steadied Chasity. She was only too familiar with her mother's self-righteous bending of the truth.

"How considerate of you," Chasity thanked her. Her tone was dripping with sarcasm.

"Truth is, I really never wanted you in the first place. I just thought that having you would make things better between your father and me, but that backfired in my face big time."

Chasity stared at her mother, amazed once again at the woman's coldness and her level of cruelty. "Something is seriously wrong with you. You are so fuckin' screwed up."

"No bitch, what's wrong with me is *you*," Brenda charged. "But, now that's over. With you gone, I can move on with my life."

"Screw you," Chasity jeered. "You think your life will be good after all the hell that you've put me through?"

"No matter *how* my life turns out, it will be ten times better without your spoiled little ass in it," her mother shot back. "You think that you'll be better off living with my bitch of a sister, but it will just be a matter of time before you ruin *her* life too. The difference is, *she* deserves it." Brenda Parker turned on her heels, walked calmly to the door, and slammed it on the way out.

"Who the hell are you are staring at?" she yelled, tripping over Sidra. "Get out of my way."

Sidra followed the rude woman's progress down the hall. She could have run up and tripped her, but her main concern was for her roommate. Sidra walked slowly into the room, only to find Chasity pacing with her hand on her forehead.

Sidra put her books down. "Chasity, are you okay?"

Chasity looked over at Sidra, eyes glistening with tears. Such bad timing on Sidra's part.

"You were listening, weren't you?"

"Yeah. I'm sorry. If you need to talk—"

"I *don't*," Chasity cut Sidra off, and sought the only privacy available. She locked the bathroom door and sat down on the floor, her back to the door.

"Chasity, I'm going to go out for a while and leave you alone, okay?" Sidra called softly.

"Fine."

"Um. Do you want anything while I'm out?"

"No."

Once Chasity heard the outside door close, she broke down, and sobbed.

Shaken, Sidra made it only to the steps outside the dorm and sat down, the cold stone never registering, and buried her face in her hands. The conversation she'd overheard repeated in an awful playback loop, over and over in her head. *Imagine having to live in the same house as that evil ass woman. I'd tell her to go to hell, too,* Sidra swore.

"Hey, girly," Malajia sang. "We've been waiting for you. You were supposed to meet us in the lounge so we could go to dinner." Malajia shook an accusing finger at Sidra.

"Sorry, I got held up."

Sidra's reply was so wan, so flat, it set off alarm bells. Instead of ripping into her, as Malajia had planned, she leaned against the wrought-iron railing. "What's wrong?"

Betraying confidences was high on Sidra's list of Don'ts, but she couldn't keep it bottled up, and the whole incident came tumbling out.

"You should have heard the things that her mom said to her, it was unbelievable."

"Kicked out? Shit, I'd tell the old bitch to go to hell too."

Hearing Malajia echo her own verdict, and in almost the same words, Sidra blinked in amazement. She and Malajia had not agreed on much since middle school. Certainly not on the big stuff, that's for sure.

"Uh, Sidra, we might want to chill on this conversation. Alex is coming up the walkway," Malajia whispered.

Alex marched up to them, her curiosity piqued. Malajia and Sidra sharing whispered confidences? "So, what's got you two so cozy and so serious?"

Sidra glanced at Malajia, who shrugged. "Might as well. She'll nag and bitch and moan until she drags it out anyway."

Sidra gave a barebones account, stripping it of detail and sticking only to the facts, the divorce and Brenda Parker's announcement.

"Well, Alex, maybe *now* you can understand why Chasity feels a certain way when it comes to mothers," Sidra suggested softly. "She hasn't had a good example of one."

"And maybe, just maybe," Malajia proposed in much harsher tones, "growing up in that rich household ain't all you think it's cracked up to be."

Alex sat for a moment, making no reply. Then she stood up, and turned toward the dorm entrance.

"Leave her alone, Alex," Sidra advised, tone traced with frustration. "You know that she doesn't want to be bothered."

"Look, I'm not going to stand here and let someone feel this bad. I'm going to go up there and talk to her," Alex protested.

"I hope Chasity kicks her nosey ass," Malajia muttered as Alex disappeared inside.

Chasity let out a heavy sigh at the sound of a knock at her door. She rolled her eyes when she opened it. Alex was standing there.

"What do you want?" she spat out.

"I came to be a friend and to talk to you," Alex declared, stepping into the room.

"Sidra told you, didn't she?"

"Yes, can you blame her? She's concerned about you; we *all* are."

Chasity again rolled her eyes. "Alex, spare me this crap, okay? I'm not in the mood for your advice, or your friendship."

"Look, I know that we haven't really been speaking to each other these past weeks—well *you* actually stopped speaking to *me*..."

"Do you have a point?" Chasity interrupted.

"Yes I do, my point is...I wanted to apologize to you, I didn't know that your mom was so crappy to you—"

"Alex, please stop acting as if you have me all figured out. Do you get off on this kind of thing? Why do you just *have* to have everyone all figured out?" Chasity's voice rose steadily.

Alex sighed. "I didn't come here to upset you, Chasity. I came here because I consider you a friend, and I want to be here for you."

"Alex, I don't need you to be here. What I need for you to do is go away so that I can be by myself."

"Why? So that you can feel sorry for yourself?" Alex admonished.

"What are you talking about?" Chasity growled. "I don't feel sorry for myself—you get on my nerves!"

"You can't push me away, Chaz," Alex promised. "Why don't you just let those ten foot steel and brick walls down so someone can be there for you?"

"I want you to leave me alone! I don't need you. When are you and everyone else gonna realize that?" Chasity shot back.

"You know what? You are so used to everyone giving up on you because of your attitude. You are used to people being afraid of you," Alex argued. "And you are okay with this, because it keeps people from getting to know the real you."

"And since you know so fuckin' much, who is the *real* me?" Chasity asked, folding her arms across her chest.

"You are more kind, caring, funny, and sensitive than you want people to realize," Alex responded. "You want to be understood and accepted, just like everybody else. And if you didn't care about anything, then this whole situation with your mom wouldn't bother you."

Chasity just stood there. She was so angry that she couldn't bring herself to say anything. Alex figured that she had said enough. But before she left, Alex put her arms around Chasity. Even though Chasity's arms never unfolded to return her hug, Alex squeezed tight. "Sweetie, if you need to talk or yell or cry or *whatever*, you have four ladies that you can call who won't judge you."

Chasity held the hard expression on her face as Alex walked out of the room. Once the door shut, her eyes began to well up with tears.

"Trisha, I really don't want to talk about it anymore." Chasity plumped up the pillows on her bed and checked the time on the phone. *Twenty minutes,* she thought, *twenty fuckin' minutes I've been listening to my aunt rant.*

"I wish I'd been there. I would have killed her," Trisha fumed. Chasity was only half listening.

Trisha had hated Brenda for as long as she could remember, and the feeling was mutual. All during her childhood, Chasity had walked on eggshells, waiting for another eruption between the two siblings. When Trisha bought Chasity a Miami condo, Brenda had exploded. She couldn't stand having Trisha's success crammed down her throat. Beautiful Patrisha, with her glamorous life and thriving real estate business, never missed a chance to show her up, and she had to put up with it.

Chasity held the phone away from her ear as the angry tones droned on. Finally, she decided, it was time to interrupt. "Why are you more upset about this than I am?"

"Because," Trisha said, "she was supposed to take care of you, not treat you like shit."

"Yeah, I know, but what are you gonna do?" Chasity parried. "It's over. I hate her, and she hates me, so what?"

Trisha sighed. "I'm sorry that everything turned out this way. I never wanted you to get hurt."

"I know you didn't, but it's not your fault," Chasity replied, twisting a strand of hair around her finger, and wondering when she could hang up. The line went silent. "You gonna say something else, or is this conversation over?"

"I'm sorry sweetie, I was looking out my window at something," she temporized. Even though Chasity never said anything to her, Trisha suspected that Chasity knew that she was keeping something from her. "Anyway, do you want to come down to Miami next weekend? We can go shopping and hit up some clubs. You can even bring your friends."

Chasity drew in a deep breath. "They're *not* my friends."

"Shut up, girl. Let someone like you. You know that they enjoy your company, even though you are giving them hell."

"Funny," Chasity responded sarcastically.

"So, why don't you all come down?" Trisha pressed playfully.

"Sounds good, but no. I'm not in the mood, but thanks anyway."

"All right," Trisha accepted reluctantly, obviously disappointed. "Well, you and your friends have a standing invitation. Whenever you're ready, just call me, okay?" She paused for a moment. "I put some more money in your bank account. It's about five thousand, so you can go shopping or something."

Chasity bolted straight up on her bed. "What do you want?" she asked suspiciously.

"Whatever do you mean?"

"Whenever you tell me how much money you've deposited in my account, you want me to agree to something that you know I'm gonna hate." Like clockwork, Trisha automatically transferred money into Chasity's account, but never mentioned it unless she wanted something.

"Okay, you figured me out," Trisha admitted. "Your grandmother wants to have Thanksgiving at her house. She misses you, and she wants you to come."

"What?" Chasity exclaimed. "No. I don't wanna be around those people. Grandmom is cool and all, but everyone else makes my face hurt."

"Ahh, you thought that you had a choice?" Trisha teased. Chasity's eyes glinted with anger. Her aunt always couched her proposals, so they gave the appearance of choice, but only the appearance. Even when Chasity said "no" initially, she ended up doing what Trisha wanted.

"Anyway, I have to go now," Trisha said abruptly, before Chasity could get another word in.

"Wait! No, I'm not done yet"

"Love you, miss you, bye-bye." When Trisha hung up, Chasity stared at her phone for a few seconds, then pushed the "end call" button.

Chasity frowned in concentration, her fingers flying. She was determined to beat her best score on Ski Ball. When her final tally flashed across the screen, she clapped her hands, thoroughly pleased, sighing in satisfaction.

Sidra watched the points accumulate. "Geez, Chasity, how did you learn to play like that?"

Sidra was relieved to have the game as a buffer. The last couple of days, she'd been treating Chasity with kid gloves. Chasity's mom was the proverbial elephant in their room. If Sidra brought the subject up, she might remind her roommate that she had blabbed to Malajia and Alex. But if she didn't talk about it, Chasity might think she wasn't concerned and she *was*.

"So…how are you doing?" she finally asked.

"I'm fine," Chasity said, pushing a button and starting the game over.

"You don't *sound* fine," Sidra pointed out.

"What? Do you and Alex subscribe to the same 'let's figure Chasity out' magazine?" Chasity exclaimed, exasperated.

"I'm just concerned," Sidra replied.

"Don't be. I'm fine. I don't care that my mom hates me. Guess what? I hate her too. So stop talking to me as if I'm a broken child, and *stop* feeling sorry for me."

Sidra shook her head and looked Chasity squarely in the eye. "I'm not pitying you. I'm just trying to be a good friend."

Chasity had to admire Sidra's guts. She'd been so careful, so tentative around her, that Chasity knew she was feeling guilty about blabbing to the others. "Okay," Chasity relented, feeling bad for snapping. "I'm just not used to people being all up in my business. I'm used to being by myself a lot. And I know that I'm not the easiest person to get along with, but that's just me."

"Fine. I understand," Sidra nodded. "But don't *ever* confuse me with Alex, because *she's* just nosey."

"Trust me. I'm aware," Chasity admitted, "and contrary to how I act or what you might think, I *do* appreciate you asking how I'm feeling."

"Anytime," Sidra replied, pleased to have normal relations with her roommate restored, if relations with Chasity could ever be classified as normal.

"So, is everyone ready to go?" Alex asked, walking up to the space with Malajia and Emily.

"Yeah," Sidra replied. At a groan from Emily, she spun around. "What's wrong with you?"

"Ice cream, fries, and greasy pizza, deadly combination," Malajia put in. "I swear, next time we go out, the child stays home."

"I think that I'm gonna be sick," Emily gulped, clenching her stomach.

Malajia grabbed Emily's arm and yanked her forward. "Ugh, let me take her to the bathroom before she vomits."

"Malajia, don't. She's gonna—"

Before Alex could finish her sentence, Emily threw up. Vomit splattered on the floor and hit the tops of Malajia's red boots. Chasity, Alex, and Sidra took a step back and covered their noses.

"My shoes, you threw up on my shoes!" Malajia screamed as Emily made a beeline for the bathroom.

"Gross," Sidra scoffed, face not hiding her disgust.

"Those two," Chasity warned, "are *not* riding in my car."

Chapter 15

Alex woke up feeling uneasy. She was also cold. Sometime during the restless night, she'd kicked off her comforter. Alex rolled over and punched her pillow. Pieces of a weird dream kept swirling around in her head. She pulled the comforter up and dove under, hoping to shake the images of Paul cheating on her, but she couldn't. They'd been on edge with each other for weeks, ever since he'd hung up on her.

She'd never be able to go back to sleep, Alex realized, and quietly got up, careful not to disturb Emily, who was still suffering the aftereffects of the abundance of junk food from the other night.

When the telephone rang, she scrambled to answer.

She smiled, recognizing her friend Victoria's voice, but the smile soon froze as she listened to the information spilling from Victoria's mouth.

"Vicki, are you sure? I can't believe this. He's *really* cheating?"

"Girl, I wouldn't lie to you. I saw him. I even approached him."

"Well, what the hell did he say?"

"That she was just a friend, and it shouldn't matter who he's out with, because you're up there with a bunch of college guys, and it's not like you're thinking about him."

"The bastard, he said that?" Alex hissed into the phone. "He's mad at me because I'm in college. It's not *my* fault that he didn't graduate on time."

"I haven't told you the worst part."

"Huh?"

"The girl that he was with…it was Sherry Armstrong."

"What? The girl that slept with half our graduating class? No way. He said he would never date someone like her."

Alex had always known that Sherry had the hots for Paul, but she never dreamed Paul would go for it. They'd been together for three years, for God's sake, and he'd throw it all away for some cheap thrill.

"Yep, and believe me that girl was looking all stank. She had on this skintight hooker looking outfit too. I'm surprised she could breathe."

"You know what," Alex said, seeing Emily stir, "I gotta go."

"Okay, give me a call if you want to talk, girl."

"Yeah. Thanks for looking out for me." She stood by the phone for a minute and felt tears welling up in her eyes. "I'm not gonna cry. I'm *not* gonna cry, he's not worth it," she murmured. After all of the arguments, all of his threats, he had actually cheated on her and with someone she despised.

Malajia walked in, catching Alex by surprise, and sprinted over to her dresser. "Hey girl, I need a jacket. It's chilly out." Malajia foraged around in her closet, and pulled out a red coat. "What's with you? No 'hello, how you doin'?" she jeered when Alex didn't acknowledge her.

"Malajia, I'm not in the mood okay," Alex responded, unenthusiastically.

Malajia frowned. "Well, Ms. Sunshine. What the hell got into *you*?"

Alex looked up and saw only the short, tight red-and-black dress paired with six inch high heels—an outfit Sherry would happily wear to advertise her wares. "I said that I'm not in the mood, okay!" she yelled.

"Why are you yelling at me? What did I do to *you*?!" Malajia shouted back.

Alex snapped, losing the last ounce of control she had. "I'm sick of cheating men, I'm sick of arguing, and I'm sick of women like *you*."

Emily rolled over in the safety of her blankets and looked at them. "What's going on?" she asked, her voice still fuzzy with sleep.

Malajia ignored her and watched Alex angrily grab her robe and bathroom essentials.

"Wait a minute," she ordered, blocking Alex's way. "What the hell do you mean by women like *me*?"

Alex spun around, enraged. "I mean women who walk around in their skimpy little outfits, parading their tits and asses in guys' faces, willing to do *anything* for a guy's attention. Women who go out with a guy even if he already has a girlfriend. You just want the satisfaction of knowing that you can get any guy that you want. You just want to add another guy to your little list of conquests—*that's* what I mean by women like *you*."

Malajia stared at her, stunned at the venom pouring out of the girl who was usually the voice of reason. "Are you kidding me? You're implying that I fit into the same category as a whore? Is that what you're implying, Alex?" Malajia's fists clenched around the jacket and she paused, looking Alex up and down. "Because *if* that's what you're implying, then you *know* where you can put that bullshit!"

Malajia stormed out and slammed the door. Alex stood there, shaking. She felt betrayed, sore deep down, and too angry to care if Malajia's feelings were hurt.

Emily hid her face in her pillow. Until the dispute, she was actually feeling better, ready to join the land of the living.

After she showered and dressed, Alex escaped outside. She wandered around, looking for someone with a cell she could borrow. She wasn't going to let this go without giving Paul a piece of her mind, but this was one conversation she didn't want Emily to hear. Alex had already embarrassed herself enough, losing control and lashing out at the first victim she saw.

She spied Chasity sitting on a bench outside the science building, and walked up to her. "Can I use your cell phone?"

Chasity looked up, irritated at the interruption, particularly when it was Alex. They were barely on speaking terms, and now she calmly asked for a favor? "Wow, no 'hi' or nothing?"

"Chasity, I'm not really in the mood for your smart comments right now," Alex sneered. "Can I use your cell phone or not?"

"Is the phone in your room broken?" Chasity mocked.

"Forget it," Alex hissed.

"What the hell is your problem?"

"I'm just going through some things right now and I need to make a private call," Alex stated, frustrated.

"And you know *all* about privacy." After subjecting Alex to a long, measured look, Chasity fished her cell out of her bag and handed it to her.

Alex hurried down the path and dialed Paul's number. After five rings, she got switched to voice mail. "Paul, this is Alex. Victoria told me that she saw you the other day. We need to talk, and I mean now. So call me back." Frustrated, she stomped back up the path, and shoved the phone at Chasity. "Don't bother asking me, because I don't wanna talk about it."

"You better not have broken my damn phone, I know *that* much," Chasity warned, dropping the cell back into her bag.

"Yes, Mark, we have your list...I understand that your mom is going to kill you if you don't pass this class...Okay...Stop yelling in my ear! I said we'd get them." When Mark called, Sidra was waiting for Chasity. They were taking her car to Mega-Mart to pick up some food and supplies for a class project.

"Where is Chasity? She knew we were going to be out here." Malajia craned her neck around, searching the parking lot. "Finally! It's about damn time."

"Don't start with me," Chasity shot back, fumbling with the keys.

Sidra noticed that one of her hands was tucked away in her jacket. "Why are you hiding your hand?" she asked, amused. "Don't tell me your hands are cold already."

Chasity let out a heavy sigh, and slowly, painstakingly, pulled her hand out of her jacket. The entire area from palm to four inches up her arm was wrapped in an Ace bandage, with a few pulls between the thumb and index finger to secure it in place with a small metal clip.

Sidra changed from amused to concerned. "What happened? Why is your hand all bandaged up?"

"I was in that stupid health and wellness class, and we had to lift fuckin' weights. I picked up a barbell that was too heavy, and my wrist bent back."

"Ouch," Malajia commiserated, rubbing her own wrist.

"They said that I sprained it. But now I can't drive."

"I would offer to drive, except I left my license in my other purse," Sidra apologized.

Malajia stomped her foot on the ground. "Chasity, you're messing up our damn plans," she joked.

Chasity shot her a confused frown. "How the hell is my hurt wrist messing up your plans?"

"We need you to drive, and you *could* have if you hadn't tried to be all extra hype and prove how strong you're *not* and ended up spraining your damn wrist."

Sidra couldn't make head nor tails of Malajia's tortuous explanation, and neither could Chasity; her eyes had glazed over.

"Girl, I don't know what that fool is talking about, so don't even ask me," Sidra said, picking up on Chasity's confusion.

"She's your damn friend," Chasity pointed out.

"She's yours *too*," Sidra laughed.

"Fine, *I'll* just drive," Malajia offered, holding her hand out for the keys.

"That would be a fuckin' no," Chasity declared bluntly, earning a glare from Malajia.

Alex and Emily came up just in time to see Chasity move her hand out of Malajia's reach. As soon as Malajia saw Alex, she froze. "I am not riding in the car with her."

"What happened?" Sidra asked.

"I don't wanna talk about it," Malajia said, turning away.

"Okay." Sidra shrugged and turned her attention to Alex. "Alex, do you have your license on you?"

"Yeah. Why?"

"Chasity hurt her wrist and can't drive." Sidra sent Chasity an apologetic look. "Is that okay with you?"

"Sure, whatever," she said and tossed Alex the keys.

Without another word, Alex walked over to the driver's side of the car, and slid behind the wheel.

As Malajia climbed into the back seat, Sidra nudged Emily. "What's wrong with Alex?"

"She and Malajia got into it this morning, maybe that's it. But something has definitely upset her. She didn't say a word on the walk over here," Emily whispered.

They'd almost reached the Mega-Mart when Chasity's cell phone beeped.

"Yeah?" she answered, juggling the cell in her good hand.

"Hey, it's Jason."

She frowned. "Jason? How did you get my number?"

"Malajia gave it to me."

"Oh she *did*, huh?" Chasity turned, glaring over her shoulder at Malajia. "Well, what do you want?"

"I just wanted to ask you to let Sidra know that she doesn't have to pick up the supplies for Mark's project. I'm already at Mega-Mart, so I'll pick them up. Mark called me a few moments ago, he was afraid that Sidra was going to forget."

"So why call *me*? You should've called Sidra."

"It was a good excuse to hear your voice," he replied with a laugh.

"Whatever," she drawled, and promptly hung up on him. "So, you gave Jason my cell phone number, huh?" She hissed at Malajia.

"Yes, I *did*," Malajia admitted frankly. "The man likes you, cut him a damn break. Besides, he asked me for it, and who am I to deny someone that gorgeous?"

"No," Chasity argued, "I bet he didn't ask you for my number. I think that *you offered* it to him."

"So what if I did?" Malajia retorted "Get over it."

Alex pulled into Mega-Mart's immense parking lot. "We're here," she announced, breaking her silence. She hadn't said a word in the car. Once inside the mammoth store, they headed straight for the stationery aisles.

"Damn," Malajia complained, "I can't believe how much this calculator costs. Makes no damn sense."

"Hey!" Jason called out as he sprinted over to them.

"Hey, Jase. Did you get everything for Mark?" Sidra asked. "He'll be on your back all night if you forget anything, trust me."

"Almost," he sighed, then pointed to Chasity's bandaged wrist. "What happened?

"I hurt it," she responded dryly.

"No kidding," he mocked. "I meant *how* did you hurt it?"

"I sprained it, if you *must* know."

"Well, I can take care of that for you. I've had a lot of experience with sprains."

"No thanks, I'm fine." Without thinking, she picked a heavy ream of paper off the shelf, wincing as her injured wrist gave way.

Jason quickly picked up the fallen item and returned it to the shelf. "See, you're not fine. I know that it hurts, but, of course, you think you're sooo tough and so damn stubborn." Discouraged, he ran his hand over the back of his neck. "Listen, make sure you ice it; keep the bandage tight, and keep the wrist elevated. That should help."

"Fine, I will. Thanks."

"If you need me to ice it for you—"

"That won't be necessary," she interrupted so quickly that he chuckled.

"Okay. Gotta go. Take care."

"Malajia, did you see any graph paper?" Alex asked, only to be treated to a stony silence. "Malajia, did you hear me?"

"Yeah, I heard you," she retorted. "But I don't have time to talk to you. As soon as I'm finished here, I'm gonna go find some guys to seduce with my slutty self."

Malajia stalked off, leaving Alex speechless.

Shopping finished, the girls piled into the car. They were barely out of the parking lot when Sidra pounced. She couldn't pass up an opportunity to tease her roommate.

"Chasity, I saw you talking to Jason."

"So?"

"Just know that when you guys get married, I want to be a bridesmaid," Sidra warned, coaxing a giggle out of Emily.

"Girl, please," Chasity scoffed.

"Shit. *Damn* the wedding. If I were you, Chaz, I would look forward to the honeymoon," Malajia broke in. "That man looks like he can lay some pipe."

"Malajia!" Sidra scolded as Chasity shook her head.

"C'mon," Malajia protested. "You can't tell me that Chasity hasn't been thinking the same thing."

"I haven't," Chasity confirmed, annoyed by the sound of Malajia's voice.

"Yeah, whatever you say," Malajia teased.

Alex glanced at Malajia in the rear-view mirror and shook her head.

"What's the matter, Alex? You mad I made that comment?" Malajia inquired, eyes flashing. "I'm sure it confirms your opinion that I'm a whore, huh?"

"Malajia, what are you talking about?" Sidra asked, disturbed by Malajia's anger. She wasn't just simmering; she was about to boil over.

"Ask Alex," she answered coldly, folding her arms.

Alex let out a sigh. "Malajia—"

"Don't you talk to me," Malajia hissed.

"What's going on?" Sidra broke in. "Are you two fighting?"

"Alex thinks that I'm a whore."

"A whorish virgin? *That's* new," Chasity interjected with a laugh.

"Stay out of it, Chasity," Alex warned. "Malajia, I was angry at my boyfriend, not *you*. You were just unlucky enough to come along at the wrong time. I realize that I was a bitch, and I'm sorry."

"Whatever, Alex," Malajia snarled. "You meant every word. Didn't *you* inform us that you always tell it like it is? You are so fake. Deep down, you think that I'm a whore."

"What? I'm not allowed to be upset? I can't be human?" Alex shot back. "My boyfriend is cheating on me and when I looked at you, I saw the girl that he was cheating on me *with*!"

"I am *not* that girl," Malajia argued.

"I *know* that, I just got angry," Alex stammered, her voice cracking.

"Forget it, I'm just gonna shut my trampy ass up." Malajia leaned back in her seat and looked out the window.

Back on campus, Malajia, not wanting to be anywhere near Alex, followed Chasity and Sidra. "You two have any food?" she asked once they got to the room.

"Yeah, but it's junk food," Sidra cautioned.

"That'll work." Malajia tossed her purse on the loveseat and flopped down.

Chasity, checking out her text messages, let out a groan. She half expected to see multiple hits from her aunt Trisha. What she got was equally irksome, but for altogether different reasons. Damn Malajia for giving him her number.

"I wish he'd kill the nonsense," Chasity muttered and tossed her jacket on the chair. She managed to knock her bad wrist on one of the wooden arms, and hissed in pain.

"Calm down," Sidra advised, peeking over Chasity's shoulder at the message. She stifled a giggle when she saw the little red heart and kissy face emoji. "Aww, that is so cute," she simpered, earning a glare from Chasity.

"Shut up," Chasity ordered through clenched teeth, but Sidra just laughed and tossed a bag of cookies at Malajia. "Here child, maybe those will fix your mood."

"I doubt it," Malajia sulked.

"So, Malajia, when are you leaving?" Chasity asked, watching Malajia tear open the cookie bag and settle back against the couch cushions. "Or do you plan on gracing us with your presence all night?"

"Yep, all night," she returned between bites. "I'm not gonna sleep in the same room with someone who thinks so little me."

"Yet you're gonna sleep in the same room with me?" Chasity mocked.

Sidra shook her head. "Malajia, you can't let Alex run you out of your room. Come on, girl. That's not the Malajia I know."

"Oh shut up, you just don't want me to spend the night here," Malajia scoffed, brushing cookie crumbs off her jacket.

"Honey, you know that's not true," Sidra protested.

"*Yeah*, it is," Chasity interjected, then ducked as Malajia threw a pillow at her.

"Look, Malajia, I understand why you're upset at Alex, I would be too," Sidra confided. "But she's *still* your friend, and I know that she's sorry for whatever she said to you."

"Don't want to hear it," Malajia said flatly.

Sidra sat down on the couch and brushed the last few crumbs from Malajia's jacket. "Look, maybe I'm confused, but we always laugh and joke with each other, at least we used to. You didn't take the insults seriously. Why now? Help me understand."

Malajia sighed. "Well, I've always been considered a whore because of the way that I dress and act. I've gotten used to it, because it only comes from people who don't know me. I know we joke and tease each other and I know that I've heard worse...but...I don't know how to explain it...It's different coming from Alex."

The look on Sidra's face told Malajia that she was beginning to get through to her. "You and I have cracked on each other since we were kids, and Chasity is just mean. I know that, and I accept that. But Alex, posed herself as someone who always treats her friends with respect, and she just totally disrespected me today. You should have seen her face—she was really serious."

Sidra saw how hurt Malajia was and ached for her. She'd had that same look on her face in middle school, when her parents forgot her birthday. Sidra put an arm around Malajia, who sighed and munched on another cookie.

Alex and Emily waited for Malajia, and waited, neither saying much. Finally, Alex gave up, drew back the comforter on her bed, and grabbed her diary off the floor.

"I guess she's not coming." Alex switched off the overhead lights and flicked on her reading lamp.

Emily rolled onto her side. She could just make out Alex's outline in the shadows. Seeing the diary propped up on bent knees, Emily smiled. Recording the day's events was a nightly ritual for Alex. But today's entry didn't seem to be going so well. She wasn't writing anything, just tapping her pen on the page. "Alex, are you okay?" Emily asked after a while.

"Um...no, not really, sweetie."

"Do you wanna talk about it?"

"No, not right now."

"All right then...Good night."

"Night," Alex murmured. She'd done some serious soul-searching over the past hour waiting for Malajia, and she didn't like what she saw. She'd always lambasted people who used criticism as a weapon, and here she was attacking Malajia, taking her anger and frustration out on someone who meant a lot to her. Paul, she finally admitted, brought out the worst in her. After a quick glance to make sure Emily was asleep, she picked up the phone and dialed Paul.

"Hello," he answered.

Surprised and relieved that she didn't get routed to voice mail yet again, Alex jumped right in. "Look, I'm not going to bring up the fact that you haven't returned my phone calls, and I'm not going to mention that you went out with that girl to get back at me for doing something great with my life."

"Alex, listen—"

"No, *you* listen," she barked. "I'm through listening to you. I don't like the person I am when I'm with you. I called you to do you a favor...this relationship is over. See who you want, *do* who you want, I don't care anymore. You stay there and you fail the twelfth grade *again,* but you will *not* blame me for your life, because I'm moving on with *mine*." As soon as she got out everything she had to say, she hung up. She knew Paul would throw words and arguments at her, and she didn't want to hear them. Alex was tired of the nonsense.

The next morning, Alex felt lighter, freer than she had in a long time. But she still had a major problem to fix. After breakfast, she was determined to make things right with

Malajia. She was not going to let her stupidity, her senseless attack, ruin a friendship. She spotted Malajia on her way to English and ran up to her.

"Malajia, we need to talk."

Malajia glared at her and turned to walk away. "I don't want to hear it."

Alex grabbed her arm. "Listen, I know that I hurt your feelings. What I said was insulting, degrading, and unforgivable. Paul was messing around with some stank ass girl, and I just lost it. My tantrum had nothing to do with you. You were just a convenient target, and I am so, so sorry."

"Alex, I *get* that you were hurt, but that's no excuse," Malajia chided.

"I know," Alex admitted, looking at the floor.

"I mean damn, have I ever given you the idea that I'd go around stealing another girl's man?" Malajia paused, thinking of her provocative clothes. "Wait, don't answer that."

"Malajia, seriously? You may be loud and love attention, but you would never do something like that," Alex assured. "You need to be the center of attention, so a man who already has someone is out of the question."

"Damn right." Malajia folded her arms, then a smile crept across her face. "Okay, I forgive you. I hate to admit it, but I miss talking to your nosey ass."

Alex threw her arms around Malajia and gave her a big hug.

"All right, all right—get off me. You're gonna mess up my hair."

Chapter 16

"So who's riding in the car and who's taking the bus?" Mark asked.

"Um, the *girls* are riding in the car, and the *guys* are gonna hike it on the bus," Alex stated. "Sound fair?"

"Hell no," the guys responded in unison.

"Too bad. Better move it, here comes your ride," Alex advised. Seeing the bus lumbering toward the stop, the guys took off.

"Wait. My pants are falling down!" Mark yelled as he tried to hike up his pants.

"Why do we hang out with them?" Malajia asked and shook her head.

"I still haven't figured it out," Alex tossed over her shoulder and slid into the driver's seat.

"That's not fair, how come Alex gets to drive again?" Malajia whined.

"Because I asked her to," Chasity responded nonchalantly. "My damn wrist still hurts, and I just don't want you driving my freakin' car."

"I still don't believe Emily copped out," Sidra remarked, strapping on her seatbelt. "I mean it's Halloween, we're supposed to have fun."

"'But I've never been to a haunted house'," Malajia mimicked. "I almost smacked her right in her damn face before we left. She gets on my nerves."

"I don't even want to hear about her pathetic ass anymore," Chasity hissed. "She needs to get a life."

"Damn, I guess Emily's the *only* one who stayed home. Look at that long ass line," Malajia complained as they drove up and parked. The queue for tickets snaked around the haunted house, two or three deep in places. The guys' bus lurched to a stop and promptly emptied.

"This is gonna be off the chain," Mark predicted, sidling up to Sidra in the line. "I heard that you go from one room to another, starting with the asylum, and that there's a big surprise waiting for you at the end."

"I bet you get scared," Josh stated, voice filled with laughter.

"Please, nothing can scare me," Mark scoffed.

"Oh yeah, I'm gonna see Chasity get scared, I'm gonna see Chasity get scared," Malajia chanted, clapping her hands.

"I hope you die in there," Chasity shot back.

"Anyone who votes for Malajia to be in front, raise your hand," Mark proposed, then quickly threw his hand up in the air.

Malajia glared at him. "You would do that to me, really?"

"Hell yeah," Mark said. "Better you getting sliced, than me."

"Asshole," Malajia spat, folding her arms.

"God, can we just get through this without you two going at it?" Alex groaned.

"Nope," Malajia and Mark answered in unison.

"I swear, Emily has no idea what she's gonna miss," David said happily.

The line moved quickly. After getting their hands stamped, they walked into the factory. Fog and eerie lights, and sounds filled the dark interior.

"Oh, please," Mark jeered. A sudden screech pierced the quiet. Startled, Mark jumped behind the girls.

"That's good, Mark," Alex put in, "We need someone on the back end."

Soon, noises of all kinds bombarded them. A blood streaked hand reached out of a wall and grabbed David's arm. At a fork in the road, they paused.

"Um, which way should we go?" Sidra asked, clutching Josh's arm.

"Uh Sid, as much as I enjoy you touching me, you're cutting off my circulation," Josh joked.

"Sorry," she replied completely unaware of how tightly she was squeezing him.

"We're *not* splitting up," Alex said with authority as the eerie noises, blood-curdling screams, and insane ranting grew louder and louder.

"Come on, Alex. It's a haunted house; it's not real," Mark said, giving Alex a playful nudge. "Besides, I could never leave you guys anyway."

Suddenly, the loud speaker crackled to life. "Everyone back to your rooms. The patients have escaped. They're gonna kill us, they're gonna kill us all!" The sound of a chainsaw blared from the speakers. At the announcer's scream, everyone huddled closer together.

"Man, fuck this," Mark yelped, pushing past his friends.

"Are you kidding me?" Malajia yelled at him as they watched him run away.

"I'll miss y'all!" they heard him shout. Then, without warning, a crowd of mental patients with blood-stained clothes and chainsaws jumped from the walls. Everyone scrambled to get away. Jason, Malajia, Chasity and Alex ran one way; Sidra, David and Josh another.

Everywhere they turned, things popped out of the walls, and the patients still chased after them.

"Oh my god! Oh my god!" Malajia screamed at the top of her lungs as a heavy-set woman, covered in blood and holding a machete, chased them.

Chasity froze as another crazed patient jumped in her face. She screamed as the blood covered man reached for her. Jason grabbed Chasity's arm and pulled her along. "This is crazy," he concluded as the two of them took off running in another direction.

Malajia and Alex ran until they couldn't run anymore. "I can't breathe; I swear to god I'm gonna pass out," Malajia panted as she leaned against the wall. Something reached out and latched onto her arm. She screamed at the top of her lungs.

"I'm gonna die, I don't wanna die," she screamed.

Alex grabbed the hysterical Malajia. "Mel, calm down." Sensing that Malajia was reeling out of control, Alex slapped her.

"You mop headed bitch!" Malajia shouted, shocked back to normalcy. "I outta drop kick you."

"I'm sorry, but you had to calm down—you were gonna hyperventilate." Rounding the corner, they stumbled over a familiar figure.

Mark was crouched in the corner.

"Boy, get the hell up and come on, you punk," Alex commanded, pulling him up by the shirt collar.

"What! I'm not scared," he lied as he hopped up, straightening out his shirt.

"You left us," Malajia spat.

"What?" He exclaimed. "You mean ya'll weren't behind me?"

"Oh please! You left us. That was so wrong!" Malajia hollered. While Mark and Malajia were arguing back and forth, Alex heard a slow dragging sound approaching them. She turned her head to see where it was coming from.

"Umm, guys," she said nervously as she continued to look around. Then the noise started getting closer and closer. "Guys," she repeated, her voice cracking.

"You are such a punk," Malajia shot at Mark.

"No see what happened was—when I turned around and saw that ya'll weren't there, I went to run back, but something grabbed me and said 'naw man, don't go back for them' and so I was like 'man you got a point' and we was cool and everything—"

"Oh please," Malajia interrupted.

"Guys!" Alex shouted as the noise stopped.

"What is it?" Malajia asked.

"Something's here." Suddenly a light flashed on a huge guy carrying an axe dripping with blood. "Okay, I'm done," Alex cried. "We're outta here."

Panting and coughing, they threw themselves onto the grass outside the haunted house.

"We missed the funhouse," Mark moaned.

Malajia shot him a glare. "Shut up, with your scared ass. Leaving us and shit."

"You *still* on that?" Mark questioned.

"How was the funhouse?" Alex asked as the rest of the group sat down on the grass.

"Alex, don't ask me about that stupid funhouse. I freakin' hate clowns," Sidra scoffed.

"The guy hanging on a hook in the meat room, with his insides hanging out wasn't a good time either," Jason laughed.

Chasity glared at Malajia. "Let's go to the haunted house, Chasity. It's gonna be fun, Chasity. Stop being so mean, Chasity," she mocked, mimicking Malajia coaxing. "Getting stuck in a room with spinning mirrors and crazy people was *such* an awesome experience," Chasity drawled, "thanks for the invite."

Malajia rolled her eyes at Chasity's sarcasm.

Rather than wait for the bus, the guys all piled into Chasity's car.

"Chasity screamed like a girl," Sidra said, relishing the rare chance to tease her roommate.

"At least she's not scared of clowns," Josh pointed out with a grin.

"Emily is gonna be so salty she missed this," Malajia laughed.

"Halloween's over. Now Thanksgiving's just a couple of weeks away," Malajia observed. "So what are you heifers gonna do for the break?"

"Always with the name calling," Sidra huffed, "You need to broaden your vocabulary."

Alex chuckled at the half-hearted glare that Malajia shot at Sidra. "Anyway, I think that we're all going home for Thanksgiving."

"You gonna see Paul?" Emily asked. Alex had finally told everyone what was going on with her. Keeping the news bottled up had backfired, big time.

"Probably," Alex said. "Our families are close. It'll be okay. We were headed for a split anyway."

"Well, for someone who just broke up with her boyfriend of three years, you sure seem chipper," Sidra put in.

"Look, I'm not gonna let one fool ruin my life," Alex said with a shrug.

"Enough with Alex's drama," Malajia joked. "We should do something for the holiday."

"Um, no," Chasity said, shaking her head emphatically.

"Why not?"

"Because my aunt is making me stay with *her* the whole damn time," Chasity bit back.

"What?" Sidra feigned astonishment. "Someone is *making* you do something?"

"*She's* the only one who *can*," Chasity stated flatly. "Not to mention that I can't stand you people."

Malajia sucked her teeth. "You people are making me sick with your boredom."

"What Malajia? What do *you* wanna do, huh?" Sidra asked. She was beginning to become annoyed with Malajia's whining.

"Look, I'm trying to suggest we do something fun during our break. I don't know about *you*, but *I* don't wanna spend the whole time with my dull ass family."

"Sounds like a personal problem to me," Chasity ventured.

Malajia stomped her foot on the ground. "Look, if you don't wanna listen to me, just get up and leave!"

Alex, Sidra and Chasity looked at Malajia, and stood at once.

"You know what?" Malajia hissed, "I'm about sick of your attitude toward me."

"Don't care," Chasity responded flippantly.

"Ooh, I should pull your hair right out your head," Malajia snapped.

"Do it and die, bitch," Chasity threatened.

Sidra shot her a disapproving look. "Must you two be so nasty and belligerent *all* the time? Can't you act like ladies, just *once*?"

"No," Chasity responded nonchalantly.

"For what?" Malajia asked, turning her nose up. "What's the fun in being all stuck up and prissy?"

"Call me prissy all you want. But, at least I know how to act like I have some sense," Sidra ground out, flipping her hair over her shoulder.

Malajia leaned in close to Chasity. "Was flipping that ponytail supposed to scare us?" she asked.

"Malajia, I swear to God, you need to get out my face," Chasity snapped.

Sidra tried to stifle her laugh at the look of embarrassment on Malajia's face, but was unsuccessful. "Mel, you should see your face."

Malajia waved her hand dismissively. "Anyway, like I was saying, we should meet up during break," she persisted. "We don't live that far apart; we could pick somewhere central."

"Ummm," Emily started.

"Oh what, Emily? Mommy's not gonna let you out of her sight?" Malajia mocked, anticipating Emily's excuses.

"Malajia, will you leave the girl alone?" Alex protested.

"Listen, my mom is going to want to spend the whole holiday with me." Emily hugged her books to her chest. "I don't think that's such a bad thing."

"Come *on*, Emily. You are such a damn child," Malajia barked.

"I am *not*," Emily whispered.

Chasity's face frowned in confusion. "What the fuck are you whispering for?"

The brusque question made Emily look down at her pink boots in embarrassment, which succeeded in bringing Malajia to burst out laughing.

Alex sucked her teeth as she adjusted her book bag on her shoulder. "Emily sweetie, pay evil one and evil two no mind. They have no sense whatsoever"

"Emily, you really need to toughen up a little. If one of us cracks on you, just tell us off," Malajia advised, turning to Chasity. "See, watch this…Chasity you're a bitch."

"Screw you," Chasity retorted.

"See what I mean?" Malajia asked.

Sidra shook her head. "Sweetie, don't take after them. Please don't."

"Just shut up," Chasity muttered.

"Hey," Sidra shot back, "I heard that."

Chasity rolled her eyes. "I'm leaving."

"Wait, we still haven't made any plans for Thanksgiving," Malajia wailed at Chasity's departing figure.

"Relax," Alex put in, stifling a laugh. "You have two weeks to work on it. But right now, I've got to go study for my math test."

Two hours later, Alex was still at her desk, puzzling through calculations. "Limits, huh; well I've just about reached mine," she muttered.

The door swung open and Malajia came in, dropping a bag of groceries by the door.

"Hey Al—"

"Shut up, I'm studying," Alex cut her off.

"Oh, sorry," Malajia whispered. Then, hearing the phone ring, she dashed for it. "Don't get up. I'll get it."

"Okay, thanks," Alex mumbled, trying to regain her focus.

"Hello?" The exaggerated cheerfulness with which Malajia always answered the phone was followed by an ear-piercing scream. "It's my friend Erica from high school," Malajia exclaimed as she held her hand over the receiver.

"How nice," Alex responded tartly, thumping her pencil on her workbook.

"Oh, you're studying. Sorry," Malajia apologized, but then a stream of chatter gushed into the phone, punctuated by gurgles of delight.

Exasperated, Alex slammed her workbook shut, and gathered up her papers. "You are so lucky that I'm in a good mood. I'm going to find someplace quiet."

By the time she reached the library, her good mood had soured. It didn't improve when she noticed Chasity about to go into the stacks.

"Oh my goodness. *You're* actually in the *library*?" Alex teased.

"And what is *that* supposed to mean?" Chasity demanded.

"Shhhhh," students nearby scolded.

"Oh, shush your damn self," Chasity barked.

Alex pulled Chasity down into the seat next to her. "Girl, shut up before you get thrown out of here."

"So what, it's not like I really want to be in here anyway."

Alex chuckled, "Girl, who you tellin'? I would rather be in my room, but Malajia is running her loud mouth on the phone."

"No surprise there," Chasity commented, pulling a book from her book bag and putting it on the table.

"Graphic design?" Alex looked at the title of the book. "You like computers?"

"*No*, but I like to design websites. I did them for my aunt Trisha when she started her real estate company." Chasity's eyes narrowed at Alex's look of surprise. "What? Just because I'm a moody bitch, doesn't mean that I don't know how to do anything."

"You're taking the intermediate class?"

"Yeah, I'll really get into my major next semester."

"Wow Chaz, that's really great." Alex was impressed. "I'm going to major in English and go into editing," she tossed her pencil down. "But I've been stuck with this damn math for hours. Why do I need *math* for *editing*?"

"I don't know, Alex." Chasity shook her head. "The majority of our classes this semester don't have *anything* to do with our major."

"Yeah," Alex agreed. "Sidra is a Criminal Justice Major, Emily's is Education..."

"Education? Don't tell me she wants to be a teacher," Chasity muttered, aghast.

"Uh huh."

"*Her* scared ass? A *teacher*? She can't even tell people to shut up. How in the hell is she gonna control a classroom full of bad-ass kids?"

"Will you leave the girl alone? She's lived a sheltered life. I bet by the time she graduates, she'll be over her shyness," Alex predicted.

"Yeah, whatever." Chasity remained unconvinced.

"Anyway what was I saying?...Oh, yeah. Malajia's major is fashion...well more like Design and Business."

"God help the world of fashion when that idiot graduates," Chasity jeered.

"Stop it," Alex scolded, giving Chasity a poke. "She's really talented. *You've* seen what she can do with a T-shirt, glitter, and some scissors."

Jason crept up behind Chasity and put his hands over her eyes. "Guess who?"

"Fuck my life," she complained.

"It's your future husband and father of your children," he teased, prompting a giggle from Alex.

"Guys, please," Alex begged. "As much as I'd like to be amused, I've got to finish going through these math formulas. Can you two take your conversation elsewhere?"

"I'm not even talking to him," Chasity exclaimed, pointing to Jason.

"Less talking, more moving," Alex teased. "Jason please, can you take it elsewhere?"

"Sure," Jason agreed, pulling Chasity away. "Let's go out Friday," he asked her when they reached a secluded spot.

"No."

"Damn, do you have to be so evil about it?" he rebuked.

She folded her arms. "What is it that you want from me, Jason?"

"I want you to lighten up a little."

"No. Stop bothering me. You're annoying," she hissed.

"Am I really?" he asked, staring at her intently.

"Why are you staring at me like that?" she questioned after a few seconds. "Is that look supposed to make me *want* you?"

"You know what?" He laughed. "I can honestly say that you are the most challenging, stubborn women that I have ever met."

"And your point *is*?"

He closed his eyes for a moment. "You keep me on my toes," he said quietly. "I also know that if you didn't like me at *all*, you wouldn't even speak to me."

Chasity glared at him. *Damn it,* he was right. But she wouldn't give him the satisfaction of admitting it.

"Jason, get out of my face."

"Okay I'll go...for now," he said. "But you'll be mine one day."

"Don't hold your breath...Better yet, go *ahead* and hold your breath. That way you'll die, and I won't be bothered anymore."

"Ooh, is that all you got?" he asked playfully, holding his hand over his heart. "It doesn't faze me. I'm a very patient man, Miss Parker."

"Whatever," Chasity muttered. She turned on her heel, and left him in the stacks to return to her studies.

Chapter 17

Malajia speared a piece of romaine lettuce with her fork. "I have an idea about what we should do during Thanksgiving break."

"You're *still* on that?" Sidra asked, then bit into a dinner roll.

"Yeah, so?"

"Mel, we've been away from home for months. I'm pretty sure people would prefer to just stay home," Sidra argued.

"First of all, Thanksgiving break is four freakin' days. We can spend Thursday and Friday with our families and *still* do something Saturday and Sunday."

"Okay, ladies," Alex laughed, "let's hear Malajia's plan before she gets indigestion."

Malajia moved some hair off her face. "Thank you," she said. "I was thinking that we could stay at a luxury hotel for the weekend."

"Why?" Chasity asked, picking at her turkey wrap.

"We don't have enough time to go on a trip, but we could still do something fun on the weekend."

"So, where do you plan on renting this luxury hotel room?" Alex asked, not quite ready to prick Malajia's bubble.

"I haven't quite figured that out yet, but I will."

"Time out here," Sidra interjected. "Be realistic. Staying in a luxury hotel for a weekend is going to cost a lot."

"Yeah, I don't have that kind of money," Alex put in. "Actually, I have *no* money."

"Why are you two even entertaining this nonsense?" Chasity asked. "Malajia's little plan is never going to happen."

"Look rich girl, I'll find a damn way," Malajia shot back. "I am *not* staying in that house with those damn Simmons people for four days straight."

"Um, Malajia?" Emily tapped Malajia's arm.

"Emily, shut up. You're *going*."

"No, I was gonna tell you that it's time for your class to start."

Malajia looked at her watch. "Oh shit!" she shrieked. "I have to go, we'll talk later!"

"Malajia, slow down. You're going to fall in those heels," Sidra shouted after her.

Midterm grades came out the week before Thanksgiving break, and students were clustered around their mailboxes anticipating the results.

"I know I got all A's, I know I got all A's," David chanted happily and ripped open his envelope. "Yes, I knew it."

"Man, shut up. I'm sick of you," Mark grumbled.

"Aww, what's wrong, 'F' man?" David teased.

Mark snatched open his envelope. "Ha, ha. You're salty, I didn't get not one damn F."

"Just a couple of D's," Jason observed, looking over Mark's shoulder. "If I wasn't on this athletic scholarship, I would probably be screwing up too."

"No, you wouldn't," Josh contradicted.

"You're right. I wouldn't."

"How'd you do, Jase?" one of Jason's teammates called out.

"B's."

"Ah, typical freshman. When you're an upperclassman, you'll learn you can get by with C's."

"Get outta here, Carl," Jason said with a laugh.

"All right, dude. See you at practice." Turning, Carl bumped into Chasity.

"You wanna watch where you're going?" she snapped.

"Hey ladies," Carl grinned. "Coming to the game this Sunday?"

"Not to see *you* play," Malajia brushed him off. This wasn't the first time Carl had tried to hit on them. He had a reputation for being a player.

"That's okay, I'd much rather see your friend here anyway," he said, looking at Chasity.

"Sorry, sweetie," she said, sizing up the short, stocky guard. "You're a bit too small for me."

"Well, you know what they say..."

"Carl, back off," Jason warned, going into protective mode at the sight of Chasity's frustration.

"Ugh, he makes me sick," Malajia said, watching his retreating back. She turned her attention to Mark. He was leaned up against a wall of mailboxes, preventing her from getting to hers. "Could you move please?"

Mark, feigning niceness, moved aside and let her pass. As Malajia went to open her mailbox, he unzipped her book bag, spilling its contents on the floor. Malajia cursed as she nudged him away from her.

"Mark, just leave her alone. You play too much," Josh advised, watching Mark laugh at the sight of Malajia picking up her papers.

"So," Alex asked, shaking her head at their antics. "You guys survive midterm grades?"

"Barely," Mark admitted.

"Yep," Jason nodded.

"Make that a mega-yes," David added.

"Shut up already," Mark complained. "Nobody says 'mega-yes'. You nerd." David sucked his teeth at Mark's snide comment.

"That's what you get, Mark, for always playing—a bunch of C's and D's," Alex put in.

"How did you know what I got?" He frowned.

"I guessed. And by the look on your face, I was right."

"I don't have time for this bullshit," he scoffed. On the way out of the mailroom, Mark deliberately bumped Malajia, and her mail went flying in all directions.

"I hate you!" she screamed, stooping to pick up her grades.

"Anyway, how did you ladies do?" Josh asked when he stopped laughing.

"All right," Emily answered cautiously. She was a little worried about the two C's; her mother would not be pleased.

"These grades are only to show you how you're doing so far. These are not your final term grades," David informed.

Chasity's cell phone rang. "Hello? Yeah….five B's and a D….So, I hate math anyway…..Yeah whatever….I already told you I'll be there. Bye."

"Your aunt Trisha?" Malajia asked.

"Yes, nosey," Chasity responded, shoving her phone back into her bag.

"Well, I'm *this* close to getting a D too—in that stupid Public Speaking class," Sidra moaned.

"Sidra, that class isn't so bad." Alex shook her head, and then looked over at Chasity. "What did your aunt say?"

"That I should try to bring my D up by the end of the semester."

"Or else what?" Jason asked.

"Or else *nothing*."

"Jason, Chasity's aunt spoils the crap out of her. She could bring home straight F's and she'd *still* get a diamond tennis bracelet," Malajia sniffed.

"Shhh, don't get jealous, sweetie," Chasity cooed, walking out of the mailroom.

"Chasity, I can tutor you in math; I'm pretty good at it," Jason offered, heading out behind her.

"Ugh, time for me to call my nosey ass parents and tell them my grades. I'm gonna hear my Dad's mouth about it, I just know it," Malajia sulked as she walked out.

"Now, you wouldn't be stressing so much if you all had…"

"*A's,* if we had all *A's,*" Sidra interrupted David's teasing. "We know that you get A's every time David. We *get* it."

"Ah, the sound of envy, I love it," he joked and Sidra playfully elbowed him in the ribs.

The girls walked back to Torrence Hall. They were about to go up to the room, when the resident adviser called out.

"Sidra, a package came for you."

"Since when do packages come to the dorms?" Malajia asked. "I thought they were supposed to go to the post office."

"Since Sidra's mother had it delivered here," the adviser sniffed, flicking to another page in the magazine she was reading.

"How come my parents don't send *me* any damn packages?" Malajia complained.

"Please stop whining," Chasity demanded.

"Come on, ladies. Let's go," Sidra said as she grabbed her package off the counter.

As soon as they got to the room, Chasity tossed her books down on the chair, and walked over to her mini-refrigerator.

"Ooh, you got food!" Malajia exclaimed, sprinting over.

"Get your greedy ass away from me," Chasity snapped and shut the refrigerator door. Malajia was really hungry; she'd missed lunch because she'd spent hours talking on the phone instead.

"You're gonna *give* me some food," she ordered, struggling to reach the refrigerator door. "I'm hungry."

"It's not my problem you missed lunch," Chasity shrugged, knocking Malajia's hand away. "You shouldn't have been running your damn mouth on the phone."

"But I was talking to my sister, Geri."

"I don't give a shit," Chasity shot back.

"I cannot believe that you two are old enough to be legal adults," Alex grinned as she watched them tussle over the fridge. "You act like children."

"Girl, move!" Chasity ordered, giving Malajia a push out of the way.

"Will you just share?" Malajia shouted and tossed a pillow at Chasity, catching her on the arm. "I hope that your wrist still hurts."

"Well, it *doesn't*," Chasity taunted, throwing the pillow right back at her.

Sidra laughed, taking a seat on her bed to open her package. "Yay! Mama sent my winter clothes."

"You sure you have room in that closet?" Chasity asked as she combed her hair back into a ponytail.

"I hope your hair falls out too," Malajia muttered.

"Will you shut the fuck up?" Chasity yelled.

"I just want some food," Malajia protested.

"You know what," Chasity barked, flinging a bag of bagels and plastic container of cream cheese at Malajia. "Take the damn food and shut up."

"Thank you, darling. You're so sweet," Malajia said, tearing open the bag.

"Oh, my gosh," Sidra gasped.

Surrounded by winter clothes, she clutched a little rectangular box. "Condoms. My mom sent me *condoms!*" She ripped off the attached note. "'Don't come home with any babies,'" she read aloud. "My mama is crazy."

Malajia took the box out of her hands. "Ooh, the ribbed kind. What does Mother Howard know about ribbed condoms?"

"What do *you* know about them?" Chasity asked smartly.

"No more than *you* do," Malajia shot back.

"Is there something that you're not telling us, Miss Princess?" Alex teased, leaning up against the dresser.

"No, it's just that my mom is absolutely petrified that I'm going to get pregnant," Sidra said with a laugh.

"Trisha gave me a box of those for my sixteenth birthday," Chasity offered.

"I don't know *why*. It's not like you let anyone touch you anyway," Malajia mocked. "Sidra, since you're not gonna use them, just give them to me."

"Oh *why*? What are *you* gonna do with them?" Alex asked, cocking her head at Malajia.

"You know what, let me just put them away," Sidra decided and shoved the box in the top drawer of her dresser.

"Are we going to dinner?" Emily asked meekly.

"Yeah," Alex said as she stood up. "All this drama is enough to work up an appetite."

"These coats are ugly," Malajia scoffed, putting another one of the garments back on the rack. Her winter coat had a hole in it, and after hours of whining and pleading, her father had finally given up and agreed to put money in her checking account.

"Malajia, please, come on," Chasity urged. She hadn't gotten much sleep the night before, and she was paying for it. She dreaded Thanksgiving break, but there was no way to wiggle out of her aunt Trisha's plans. Trisha's daily phone calls made sure she realized that.

"Look, if the coat has to last me all winter, then I'm gonna pick the cutest one," Malajia stated and wandered out of the store.

Her eyes lit up when she saw the mid-length red coat in the window display. "*That's* the one," Malajia cried with joy, and hurried into the elegant boutique. "I have a pair of boots that will be *perfect* with it."

Chasity casually fished inside the coat's sleeve for the price tag. "Malajia, this coat costs eight hundred dollars."

Malajia peered over her shoulder. "I see that. I can *read* a price tag," she shrugged. "I better find an ATM machine and check how much money my dad put in this morning."

"Just hurry the hell up," Chasity insisted. "I saw one outside, a couple of doors down, across from the fountain."

Malajia skipped to the machine, slipped in her debit card, and clicked out her pin number. Chasity watched as Malajia frowned.

"What," she exclaimed, "Two hundred dollars? Are you kidding me? Two hundred dollars?"

"Malajia, you're yelling at a machine," Chasity pointed out.

"I want that coat," Malajia whined.

"You don't have enough for it, whiny," Chasity jeered.

"Don't you think I *know* that?" Malajia yelled, "I just saw my balance on the screen,"

"You've got *one* more time to raise your voice at me, then your ass is walking back to campus," Chasity warned, holding up a gloved hand.

Malajia stomped her foot on the ground. "That's not fair. I can't get a coat with just two hundred dollars."

"Sure you can. Just go back to the other store, and buy one of *those* coats," Chasity advised in a tired voice. "Or just ask your Dad to put more money in."

"Are you kidding me?" Malajia scoffed. "My parents didn't even want to give me *this*. My cheap-ass dad probably had a heart attack when he deposited this money." She broke off and surveyed Chasity. She'd always liked that double-breasted black coat. "Sell me yours."

"Malajia, this coat cost me a thousand dollars, and I like it." Chasity shook her head.

"Please, Chasity, you can buy another one," Malajia whined.

"No, Malajia," Chasity barked. "I'm leaving."

"Come on, please?" Malajia begged as she followed her out the store.

"No."

Chapter 18

"Chasity, I can't find my hair dryer. Can you check my closet and see if it's in there?" Sidra called out.

"Sidra, it's not in there," Chasity replied dryly. "I already checked after you asked me the *first* time."

"Are you serious?" Sidra yelled, "It *has* to be in there!"

"Why are you yelling at me?" Chasity objected, frowning.

"I'm sorry, Chaz. I just hate packing. I always feel like I'm forgetting something. It drives me crazy," Sidra sulked.

"Will you calm down, girl? We're only going to be gone for a few days," Alex interjected with a laugh, dropping her book bag. Chasity was giving her a lift home.

"I *know* that, Alex. I've been up since seven this morning; I'm tired and I'm irritated." Sidra rubbed her hands over her low ponytail. "I need coffee."

"Oh no, the last thing you need is to be irritated *and* wired," Alex pointed out.

"All right, fine," Sidra sighed, sitting on her bed.

"So what time are we leaving, Chasity?" Alex asked, grabbing a bottle of juice out of Sidra's mini refrigerator and taking a drink.

"In a few minutes. Is that all you're taking?" Chasity pointed to Alex's bag.

Alex shook her head. "I've got a duffle bag back at the room." A grin blossomed on her face when she heard the rap on the door. "Uh oh."

"Crap," Sidra moaned as her mother walked into the room, surveying her daughter's open suitcase and the clothes scattered on the bed.

"Um hmm," Mrs. Howard laughed and pulled her daughter into a hug. "I knew you wouldn't be ready, Princess. Finish up and introduce me to your friends."

"Oh sure. Mama, this is Alex, she's nice but bossy...and nosey," Sidra joked. "And this is Miss Chasity, my roommate."

"Hi, sweetie. Are you a new roommate?" Mrs. Howard asked, puzzled.

"No. I'm the same one that she complained to you about in the beginning of the semester," Chasity confirmed.

"*This* is the snobby, ignorant witch?" she asked, looking at Sidra.

"Yep," Chasity validated, shooting Sidra a side glance.

"Mama," Sidra exclaimed, mortified.

"Never mind. Give me a hug, sweetie," Mrs. Howard said with a wave of her hand.

Chasity wasn't big on hugging people, but she found herself wrapped in Mrs. Howard's ample arms.

"And as for you, young lady, when I called half an hour ago, you said that you were finished packing."

"I *did*?" Sidra stalled.

"Don't play with me, child. Throw the rest of your things in that suitcase and close it. We have to go. I told your father and your brothers not to eat until we came back. The last thing that I want is a bunch of hungry men in my kitchen."

"Okay. Chaz and I need to get on the road too, Mrs. Howard," Alex said, tossing her empty juice bottle in the trash. "Have a safe trip."

"See you, girl," Sidra said, hugging Alex and then turning to Chasity, arms stretched out ready for a hug.

"Nope," Chasity teased, backing away. "You called me a witch."

"So mean," Sidra laughed as she shut the door behind her friends.

"Don't take forever," Chasity cautioned. "I want to beat some of that rush hour traffic."

"I don't think you'll really beat it, Chaz. Thanksgiving is tomorrow after all; everybody will be on the road all night," Alex advised.

"I didn't ask for your commentary, just hurry up," Chasity hissed, turning her car off.

"All right, calm down, cranky. I'll just be a minute," Alex promised and jumped out of the car. Alex was out of breath by the time she reached the room.

Malajia looked over at Alex, who had just fallen onto the floor the moment she opened the door. "What the hell? Why are you on the floor?"

"My big ass just ran up four flights of steps," she informed, sitting up. "Next year, I'm gonna make sure I end up in a dorm with an elevator," she vowed.

"Are you and Chasity about to leave?" Emily asked, looking up from her task of folding her clothes.

"Yeah, she's downstairs waiting for me," Alex nodded, grabbing a large green duffle bag off the floor.

"What? She's not coming up to say goodbye? Ugh, some people," Malajia scoffed. She picked up her phone and dialed Chasity's number.

"What?" Chasity answered abruptly.

"Excuse me, but you could at *least* come up and say goodbye, with your rude ass," Malajia barked.

"Malajia, don't you have packing to do?"

"Don't you worry about what *I'm* doing," Malajia snapped.

"You know what—Mark if you don't get away from my car I'm gonna run you the fuck over!" Chasity shouted.

"Is Mark bothering you?" Malajia asked unnecessarily. Even over the phone, she could still hear him.

"Yes—he's got his damn face plastered to my window."

"Well, serves your ass right for not saying goodbye to us," Malajia teased, then the phone went dead. "Hello? Hello? That bitch hung up on me."

"I better get down there," Alex sighed, slinging her bag over her shoulder. "Mel, I'm sorry your little Thanksgiving getaway didn't work out. Maybe next time."

"I don't wanna talk about it," Malajia said sharply.

"Don't be mad, Malajia," Emily put in hastily. The Thanksgiving getaway was still a sore spot.

"Well, I *am*," Malajia retorted. "Now I have to be home with those freaks the whole time."

"Look, you ladies take care," Alex cut in. "See you next week."

Alex lugged her duffle bag to Chasity's Lexus and, sure enough, there was Mark sitting on the hood.

"Boy, what are you doing?"

"Making our friend here mad," he responded with a laugh. "And I think it's working."

Alex shook her head and popped the trunk. Mark slid off the hood and followed her.

"Quit it," Alex warned when Mark started poking her.

"Oh, stop being so uptight," Mark laughed.

"Mark—do you *want* me to punch you? Because I'd be happy to do it."

"No, I'm good," he said and ran a hand over his hair. "Do I get a hug?"

Alex looked at him for a second before smiling, wrapping her arms around him none too tight. "Be safe," she said.

"You too," Mark said as he let go. Then he knocked on the car window. "Bye sexy!"

"Fuck off!" Chasity shouted.

"I love to see her get mad," he said with a grin.

"Boy, get on, before David and Josh kill you for making them wait," Alex urged.

"Please. They're riding in *my* father's car. They can wait a minute."

"Bye, Mark," Alex said, getting into the car. "All right Mama, let's go."

"It took you long enough," Chasity sneered.

"Oh hush," Alex scolded, leaning back in her seat to get settled for the long drive home.

Sidra's mother had always had a soft spot for Malajia. When she discovered that her "play daughter" was taking the train home, she wouldn't hear any arguments. Mrs. Howard and her daughter would drop Malajia at the station and see her safely on board.

"She better be on her way down," Sidra said as she filed her nails.

"I'm sure she is," Mrs. Howard added dryly. "No one could take as long as you to pack."

"Oh, *Malajia* can," Sidra protested, pointing her nail file to the steps where Malajia was struggling with a mammoth-sized suitcase. "Wow, that bag must hold enough clothes for a month. No wonder it took her so long."

"Please don't fall, please don't fall," Malajia muttered to herself, letting out a screech as the bag tumbled down the stairs. "Are you kidding me?" she yelled.

"The poor girl needs help, Sid," Mrs. Howard suggested, trying not to laugh. When Malajia tripped and fell, she was out of the car in a flash. "Oh sweetie, you okay?"

"No, not really, Mother Howard," Malajia said as she dusted herself off.

"Are you okay, trippy?" Sidra teased as Malajia shuffled into the backseat.

"Very funny, Sidra. Very funny," Malajia hissed, giving Sidra's ponytail a quick yank.

"Mama, did you see what she just did to me?" Sidra demanded.

Mrs. Howard couldn't help but laugh. She had missed the way that these two interacted. She was glad that they were friends again.

"You girls are so silly," she finally said, shaking her head with a smile.

Chapter 19

"How many potatoes do you think we need?" Emily asked, slitting open the bag.

"Might as well use them all."

Emily filled a large pot with water, tossed in some salt, and set it on a burner to heat.

"Mommy, I really wish that you would give my friends a chance. They're good people."

"Emily, those heathens are *not* your friends." Ms. Harris stopped seasoning the turkey. It irritated her to no end to hear Emily prattle on about her friends.

Jazmine breezed into the kitchen and took a soda out of the refrigerator. "Well, Mom, you must be glad to have your personal servant back. When she's finished doing your bidding, maybe she could make my bed," Jazmine taunted, shoving Emily out of her way.

"Jazmine, don't you put your hands on her again!"

"Whatever," Jazmine shrugged. The older sister flicked open her can of soda and retreated to the living room.

"Are you okay, baby girl?"

"I'm tired of getting picked on," Emily gulped, wiping the tears from her face.

"Sweetie, she's just jealous because you're the youngest and get all of mommy's attention. Don't pay her any mind, you hear me?"

Emily nodded and began peeling potatoes.

"Oh, I forgot to tell you—your father is coming over for Thanksgiving dinner."

Emily smiled faintly at the news. She was excited to see her father, but it bothered Emily that her mother kept on brushing off any moment of conversation that had to do with the parts of her life that didn't include *her*.

"Oh and Emily?"

"Yes, Mommy?"

"I'm thinking about getting your room changed."

Emily dropped the potato she was peeling and shot her mother a quizzical look. "Huh?"

"Your dorm room," Ms. Harris clarified. "I'm going to see if I can pull strings and get your room changed. I think that you would be better off in a single room."

Emily shut her eyes tight. She was ready to scream. "Um Mommy…there are no single rooms right now. They haven't finished building the new dorms."

"Well, I'm going to see for myself. I feel that you need your own space away from those troublemaking girls."

"That's not fair!" Emily exclaimed.

"Don't raise your voice at me, Emily Kelly Harris. Now you've just proven my point. Hanging around those girls is causing you to lash out at me."

"But you're controlling my life," Emily cried.

"Emily, I am your mother and I know what's best for you."

Emily threw the peeler into the sink and stormed out of the kitchen.

"Mama, the apple pie that I made should be done in a few minutes," Sidra informed, removing her apron and placing it on the counter.

"Good job, Princess," Mrs. Howard gushed.

Sidra smiled. "Thanks. It's my first one, so I hope it goes over well."

"Oh, I'm sure it will. If anything your father and your greedy brothers will tear it up," Mrs. Howard assured, stirring the gravy.

Sidra's giggle was interrupted by the doorbell. "I'll get it." She let out a sigh as she saw who was gathered on the other side of the door. "I'm not surprised."

"Sid-ra," Mark greeted, voice carrying through the house.

"You guys ate already?" Sidra asked as she moved aside to let Mark, Josh and David into the house.

"No, Mom's not gonna be finished cooking for a while, and I'm hungry *now*," Mark replied, rubbing his flat, toned stomach.

"Nobody cooked at my house," Josh put in. "Dad had to work this year, and I didn't feel like going all the way to Jersey to visit Mom."

"Oh, well, have you spoken to Sarah?" Sidra asked. "What is *she* doing for the holiday?"

"You already know that I have no intention on talking to my sister," Josh responded. The bite in Josh's tone, told Sidra to not press any further about his older sister.

She turned her attention to David. "And *you*?"

"Um, Dad can't boil water, so yeah, I'm hungry," David joked.

"Mama," Mark exclaimed, hugging Mrs. Howard as she was about to pass them.

"Hi boys, how are your parents?" Mrs. Howard asked.

"Good," Mark replied. "Oh, my mom wants you to call her."

"I will," Mrs. Howard responded. "Have you three eaten already?"

"No Mama, they came to freeload off of us," Sidra informed. She looked from her mother to the guys. "*Again.*"

Mark sucked his teeth at her.

"Oh, well, we'll be eating in about a half hour. And don't go overboard, Mark," Mrs. Howard said with a chuckle.

"Why did you have to direct that towards me?" he asked, shocked, pointing to himself.

"Do you *really* want me to answer that?"

"Mama, you know you love it when I come over," Mark teased. Mrs. Howard laughed as she retreated to the kitchen.

"What's goin' on fellas?" Marcus, one of Sidra's older brothers, asked as he came flying down the stairs.

"We hungry," Mark responded.

"Yeah, I know the feeling," Marcus agreed, patting his stomach. "That pie almost done, sis?"

"Yes, greedy," Sidra replied, smoothing her long-sleeved, blue sweater dress with her hands.

"Oh guess what! I brought six new games for the game station," Marcus informed.

"Ooh, games!" Mark cried out. All four guys pushed past Sidra and ran upstairs, their hunger immediately forgotten.

Sidra shook her head. "Boys," she said to herself.

Malajia and her two older sisters were hiding out. No one felt like spending any more time in the kitchen.

"I made the pecan pies," Geri rationalized.

"So? Nobody's gonna eat those nasty ass pies," Malajia scoffed, leaning back on her bed.

"You *still* mad that you had to ride the train for two hours yesterday?" Geri questioned. She remembered how Malajia had walked through the door yesterday evening, whining and complaining about having to take the train home from school. Every chance Malajia got, she brought it up.

"Sure *am*. Dad could've come and picked me up."

"So, Malajia, give us the scoop," her older sister Maria pressed, changing the subject. "Do you have a boyfriend?"

"Maybe," Malajia replied with a big smile.

"Oh please, Maria, you know damn well that girl doesn't have a boyfriend," Geri put in.

"And just how do *you* know?" Malajia asked, bristling.

"Girl, please." Geri shot Malajia a knowing look. "No man wants someone who whines all the damn time."

"Well, that explains why *you* don't have a man," Malajia retorted, sticking out her tongue at her older sister.

"Girls," Mrs. Simmons yelled, barging in their room, "get down here and help me with this food before I go insane. Oh, and before I forget, Malajia, your aunt wants you to babysit tomorrow."

"Mom, no," Malajia whined. She hated babysitting those kids. They were so loud and uncontrollable; she was sure her aunt loaded them up on sugar before passing them off to her.

"Why not? You do it every year. You should be used to it by now," Mrs. Simmons laughed.

"Why can't one of *you* do it?" Malajia asked her sisters.

"Because *we* have something to do," Maria responded. "We're going to an office party."

"Neither of you even has an office," Malajia pointed out. "With y'all party crashing behinds."

"But my boyfriend *does*," Maria mocked. "That's where it's being held."

"Oh...Well I wanna go."

"No."

"Why not?"

"Because you don't even like him," Maria retorted. "And every time you get around him, you start making fun of him."

"Well maybe if he wasn't so ugly—"

"That's it, I'm done with you," Maria snapped, effectively cutting Malajia off.

"I'm kidding, Maria, I'm just kidding," Malajia apologized with a laugh to hide just how serious she was. Desperate, Malajia tugged on Maria's arm. "Can I go? Please, please, please?"

"You promise to be good?"

"Oh, I swear on your boyfriend's face," Malajia promised, holding up her right hand.

"You swear on my boyfriend's *face*?" Maria asked, her temper rising.

"What? Don't get mad," Malajia said, trying to placate her sister. "I promise, for real this time. I'll be good."

"Okay, fine," Maria finally acquiesced after a long pause.

"Okay, that's enough girls." Mrs. Simmons broke into Malajia's squeal of delight. "Get down here and help me."

A couple of hours later Malajia flopped down on the couch, thinking if she never saw another collard green or yam again, it would be too soon. She leaned back and closed her eyes.

"Malajia, Malajia," her ten-year-old sister screamed and pounced on her lap. "Mommy said that you have to take me to the store."

Malajia opened one eye. Dana was a troublemaker, and her mission in life was to make Malajia miserable. "Girl, get away from me. I know damn well Mom did not say that I had to take you to the damn store."

"I hate you," Dana yelled. "And I'm telling Mommy and Daddy that you cursed at me. So *there*."

"No, Dana, no," Malajia pleaded, taking a dollar out of her jean pocket. "I'll give you a dollar if you don't tell."

Dana snatched the dollar from Malajia's grasp. "Thanks. I'm still telling. Ha ha," she teased before running off.

"You ugly brat!" Malajia yelled after her.

Malajia stood there for a few seconds and counted. "Five, four, three, two, one...and right on schedule," she muttered to herself, as she heard her father shout.

"Malajia, did you curse at your sister?"

Malajia rolled her eyes. "No!"

"Yes, she did!" Dana yelled.

"Shut up, you little jerk!"

"Malajia, get in here now," Mrs. Simmons demanded.

"I hate her, she makes me sick," Malajia swore, stamping her foot on the floor.

"Malajia Lakeshia Simmons, what did I just say?" Mrs. Simmons shouted.

"All right Mom! Dang, what are you gonna do? Spank me?"

"Guys, turn the game off and come help me in the kitchen," Jason's mother ordered, standing by the television.

"Honey, isn't that why your sisters are here?" Mr. Adams asked, grabbing the remote off the coffee table.

"I'm going to pretend like I didn't hear that," she huffed. "At least turn the TV *down*. I can't even hear myself think."

"But honey, the game is more exciting when it's up loud," Mr. Adams protested.

"You're riding my last nerve; turn it down, please!" Mrs. Adams snapped.

"Dad, turn it down; that vein is popping out of her neck again," Jason said as he nudged his father.

"Way ahead of you, son."

Jason shook his head and smiled. His mother didn't take crap from anyone, not even her own husband and sons. And because of that, he had always admired and respected her. His smile widened as he watched his father turn the volume up, little by little, once his mother headed back for the kitchen. He had always known that he had gotten his sense of humor and playfulness from his father.

"Dad, you know she's gonna kill you, right?" Jason joked.

"Yeah, I know," he replied with a laugh.

"Hey, Kyle, where have you been hiding?" Jason asked his thirteen-year-old brother as he ran downstairs.

"Playing your video game," the smiling teen answered.

"Did you beat my score yet?"

"Nope, I was *this* close," Kyle said, leaving an inch of air between his thumb and index finger. "You have a girlfriend yet?"

"I'm working on it. *Trust* me." he said and then smacked Kyle in the face with a pillow.

"How's football?" Mr. Adams asked.

"Oh, it's going great. Coach said he's really impressed with my skills."

"Good, good," Mr. Adams said, patting Jason on the back. He'd played football in college, and was proud of his son.

One of Jason's uncles poked his head through the doorway. "Hey, I've got a great idea."

"Oh no," Jason muttered, knowing what was coming next. Every time his uncles and his father got together, they wanted to play football with Jason. He enjoyed it at first, but they never seemed to want to quit.

"Come on son, let's show these old men how the game *should* be played," Mr. Adams urged.

"Um, Dad, I'm a little tired right now. Can I just sit this one out?"

"No way, son," Mr. Adams said as he grabbed a jacket off of the coat rack next to the front door.

"Have fun," Kyle teased, then started laughing.

"Don't laugh too hard, Kyle," Mr. Adams said as he opened the door. "You're coming too."

Kyle stopped laughing. "Aww, man. I should've stayed upstairs."

"You and me both, little bro," Jason chuckled.

"We are going to have a late Thanksgiving dinner," Alex's mother said as she cut some greens.

"Ma, cut yourself some slack. You didn't need to get up at the crack of dawn to put the turkey in. You were tired with all the prep work."

In a few hours, the Chisolm home was going to be filled with aunts, uncles, cousins, and grandparents. Their house wasn't as big as some in the family, but it was always so warm and inviting that everyone liked gathering there.

"So, Alex, when do we get to meet your friends?"

Alex smiled. Ever since she'd come home, her fourteen-year-old sister had been interrogating her. Sahara wanted to know everything about college and her big sister's life.

"I'm not sure, but soon, I promise," Alex answered just as the phone began to ring. "I'll get it."

"Sahara, what are you doing?" Mrs. Chisolm asked, looking at her daughter skeptically.

"Um, I'm just putting some salt in the potatoes," she answered dubiously.

"Girl, that was sugar! You used the wrong shaker," her mother scolded, tossing a spoon in the sink.

Alex walked back in the kitchen just as Sahara began washing the potatoes off. "Everything okay in here?"

"Who was that?" Mrs. Chisolm asked, ignoring Alex's question.

"Mrs. Donahue," Alex replied. "They're going to drop by after dinner."

Her mother stopped what she was doing and looked up. "Paul's mother?"

"Yes," Alex laughed. "Those are the *only* Donahue's that we know, Ma."

"Honey, are you sure? What if Paul comes too?"

"Ma, I'm fine. Don't worry," Alex answered. Trying to reassure her mom, Alex bent the truth a little bit. She had no problem with seeing Paul's parents. But, still feeling raw, she wasn't all that okay with seeing Paul so soon. She had an urgent need to talk to one of her friends.

Suddenly the kitchen was filled with aunts, uncles, and cousins. "Debra, you're not finished yet?" one of her aunts observed, lifting lids off pots.

"Does it *look* like I'm finished?" Mrs. Chisolm answered with some bite.

"Okay, hand us some aprons," another aunt requested. "Sahara, Alex, move out of our way. This is no place for youngsters."

Alex put her hands on her hips. "Excuse me, Auntie, but I'm grown," she said playfully.

"Child, if your age ends with 'teen,' you're not grown. Now out," she retorted, scooting her nieces out of the kitchen.

"All right. I'm going to run out for a bit. I'll be back around six," Alex said, grabbing her coat out of the closet.

"Sweetie, make it eight," Mrs. Chisolm amended.

Chapter 20

Jason recognized the solitary figure trudging along the sidewalk, and pulled over to the curb.

"Hey, Alex, get in," he invited, leaning over to open the car door. "I bet I know where you're headed."

"Umm hmm," she said, piling in and closing the door behind her. "It's a madhouse at home."

"So you've come to seek sanctuary with the calm and peaceful Chasity huh?" he joked, putting the car in gear.

"Yeah. I *was* going to hang out with one of my friends from high school for a bit," Alex informed, removing the leopard print earmuffs from her ears. "But when I called her, all she wanted to talk about was my ex-boyfriend. So I figured an hour ride on the bus to West Chester was a much better alternative."

"Yeah, I don't blame you," Jason chuckled. "I only live a few minutes away from Chaz. So I figured, I'd just show up unannounced and annoy her."

Alex stifled a laugh as she relished the heat coming from the vents. "And annoy her, you *will*," she agreed. A few minutes later, they rolled to a stop in front of a large stone colonial. "This should be it."

They walked in companionable silence along the flagged path, and rang the bell.

"Hi, is Chasity here?" Jason asked the brown-skinned girl who opened the door a crack.

"She's around somewhere being a bitch."

Jason and Alex exchanged a quick look of surprise at the sullen reply. "Maybe Chaz wasn't so off not wanting to spend the break with her family," Alex muttered under her breath.

"Look, it's a little chilly out," Jason said, "so could you please let her know that Alex and Jason are here?"

"Whatever." The girl shrugged, ducked her head back inside and shouted up the stairs. "Chasity, you got company."

A few seconds later, Chasity clattered into the entrance hall and came to an abrupt stop.

"What the hell are you two doing here?" she asked, both startled and suspicious.

"I'm escaping from a touch football game," Jason explained, unsure about the wisdom of this little visit now that Chasity was actually standing in front of him. "My dad and my uncles will be going at it for hours. I couldn't take it anymore."

Chasity smirked. "Such a baby."

"Chaz, they had me playing for almost two hours," Jason responded, full of animation. "I'm telling you, they're crazy."

"And I was kicked out of the kitchen by my aunts," Alex put in. "Too many cooks, you know?" Stepping inside, Alex looked around, taking in the polished antiques and winding staircase. "Wow, nice house."

"It's my grandmother's," Chasity interrupted. "I don't live here. I'm living at my aunt's house about five blocks from here. The house is finally done so I have it to myself...at least until she moves back up here from Florida permanently."

"Girl, if I were someone else, I'd be totally jealous right now," Alex joked.

Chasity shook her head. "Trust me, you wouldn't be," she assured. "Anyway, why are you two *really* here?"

"To meet your charming relatives?" Jason queried.

"What are you talking about?" Chasity asked, folding her arms.

"That girl who answered the door seems pretty um....yeah, charming," Alex put in.

"Who, Melina? Yeah, that's my cousin, and that bitch is far from charming," Chasity jeered. "She used to bully me."

"She bullies you?" Alex was shocked.

"I said *used* to," Chasity corrected. "On my birthday a few years ago, she tried to snatch the diamond earrings my aunt Trisha gave me, out of my ears."

Jason frowned. "Really? What did you do?" he asked.

"I beat the bullshit outta her," Chasity nonchalantly replied.

"Yeah, I figured," Jason laughed.

"She's been walking around here, saying smart shit all night," Chasity revealed, unfazed. "But I bet you, her old ass won't put her hands on me again."

Alex raised her eyebrow. "Old?"

Chasity waved her hand dismissively. "She's got me by three years."

Alex chuckled. "Well that's one beat down I would have loved to see. I hate bullies."

"Uh huh," Chasity said absently, she glanced at her watch.

"Ready for us to leave already?" Alex joked.

"No...well yeah," Chasity responded. Alex resisted the urge to giggle at her smart response, and just shook her head. "But really, I'm waiting for my aunt. She went to the bakery to pick up the desserts. I wish she would hurry up; I want to get this stupid, fake display of holiday happiness over with."

While Chasity paced back and forth, her heels clicking on the marble floor, Jason spotted an album, tucked away and half-hidden behind a huge floral arrangement on a side table. He started to grin as he leafed through it.

"What are you doing?" Chasity demanded, snatching the book from him.

"Looking at pictures of you when you were younger and nicer," Jason shot back.

A half an hour later, Chasity looked at her watch again. "Shouldn't you two be leaving?" she sighed.

"Nope, I have another hour to go," Alex said, relaxing against the sofa's down cushions.

"I'm not ready yet," Jason replied, resting his head against the pillows.

"Okay, let me rephrase that…It's time for you two to leave," Chasity corrected.

"Sweetie, stop being mean and introduce me to your friends."

Jason and Alex looked over to where an elderly woman, all soft curves and wispy salt and pepper hair, stood beaming at them from the doorway.

"Why?" Chasity moaned. "Grandmom, I don't want to."

"Come on, sweetie," Chasity's grandmother urged, pleased that Chasity had made friends at college. Her granddaughter had always been such a loner. Besides, she liked the look of these two.

"I'm Jason," he intervened, stepping forward with his hand stretched out.

"Grandmom, come *on*. How many people did you invite?" Chasity huffed as a knock on the door interrupted the introductions. "I swear, if this is Uncle Johnny and his ugly girlfriend, I'm going home."

A soft laugh erupted from Chasity's grandmother. "You're so silly," she mused.

Chasity let out a loud sigh as she flung the door open. "Oh, hell no," she hissed and tried to slam the door.

"Is that any way to greet your mother?" Brenda Parker slurred, stopping the door with her hand.

"You're drunk, aren't you?" Chasity accused.

"That's none of your business, little girl," Brenda responded with the careful, exaggerated speech of the habitual drunk.

"I'm not in the mood for this, leave me alone," Chasity said as she slammed the door in her mother's face.

"Chasity, why did your grandmother invite your mom here after what she did?" Alex asked, bewildered.

"Because she doesn't know," Chasity responded. "Look, you guys have to go. This is going to get ugly."

"No, I think we'll stick around for a bit," Jason said, his jaw clenched.

"Just be the bigger person," Alex put in, "and walk away if she starts to upset you."

"Yeah, right," Jason muttered as Chasity rolled her eyes at Alex's suggestion. "Like Chasity is about to back down from anything."

"What on earth?" Chasity's grandmother exclaimed, her voice unsteady, when the front door swung open and Brenda barged in.

"This is *my* mother's home. I have every right to be here!" Brenda yelled.

Chasity shook her head and turned toward Alex and Jason. "Go home, you guys."

"Chasity, I think that we should stay," Alex protested, full of concern.

"Alex, I don't care what you think—go home," she repeated and pushed them out the door; her only thought was to escape upstairs. Chasity couldn't face another argument with her mother and she didn't want to upset her grandmother.

"Where are you going?" Brenda shouted.

Chasity turned around. "Don't start with me. I'm not in the mood."

"Still a disrespectful brat, huh?"

"Whatever, Brenda," Chasity spat before turning to walk away.

"Don't walk away from me, you bitch!" Brenda shouted and threw her empty glass at her daughter. Luckily, Chasity's quick duck caused the glass to hit the wall instead of her head. The glass shattered, scattering shards all over the floor.

"Are you crazy?" Chasity yelled.

"I told you, never to walk away from me while I'm talking to you!" Brenda screamed.

"Leave me the fuck alone, Brenda," Chasity demanded as she flicked little pieces of glass out of her hair. "Why are you here anyway? Nobody wants you around."

"*Me*? Oh no Chasity, the person that nobody wants around is *you*. Why don't you do everyone here a favor and leave?"

Chasity took a long look at the crazy, drunken woman in front of her, and snapped, "You know what? *I'll* leave."

"What in God's name is going on?" Chasity's grandmother scolded, holding herself stiffly upright.

"Grandmom, I'm sorry, but I have to go," Chasity stated, voice shaking as she felt herself tear up.

"No, you're not going anywhere."

"Grandmom, just let me go. I gotta get out of here."

"No, you stay put," she ordered, placing a restraining hand lightly on Chasity's arm. "Brenda, why are you treating this child this way? I raised you better."

"That girl is nothing but trouble," Brenda spat, stumbling against the wall. "It's about time that you woke up and saw her for what she really is."

"Brenda, you're drunk," Grandmother Duvall cautioned. "You need to calm down."

Desperate to get away, Chasity made a dash for the door, leaving her coat behind.

"Chasity," Brenda slurred. "Did I ever tell you how much I hated you?"

"Brenda!" Grandmother Duvall gasped as Chasity stopped, and spun around to face her mother.

"You tell me every time you see me," Chasity shot back. "You're just mad because your life is trash. You're nothing but a disgusting drunk."

"It's *your* fault!"

"It is *not* my fault," Chasity hissed. "*You're* the one who turns to the damn bottle every day, *not* me. *You're* the one who lost your job because you kept coming into work drunk, *not* me. *You're* the one who drove Daddy away, *not* me."

"Everything was perfect in my life before you came around," Brenda groaned, sinking into one of her fits of maudlin self-pity.

"But I'm not even *around* you anymore," Chasity protested. "You flew to my school, just to tell me that you never wanted me to come back home."

Chasity's grandmother grabbed the nearest table for support. She was shocked. She'd never heard any of this. She was so angry and disappointed in her daughter, she could have spit nails.

"You see that?" Brenda asked, looking around at her stunned audience. "You see how she talks to me?"

"You've got to be fuckin' kidding me." Chasity shook her head. "Do you hear yourself? Do you think that you can stand here, try and tear me down in front of everybody, and I'm not gonna say anything back? You're crazy."

"Don't talk to me like that!"

Chasity felt her head pound. She was sick of her mother and her endless tirades. "You know what? You make me sick. I'm leaving."

"I said, don't walk away from me!" Brenda darted up to Chasity, grabbed her by her arms, and slammed her against the wall.

"Get off of me," Chasity hissed, pain radiating up her back and neck.

"For God's sake, Brenda, let her go," Grandmother Duvall shouted.

"I should squeeze the life out of you right now," Brenda swore and tightened her grip on Chasity, her long nails gouging into Chasity's soft skin. "Just like you squeezed the life out of me. I should never have brought you home from that damn hospital the day you were born."

"Why *did* you?"

"I don't know, but I'll tell you one thing. I didn't do it because I wanted you. You were a mistake, not the product of some precious love, and *I* was left to take care of you."

Chasity stared at her mother with shock. "What the fuck did you just say?" she asked in faltering tones.

"You heard me," Brenda panted. "Your *real* mother should have gotten rid of you like she was supposed to. But what does she do? She leaves me to take care of her garbage."

Chasity broke free from her mother's grasp and shoved her away. Brenda rounded and charged at her, delivering a stinging slap across Chasity's face. Chasity steadied herself, her self-control gone, and punched her mother in the stomach.

Brenda doubled over and fell, allowing Chasity the opportunity to jump on top of Brenda and rain punches down on her.

"Get her off me!" Brenda screamed as she tried to ward off her daughter's blows.

"Oh shit," Alex gasped as she and Jason barged through the door upon hearing the commotion. They had refused to leave without knowing that Chasity was okay.

Jason pushed his way past Chasity's grandmother and grabbed Chasity around the waist. "Enough, Chaz, enough," he said calmly, pulling her off of her mother. "Come on, let her go."

As Jason and Alex escorted Chasity outside, bruised and bloodied Brenda got to her feet. "Mom, did you see..."

"Get out," Grandmother Duvall shouted, tears streaming down her face. "Get out now, Brenda."

"What?"

"Take your drunk behind out of my home," she said with ominous quiet and pointed to the door.

"Grandmom, at least let her clean her face up first," Melina argued and shepherded Brenda toward the bathroom.

"Chasity, take a deep breath," Alex soothed, putting a comforting hand on Chasity's shoulder as she paced back and forth in front of the steps.

"Alex, don't touch me," Chasity snapped, knocking Alex's hand away.

"Baby, at least take my coat, it's cold out here," Jason suggested, trying to place his coat on her shoulders.

"I said don't touch me," Chasity hollered, knocking the black coat to the ground. "Didn't I tell you to go home?"

"We couldn't leave you like that," Jason protested. Chasity was seething; she could have punched him and Alex both in the mouth.

Before Chasity could say another word, Trisha pulled up in her silver Mercedes Benz. "Baby girl, what are you doing out here without a coat on? You'll catch a cold," she said, stepping out of the car.

Chasity didn't say a word; she only stared at her aunt with pure anger.

Trisha frowned with concern at the sight of Chasity's eyes welling up with tears. "What's the matter? What happened?"

Chasity gave no response as she stormed around to the back of the house. Trisha turned to Alex and Jason. "What the hell happened?"

"She got into a fight with her mother," Jason replied, picking his coat up off the ground.

"What?!" Trisha didn't need to hear another word.

Trisha stormed inside the house, coming face to face with her mother. "Mom what happened? Where's Brenda?"

"Cleaning herself up," Grandmother Duvall solemnly answered, sweeping up the broken glass in the corner with a broom and dust pan.

"What is she doing here? Why did you let that woman in the house?"

"I invited her over for Thanksgiving dinner. I thought that it would be nice to see her," Grandmother Duvall said, placing the broom in the corner. "Why didn't you tell me Brenda had kicked Chasity out of the house?"

"Mom, we didn't want you to get upset."

"Too late, daughter." Grandmother Duvall skewered Trisha with a piercing look. "It was terrible. Brenda was screaming about how much she hated Chasity, and that the poor girl was a mistake. She even said that her real mother should have gotten rid of her. What was she talking about? Chasity's not adopted."

"She *said* that? Where is she?" Trisha hissed.

"Patrisha, what was she talking about?"

"Mom, where is she?" Trisha demanded, then caught sight of Brenda coming out of the bathroom with a towel held to her swollen jaw. "You bitch!"

"Trish," Grandmother Duvall cautioned. "I've had enough violence in my home for one evening."

"Brenda, how could you say that to her?" Trisha charged. "How could you tell her that she was a mistake and that her mother should've gotten rid of her?"

"She *was* a mistake and you *know* it," Brenda shot back. "You're so fuckin' evil."

"Are you two saying that Chasity was adopted?" Grandmother Duvall ground out. The two women were silent. "Answer me."

"Yes, Mom, she was," Brenda revealed. "And if you want more details, why don't you ask your favorite daughter?"

"What do you mean *favorite*?" Grandmother Duvall objected. "I love all of my children equally. I don't have a favorite."

"Oh, please," Brenda sneered. "Ever since Trisha bought you this damn house, you've forgotten about all the shit she put you through as a teenager."

"She changed, Brenda."

"Whatever, Mom."

"So *now* you're mad because Mom doesn't hate me like you do?!" Trisha shouted at her sister.

"Go to hell where you belong," she hissed as she walked toward the door.

"Brenda," Trisha called, stopping Brenda in her tracks. "If you *ever* put your hands on Chasity again, I swear I'll kill you."

Brenda simply rolled her eyes and walked out the house. As the door slammed shut, Grandmother Duvall looked at Trisha.

"Trish, what's going on here?"

"Mom, this is not the time. I have to find Chasity." Knowing that Chasity couldn't have gone too far without the keys to the house that they were now sharing, Trisha walked out the back door and into the massive back yard of her mother's home, scanning the grounds. Finding nothing, Trisha checked the small pool house off to the side, and found Chasity inside, sitting on the floor.

"Sweetie, I was so worried about you," Trisha said as she crouched down next to Chasity.

"Please don't touch me," Chasity said, holding up a warning hand.

"Honey, do you want to talk about it?"

"No, not really, I'm fine. Thanks," Chasity hastily replied, standing up from the floor

"Chasity, please don't shut me out," Trisha pleaded.

"I *said* that I don't wanna talk about it!"

"Baby, I know that you're hurt."

"I don't care!" Chasity shouted.

"I know you better than that. I know that you do care and that you are hurt. I don't want you to go to bed angry, just talk to me," Trisha urged, tears streaming down her face.

"Fine, you want to talk?" Chasity snapped. "You wanna talk *sooo* bad? Fine. Let's talk about my *adoption*."

"What? I—"

"Please, tell me that you didn't know about it, and that you're just as surprised as I am."

"Chasity…"

"Please tell me that you haven't been lying to me my whole life," she ground out, her voice cracking, getting higher in pitch as the tears began anew.

"I wish that I could. But I *can't*," Trisha confessed. "I knew that you were adopted."

Chasity shook her head. "You're so full of shit."

"I know that you're pissed at me right now, but this doesn't change anything. You are my family," Trisha assured her.

"You know what, I'm actually relieved," Chasity confessed. "Now I can cut all ties with this fucked up family."

"It's not that simple," Trisha cried.

"Oh no?" Chasity asked, cocking her head. "Let's see. Birth mom thought I was a mistake, didn't want me, and gave me up without thinking twice. Sounds pretty simple to me."

"It wasn't like that," Trisha protested. "Your mother wanted you. She only did what she thought was best for you at the time."

"Best for *me*, or best for *her*?"

"Sweetheart, please don't do this to yourself," Trisha pleaded. "You have never been unwanted. You were not and have never been a mistake."

"Patrisha, stop," Chasity said. "My head hurts and I'm tired. Just leave me alone."

Trisha let herself out of the pool house, and crumbled against the wall, sobbing. She loved her niece more than life. She wanted more than anything to make the hurt stop, to make everything better, but she knew that she was powerless to do so.

After a while, Trisha gathered herself, smoothing her hair and brushing away the tears. Slowly, she walked back into the house where Alex and Jason remained in the living room, waiting. She had to confront them, as their obvious worry and stubborn jaws told her that they would demand an explanation.

"This is all my fault," she began. "Chasity didn't want to come here for Thanksgiving. I forced her."

"Her grandmother didn't know what was going on," Jason charged, face frowned. "But *you* did. Why didn't you protect her?"

If Trisha thought it odd to be subjected to an inquisition from a college freshman, she didn't let on. "It was a mistake. She won't stay here, and I'm sure she doesn't want to come home with me. She's very upset with me right now...rightfully so."

"I'd invite her to stay at my house," Alex put in. "Though, I'd doubt she would come with me."

"No, she definitely won't," Jason added.

"No, no," Trisha interrupted. "Look, this holiday has been crap so far for Chasity. I know my niece. She doesn't share her time or her space with just *any*body. I thought you could get the rest of your group together and go have some fun. Maybe the Wyngate Hotel in Philadelphia."

"That's a great idea, Ms. Trisha. But I can't afford a luxury hotel," Alex interrupted. "I'm the broke student in the group."

"No, sweetie," Trisha said, holding up a hand. "My treat—I'd pay for everything. Do you think you could persuade her? She needs to get away."

Alex and Jason exchanged looks, then Jason nodded.

"Don't worry, I'll take care of her," he assured her.

Jason left the house and slowly walked across the grounds until he reached the pool house. He hesitated a moment before knocking quietly, and letting himself in.

"Did I seriously forget to lock the fuckin' door?" Chasity spat as if she were still alone in the room.

Jason just looked at her sympathetically. He had come not only to pass on the message from Trisha, but to see if she was okay for himself. "This may be a stupid question but...are you okay Chaz?"

Chasity looked at him, eyes still red. It was obvious she'd been crying. "You're right, it was a stupid question," she hissed. "Get out, Jason."

"I'm here as a messenger," he explained, taking a step towards her.

"I don't want any messages from anybody in that damn house."

"I figured that, but I told your aunt that I would talk to you…she wants to send you and the rest of our group to the Wyngate Hotel for the weekend. So you can get away."

"Oh, how cute," Chasity said in a bitter tone. "A typical Trisha Duvall bribe, and with your cooperation. What else do you get out of convincing me to go?"

"That's not fair," he protested, sitting down on the loveseat next to her. "Your aunt, like me, just doesn't want to see you upset. She's trying to make things better."

"I don't need for you to be Captain Save-the-liar," Chasity scoffed.

"I'm not *trying* to be."

Chasity was tired of the back and forth; she just wanted him to go so that she could sleep. "Whatever Jason. If it'll get her and *you* off my damn back, then fine. I'll go on this little guilt trip. Happy now?"

Jason stared at her intently. "It's not about *me* being happy, Chaz."

She rolled her eyes. "Whatever. I'm over this, just leave."

"You know that I can't do that, not with you hurting like this," he said as he put his arm around her.

"I'm *not* hurting," she muttered, fighting to hold it together. "Can you just—can you just go? Please?" Tearing up again, she felt herself nearing a breakdown as she recalled the nights events and everything leading up to it. "Damn it," she cried, no longer able to fight her emotions. Jason drew her close, nestling her head against his shoulder. He sat quietly and just held her as she let the tears take her.

Chapter 21

Jason stayed with Chasity until she finally fell asleep. It was after midnight when he slipped out of the pool house and went back into the main house.

"She's asleep," he told Trisha and Alex, rubbing his neck and stifling a yawn.

"Did she agree to go?" Trisha asked anxiously.

"Yeah, after some persuading."

"I bet," Alex put in. "The last thing that she's gonna want is to be around a bunch of people."

"What Chasity thinks she wants and what she really needs are not always the same," Trisha observed with a tired gesture. "Can you get everything ready? Get in touch with your friends?"

"I'll let the guys know," Jason offered, "and Alex can handle the girls."

"All right. By the time you get back up this way, she'll more than likely be at our house since she has to pack up her stuff," Trisha stated, grabbing a notepad from a nearby side table. Chasity had spent Wednesday evening at home before heading over to her grandmothers on Thanksgiving, so all of her belongings were where she left them. "Here is the address, I'll see you later."

Jason had barely pulled away, before Alex hurried into her house. "Ma, you up?" she called.

"In the kitchen," Mrs. Chisolm responded, then grinned as her daughter ran in and hugged her tightly. "What was that for?" she asked, swatting her daughter on the behind with a dish towel. "You think a hug is going to make up for missing Thanksgiving dinner? You weren't avoiding Paul, were you?"

"No, Ma," Alex apologized, with a sharp shake of the head. "One of my friends is in trouble and we're taking her away for the rest of the break."

Mrs. Chisolm frowned as Alex grabbed a piece of leftover turkey off of a plate and popped it into her mouth. "Trouble? Do you need to call the police?"

"No, no, no. Nothing like that. It's a family problem," Alex clarified. "It was hard to watch actually. I mean I had no idea the crap that she was dealing with from her mom." She then shook her head as if she were trying to get last night's images out of her head. "Anyway Ma, I'm sorry to be skipping out again."

"And just *where* are you skipping to?"

"The Wyngate Hotel downtown. My friend's aunt is putting a group of us up."

"Well, I hope the trip makes your friend feel better, and I hope that you have fun," Mrs. Chisolm said with an attempt at a smile.

Alex gave her mother another hug. "Thanks, Ma."

"For what?"

"For being you and not asking too many questions." Alex bent forward and kissed her mother's cheek. After the close encounter with Brenda, Alex realized just how lucky she had been in the mother department. "Now, I've got some arrangements to make."

"Malajia's house of boredom, home of the bored, Malajia speaking." Malajia's tone was dry.

Alex laughed into the receiver. "Girl, get up."

Malajia twirled a strand of hair around her finger as she lay in her bed. "Shut up, Alex. What's going on?"

"Well, I have good news for you. Chasity's aunt Trisha has booked us into a suite at the Wyngate Hotel, all expenses paid." Alex held the phone away from her ear; Malajia had begun to scream into the phone.

"Malajia, shut up!" Geri could be heard yelling to her loud sister.

"Are you serious?" Malajia exclaimed, ignoring Geri entirely.

"My ears," Alex complained, laughing.

"I'm so hype, this is awesome," Malajia yelled, standing up on her bed. "I'm gonna call Sidra right now."

"Okay, I'll call Emily."

"Alex, please. Her mom is never gonna let her go," Malajia pointed out. "But forget her, this is gonna be so much fun!"

"Mel, remember—you all have to make your way to Philly. The hotel is here," Alex informed.

"That's no problem. David will probably drive his father's car. He can pick those Delaware fools up, and I'll get Daddy to drive me."

"All right, girl," Alex agreed. "Jason is picking me up, so if you have any more questions, call Jason's cell."

"See ya, girl," Malajia said happily, bouncing up and down on her bed. After giving the mattress a real workout, she picked the phone back up and dialed Sidra's number.

"Hello," a groggy Sidra answered, rubbing her eyes.

"Sidra, you won't believe what I just heard. Get up, get up, get up," Malajia screamed.

Sidra moved the phone away from her ear. Malajia's high pitched voice was not what she wanted to wake up to. "Oh God," she moaned, glancing at the alarm clock on her nightstand. "Girl, it's seven thirty in the morning. What do you want?"

"Guess what? We are all going to the Wyngate Hotel in Philadelphia."

"Malajia, what are you talking about? Those plans fell through."

"No listen, Chasity's aunt is paying for everything. Do you hear me? *Everything*," Malajia informed.

"Why?"

"Who *cares*? Just call the guys, and get ready."

Sidra, suddenly wide awake, sat up straight in her canopy bed. "Okay, let me get this straight. We have reservations to stay at the Wyngate Hotel for the weekend, right?"

"Yep. You just need to call the guys and get to Philadelphia."

"Wait. What about Emily?" Sidra asked, rubbing her eyes.

"What *about* her?" Malajia scoffed.

"You know she's not going to be able to go," Sidra pointed out, dragging her suitcase out of the closet. "She's going to feel bad."

"That's not *my* problem," Malajia retorted.

Sidra sighed as she began to pack, "Mel, that's not right."

"Okay, okay, we'll think of something. Geez," Malajia temporized, "I have to get ready. Call Jason for the directions, all right?"

"Bye."

As soon as Malajia hung up, she ran into her parents' bedroom.

"Daddy!" she shouted.

"What? What happened?" Mr. Simmons popped up in bed. Noticing the big grin on Malajia's face, he sighed. "Malajia, what is it?"

"I need you to do me a favor," she said, doing a little dance.

"No," he groaned and put a pillow over his head.

"Daddy, listen. My friend's rich aunt is paying for us to stay in a hotel suite for the weekend. The thing is, it's in Philly, so I need you to drive me."

"Malajia, are there going to be boys in this hotel suite?" her father asked, his eyes narrowing with suspicion.

Malajia put her hands on her hips. "Just stupid Mark, Josh and David, and you know them. And Jason. But he's only interested in my friend Chasity, not me, so you don't have to worry about a weekend orgy."

"Mel, you just got here," Mrs. Simmons objected, hoisting up on one elbow and regarding her daughter sternly. "Don't you want to spend more time with your family?"

"No," Malajia responded instantly and then just as quickly regretted it, catching her parents' glare. "Um...well...okay I couldn't think of anything nice to say. Listen I've been around you guys for nineteen years already. I want to spend time with my friends."

"All right child, you can go," her mother relented and settled back into her pillows.

"But I was going to go *anyway*," Malajia put in. "I just need a ride."

"Malajia," her father rebuked. "Don't be a smart ass."

"All right Dad, dang. Can you give me a ride or not?"

"Not," he responded in even tones. "You know the van is in the shop."

Malajia's mouth fell open. "The shop? How was I going to get back to school then?"

"The train," he retorted. "Same way you came."

Malajia let out a groan and stomped out of the room. Mr. Simmons looked at his wife.

"That's *your* child," she said before he could get a word out.

Malajia stormed into her room and slammed the door. "What's wrong? Daddy yell at you again?" Geri smirked, ducking when Malajia threw a pillow at her.

"Mind your business," Malajia hissed. At least she had Sidra on speed dial.

"Hello?" Sidra answered.

"Sidra, you have to help me! You would not believe—"

"Okay Malajia, you've got to stop screaming," Sidra demanded, dripping water on the floor. "I was in the shower. What's going on?"

"You guys have to pick me up."

"But that's going in the wrong direction," Sidra complained. "What happened to your dad?"

"The stupid van is in the stupid shop," Malajia yelled.

Sidra looked at the phone. "Did you just yell at me? Again?"

"I'm Sorry Sid," Malajia pleaded in a whisper. "Come and get me. Pleeaasssseee. I can't take this house anymore."

"All right, all right, stop whining," Sidra relented. "I'll call you when we're close to your house."

Chasity headed down the steps and placed a few last items into one of her packed bags. Trisha, who was fixing breakfast as she patiently waited for Chasity to come from upstairs, was relieved to see her bags packed. She didn't know what to think after Chasity snuck away from her mother's home and back to their house earlier that morning without a word to her. "Chasity?"

"Yes?" Chasity replied, turning to face her.

Trisha flinched at the monotone, curt reply. "Are you going to go straight to school from the hotel room?"

"Probably." Chasity's tone had not changed.

"I'll miss you."

Chasity rolled her eyes. She would rather sit in the car and wait for Jason and Alex, than to have to listen to Trisha talk. "Whatever," she threw out, heading for the door.

"Chasity, wait," Trisha urged, halting Chasity's progress. "Please don't be mad at me."

Chasity sighed. "I'm trying not to be. But I don't like being lied to. And you've done that my whole life."

"I know, sweetheart, I know. But if I had gone behind Brenda's back and told you the truth, she…" Trisha couldn't get the words out. It was too hard for her to talk about anymore. As much as she wanted to be honest with Chasity, she was convinced the truth would hurt her even more.

"Look, I appreciate everything that you've done for me, but—"

"Stop it," Trisha interrupted. "Nothing is going to change between us. Okay? I'll make this right, I promise you. You're my family and that is the bottom line." Chasity stared at her with cold hazel eyes as Trisha wondered if she should attempt to hug her or not.

Trisha didn't get a chance to decide either way. She heard three taps on the front door. "That must be Alex and Jason."

"Must *be*. Bye," Chasity said abruptly. She had no desire to stand around while her aunt exchanged chitchat with her friends. She just wanted to get out of the house.

"Nice to see you both again," Trisha called after them. "Chasity, I'll call you, all right? Enjoy yourselves."

No one spoke as they walked to the cars. Jason popped the trunk of a white Mazda sedan. "Let me put our stuff in your car; then you can follow me so I can get my dad's car back to him."

"Fine," Chasity agreed, sliding behind the wheel of the Lexus.

As Chasity adjusted her rearview mirror, Alex shot her an appraising look, not liking what she saw. "Are you sure you're…?"

"Yes, Alex. I'm okay," Chasity hissed.

"I'm sorry. I was worried about you."

Chasity let out a loud sigh as she turned the key to her car. "Look, please stop asking me how I'm doing. I'm already mad at you for staying last night anyway."

"I don't *care* if you're mad. I'm your friend, and I wasn't going to leave."

"Whatever," Chasity said with a dismissive wave of her hand as she pulled off after Jason.

"Come on, Sid," David urged. "We still have to go pick up Malajia."

"I'm coming! Bye, Mama. Bye, Daddy!" she tossed over her shoulder as she ran out the door.

Her parents were disappointed that Sidra was leaving early, but they wanted her to have a good time. They didn't think she was silly enough to do anything stupid. David certainly wouldn't try anything. Mark, they weren't so sure about. But Josh was always the gentleman, her mother thought, watching him jump out of the car to help her daughter with her bags.

"Damn Josh, don't fall out of the car," Mark joked.

"Man, shut up," Josh said as he slammed the door.

As Sidra walked up to the car she noticed Mark was sitting in the front seat. "Um, excuse me," she drawled, "but you're in the wrong seat. I always ride in front."

"Not *today* you're not," Mark argued. Sidra raised her eyebrows, staring at him.

"Mark, man, get in back," David chimed in, pointing to the back seat.

"What?"

"Mark, just move your ass to the back," Josh shouted from outside.

"Man, this is bullshit," Mark groaned, snatching off his seatbelt. "Now I'll have to sit in the back with stupid Malajia."

Sidra smiled as she hopped in to the front seat of the car. "Thank you, love."

"Shut up," he shot back as he scrambled into the back seat and shut the door.

"Anybody talk to Emily?" David asked, pulling off.

"Yeah. She can't come," Sidra replied, fastening her seatbelt. "Her mother is being a jerk."

"Damn," Mark said, exasperated. "The girl is in college and she can't do *anything*."

After Jason returned his dad's car and keys, Chasity unlatched her seatbelt and got out. "Jason, you drive."

"You sure?" he asked.

"Yeah, I don't feel like driving," she replied. "Alex, move your ass to the back."

"All right, all right," Alex grumbled and hopped out of the front seat. "You two didn't do anything last night, did you?"

"Alex, what the hell are you talking about?" Chasity demanded.

"Well, things seem a little awkward between you two."

"Alex, she asked me to drive her car, there's nothing awkward about that," Jason snapped.

"Look, I'm used to *you* cracking jokes and *her* cursing you out, that's all," Alex explained and sat back in the seat.

"Alex, nothing happened between us all right, so shut up," Chasity barked.

"Well," Jason grinned, "it would've been nice if—"

"You shut up too," Chasity interrupted, cutting off the smart remark that she just knew Jason was about to make.

"Man, it's hot in this damn car," Mark complained after an hour on the road.

"Look, I already told you that I can't turn the heat down," David said as he looked at Mark through the rear view mirror.

"Well, do *something*," Mark grumbled. "There's too many black people in this car, it's hot."

Sidra giggled. "Boy, just roll down the window," she suggested.

"But it's *cold* out *there*," he quibbled.

"You know what?" Josh broke in, leveling a sharp look at Mark. "The complaining has got to stop."

"I'll bet you anything that this is Malajia," Sidra predicted when her cell rang. "Hello?...Yes, Malajia...We'll probably be about another hour or so...David is not going to floor the gas, just be patient...Chill the hell out...I don't care if your Dad is threatening you...Well, you shouldn't have yelled at him...Malajia, get off my damn phone."

"What's she talking about?" David asked.

"She wants you to floor it and get there faster," Sidra said, pocketing the phone and rolling her eyes.

Malajia spent the next hour and a half pacing up and down in the living room, alternately checking her watch and looking out the front window every five minutes.

"Geez," Maria observed, "if I didn't know better, I'd say you were anxious to get away from us."

"And? A day is more than enough," Malajia retorted, "I'm sick of you people, I'm ready to go."

Maria shook her head. "You're so rude," she concluded.

Malajia broke into a huge smile when she heard a car horn. "That's them, gotta go!" she exclaimed and grabbed her bags.

"Aren't you gonna say goodbye to Mom and Dad at least?" Maria asked.

"Nope!" Malajia hollered, sprinting out of the door. She grimaced when she saw Mark in the back seat. "Ugh. Sidra, can I ride up front please?"

"No, get comfortable," Sidra advised, "We have three long hours ahead of us."

"Don't touch me, Malajia," Mark warned as Malajia crawled over him.

"You want to sit in the middle?" she challenged. "If not, shut the hell up."

Chapter 22

"Wow," Alex exclaimed, kicking off her boots and luxuriating in the plush carpeting. "A couch and loveseat, a flat-screen TV..."

"And a mini-bar," Jason put in, opening it to take out a soda.

Chasity plopped down on a couch. She didn't need a tour. She'd been to the Wyngate Hotel with her aunt before.

"I'm almost afraid to touch anything," Alex said with a chuckle as she peaked into the bedroom. "Ooh, two queen-size beds." She wandered over to a closed door. Flinging it open, she gasped. "Wow, look at all that marble, and a glass shower with a gazillion shower heads."

Jason poked his head in. "Nice."

Chasity sat up, annoyed. Her cell was vibrating again. "God, leave me alone," she hissed, tossing it onto the floor.

"What's wrong?" Jason asked as he lounged on one of the chairs.

"My Grandmom and Trisha keep calling me. I told them that I didn't want to be bothered."

"Chasity," Alex chided, "they love you. Cut them a break."

"Don't tell me what to do," she snapped before standing up and walking into the bedroom.

"Chasity is gonna shut down eventually if she doesn't talk to somebody," Alex predicted in a quiet aside to Jason.

Jason shook his head. Chasity had her own way of dealing with things. Talking about her feelings was not an option for her. "Alex, don't keep bothering her about it, okay? Let her work things out in her own way."

Alex threw her hands up in the air. "All right, fine, I will."

"We need a key to our room," Malajia announced happily at the front desk, her spirits revived on arrival. The drive had been awful. Sitting next to Mark was bad enough, but then they had gotten lost, and she'd been forced to endure an extra two hours in the back seat.

"You will need to check in first," the concierge advised. "Your name?"

"Malajia Lakeshia Simmons."

"Not *your* name," Sidra whispered. "He needs the name that the reservation is under."

"Oh," Malajia huffed. "What's her name? All I know is Trisha."

"Then tell him that," Sidra recommended. Malajia rolled her eyes and turned back to the rep.

"The name is Trisha."

"Trisha *what*? I need a last name," the concierge replied.

Malajia shot him a nervous smile and angrily turned on her friends. "Why do you guys have me up here looking like an ass?" she snapped. The concierge shook his head as the group started arguing among themselves.

"*I* don't know what her last name is," Malajia exclaimed, annoyed that they weren't getting anywhere.

"Her last name is Duvall," Chasity said as she walked up to them. "You should probably make an effort to learn her last name, if you're going to be spending her money." The group looked down at the floor in shame as a result of Chasity's scolding.

"Oh, Trisha, as in *Pa*trisha Duvall," the concierge beamed, slipping her a check-in card. "She's a regular here. And you must be her niece?"

"Yeah," Chasity responded as she signed the paper. "*Unfortunately*, they're with me," she said, pointing to the crew gathered around the front desk.

"Enjoy your stay. Please feel free to use all our facilities, and let us know if you want or need anything," he said, anticipating a big tip at the end of the niece's stay.

"This is so awesome!" Malajia exclaimed, trailing behind Chasity. When they got to the suite, her enthusiasm bubbled over. "Chaz, if you weren't so mean, I'd hug you right now for having such a generous aunt."

"Don't try it," Chasity warned, pointing a finger at her.

"What's up *your* ass?" Malajia pouted with her nose turned up, inciting a glare from Chasity.

"Come on," Alex urged. "Let's not start with the fighting. We're here to have a good time."

"*I'm* cool, just as long as that heifer over there doesn't mess with me," Malajia said as she sat down.

"Malajia, don't get slapped," Chasity shot back.

"Hey, be nice," Alex said as she sat between them. "The point of this trip is to have a good time. Too bad Emily couldn't come."

"Can't say that I'm surprised," Malajia put in.

"Me neither," Sidra said, moving her bangs to one side of her face.

"I even offered to ask her mother, but she wanted to try herself. It never happened. That woman really has a serious problem with us," Alex said.

"Cause she sees how *evil* you all are," Mark teased as he opened a bag of chips and stuffed one in his mouth.

"I hope you choke to death," Malajia hissed, walking over to the fridge in her high-heels to inspect the contents.

"So, guys, what are we going to do?" Sidra asked, playing with the fringe on her royal blue scarf.

"Sleep," Chasity murmured, resting her head on the arm of the couch.

"No, you're not," Alex countered, pulling her up. "We're gonna have some fun."

"What's your problem?" Malajia asked, glaring at Chasity. "Damn, we just got here and you're already miserable."

"Stop talking to me," Chasity warned.

"Malajia, stop aggravating her," Jason scolded.

Malajia rolled her eyes and let out a frustrated sigh. "Am I supposed to deal with her anger *all* weekend?"

"God, will you shut up?" Mark yelled, waving a potato chip at Malajia.

"Who the hell are you talking to?" Malajia shouted back.

"You! You talk too damn much," Mark retorted.

"Listen, you two, enough with this pointless arguing," Sidra interrupted. "Let's go to the pool."

"How about the hot tub instead?" David suggested as he hopped up.

Mark jumped off the chair. "Finally, I'm gonna see ya'll girls in bathing suits." He immediately tripped and nearly fell, darting for his bag. "Y'all didn't see that."

Malajia shook her head. "Damn, I was hoping he would fall," she scoffed.

"Last one in the hot tub is buying dinner," Mark challenged when they'd all changed into their suits.

"Everything is paid for already, you fool," Jason mocked.

Towels and fluffy robes were tossed on the chaises, and one by one they each lowered themselves into the swirling water. Malajia waited until everyone got in before dropping her towel on the marble tile. Strutting, she pranced to the tub and did a spin.

"Oh come *on* Malajia, that was totally uncalled for," Sidra charged, her eyes glued to Malajia's flaming red thong and itsy-bitsy bikini top.

"Really? Did you have to wear that?" Alex asked, crinkling her nose up.

"Yes, I did."

"She knew that we were gonna be disgusted. *That's* why her ass waited to be the last one in," Chasity said, splashing warm water over her shoulders.

"You bitches are just jealous, so I'm not fazed by your comments," Malajia said, with a dismissive wave of her hand.

"Can you refrain from calling us bitches?" Alex scolded. "It's uncalled for."

"Like I said before, if your body had a different face, *then* I'd like it," Mark commented, his legs bobbing in the swirling water.

"Ooh, it's hot," Malajia complained when she stepped into the tub.

"That's why it's called a hot tub," Chasity snapped. "I swear, I cannot deal with your stupidity all weekend."

"You know what? All you do is complain," Malajia shot back. "You need to get laid. Maybe then you'd shut up."

Chasity glared at her, her jaw tightened.

"So, how was everyone's Thanksgiving?" Josh asked, hoping to ease the tension.

"Boring," Malajia declared, "mind-numbingly boring."

"A waste of time," Chasity responded after a pause.

"Well, *mine* was great," Mark interjected. "I ate sooooo much."

"We *know*," Sidra, Josh and David said in unison. After filling up on Thanksgiving food at Sidra's house, the four of them made their way to Mark's house, were he stuffed himself some more.

"What's *that* supposed to mean?" he objected.

Sidra shook her head. "Boy, I've always wondered why you're not fat, the way you eat," she said.

"Yeah, so do *I*," Mark said with a laugh.

"What exactly happened with Emily?" David asked.

"Well, I called and told her about the trip. She was really excited," Alex replied.

"Oh my god, nobody cares," Malajia sneered. "She is such a damn baby, letting her lonely ass mom control what she does."

"Mel! Don't talk about her like that, she's not here to defend herself," Sidra scolded.

"Oh please, even if she *was* here, that chick *still* wouldn't defend herself," Chasity chimed in.

Sidra glowered at Malajia and Chasity. "That's not the point, evil-ass one and two."

"If I can finish my story," Alex protested.

"Go ahead, girl," Sidra said, "we're sorry."

"Anyway, before Emily had a chance to ask, her mother picked up the damn phone and started screaming at me to leave her daughter alone. She said we weren't good enough to be around her."

"Are you serious?" Josh asked, his eyes widening in shock

"Oh yes. I tried talking to her, but I couldn't get a word in."

"I swear to beans, I want to punch that cow right in the mouth," Malajia groused.

Mark scrunched his face up. "You swear to *what*?" he asked, sending a splash of water her way.

"Beans," she responded with a shrug.

"You swear to *beans*?!" Mark sneered. "You get on my damn nerves. Stop trying to make up new shit!"

"Damn, Mark," Jason interjected with a laugh. "Why are you mad?"

"Cuz she always does that. She gets on my nerves," he responded.

"Boy, please," Malajia jeered. "You're just pissed because that dumb ass phrase that you made up didn't stick."

"Hey. 'It's cooler than a penguin with shades on' would have stuck if you had kept saying it like I *told* you to!" he shot back.

"*This* is what I had to put up with my whole childhood," Sidra lamented and then giggled when she looked at her hands. "Eww, my skin is doing that pruney thing. I'm going up for a shower."

"Last one dressed, buys dinner," Mark once again challenged, hopping out of the tub.

Jason shook his head. Not even bothering to repeat his earlier response.

Muscles relaxed from the long soak in the hot tub, Sidra leaned back in her chair. She and Chasity had claimed first dibs on the bathroom and, showered and dressed, were in the hotel restaurant waiting for the others.

"This is so nice," Sidra said casually, smoothing her hand on the white table cloth. "I'm going to owe your aunt a big thank you note."

"Yeah, whatever," Chasity responded dryly and picked up the menu.

Sidra frowned at the irritation in Chasity's voice. "What's the matter with you?"

"Nothing, I'm fine."

"No, you're not. What happened between the time you left school and now?"

"Sidra, please," Chasity protested, tossing down the menu. "I don't want to talk about it."

"You're right," she mocked. "Keep it all bottled up inside and see how long it takes to explode. Better yet, we can go back to not talking like we did when we started rooming together because you are too damn angry to talk to anybody."

Chasity folded her arms. "Why are you so damn determined to get in my business?"

"My *goal* isn't to get in your business," Sidra said, gritting her teeth. "I don't know about *you*, but I feel that we're friends, and *friends* are supposed to talk to each other."

"*Not* if they don't *want* to," Chasity argued.

"Fine," Sidra conceded, picking up her menu. "I won't bother you anymore."

Chasity picked up her fork and started drawing patterns on the tablecloth. Deep down, she did want to talk to someone about the hurt she was feeling, and Sidra was probably the only one in their circle who wouldn't make jokes or try to lecture her.

"Sidra," she began softly.

Sidra never got to hear what Chasity was about to say. Mark dropped into the chair next to her and Chasity clammed up.

"We'll talk later," Sidra promised. Chasity nodded.

"So what's good here? Do they have any pizza?" Mark asked, trying to take the menu from Sidra.

"No, they don't have pizza. This place is a little classier than the Pizza Shack at school," Sidra mocked, moving it out of his reach.

"How about we order a bottle of that expensive champagne?" Malajia suggested, rubbing her hands together.

"How about we all get thrown in jail for under-age drinking?" Alex retorted.

"You're corny. Why couldn't you stay home with Emily?" Malajia complained, unfolding her napkin with an angry flick.

"Why couldn't we have left *your* bored ass in *Baltimore*?" Alex shot back, grinning at Malajia's blank stare. "What's everyone thinking of ordering?"

"I'm going for the linguini and shrimp scampi," Sidra declared.

Malajia slammed her hand on the table in frustration, grabbing everyone's attention. "Damn it Sidra, just say *pasta*," she sneered. "What the hell is a linguini?"

The entire table shot Malajia confused expressions. "Linguini is a type of pasta, you flippin' moron," Sidra jeered.

"So what? I just don't like the way you say it," Malajia shot back defensively, flicking her hand in Sidra's direction.

"Wow," David laughed at the silly banter.

"This service is great. So fast," Alex murmured when their entrées arrived fifteen minutes later; the waiter set the plates down with a flourish.

"Mmm, you guys should try this dish," Sidra mumbled between bites. "It is so good."

"I don't want this prissy ass food," Mark scoffed. The pasta noodles kept slipping off his fork.

"If you didn't want the fettuccine, you shouldn't have ordered it," Alex argued, taking a bite out of a breadstick.

"I thought it would be good," he protested. "I really wanted some pizza."

"Mark, enough with the damn pizza. Stop being a jackass, and eat what you ordered," Malajia scolded.

"I'm not eating this damn food!" Mark yelled.

Fed up with Mark's constant complaining, Chasity slammed her hand down on the table, and picked up her knife. "Listen, boy," she warned, pointing the sharp blade at Mark, "you ordered that food with *my aunt's* fuckin' money, so you better eat it!"

The table went silent at Chasity's outburst. Everywhere in the dining room, heads turned in their direction.

"Everything is fine," Alex announced to the curious. "We just have an idiot with us."

Mark sat in silence for several seconds. "All I was talking about was pizza," he mumbled.

"I've had enough of this bullshit," Chasity ground out, pushing her seat back from the table. "I'm sick of his stupid ass."

"Wait a minute, where are you going?" Jason asked, rising from his chair.

"Jason, leave me alone," Chasity ordered and walked off

The girls shot Mark glares. "Next time, leave his stupid self home," Malajia sneered, tossing a balled up napkin at him.

"Gladly," Sidra seethed.

Mark, for once, stayed silent, and stared down at his plate.

Chapter 23

Chasity enjoyed a whole hour of peace, relaxing on a chaise lounge with her music blaring through her cell phone, until the troops invaded.

"Chasity, dumbass has something to say to you," Sidra announced, pushing Mark forward.

"I don't want to hear it," Chasity bit out.

"That's okay," Sidra maintained, shooting Mark a look, "but he's gonna say it *anyway*. Mark, start talking."

Mark knew that look; he grew up with it. Every time he, Josh, or David did something childish or stupid, she'd give them that look. If they didn't do as she said, she would turn ugly real fast.

"Okay, okay," he said, putting his hands up before kneeling next to Chasity. "I'm sorry that I was being stupid tonight. I'm a jerk, I know it, and I ate all of the food."

Chasity stared at him, trying not to laugh at the silly, hopeful smile on his face. "Boy, get away from me," she said, nudging him off.

Apology accepted, he realized, when she didn't freeze him out or punch him. "Aww, I love you to…"

"That doesn't mean that you can touch me," she warned, blocking his outstretched arms.

"So, what are we gonna do now?" Josh asked as he sat on one of the smaller chairs.

"*I* know," Mark said with a sinister smile. He rose to his feet and walked over to his coat. David and Josh's eyes widened as Mark pulled out a deck of cards.

"Oh no," Josh groaned.

"Oh *yes*. Let's play spades, baby," he shouted, waving the box of cards around.

"Mark, nobody is playing that game with you," Sidra objected. "You get crazy."

"Why? Why won't you play?" Mark bristled. "You mad because I beat you every time."

"You do not!" Sidra shot back, shaking her head.

"Do *so*. And I'll prove it," he challenged. "Let's have a tournament. Everyone, pick your partners."

Josh and David exchanged looks and gave each other a high five. "Let's beat this fool," Josh said.

"Oh no," Jason groaned when Mark glanced his way.

"Jason, my man!" Mark shouted.

"Yeah?" Jason replied, pinching the bridge of his nose with two fingers.

"You're my partner."

"Yeah, I figured," Jason responded with a total lack of enthusiasm as he walked over to the table.

"Okay, roommate, you're my partner," Alex said, motioning to Malajia.

"Hell no," Malajia exclaimed, turning up her nose.

Alex looked surprised. "Why *not*?"

"Because the last thing I need is you telling me what to do."

"What?"

"No. I want to partner with Chasity," Malajia wheedled.

"Hell no," Chasity protested.

"Shush, you have no choice. Besides, it's perfect," Malajia argued. "I hate Mark, you hate Jason, and we can brag once we beat 'em."

"Sidra, don't do this to me," Chasity begged after starring at Malajia's wide grin.

"Sorry, Chaz," Sidra shrugged, "I'd rather play with Alex."

Chasity's mouth dropped at Sidra's honesty.

"Aww, honey, you know you're a witch," Sidra teased.

"Look, it doesn't matter who partners up. All I know is that every last one of y'all is going *down*," Mark predicted with glee as he shuffled the cards. "Come on. Game goes to six hundred, we're gonna kick your ass."

"Just deal," Alex prompted, taking a sip of juice. "Remember: the two of diamonds is higher than the two of spades."

"We *all* know that, Alex," Malajia complained and slapped her hand on the table. "This is why I didn't want to partner with you."

"Don't start with me, you roommate traitor," Alex joked.

After all of the cards had been dealt, they started counting their books. "How many do you have Sid?" Alex asked as she frowned at her hand.

"One," Sidra responded with an attitude.

"One? Are you serious?" Alex's head jerked up. "*I* only have two, maybe three if I'm lucky."

"Mark dealt me these stupid ass cards," Sidra sighed. "We just have to go board."

"Lousy hands," Alex complained. "What do you guys have?"

"Five," Jason replied, adjusting his cards in his hand.

"I only got two," Mark added.

"Stop lying," Sidra shouted, pounding her fist on the table.

Mark started laughing. "*When* Jason and I get all ten books, ya'll will bust."

Sidra gritted her teeth. Playing spades with Mark always brought out the worst in her.

"Girl, don't worry," Alex murmured. "Just because we're starting off badly, doesn't mean that we're gonna lose."

Four hands later, Sidra remained unconvinced. "Alex, what the hell are you doing?" she exclaimed.

"Calm down, I know what I'm doing," Alex assured her skeptical partner. "I paid attention to the cards."

"I swear Alex, you better win this hand," Sidra threatened. "If you lose it, don't set foot in my dorm. You'll be banned."

"I hate you, heifer," Alex laughed as she threw her card down. "See, we won this hand, I told you that I know what I'm doing." But skill didn't match her confidence or her cards.

"That's it. Alex, you're banned," Sidra hissed, tossing her cards onto the table after losing the game. "We lost damn near every hand. I told you to start bidding higher, but noooo, you wanted to play it safe!"

"*Excuse* me, some of those so-called books that *you* had weren't even strong," Alex yelled back.

"I'm not partnering with you next time," Sidra seethed.

"Forget it, we lost, it's over," Alex said as she stood up.

"Isn't it lovely to see friendships fall apart because of this game?" Mark asked Jason jokingly. "Ah, I love it."

Mark leaned over and got in Sidra's face. "Come on, loser. Get up from the table. Time for someone else to lose now."

Sidra plucked him on the nose before angrily standing up and forfeiting her place.

"Did she just pluck me?" Mark asked Jason, who was laughing at the expression on Marks face.

"David, Josh, kick his freeloading ass," Sidra commanded.

"With pleasure," Josh smiled. "Mark, be prepared to get your ass kicked."

"I can't wait to humiliate you in front of your girl," Mark said as he rubbed his face.

"*Whose* girl? Josh's?" Malajia asked, afraid she'd missed out on some excellent gossip.

Under the table, Josh kicked Mark hard in the shins.

"What the hell?" Mark yelped. "Man, I'm getting sick of you all abusing me."

"Then stop being so damn stupid," Josh advised.

"Can we just play?" Jason asked calmly. "It's my deal."

Midway through the game, Josh watched Jason pick up yet another of their books and scowled. "David, can you pay attention please?"

"Josh, get off my back. These cards that you dealt suck," David shot back, pushing his glasses up on his nose.

"I *told* y'all that I'm the best," Mark gloated.

"Shut up," Josh and David grunted in unison.

"Come on, guys. Do something. I know that you can play better than this," Sidra leaned over and patted Josh's shoulder.

He frowned. He loved the smell of her perfume, but it was wreaking havoc on his concentration.

"Sid, it all depends on the cards," David said as he flipped through his hand.

"Right," Mark sneered, a goofy smile on his face. "It all depends on the cards."

"Somebody please wipe that damn smile off of his face," Sidra begged.

"Don't worry, girl," Malajia joined in the fray. "Chaz and I got this fool."

"Hold up, the game isn't over yet. We can still beat him," David objected, but a few minutes later Mark snatched the one book that would have won the hand, off the table.

"You lose," Mark proclaimed with a triumphant grin.

"Mark, you cheated man," David said with disgust and pushed away from the table.

"Yeah, yeah," Mark laughed. "Next victims."

"Victims, my ass," Malajia sneered as she sat down across from Chasity.

"Hey, baby, you feeling better?" Jason asked as he rubbed Chasity's shoulder.

"Boy, get off me," she said and brushed his hand away.

"Don't try to butter her up, you're going down dawg," Malajia taunted.

"Please, please kick Mark's ass," Sidra pleaded.

"Aww, what's the matter Princess?" Mark chortled. "Can't stand losing to the master?"

"Just deal the cards," Chasity suggested. "Always running your goddamn mouth."

Waiting for his cards, Mark started cracking his knuckles and moving his neck from side to side.

"Is that supposed to scare us?" Malajia asked, cocking her head.

"Scared or not, you *will* take this ass whooping that we're about to give you," Mark shot back.

"This is going to be a long game," Jason predicted with a laugh.

Sidra peaked at Chasity's cards and squealed with pleasure. "You bastards are going down."

"Sidra, move," Chasity ordered and nudged her away.

"Damn, Sid," Jason protested. "Why I gotta be a bastard?"

"I'm sorry, baby," she corrected. "That label was meant for that black-ass, freeloading bitch across from you."

Mark threw his hands up in the air. "Damn Sidra," he exclaimed. "Why I gotta be all that?"

"Books?" Jason asked, shaking his head at the banter.

"I have five," Chasity said.

"Are you sure, Chaz?" Malajia asked, directing an intense stare at her partner.

"Yes. Stop looking at me like that," she sneered.

"I just wanna make sure cause…"

"How about you worry about your own damn books? How many do *you* have?" Chasity snapped.

"Calm down. I have about four," Malajia responded.

"*About*?" Chasity asked, raising an eyebrow.

"Three and a possible," Malajia clarified.

"We're going eight," Chasity declared and looked at Jason, who was keeping score.

"What about my possible?" Malajia whined.

"*Fuck* your possible!" Chasity growled.

Alex giggled. "It looks like Mark isn't the *only* one who's competitive."

"I got four books," Jason announced.

"Are you...."

"Mark, don't start with me," Jason said as he cut Mark off.

"I'm just kidding," Mark laughed. "I know you're sure. We can go six."

"Didn't you just hear them say that they're going eight?" Jason frowned at him. "How can we go six? If they get nine with Malajia's possible, we bust."

"Man, they're lying," Mark scoffed. "They're overbidding. *I'm* not scared." Jason glared at Mark as he threw down his first card. "Ace of hearts! Beat that," Mark boasted.

Malajia threw down a five of hearts.

"You can't beat that, I said you can't beat that," Mark chanted as he did a dance in his seat.

Jason put down a six of hearts.

Mark stared at Chasity and taunted. "Come on, crazy. What you gonna put down? Come on so I can snatch the book off the table." Chasity's three of spades caught him off guard. "Oh, noooooo," Mark yelled.

Jason slammed his hand on the table. "Man, I *told* you."

Malajia shrieked with delight and snatched the book off the table.

"You're going down," Sidra exclaimed, clapping her hands.

"It ain't over," Mark pointed out.

After losing the next few hands, Mark began to lose his cool. "What the fuck is going on?" he shouted, watching Malajia snatch up another book.

"It looks like you're losing another hand," Malajia taunted.

Mark pointed a finger at the girls, "I swear, you two are cheating," he declared.

"How do you figure?" Chasity questioned, looking up from her cards.

"Kill the innocent act, Chasity," Mark snapped, pounding his fist on the table. "You look like you cheat all the time, you little evil witch."

"Wow, *you're* upset," Chasity calmly shot back.

"Mark," Jason called, grabbing his attention. "Will you shut up and just fuckin' play? Damn." Jason watched with frustration as his partner began shuffling around in his seat, trying to decide on what card to play. He was so over this game. "Will you come on!" he yelled.

Mark flinched at the base in Jason's deep voice. "Okay fine."

Mark threw down a king of clubs; he knew that Malajia had played the ace early in the game. He watched with agony as Chasity chose a card from her hand and was relieved to see that it was a six of clubs. Jason threw out a nine of clubs. Mark knew that Malajia had a club, but to his surprise, she threw down a four of spades.

"What the fuck?" he shouted, banging on the table as Chasity scooped up the book.

"Mark, there are other people in the hotel," Alex scolded.

"Shut up, you curly haired freak."

"Really? Was that necessary?" Alex queried as she placed her hands on her hips.

"You're not gonna *cry* are you, Mark?" Malajia asked with malicious intent.

Jason threw out a jack of clubs to start the next book. Chasity watched as Malajia threw out a ten of clubs; Mark threw out a five of clubs. Quickly throwing out a five of spades, Chasity grabbed the book and put it on her side. She glanced at Malajia. They both knew that Malajia had just thrown off clubs with a spade in the other round. They stood to lose three of their books if the guys caught that. While the guys were caught up in an argument, Chasity slowly tucked the book in question under all of the other books.

Malajia gave a knowing nod to her sneaky partner. "Are you two ready?" she asked the guys, who were still squabbling.

"This is bullshit," Mark shouted.

"If you stop running your damn mouth and play like you have some sense, maybe we can win a hand," Jason argued.

"Yo, get off my case...wait, what suit did we just play?" Mark asked.

"Why?" Malajia asked, feigning innocence.

"What suit?"

"*Clubs*, man, why?" Jason asked.

Mark slammed his cards down on the table. "The hand before this one, I played the club card. Malajia threw out a damn spade and now all of a sudden she has a *club*? Y'all are cheating."

"He's right," Jason interjected.

"No, she didn't," Chasity lied. "You can't prove that she *did*."

"Chasity, you're cheating. You *know* that she reneged," Jason argued.

"Look, if you're so fuckin' sure that I'm a cheater, it should be no problem for you to find that book and gain three of ours," Malajia challenged, feigning hurt.

"Malajia, how can you sit there with a straight face?" Mark complained. "I know that you cheated."

"Prove it," Malajia shot back.

"Fine, here it is," he snapped, reaching for the top book and examining the cards. His eyes widened when he came to a realization. "Chasity, you moved it."

"You thought I would keep it there?" Chasity scoffed. "Yeah, *that* would've been real smart."

"Um," Malajia crowed, "you guessed wrong, and now we get three of your books."

Mark started grinding his teeth as Malajia slowly grabbed three of the guys' books. "You lose," she smiled.

"Watch what Mark does," Josh whispered to Alex, knowing all too well how much his best friend hated losing.

Mark got so angry, he started shaking. Then he flipped the table over, sending the cards flying and his friends darting away. "I want a rematch and I want it now!" he hollered.

"You lost," Malajia yelled back. "Get over it." Too angry to think of a retort, he stuck his middle finger up at her.

"What's the matter, *loser*?" Sidra teased. "You gonna stand in the loser corner?" Her laughter was halted by several cards hitting her arm. "Seriously, Mark?" she exclaimed. "Is throwing cards necessary?"

Chapter 24

The waiter rolled the breakfast cart into the bedroom and started fussing with the plate of pastries.

"Thank goodness," Sidra said, grinning at the waiter. "I need some caffeine bad."

"The coffee is in the thermos, Miss, and cappuccinos are in the covered mugs. Enjoy." Malajia, still in her bright red nightgown, stumbled toward the cart and reached for a muffin.

"The guys are *still* asleep," Malajia complained.

"Damn Mel, you wake *up* complaining," Sidra teased, stretching. "I wonder if they were comfortable. I saw them laid out on the floor in the other room."

"Who gives a shit?" Malajia scoffed, putting jelly on her muffin with a butter knife. "They shouldn't get none of this food." Her mouth curled up in a mischievous grin and she looked over at Chasity, who was grabbing a donut off of a nearby tray.

"Hey, Lucifer," she said, "you wanna be evil this morning?"

"Always," Chasity smirked and walked over to the waiter. "Hey you," she said, drawing him aside. "If I give you fifty dollars right now, can you make sure room service won't take breakfast orders from any man in this suite?"

"But, we serve breakfast until eleven," he stammered.

Chasity frowned at him. "I didn't ask you that," she replied snidely.

"We're playing a trick on our friends out there in the other room," Malajia broke in, then clasped her hands together. "Please, please will you do it? You won't get into any trouble."

The waiter looked from Malajia, who was grinning to Chasity, who was waving a fifty-dollar bill in his face.

Smiling, he took the money, clinching the deal. Sidra, having overheard her friends plan, just shook her head.

"You two are terrible," she commented, taking a ripe strawberry off one of the trays.

"Yeah, we know," Chasity replied, sitting on one of the beds.

"What are you guys doing?" Alex asked, from the bathroom doorway.

"Getting ready to make the guys life miserable," Malajia laughed. "Now hurry up and eat, so we can hide anything that's left over."

Alex finished drying her hands on a small towel. "What's the point of that?" she questioned. "They'll just order more from room service."

"Why you gotta ask so many damn questions?" Malajia protested, tossing her arms up in frustration.

Alex glared at Malajia, putting her hands on her hips. "Because I *can*?" she suggested.

Malajia stuck her middle finger up at her in retaliation.

"Anyway…" Alex was distracted by Sidra grabbing the last of the strawberries off of the tray.

Sidra caught her stare. "What?" she questioned.

"Are *we* not allowed to have any strawberries?" Alex teased.

Sidra dropped her handful back onto the tray. "Sorry it's my favorite fruit," she replied.

An hour later, the coffee thermos was empty and the bulk of the food hidden, only crumbs remained on the trays. There was, however, a bunch of grapes.

"I feel like waking the boys up," Malajia announced and snatched up the grapes.

"Malajia!" Alex cautioned, suspicious of the glint in Malajia's eye.

"Calm down, *Mom*," Malajia shot over her shoulder. "C'mon, Chasity, I know *you'll* have fun with me. Alex and Sidra are corny."

Holding out her hand for Malajia to give her some of the grapes, Chasity followed her partner in crime into the living room. Sidra and Alex hovered in the bedroom doorway as the two girls crept to within a foot of the sleeping guys and started tossing grapes at them.

"You girls are terrible," Alex laughed as grapes rolled off of noses and around the floor.

Then Malajia tossed a grape into Mark's open mouth. He choked, bent over in a fit of coughing, and the grape popped out.

"What the hell?" he mumbled, looking at the grape on his pillow and scratching his head. "How did that get in there?"

The guys began to stir and sit up. "Did you guys sleep well? That floor looks pretty hard," Malajia asked, feigning concern.

Mark stared at her for several seconds, confused. She was acting completely weird. "Uh, the floor was fine," he answered, running his hand over his head. "Anyway, where's the rest of the food? I know ya'll got some."

"Yeah, we ate breakfast already," Malajia replied. "It was good too."

"Any left?" Josh asked as he rubbed his eyes. "I'm starving."

"Nope," Sidra answered, tying her blue satin robe closed.

Josh looked at her. "Are you serious?" he asked.

"Yep," Malajia put in, grinning widely.

"Naw, there better be some damn food in there," Mark warned and stormed into the bedroom.

"Sorry guys, it's all gone, we only ordered enough for us," Alex added, now willing to participate in the prank.

"Why would you order only for you?" Jason asked, frowning.

"Cause we're selfish and we wanted to," Chasity answered. Jason, narrowing his eyes, pointed a warning finger at her. She just made a face at him.

"This is bullshit, man!" Mark snapped as he stomped back into the living room. "There's not a damn thing left. I'm fuckin' starving."

"Why do you have to curse all the time?" Sidra asked with an attitude.

Mark up his hand up at her. "Not now, Prissy, not now," he hissed. He walked over and stood in Chasity and Malajia's faces.

"Come on man, I'm hungry!" he hollered.

Malajia covered her nose as Chasity made a face in disgust. "You *do* know that your breath smells like somebody took a shit in your mouth, right?" Chasity asked him.

"And I will follow you around and breathe on you all damn morning if I don't get some damn food," he shot back.

"Eww, move," Malajia screeched as she pushed him away from her.

"Mark, forget them. We can just order room service," David pointed out as he picked up the phone.

Mark jumped over to David and snatched the phone. "We don't need y'all, ha ha," he crooned as he dialed.

"Wyngate Hotel room service," a male voice answered.

"Hey, yes, this is room 907. We would like to order breakfast," Mark replied.

"I'm sorry, sir, we are no longer serving breakfast."

Mark frowned, looking down at the time on the phone. "Stop playing, man. Send up some food. The same stuff you bought up here earlier. And make sure you throw some cheese on those eggs," he responded.

"I'm sorry, sir. We can't."

Mark tried to laugh off his frustration. "Just send up some food."

"Room service is closed."

"Damn it!" Mark hollered, as he threw the phone on the couch. "They talking about room service is closed."

"There must be some mistake. It's only ten fifteen," David picked the phone up and dialed. While he waited for someone to pick up, he fixed his glasses. "Hello…We would like to order for room 907…There must be some mistake. It's only ten fifteen…Oh I see…Thank you."

The guys stared at David as he hung up the phone. "Well?" Jason prompted.

"Room service is apparently under strict instructions not to accept any orders from this room placed by men."

He and the other guys then shot accusing looks at the girls, who were simply standing there, smiling and fighting to contain their laughter.

"I knew it," Josh exclaimed.

"Are you serious? Were you *that* bored this morning?" Jason asked. The girls shrugged.

"So, what are you saying? That they won't send up any more room service if a guy calls?" Mark asked angrily.

"That's what I just said," David responded.

Mark rubbed his hands together. "Okay, who among us sounds feminine?"

Three pair of eyes fixed on David, who looked back at them with shock. "Get out my face," he shouted.

"Naw, David's right. He just sounds like a nerd," Mark teased, then ducked as David tossed a pillow at him. "Josh, *you* call."

"Mark, I'll smack the bullshit outta you," Josh barked.

"That's a *lot* of smackin'," Malajia commented.

"Malajia, shut up," Mark shot at her as she started laughing. "To hell with it. *I'll* do it." He picked up the phone, dialed and cleared his throat. "Hello," he answered in his best falsetto. "I'm a girl in room 907 and I want to order room service..."

"What is he saying?" Jason asked, laughing.

Mark could no longer hold it together, and laughed as he hung up the phone. "He laughed at me," he said.

"Well, you sounded stupid," Alex put in.

"Man, fuck it, I'm eating these grapes off the floor," Mark said as he walked around the room picking up the grapes.

"Eww," Sidra scoffed as he popped a grape in his mouth.

Josh looked at him and held his hand out. "Can I have one?"

"No," Mark yelled, pushing his hand away.

The girls finally relented and gave the guys the rest of the hidden food, after watching them nearly come to blows over the few grapes that were lying around on the floor. With metabolisms restored, they ventured out to explore the city. They even decided to give ice skating a try in the park by the Museum. To everyone's surprise, David turned out to be a whiz.

"I don't know about you," Malajia whined as she sat back on the couch later that evening, "but I'm tired and my damn feet hurt."

"That's probably because you kept trying to tip-toe on those cobblestones," Alex observed. She'd warned Malajia that the trendy mid-thigh, high-heeled boots would be a problem.

Malajia shot Alex a glare as she rubbed her feet. "I'd rather suffer, than wear those ugly ass man-boots that you had on."

"It's after ten and we have to get up early tomorrow to check out," Alex pointed out, completely ignoring Malajia's insult.

"Yeah, I'm exhausted," Sidra agreed and rubbed the back of Josh's head. "Good night boys," she threw over her shoulder as she walked into the bedroom.

Mark couldn't miss the stupid smile on Josh's face. "Could you be any more obvious?" he wondered loudly. Josh quickly stopped smiling.

"How about a goodnight kiss?" Jason proposed, getting in Chasity's face.

"Ugh," she scoffed and stood up from her seat.

"Hey, why do *we* have to sleep out here again?" Mark asked.

"He's right," Josh put in, rubbing the back of his neck. "You girls had the bedroom last night. Why don't you let us have it tonight?"

"Unless they're willing to share the beds. What do you say, my future wife?" Jason grinned at Chasity.

"Give it a rest, you horny bastard," she snapped as she walked into the bedroom, inciting a chuckle from him.

"Come on man!" Mark hollered, slamming the sweatshirt that he just removed on the floor. "That's not fair. Y'all have two beds in there. And where are you going with the couch Alex?"

Alex stopped pushing the cream couch towards the bedroom and looked up. "Um, Chaz said she isn't sharing a bed again sooooo I'm gonna sleep on the couch...in there," Alex admitted, gesturing to the bedroom.

The guys stared at her. "Sooooo y'all just aren't gonna leave us with no cushion to sleep on huh?" Mark asked.

"Nope," Malajia replied before standing from her seat and limping into the room.

"Night, guys," Alex said, pushing the couch the rest of the way in and shutting the door.

"Man, this floor is hard as shit," Mark complained, flopping down on the carpeted floor.

"I should go get in Chaz's bed," Jason said, trying to stretch his long frame out on the loveseat.

"Please. She would kill you if the other three didn't," Josh pointed out.

"Man, you're a punk! You're just scared to upset Sidra," Mark barked.

"Mark, you're beginning to piss me the hell off," Josh swore.

"Whatever. I'll beat your ass like I did when we were kids."

Josh jumped up and pointed at Mark. "Man, I kicked your ass *every* time we fought as kids."

"So?" Mark shouted, realizing that Josh was right. "Bet you can't do that shit *now*."

"All right fellas, calm down," David intervened, trying not to laugh. He could still picture Mark and Josh flailing away at each other when they were kids.

Mark tossed and turned, then sat up. "Man, I can't get to sleep. Ya'll feel like getting back at the girls?"

"What do you have in mind?" Jason asked, suddenly alert.

Mark grabbed a mug from the kitchenette and filled it with water. "Pay back," he said, holding the mug up. The guys laughed and scrambled to fill their own cups. Then they tiptoed into the bedroom, and threw the water on the unsuspecting girls.

"My hair!" Malajia screamed.

"What do you think you're doing?" Alex demanded, pulling up the cover. The guys laughed as they ran out of the room with the girls chasing behind them.

"Are you out of your damn mind?" Chasity yelled, holding her wet shirt away from her skin.

"You don't *like* being messed with, *do* you?" Mark teased.

"You ruined my hair!" Malajia yelled at Mark through clenched teeth.

Mark stared at her. "What? You're not gonna *cry*, are you?" he scoffed, echoing her words when he was losing at spades.

"That's it," Alex huffed as she stormed over to the sink. Turning the water on, she started spraying the guys with the sink hose.

"Oh it's on now baby!" Mark shouted as he and the rest of them ran for items to fill with water.

Getting into the mix, Sidra snatched an opened bottle of spring water off the counter and tossed it at Josh. Malajia picked up an empty plastic water bottle and hurled it at David, hitting him in the face.

"My glasses," he exclaimed.

Chasity stood there and folded her arms as she watched the rest of the group play. She was in no mood to participate in the nonsense and became fed up when she saw Malajia pick up a large potted plant.

"Everybody cut it the fuck out," Chasity yelled, stopping everyone in their tracks. She pointed to Malajia. "Malajia you idiot, put that damn plant down," she ordered. "What the fuck were you gonna do with that?"

Malajia looked down at the pot that she was holding. "Um...I was gonna throw it at..."

"You were gonna *throw* it? The whole goddamn thing?" Chasity questioned, frowning. "If you break something, who the hell do you think has to pay for it, stupid?"

Malajia slowly placed the plant down on the floor. "My bad sis," she apologized, realizing that any damage done to the room would fall on the pockets of Chasity's aunt Trisha.

"Malajia, you always gotta take shit too damn far," Mark huffed, slamming his cup on the counter.

Malajia shot him a venomous look. "Y'all guys started it," she exclaimed. "I bet *you* were the damn ring leader, you ugly ass turd."

"Okay, enough with the arguing," Alex intervened, surveying the room and mentally tallying up the damages. Thank goodness, they'd just got started. "Fun's over. Let's get some sleep."

"I swear I'm gonna beat somebody's ass tonight, just wait 'till y'all go to sleep," Mark threatened, plopping down on the floor.

"What? You mean like when we were kids?" Josh teased. Mark sucked his teeth and tossed a wet pillow at him.

"Well *I'm* not going to sleep. I don't trust none of y'all," Malajia stated flatly, folding her arms over her chest.

"Fine. Whoever goes to sleep first is getting rolled on," Mark promised.

"Man, nobody has time for this shit," Alex objected. "We have to get up early tomorrow."

"Okay. When you wake up with a foot in your mouth, don't say nothin'," Mark scoffed.

"Boy, I will cut you," Alex shot back.

"Don't go to sleep then," Mark threatened, rubbing his head.

Nobody wanted to be the first to doze off. Tired, Alex lost her patience. "Come on guys, this is childish. Let's just go to sleep."

"*You* go to sleep," Malajia challenged. "Go ahead so I can watch them write on your face."

After ten minutes, still waiting to pull a prank, Mark pulled his hands down his face, stretching it. "Somebody please fall asleep," he tiredly complained. As if on cue David nodded off, rolling on his back. "Yes!" Mark exclaimed, hopping up from the floor.

"Oh come on Mark," Sidra objected as she watched him grab a small yogurt out of the refrigerator. "You're not really going to do anything to him are you?"

"Stop acting like you don't know me Sid," he responded, kneeling down next to his sleeping friend. Mark snickered as he poured the yogurt onto David's hand. Malajia then tickled his cheek, causing him to smack himself in the face with his yogurt covered hand.

"Come on," he complained, turning over. "Y'all play too much."

The next few to fall asleep were Josh, Sidra and Alex. There was continuous laughter from Chasity, Jason, Malajia, and Mark as they harassed their sleeping friends. Alex woke up and found that Mark had tied some of her hair to a shoe. They lost count of how many times Jason and Mark plucked and pinched Josh and David as they slept.

Convinced that the pranking was now over, Mark had fallen asleep. Jason looked at Malajia and Chasity and laughed, then he slapped the sleeping Mark on his face.

"What the fuck?" Mark shouted as he popped up to find the three of them snickering. He must have been half asleep because he just flopped back down.

"I'm glad that you guys had a good time," Emily said as she played with the strings on her sweat shirt. She was still reeling from the argument she'd had with her mother. She could hardly bear to face Alex after the awful things her mother had screamed over the phone.

"Emily, I'm really sorry that you couldn't be there," Alex sympathized.

"I know. Thanks."

"It's a shame, baby girl. We really did have a good time," Mark said as he stretched out on Alex's bed.

"You don't have to rub it in," Alex scolded. "And get off my damn bed."

"Back off," Mark advised, settling in.

"How you gonna talk trash lying on *my* damn bed?" Alex demanded, grabbing a pillow and hitting him with it.

Malajia walked into the room with a shiny substance all over her face.

"Good god, what the hell is that?" Mark teased. "Alex, quit it," he warned, trying to shove Alex away as she tried to pull him off of her bed.

"Malajia, what is that stuff on your face?" Alex gasped, smacking Mark's arm down.

Malajia adjusted the towel that was slipping off her shoulders and shot Alex a cool glance. "It's a cleansing mask, okay?"

"Just asking. Don't be so defensive."

"Whatever. This damn pimple on my face won't let me be great, and this is supposed to help," Malajia explained.

"It was probably all that junk food you ate this weekend," Sidra assumed.

"Maybe," Malajia shrugged. "Hey Em…You missed a hilarious time, girl. We—"

"Malajia," Alex interrupted when she saw Emily visibly flinch.

"What?" Malajia asked.

"Emily's already disappointed enough. Don't make it worse."

"It's not *my* fault that her mommy wouldn't let her go," Malajia protested.

Alex just shook her head as Chasity walked in with Jason and blinked. "Eww, what the hell?" Chasity complained, staring at Malajia. The facial mask had turned white and was peeling off in patches.

Malajia glared at her. "You're a hater. This stuff makes my face glow, and you're jealous."

Chasity smirked. "Yeah okay," she dismissed, turning away. "I hope it gets rid of that zit on your forehead."

"You can still see it?" Malajia exclaimed, darting to the mirror.

"Malajia, you *do* look like shit," Mark butted in.

"Even with this mess on my face, I *still* look better than any girl you think you can pull," Malajia scoffed.

"You wish, you damn alien," he chortled, rolling around the bed laughing.

"That's it. Get the hell out," Alex commanded and pushed him off of her bed.

"Aww, come on. Don't be that way," he coaxed. "I'll let you kiss me."

"Out," Alex shouted and pointed to the door.

"Fine, I'm hungry anyway," he said as he got to his feet. "Jason, you wanna grab a pizza?"

"Yeah," Jason nodded, opening the door. "But I gotta stop by my room first to get some money."

"How much money you got?" Mark asked, walking out behind him.

"Man, I'm *not* paying for you," Jason warned, shutting the door.

Sidra shook her head and sighed. "I'm so tired from the weekend. I hope no one springs a pop quiz tomorrow."

"The day after break?" Alex looked at her. "What would make you say that?"

"I don't know. I just have this weird feeling."

Malajia opened a can of soda and took a careful sip. She didn't want any more cracks in her mask. "All snide remarks aside, Chasity, that was really nice of your aunt to arrange that hotel stay. I hope it made up for the rough Thanksgiving you had."

Chasity looked at her and frowned. "And where exactly did you hear that I'd had a rough Thanksgiving?" she asked, stiffening up.

"*I* mentioned it to her and Sidra," Alex interjected.

"What the hell did you do that for?"

"I didn't want the other girls to question you about your break, so I told them that you had a rough time and not to ask you about it," Alex responded. "*Malajia*," she added, gesturing to her.

"What?" Malajia exclaimed then patted her face. "You never said not to mention it."

Chasity turned on Alex. "Why would you think that I wanted them to know my business?"

Alex turned away from Chasity to grab a shirt off of her bed. "Let's not argue about this," she said, brushing aside Chasity's obvious annoyance.

"What? You tell Sidra and Malajia *my* fuckin' business, and now you don't want me to argue with you about it?" Chasity charged.

Alex spun around and faced Chasity. "Sweetie, I'm not doing things like this to hurt you. I just feel that we're friends and we need to share things that bother us. It's good to have a support system—"

"No. You're a nosey, interfering bitch," Chasity shouted. Alex gasped at the insult, but Chasity barreled on. "You just can't stand that I don't whine and cry about every little fuckin' thing."

"That's not why I said anything!" Alex protested.

"Whatever, Alex!" Chasity hollered.

"God, Chasity, you are such a …"

"I'm a what?"

"Okay, okay. That's enough." Sidra jumped in between the arguing girls. "Malajia, you get your roommate, I'll get mine." She grabbed onto Chasity's arm and proceeded to pull her out of the room.

"Oh please. This one ain't gonna do nothin'," Malajia replied as she gestured to Alex, who was busy smoothing her hair back with her hands.

"I'll call you all later," Sidra said as she shut the door behind her.

Malajia and Emily looked over at Alex; her hand was over her forehead.

"Chaz is right," Malajia declared, "You *are* nosey."

Alex, not in the mood for Malajia's glib comments at the moment, snatched part of the mask off Malajia's face and walked away.

"It wasn't ready yet!" Malajia yelled, putting her hands over her face.

Chapter 25

Monday morning, most of the crew dragged themselves to Science class. Mark, yet to recover from the weekend, had his head down on the desk.

Jason poked Chasity when Professor Jones walked in and started writing on the blackboard. "Quiz today," Jason groaned.

"What? Now?" Chasity exclaimed loudly enough to attract the professor's attention.

"Yes, *now*. Put your books away."

Emily raised her hand. "What is it going to be on?"

"Chapters five and six. They were assigned last week before you went home for Thanksgiving break," Professor Jones answered, voice laced with frustration.

"Sorry," Emily mumbled and slumped down in her seat.

"Come on, Professor Jones," Mark objected. "How do you expect people to study over the *holiday*?"

"Because Mr. Johnson, this is college. Not high school. College. I expect you to work hard and study hard, no matter what time it is, or what *holiday*," he responded, folding his arms.

"Why don't you just do us all a favor and make the test for next week?" Mark pleaded.

"Mr. Johnson, don't make me throw you out of my classroom for stupidity." Professor Jones warned. "Now, clear your desk right now, or I'll give you a zero."

"Um, I have cramps," Chasity said, offering the only plausible excuse she could think of. "Can I take it another time?"

"Miss Parker, you're on thin ice already due to your smart mouth. Don't test my patience."

Chasity rolled her eyes and sighed as she cleared her desk.

"Damn," Jason complained, clearing his desk.

"I sure am glad I studied over the break," David murmured.

"You *would* study over a break, you dork," Mark jeered

"Make fun of me all you want," David shot back, "but don't forget to tell Mama Johnson why you failed yet another test." David's dart hit its target. Mark pounded his fist on his desk; he knew his mother didn't mince words when it came to school work.

"Wouldn't you know, Public Speaking just had to be the first class after break," Sidra complained. She hated this class. "Whole thing is a waste of time, anyway."

"It's great for Alex," Malajia said idly, frowning when she noticed the nail polish on one of her nails had chipped. "She loves giving lectures anyway, no matter how much nobody asks for them."

Alex didn't bother to reply; she just elbowed Malajia in the ribs. She would have done so harder if she hadn't been sure that Malajia would let out a scream. She couldn't believe how quickly her roommate had jumped to Chasity's defense last night.

"Knock it off," Sidra whispered, noticing that Professor Lawrence had looked up. "I don't want to attract any attention. I'm already drowning in this class."

"Let's start with your speeches," Professor Lawrence proposed, putting down the papers she had been shuffling. "Remember to keep within the five minutes allowed."

"*What* speech?" Alex asked.

"The speech on World War II that you're supposed to give today," Professor Lawrence responded.

"You've got to be kidding me," Malajia grumbled and tossed her pen down. "Who cares about World War II?"

Unfortunately for Malajia, the lecture hall had excellent acoustics. Professor Lawrence set her glasses down on the podium. "Miss Simmons, World War II was chosen for the assignment to give you practice addressing important issues and events. Shall we get on with it without you wasting any more of our time?"

Malajia rolled her eyes, "Whatever," she mumbled.

"Man, I knew that I should've done some homework over the weekend," Josh moaned. "That's what I get for messin' with y'all."

"Nobody had to twist your arm to make you come with us, Joshua," Sidra pointed out.

"Hold on. I thought that we agreed that you would never use my full name in public."

"I lied," she said, grinning at him. He hated being called Joshua.

"Oh okay. You wanna start exposing hated names huh? Sidra Ophelia Howard," he shot back, knowing full well that Sidra hated her middle name.

"Eww, what the hell is an Ophelia?" Malajia broke in laughing.

Sidra glared at Malajia, then turned her attention back to a laughing Josh. "Joshua, you are so dead," Sidra promised.

"Ah, I see that we have some volunteers," Professor Lawrence said, interrupting their exchange. "Miss Howard, you can go first."

"Huh?" Sidra exclaimed.

"Yes. Followed by Mr. Hampton." Josh let out a frustrated sigh and leaned back in his seat.

Malajia's burst of laughter came to an abrupt halt.

"Miss Simmons, you will present after Mr. Hampton, then Miss Chisolm."

"I'm so not prepared for this," Alex said as she covered her face with her notebook.

"Man," Malajia whined. "I knew I shouldn't have come to class today."

Sidra stood up and walked slowly to the podium.

"Five minutes," Professor Lawrence reminded.

"Five minutes?" Sidra echoed. "Can't I just take my zero and sit down?"

"No, that would just be too easy. Now get started."

Emily slumped in her chair. The group had gathered in one of the library's study rooms to cram for tests. But Emily couldn't concentrate.

"I completely failed that quiz."

"Stop complaining. At least you actually wrote something," Chasity snapped.

"That doesn't make a difference," Emily barked, immediately looking away. She hadn't meant to raise her voice.

Chasity shot her a glare. "Who the hell are you yelling at?" she asked, surprised to hear more than a squeak out of meek little Emily.

Alex sighed, "Chasity, get off her case."

"Bitch, don't talk to me," Chasity sneered.

Alex's mouth fell open. "Come on. You can't still be mad at me."

"I said don't talk to me," Chasity repeated.

Frustrated with Chasity's stubborn attitude, Alex sat back in her seat, folded her arms, and let out a loud sigh.

"At least you didn't have to stand in front of twenty classmates and BS for five minutes, Emily," Sidra complained.

"And bullshit you did, sis," Alex teased, giggling. Sidra slowly turned her head and glowered at Alex.

"I know, right? By the time you got to the fifth 'um the war was long and hard' I was ready to fall off my seat laughing," Malajia chimed in.

Sidra was seething so much that she started breathing hard. "Malajia, I know your simple ass isn't—"

"Sid, relax," Josh interrupted, leaning forward and giving her a comforting pat on the shoulder. "It'll be better next time."

"Yeah, right," she groused, jerking away.

"This is my first bad grade ever," Emily confessed.

"You'll get used to 'em," Malajia predicted as she scribbled on her notebook with a highlighter.

Chasity sighed loudly. "Y'all talk too damn much," she said, closing her book.

"Where do you think *you're* going?" Malajia asked, seeing Chasity stand from the table.

"I'm going to mind my damn business," Chasity threw over her shoulder as she headed out of the room.

Chasity settled in an isolated corner of the library and took her math book out. She needed to put some serious study time in. But of course, she couldn't be alone for even a minute.

"What the hell are you doing over here?" she demanded, pissed to see Jason pull up a chair next to her. She'd snapped at him several times that day for no reason, but he kept coming back for more.

"I'm here to study. Just like you," he replied, pulling his notebook out from his book bag.

"Do it somewhere else," she demanded.

"Nope," he calmly responded. Not wanting to move her seat again, Chasity just sucked her teeth and looked down at her book.

Jason was restless. He started tapping his pencil on the table.

"Could you stop that?" she asked, voice dripping with anger.

"I *could* if you asked me nicely," he replied, eyes fixed on the words in his book.

"This is as nice as I'm going to get," she stated flatly, "so could you stop it?"

He looked at her. "No, I can't."

"Why not?"

"Because you have been rude to me all day and I would like an apology."

"I'll apologize to you when hell freezes over," she sneered.

"You really think so huh?" he questioned, folding his arms. "I don't get why you're being so nasty to me."

"You make me fuckin' sick," she hissed through clenched teeth.

"No, I don't," Jason responded calmly. "And why do you have to curse at me?"

Chasity stared at him. She hated the way he kept going at it with her. "Why don't you leave?" she asked

"Why? I don't have anywhere else to be."

"Fine," she hissed and shoved her notebook into her book bag again.

"Where are you going?" he asked.

"Away from *you*," she spat, eyes flashing.

"Okay, do what you want. You always do." He chuckled as she stormed down the library corridor. "I get her every time."

Sidra, completely overwhelmed, finally snapped. She stood up on her bed and yelled at the top of her lungs.

"Girl, what is wrong with you?" Alex asked, surprised at the sudden outburst.

"I hate math," she screeched.

"You and me both," Malajia concurred, looking down at her workbook with disgust. Tired of the library scene that night, the girls decided to take their study session back to Sidra and Chasity's room.

"It's divide this and factor that," Sidra whined, then burst into hysterical laughter. "I can't even remember the quadratic equation."

Alex ran over, grabbed Sidra by the shoulders and shook her. Sidra stopped laughing and regarded her friend calmly.

"Um, Alex that didn't help me at all."

"I'm sorry, girl, but you were going crazy there," Alex explained. "If you need help with your formulas, just ask David. He knows everything, or so he says."

"Oh yeah. My buddy Dave," Sidra said, mulling over the suggestion. "I forgot that I grew up with a genius." Alex giggled as she flopped down on the love seat. A second later, Chasity stormed in the room.

"What's the matter with you?" Malajia asked, looking up at the angry expression on her face.

"Jason makes me so fuckin' sick!" she snapped.

"O-kay," Malajia drawled, fixing her gaze back down at her book.

"Shut up, Malajia!" Chasity yelled.

"What?" Malajia protested loudly. "I didn't even say anything."

"Look," Alex broke in. "Everybody's on edge with finals coming up. Let's take it easy."

Long hours spent cramming began to take its toll. As fatigue set in, tempers flared at the slightest provocation. Up all night studying, no one was in the mood to talk when the group crowded into their usual booth by the window in the cafeteria. The heavy silence weighed on Emily.

"So," she asked, "is everybody enjoying their lunch?"

"Are you serious?" Malajia scoffed, going back to her turkey wrap.

"It's just so quiet," Emily stammered, looking around. "I feel like everybody's mad at each other."

"So?" Chasity inquired nastily, raising an eyebrow.

"Not everybody has to be evil like you, Chasity," Jason interjected, trying to get a rise out of her. She was too stubborn to have an ordinary conversation with him.

She slowly turned and looked at him. "Are you trying to piss me off?"

"No," he lied. "That seems to be how you are every damn day."

"Jason, leave her alone," Alex advised.

"When are you going to learn to mind your own business, Alex?" Jason asked calmly as he continued to stare at Chasity. Alex made a face at him.

"Thank you, Jason," Malajia exclaimed, picking up a piece of red pepper that had fallen out of her turkey wrap. "Somebody else has *finally* said it." She dropped the pepper back on the plate as Alex nudged her.

"Jason, I don't know why you continue to talk to me," Chasity complained. "You know that I can't stand you."

"And you know that's not true," he shot back.

"Yes, it is. You are not good enough to talk to me. When are you gonna realize that?"

Jason's easy smile disappeared, his expression hardened. "You know what? I'll see you guys later," he said and grabbed his book bag.

Chasity closed her eyes, hoping to shut out the look on Jason's face. She couldn't believe the words that had come out of her mouth. She hadn't meant to insult him, she simply wanted him to leave her alone.

"That was so ignorant, even for you," Alex charged.

"Alex, not now," Chasity murmured as she watched Jason walk away. She was in no mood to hear one of Alex's lectures.

"Look, in Chasity's defense, he shouldn't have been bothering her," Malajia chimed in. "I mean, come on, why would he take that to heart? Mark doesn't, and I say it to him all the time."

Mark looked at her, confused. "No, you don't."

"I don't? Well, maybe I just think it," Malajia corrected and took a sip of juice. "Bottom line—Alex, leave Chasity alone."

"Why is everybody so damn cranky?" Mark asked, looking around at the tired faces.

"Because we were up all night," Josh spat out as he rubbed the back of his neck.

"Doing what?" Mark asked with a frown. "And why wasn't I invited?"

"We were studying, you moron," Malajia explained in a condescending voice.

"Why?"

"Is this 'ask dumb ass questions day' or something?" Chasity wondered aloud.

Alex shook her head. "Why wouldn't we be studying?" She tapped her fingers on the table, waiting for his stupid reply; she knew that he'd make one.

"Studying is a waste of time." He fixed his book bag on his shoulder. "All you have to do is pay attention in class, and you can pass any test." His tone was full of confidence.

"But *you* don't pay attention," Josh objected.

"Please, I got this final thing in the bag. I got it all up here," Mark claimed and pointed to his head.

"But there's nothing up there," Sidra exclaimed. "There never *has* been."

"Go pop a damn pill or something," he shot back at her, the smile wiped off his face.

"'I got it all up here.' *Please*," Josh mimicked.

"Y'all are some haters man," Mark declared, tossing a balled up napkin on the table.

Maybe it was better, Emily thought to herself, *when nobody was talking*.

"Where's Jason?" Chasity asked Mark. He looked up from the various bowling balls he was inspecting. The group had decided that they needed a breather, and a trip to the bowling alley fit the bill.

"Why? So you can insult him again?"

She narrowed her eyes at him. "Don't start it, cause *your* feelings, I don't mind hurting," she shot back.

"Instead of my feelings, how about hurting something else, sexy?" he teased and moved closer to her.

"Ugh," she groaned, pushing him away. Mark laughed and went back to picking out his ball.

"Mark, I don't know why you're taking so long," Malajia called out. "You're gonna lose no matter which ball you choose."

"Malajia, shut up for once," he responded. "Isn't it your turn anyway?"

"I'm not bowling in these damn shoes," Malajia said and pointed to her red high heels.

"Malajia, you're supposed to rent shoes, you flippin' idiot," Sidra snapped.

"Listen heifer, you need to calm down," Malajia recommended. Even when she was a kid, Malajia remembered, Sidra got cranky when she was stressed, and right now her anxiety level was off the charts.

"Can you just rent the damn shoes so we can finish the game please?" Sidra responded, exasperated. Malajia, ignoring Sidra's nasty tone, stood and proceeded to the nearby shoe counter.

Emily finished tying up her bowling shoes and glanced up. She'd been going through a rough patch, and was happy she'd been asked to tag along, although bowling was not her thing. "I'm going for some drinks, anybody want one?" Seeing hesitation all around, she laughed. "My treat."

"In that case," Alex put in and, then the orders came fast and furious. Emily's eyes widened at all of the requests that were being made of her.

"I want a cola, some nachos, two hot dogs and some pretzel bites," Mark stipulated.

"But...."

"Damn boy, are you trying to stock up for winter or something?" Alex exclaimed.

Mark rolled his eyes and let out a loud sigh. "That joke was wack, Alex."

"Orange soda and some nachos for me," Malajia put in, sitting back in her seat, shoes in hand.

"But I was just gonna buy the drinks," Emily protested as she started counting her money. The check her father had sent wasn't going to last long at this rate.

"But I want nachos," Malajia whined.

"Buy them yourself," Mark instructed and shrugged. "Can one of y'all help me out? I'm a little strapped." Everyone ignored him. "Is that how it is? Some friends."

"Man, stop whining," Josh said with a laugh. "I'll pay...again."

"Thanks dude, one of these days I'm gonna pay you back," Mark promised, eagerly rubbing his hands together.

"Boy, you've been saying that since middle school," Sidra observed, turning up her nose when Mark blew her a kiss.

Jason turned up before Emily came back with the drinks. He'd been at practice that afternoon and then met with his study group.

Chasity had been on the lookout. As soon as she caught sight of him, she walked over. "Hey," she said nonchalantly.

"Hi," he responded and turned away.

She hated feeling guilty about how she'd treated him earlier. In the past she could say anything to anybody and not give a crap. But this time she knew she had gone too far.

"You still mad about what I said to you earlier?" she asked, grabbing his arm.

"Yes, I am. You've said some pretty nasty things to me, but that cut," he said and set his book bag on the floor. "You owe me an apology."

Chasity frowned. She detested the word "sorry", and didn't want to be the one to say it. He shook his head and started to walk away.

"Wait a minute," she said, blocking his way. "Look I'm...I'm so..."

"It's not that hard to say," Jason prompted, folding his arms.

She narrowed her eyes at him. "I'm sorry," she blurted out.

Jason stood still for a few seconds, and then a big smile creased his face. "You'll apologize to me when hell freezes over, huh?"

Chasity stiffened when she heard her words tossed back at her. "What?"

"I have proved you wrong yet again. Last time I checked, hell was still hot."

Chasity gasped, anger bubbling up. "You made me feel guilty just so you could prove a fuckin' point?" she asked angrily.

"I didn't *make* you feel anything, Chasity. You did that on your own," he answered evenly. "It also proves another point of mine—that you have a heart somewhere under all that anger."

"You fuckin' bastard," she hissed. "That is the last time that I will ever feel bad over you."

"Chaz, come on," Jason pleaded, reaching for her arm.

"Don't touch me," she snapped, smacking his hand away. Jason ran his hand over his head as she stormed off.

Alex and Sidra were watching the encounter by the rack of bowling balls. "Another lovers' quarrel," Alex concluded.

"I wish that they would just sleep together and get it over with," Sidra confided. "Sure would make our lives easier."

"But a lot less entertaining," Alex said with a laugh.

On the other side of the rack, Josh and Mark had just chosen their bowling balls. The lengthy selection process involved discussing the merits of various weights and colors. Unfortunately, the holes in Mark's ball were a tight fit for his big fingers. Josh had the opposite problem.

"Guys, enough already. Just switch balls," Sidra suggested.

"I don't want his stupid ass ball," Mark shot back. "This is a lucky ball."

"And where is the luck, Mark? In your ass?" Malajia inquired, pointing to the score sheet. "Because it definitely won't show up in your game."

Mark glared at her. "I've had it with your comments," he swore.

"It's not *my* fault that your bowling sucks ass," Malajia jeered, shrugging.

He pointed to her as she took a sip of her soda. "It's not gonna be too many more 'ass' comments from you," he warned, causing her to spit some of her soda out as she chuckled.

"Josh, will you just go? Let's get this started," David prompted, gesturing toward the lane.

Josh held the ball to his chest, ready to bowl. As he drew his arm back, the ball slipped off his hand. Careening backwards, it knocked against the table. Soda cans and bottles of spring water went flying.

"Josh!" they exclaimed.

"My bad, guys. Are you all right?" Josh asked as he ran over and picked his ball up.

"Watch what you're doing, will you?" Alex scolded as she tugged her shirt down.

"He said that he was sorry," Mark yelled. "You always gotta prolong shit."

"Shut up and take your turn," Alex ordered, and pointed to the lane.

Mark walked over to the lane, squeezing his fingers into the ball. He couldn't jam them in and kept shifting from one foot to the other, making a bunch of stupid faces.

"Come on!" Jason hollered, frustrated by Mark's holding up of the game.

"All right!" he shouted back. "Here it goes." His fingers stuck, and he couldn't release the ball. The momentum sent him flying down the shiny wooden lane. "Whoa," he shouted, and landed spread-eagled on the alley.

"Oh my god," Malajia screamed with laughter. "You look like a total fool."

"Mark, you are so freakin' embarrassing," Sidra shouted.

Embarrassed, Mark picked himself up. To cut short Malajia's running commentary, he walked over, took three pretzels from his packet, and stuffed them into her open mouth.

Jason was the next up. Alex leaned forward on the bench. "Please don't embarrass us like Mark did."

"*Nobody* can embarrass us the way that Mark did," he said with a laugh.

Chasity was eating some chips, waiting for Jason to bowl, when Malajia scooted next to her. "So what were you two arguing about, huh?"

"None of your business," Chasity sneered. "Get away from me."

Malajia sucked her teeth. "Must you be so damn evil all the time?"

Chasity checked her reply when she saw Jason's arm going back. "Jason, your dick is out!" she shouted.

"Ooh, can I see it?" Malajia exclaimed, craning her neck.

Jason stumbled and dropped the ball. He quickly looked down at his pants, and then at Chasity, before retrieving his ball.

"What?" she replied innocently as Malajia laughed.

"That's real cute, Chasity," Jason bit out. "And real classy, Malajia."

"Come on, Jase," Sidra yelled encouragingly, clapping her hands together.

"Damn it," he muttered, watching only six pins fall.

"Emily, you're up," Sidra announced.

Emily hesitated. "Um, that's okay somebody else can go."

"No sweetie, it's your turn. Go," Malajia said, giving her a nudge.

Emily held the ball for a few seconds, then weakly tossed it. Her friends watched it bounce and roll into the gutter.

"Wow, you're getting better, Emily," Jason joked. "This time you got it to stay in our lane."

"Alex, your turn," David said.

"Time to make a strike," she murmured to herself as she stood up and grabbed her ball. Just as she was about to roll the ball, Mark started making loud noises and threw some pretzels at her.

"Quit playing around," she barked, tossing the pretzels back.

"Hey! Stop throwing food in here," a man shouted from behind the counter.

"Sorry," Alex muttered and rolled the ball.

The last pin wobbled, and finally toppled over. Alex did a little dance. She'd made a strike. She couldn't believe it.

"Hell no, Alex! How'd your non-bowling ass make that strike?" Mark asked in shock. "You cheated."

"How could I *possibly* have cheated to get that?" she asked, confused. "You're just mad because I did what you *couldn't* do...Fool."

Unable to think of a comeback, Mark made a face at her.

Alex was the last to bowl and everyone gathered around the score sheet.

"I suck so bad at this game," Chasity commented, getting a look at her final score.

"Finally, you're right about something," Malajia mocked.

"And I still beat *you*," she shot back.

"Last place, with an extremely sad score of seven, goes to Emily Harris," Mark teased.

"My score doesn't count," Emily said, Mark looked over at her.

"She's right, man. We said that any score less than twenty, we were gonna drop," Josh reminded him.

"So the last place prize goes to..." Alex looked at the scores. "Mark Johnson, with the sad score of forty-four."

"Did you *have* to announce it out loud?" he complained.

"That's sad man," Jason commiserated. "And after you boasted that you could beat everybody."

"Oh, shut up. I challenge everyone to a rematch!" Mark hollered.

"Boy, please," Chasity scoffed, walking away.

"What? Oh, y'all scared that I might win?" he held his arms up in the air as his friends walked away, ignoring him.

Chapter 26

"Ugh, why do I have five classes?" Sidra complained, throwing her head back against the lounge chair in frustration.

Alex chuckled as she thumbed through her notebook. "I think that's the standard, especially for a freshman," she pointed out.

Chasity looked up from her book. "Y'all don't have six classes?" she asked.

Malajia looked at her, confused. "*No.* Why would we have six classes?" she asked.

"I can barely keep sane with my five," Sidra agreed, rubbing her temples.

Chasity slammed her book shut. "Damn it! That's what I get for trying to take extra credits."

"Look on the bright side," Alex put in. "That's one less class that you have to take later on," she stated.

"That's not helping me *now*," Chasity complained.

"Guys, who cares?" Mark chimed in, resting his head on Sidra's shoulder. "Finals are a week away, why worry about them now?"

"Mark, finals will sneak up on you," Alex warned. "You really need to crack down and study."

"And there will be plenty of time to study," Mark argued, "on Sunday night,"

"Um, can you say procrastinator?" Malajia scoffed.

"Look we'll probably have three or four chapters to study," Mark declared confidently. "How hard can finals be, really?"

"Twenty chapters? The final is going to be on all twenty chapters?" Mark yelled at the professor as he wrote on the board.

"Mr. Johnson, it would be wise if you refrained from shouting in this classroom," Professor Bradley warned. "I'm two seconds away from putting you out...again."

Mark had been getting on Professor Bradley's nerves all semester. His constant outbursts and class clown behavior had caused Professor Bradley to put him out of his classroom plenty of times.

Mark shuffled in his seat. After trash talking to his friends earlier about how easy finals would be, he never thought that he would have to restudy twenty chapters of Sociology notes in a week. "Well, it's safe to say that I'm gonna fail this class," he said, tossing his pencil on his desk. Then he looked at the professor and said, "I guess we'll be seeing each other next semester, huh Professor Bradley?"

"I seriously hope not," he responded. "I'm tempted to pass you just so I don't have to see your face in my class again."

Mark smiled brightly "Really?" His tone was full of hope.

"I said that I'm *tempted*," Professor Bradley responded, before going back to writing on the board.

Mark's smile faded. "Well Jase my friend, I guess we'll be in here again," he said as he patted Jason on the back. "We all know that *David's* gonna pass."

"I refuse to repeat this class," Jason said. "Looks like you'll be in here by yourself next semester," he said as he patted Mark on the back. Mark just rolled his eyes.

"Don't worry man, I'll help you study," David quietly offered as he diligently took notes.

"Yeah thanks," Mark scoffed.

"Well forget you then. I was trying to help you out," David shot back, annoyed at Mark's nasty tone.

"I've got my schedule all planned," Emily said, fixing her pink and grey book bag on her shoulder. "These exams are a lot to handle."

"Girl, you're way ahead of me," Malajia admitted, looking at her watch.

She and Emily had finished their last class of the day ten minutes earlier, and were patiently waiting outside of the Science building for the rest of the group so they could go eat.

"About time," Malajia jeered as Sidra and Chasity walked down the building steps to meet them.

Noticing the angry looks on both of their faces, Emily became concerned. "What's the matter with you two?" she asked.

"I'm tired and stressed out," Sidra complained.

Malajia looked at Chasity. "What about *you*?" she asked her.

Chasity stared at her; "I *always* look like this," she admitted.

Malajia laughed. "True."

"I thought high school was tough," Sidra complained. "I don't know what I'm going to do if I fail a class."

"You won't fail," Emily reassured her. "You've been studying too much to fail."

"Shit, I've been studying, and I *still* expect to fail," Malajia joked and then rubbed her eyes. "I need some coffee."

"Damn the coffee," Sidra cut in. "If I don't get some food in my system, I'm gonna scream. Where are the others?" Before anyone could respond, the rest of the group approached.

"You guys wanna eat on campus or off?" Josh asked.

"Off, definitely off. I can't deal with cafeteria food today," Sidra replied, adjusting the scarf around her neck.

"Good choice, good choice," Mark agreed. "How 'bout pizza?"

"I'm cold. I should go get my car," Chasity said, fishing in her bag for her keys.

"Girl, all nine of us can't fit in that car," Alex pointed out.

Chasity smirked. "I wasn't thinking about *y'all*."

Alex playfully nudged her. "We can take the bus. It's only fifteen minutes away."

"Fine," Chasity sighed, pushing some hair out of her face

"All right, enough talking," Sidra warned. "Let's just go. I'm starving."

The Pizza Shack was a hole in the wall, but the best pizza in town came out of its brick oven. Mark and Josh pulled two tables together, so there was enough room for everyone.

"So what does everyone want on their pizza?" David asked as he looked at the menu.

"Anchovies," Josh stipulated, "with extra cheese."

"Ugh, nobody wants those nasty, salty fish," Malajia scoffed.

"Pepperoni!" Mark shouted and the short woman at the cash register smiled.

"Always have to be loud," Alex put in, rubbing her ear.

"I just want a vegetarian pizza," Chasity said as she looked at her watch.

"I'll eat a supreme," Jason said.

David rolled his eyes. "Everyone wants something different on their pizza. We are not going to sit here and order nine pizzas. Let's just compromise," he suggested.

"Dave is right. We can order three large and go half and half," Josh stated, looking at the menu. "For Sidra, Chasity and Malajia we'll get half vegetarian and for Emily and Alex we'll get half black olive and pineapples. Then on the second pizza we'll get half supreme for David, Jason and Mark and for me we'll get half anchovies and extra cheese. And then on the last pizza we'll..."

"Hold it, Josh," Mark interrupted. "Nobody at this table eats anchovies except for you."

"Yeah, so?" Josh responded.

"So that means that you'll have a whole half to yourself," Mark pointed out.

"That's right."

Mark frowned at the huge smile that Josh had plastered to his face. "Naw, naw, that ain't cool man," he complained as he shook his hand.

"What are you complaining about? We are getting a third pizza with cheese," Josh responded.

"So what man, everybody else has to share a half and you get a half to yourself!" Mark shot back.

Josh shook his head and Alex was fed up. "God, can we just order? This arguing is so unnecessary," she declared.

"We should just split the bill evenly," Emily suggested.

"That's what we were gonna do anyway," Chasity retorted sharply.

"I'm dying of hunger here," Sidra groaned. "If I don't eat soon, I'm going to slap somebody."

"No need for that," David quipped, signaling for the waiter. "Let's order."

Two harassed waiters in white shirts and black aprons finally appeared with their order. Expertly juggling the pies and pitchers of soda, they made room on the table so everything would fit. But then, one of them set a mountain of breadsticks and a plate full of Buffalo wings in front of Mark.

"There you are," she beamed. He smiled as he rubbed his hands together.

"Mark, you are *not* gonna eat all of that," Malajia exclaimed, looking at him with disgust.

He raised an eyebrow at her. "Why not?"

"You're being a greedy pig."

"So!" he yelled, taking a bite out of a breadstick. "Stop looking in my mouth, and eat your own damn food."

"Man, you're paying for that extra shit out of your own pocket," Jason declared as he grabbed a slice of pizza.

"Whatchu mean?" he asked, with a look of surprise on his face. "We're gonna split the bill."

"Dude, nobody is eating that extra stuff except you," Josh pointed out.

"Not my fault," Mark argued and reached for another breadstick.

Jason snatched the plate of wings and basket of breadsticks and moved them to the other side of the table. "Naw, you're not eating that if you're not gonna pay for it."

"Man gimme—"

"No! *I'll* pay for it and I'm taking it back with me for later," Jason argued as he blocked Mark from grabbing for the food. "Sick of you, always trying to get over."

"Mark, I'm telling your mama that you're up here acting like you're poor," Sidra said, shaking her head. "I know they send you money."

"You leave my mom out of this," he warned.

"Next time we come out, how 'bout we leave his broke ass home?" Malajia suggested, reaching for her cup of soda.

Mark sucked his teeth. "You always tryin' to get in the mix," he shot back. "Nobody was talking to you."

"So? You always trying to get free shit off of people. You bum," Malajia snapped.

"Why can't it be quiet for five minutes?" Alex complained, slamming her hand down on the table.

"And you people wonder why I try to avoid hanging out with you," Chasity commented dryly.

"Girl, please, you know you love us," Malajia teased, waving her hand at Chasity dismissively.

Emily giggled at the back and forth squabbling. "Well, I for one love everybody here," she ventured. She was about to take a bite of pizza when she noticed that Chasity and Malajia were staring daggers at her. She dropped her slice.

"Don't be scared, Emily," Alex butted in, "I'll smack these heifers before they lay a hand on you."

"You two are so damn mean," Sidra swore.

"Damn!" Mark loudly instigated.

"What? What did I do?" Malajia exclaimed, pointing to herself.

"Every time Emily says *anything*, you two get smart with her, or look at her like you want to slap her," Sidra pointed out.

Malajia's eyes widened. "I do not," she protested.

"Shit, *I* do," Chasity admitted. "Her weak ass irks my nerves."

"Emily is nothing but nice to everyone, and you two continue to treat her like shit," Alex chimed in.

"Maybe if she grew a backbone, we wouldn't pick on her. She needs to learn to stand up for herself," Malajia argued. "All she had to say when we looked at her just now was 'what the hell are you looking at?' and we would've been, like, 'you're right, Em.'"

Chasity shot Malajia a confused look. "What?" she said. The more that Malajia tried to get her point across, the less sense she made.

"She's not like that!" Sidra shouted.

"Uh, Sidra, you're yelling," Josh pointed out.

"Stay out of it," Jason warned, looking at his watch.

"Emily is not an insult-throwing person. She's sweet," Alex interjected. "Let her be."

Chasity looked at Emily, who was sitting there with her head down picking at her pizza. "Why don't you say something?" she asked angrily.

"You scare me," Emily admitted, sounding as if she were about to cry.

"I scare a lot of people, so what?" Chasity shot back.

"You see what I mean?" Sidra exclaimed, tossing her napkin down on the table.

Chasity glanced at Sidra, then looked back at Emily. "You're such a fuckin' punk. I swear, I could slap you right now," she threatened.

"Girl I wish you would. You'll have to go through *me* first," Alex warned.

"And I'll beat *your* ass too," Chasity responded, raising her voice.

"Excuse me, I have to use the restroom," Emily mumbled and pushed her chair back.

"I'll go with you, honey," Sidra said and grabbed Emily by the hand.

"That was harsh ladies," David commented once they were out of sight.

"Don't worry guys. They'll be apologizing," Alex stated confidently.

"Like hell," Chasity swore.

"Sweetie, are you okay?" Sidra asked a crying Emily. "Try to calm down okay, they're just being ignorant, don't pay them any mind."

"I just feel bad because I know that they're right," Emily sniffled. "I *should* be standing up for myself, but I just can't."

"I know. It'll take some time, but you'll get it." Sidra handed Emily more tissues as Malajia walked through the door.

"Emily—"

"Not now Malajia," Sidra objected. "You and your evil partner in crime have done enough damage for one night."

"Shut the hell up," Malajia hollered and turned to Emily. "Emily, I'm sorry. I didn't mean to embarrass you like that in front of the guys. Chasity and I took it too far. We just want you to grow a backbone, that's why we say stuff. We're waiting for you to say stuff back. We're not gonna stop being your friends just because you tell us to 'go to hell' or 'shut up'."

"Did *Alex* make you come in here and say that?" Sidra asked, eyeing Malajia with suspicion as she folded her arms.

"You know what, get out my face Sidra," Malajia warned just as Chasity came through the door with Alex following close behind her.

"Alex, get away from me!" Chasity yelled, jerking around to face Alex.

"No! You be a woman, and admit that you were wrong for what you did," Alex commanded.

"You are such a hypocrite; you always embarrass people. You embarrass *Mark* all the damn time," Chasity shot back.

"He deserves it. *She* doesn't," Alex shouted.

Chasity gave Alex the finger before taking a step towards Emily. When Emily backed away, she stood still.

"I'm not gonna hit you," she sneered. Emily was so nervous, she couldn't make eye contact. Chasity stared at her for a few seconds. "You really *are* afraid of me, huh?" she questioned with a smirk.

"Chasity, if you've come in here to rub it in, I suggest you leave," Sidra hissed.

"Shut up Sidra," Chasity ground out and turned back to Emily. "Look, maybe I shouldn't have embarrassed you in front of everybody, but you need to stick up for your damn self. You have to stop letting Alex or Sidra fight your battles. I'm telling you now, I treat everybody the same way, and I'm not gonna change the way I act or make an exception for you just because you cry. You don't like it? Say something."

"I don't fight her battles," Sidra argued.

Chasity frowned. "No? What was that back at the table then, baby Alex?" she sneered, inciting a snicker from Malajia.

Sidra made a face at Chasity as Emily began to tear up again. "Why do you hate me, Chasity?"

"I don't hate you," Chasity responded. "If I did, I wouldn't be talking to you at all. Anybody who knows me would tell you that."

"Chasity, that wasn't an apology," Alex pointed out.

"I never said that I was gonna give her one," Chasity replied, looking at Alex.

Alex slowly placed her hands on her hips. Chasity's smart mouth and defiant behavior made her want to shake her.

Malajia quickly intervened, not wanting to force the issue. Chasity seemed to have a pathological dislike of apologies.

"Listen, bottom line, we…yes *we*," Malajia began as she nudged Chasity for sucking her teeth. "…are sorry for hurting you in front of everyone. Isn't that right, Satan?"

Chasity narrowed her eyes at Malajia. "Fine…I apologize," she forced through clenched teeth.

"Now, was that so hard?" Alex asked.

"Yes."

Chasity's blunt response caused Malajia to chuckle. *This girl never fails to be a smart ass*, Malajia thought. More and more, she was finding Chasity to be someone who could always make her laugh, even at the most inappropriate times.

"Better now?" Sidra asked Emily, still concerned.

Emily nodded and wiped her eyes.

"Everything smoothed over?" Jason asked as the girls approached the table.

"Yep…For now," Alex stated as she picked up her soda.

Sidra picked up a slice of pizza. "Man! Now it's cold," she complained, tossing the pizza back onto her plate.

Mark belched loudly, causing everyone to start complaining. "Mine wasn't," he teased. Sidra glared at him as she picked a tomato off of her pizza and flicked it. Everyone laughed as the tomato stuck to his lip.

Chapter 27

"I hate math," Chasity swore. "How the hell am I gonna pass this damn final?"

"Hey, it's not as hard as it looks," Jason consoled. He'd been tutoring Chasity for days, relishing their sessions in an unused room tucked away on the third floor of the math building.

"Yes it *is*," she sneered, running her hands through her hair. "How come you know so much about math anyway?"

"Well, it's sort of necessary if I'm going to be a software engineer."

"A what?" she stammered, caught by surprise.

"I want to be a software engineer," he repeated, amused by her reaction.

"What about football? I thought you wanted to play professional."

"I'm not all jock, Miss Parker," he protested, holding up both hands. "I love football, but I don't want to play for a living. Football is just getting me through school for free."

"Okay," she said, a little unsettled by his confession. She'd had him pegged as a jock, he was right about that.

"Look, I'll help you get this. You're going to pass, trust me," Jason insisted, mistaking her preoccupation for worry. "Let's see how you did on those problems I gave you."

"I don't wanna do anymore," she whined, stomping her foot on the floor like a child.

"Get over it," he commanded. "Now come on. Your math final is next week, and you need to be ready."

Frustrated, Chasity flipped open her notebook, and shoved a couple of sheets across the table. He leaned over and tried to decipher the handwriting scrawled across the top sheet. He made a note in the margin, and accidentally brushed her arm.

"Um, do you have to sit so close to me?" she asked. The casual touch had sent tingles up her arm.

"Oh, sorry," he mumbled and shifted his chair. Tutoring Chasity, he thought, had its downside. So difficult, she was the farthest thing from a tease, but she left him hot and bothered after every session.

"Your work is getting better, Chasity," Jason said, tapping his pencil on her scribbles. "How about a break?"

"Finally," she sighed and rested her head on the desk.

"I'm gonna go get something from the machine. You want anything?" he asked as he stood up.

"A soda and a pack of cookies," she said, fishing a couple of bills out of her pocket.

"Chasity, don't insult me," he warned and handed back the folded bills.

She put a hand up submissively as she placed the money back into her pocket with the other hand. A few minutes later, he returned, items in hand.

"Here you go," he said.

"I guess thanks are in order?" she asked playfully, reaching for the can of soda he held out.

"That would be the non-evil thing to do, yes," he responded with a quick smile before sitting down next to her and digging into a bag of chips. Chasity flipped open the can and soda gushed out, spraying Jason. Both of them jumped out of their seats

"Oh my god, I'm so sorry," she said, setting the can down on the desk. Droplets of soda dripped down Jason's chin and neck.

"It's okay, it's just soda," he said with a laugh, but she grabbed a tissue out of her coat pocket anyway and started dabbing his face dry.

"Don't worry about it," he said quietly, gently taking hold of her wrist. He stared at her intently, then leaned forward.

Bewildered, Chasity took a step backwards. She didn't know how to handle his intensity, let alone a kiss.

"I have to go," she said softly and fled, leaving Jason standing there alone. He wiped his face off with his hands and sighed.

"Why can't we just give a speech like a normal speech class?" Josh questioned as he shoved his notebook into his book bag.

"Because Professor Lawrence wants to be difficult," Alex calmly stated, thumbing through index cards. Their public speaking class ended twenty minutes ago. But Alex, along with Josh and Sidra, were still sitting there reeling over the final assignment they had just learned of.

"Mel couldn't get out of here fast enough when class ended," Josh said. "She nearly screamed when Professor Lawrence mentioned the paper."

"Yeah I know. She was definitely being dramatic," Alex responded, gathering her belongings.

"I cannot believe that she is making us write the speech, give the speech in front of everyone, *and* turn in the paper," Josh complained as he rubbed his hand over his head.

Sidra, who seemed to be completely zoned out, stared at them in horror. "Wait…we have to *turn in* a paper?" she asked, shocked.

Alex frowned at her, confused. "Yes Sidra," she replied slowly. "Were you not in class with us twenty minutes ago? She explained it, what the hell were you doing?"

"I have no idea," Sidra panicked. "I completely zoned out on that part. I thought we just had to make notes on index cards."

"No crazy, that's not what she said," Alex jeered. Frustrated, Sidra threw her pencil across the room. "And now you have to go get it," Alex teased, pointing to the floor. Sidra rolled her eyes.

Malajia walked into the room and dumped two big grocery bags on the floor. Emily was pacing back and forth, the room phone pressed against her ear.

"Hey, I could use some help here," Malajia called out.

Emily gestured frantically for her to keep quiet.

Malajia rolled her eyes as she removed her coat and scarf, tossing them on her chair. Emily finally hung up the phone, sighing heavily in relief.

"That was your crazy mother, I take it," Malajia commented dryly when she noticed the dismal look on Emily's face.

"Yeah," she answered, pushing some hair behind her ear. "How did you know?"

Malajia chuckled, "Nobody *else* calls you," she joked. Her laughter came to a sudden stop when Emily plopped down on her bed and folded her arms. "My bad Em, I'm just joking," Malajia stated, sitting down on her chair. "Are you okay?"

"No. She's completely impossible," Emily whispered, wiping her sweaty hands down the sides of her jeans.

"So is *my* mother…well she's nowhere near as bad as yours," Malajia nodded. "What is it this time?"

"You don't want to know."

"Oh, I kinda do," Malajia replied. "I already have an idea that she's been talking about us."

"Well, she said I'm not to associate with you guys, even though I live with you," Emily began. "But she wants to fix that by getting my room switched to a single."

"Yeah, that's not happening," Malajia scoffed. "There are no single rooms available, so, oops! Too bad for her."

"She won't stop until she gets her way," Emily stated. "I don't want to live by myself."

"Well, tell her to back the hell off," Malajia suggested. When Emily simply looked down at the floor, rather than respond, Malajia sighed loudly. *She's never gonna stand up to her mother*, she thought. "All right, I'm done talking about her. Now help me unpack."

Emily walked over and began helping with the unpacking. "Are you sure that you have enough of that stuff?" Emily teased as Malajia took several packs of chilled coffee out of one of the bags.

"Em, these are for all of us, not just me. We're *all* going to need a little pick-me-up this week."

"Coffee will definitely do the trick," Emily said, setting a box of chocolate chip cookies on the window sill. "Except, I don't drink coffee."

"No surprise there," Malajia sneered.

"We should get going. David is waiting for us at the library," Emily reminded. "I think he's been there for a half hour now."

"I'm not thinking about David," Malajia replied tartly, folding the grocery bag and tucking it into a drawer. "I needed to get my stuff first."

Unflappable David, usually so calm and collected, was in a foul mood when they finally turned up at the library.

"Sorry we're so late," Emily whispered. "I had a call from my mother."

David's scowl lightened. "It isn't you guys. It's Mark. We're supposed to be studying for the Sociology final, and he's over there talking to some girl."

"Damn Dave, I've never seen you so mad," Malajia teased, removing a book from her book bag.

"He's playing with my time, and it's pissing me off," David admitted, tossing his pencil on the table.

Malajia glanced over at Mark and the girl that he was talking to over by a shelf. "Tatiana," Malajia commented, the recognition immediate. The long, lanky beauty in tight jeans leaning against the wall was hard to miss. "I don't know why she's even giving that fool the time of day."

Finished with his conversation, Mark sauntered over. He was met with David's piercing stare. "About damn time," he scoffed. "Can we get back to this Sociology please?"

"Chill, you nerd," Mark shot back, snatching his book off the table. "This shit is boring anyway."

"You're the one who needs help, not me," David argued. "I could have been in my room, studying, by myself."

"If I were you David, I'd let his ass fail," Malajia slid in. Emily shook her head as she began reading her text book.

Mark made a face at her. "Nobody asked for your pointless opinion," he mocked.

"Finals, remember?" David angrily put in, tapping his pencil on the desk. His stern tone caused Mark and Malajia to look down at their books.

"Nerd," Mark sneezed, inciting a snicker from Malajia. Annoyed, David gritted his teeth.

Malajia hurried into her dorm building and proceeded towards the steps, when she noticed several stacks of small boxes sitting on the front counter. "What are these?" she asked her resident advisor.

Handing three boxes to Malajia, the short, bubbly upperclassman adjusted the scarf around her neck. "Study breakers," she responded. Malajia raised an eyebrow. "The office gives us these during finals, there's one for you and your two roommates."

"Oh, cool," Malajia smiled, skipping up the steps. Moments later she threw open the door to her room, and lifted the boxes gleefully. "Ladies, we have study breakers," she announced happily to Chasity and Alex.

Alex took her box from Malajia. "I was wondering what those were," she said, setting the box on her nightstand.

"I got one of those from my RA earlier," Chasity stated as she examined the French manicure on her long nails. "I didn't open it though. What's in there?"

"Candy," Malajia began, taking a package of peanut butter cups out of one box. She picked up a small pill pack and chuckled. "And Xtra-N'ergy. They're actually trusting us with these things?"

"Don't take those," Alex advised, pointing at Malajia. "You're hyper enough as it is. One of those caffeine pills is like drinking a cup of coffee."

"I resent that," Malajia sneered, sitting the box on her bed. "I'm not hyper."

Alex rolled her eyes to the ceiling. "Yeah, okay, and the sky isn't blue," she teased. Malajia made a face before taking a bite out of her candy.

"Give me those pills. I have to pull some all-nighters," Chasity said and held her hand out. Before Malajia could give her a pack, Alex snatched it away.

"What the hell?" Chasity's head snapped around.

"What are you doing?" Malajia questioned, shooting Alex a confused look. "You all hype, snatching shit."

"I don't want you girls to start taking caffeine pills," Alex explained, clutching the packet tightly. "They can be dangerous if you take too many."

"No duh," Chasity sneered. "I'm not a moron, or a child."

"Don't care. Don't take them," Alex persisted.

Chasity smirked. "Yeah okay," she scoffed, standing from her seat and grabbing her coat. "I have my own box anyway."

"Don't you dare," Alex warned.

Her eyes widened as Chasity ran out the door, laughing. "You get back here!" Alex shouted, darting out the door after her to the sound of Malajia's laughter.

"Wait for *me*!" Malajia yelled after her friends.

Sidra flopped down on the bed and closed her eyes. She was so tired. She had a long night ahead of her, but Sidra needed a nap first. She could hardly see straight. She opened one eye at the sound of the door creaking, and groaned.

"Hey, Princess," Malajia called out.

"I guess I won't get my nap today," Sidra sneered, sitting up on the bed.

"We're sorry to disturb you, sweetie. I had to chase your childish roommate here to stop her from taking Xtra-N'ergy pills," Alex put in, voice laced with amusement.

Sidra perked up. "Xtra-N'ergy? You have Xtra-N'ergy?" she asked.

"Yeah, they came in this study breaker box," Chasity confirmed, removing the pack from her box.

"Give me those!" Sidra exclaimed as she tried to pry the pack away from Chasity, scratching her in the process.

"Damn it, Sidra, chill the fuck out!" Chasity yelled, rubbing her wrist. "What is wrong with you?"

"I'm sorry. But I need those," Sidra stammered. "I have so much work to do, and only four days to do it. I need the caffeine."

"Sid, you're trippin'," Malajia put in, eyeing her suspiciously. "You already know what caffeine does to you."

"Yes, I know what caffeine does to me Malajia," Sidra scoffed, shooting Malajia a glower.

Malajia shook her head. "Okay, crazy," she jeered.

Sidra sighed as she smoothed her hair back. "I just need *something*. I don't know how I'm going to make it through finals *and* write a paper."

"What paper?" Chasity asked, wondering if she'd missed some announcement or other.

"That bitch Professor Lawrence," Sidra hissed. "Not only do we have to give a speech to the class, we have to hand in a fuckin' paper about it. I think she has it out for me. She's been on my case ever since that stupid World War II speech."

"Whoa Sid, two curse words in one sentence. You *must* be mad," Malajia teased. Sidra rarely used profanity, and to actually hear her say it was always amusing to Malajia.

"Mel! Leave me alone, or get your trick ass out," Sidra seethed, clenching her fist. Malajia chuckled.

"Sidra, you're being paranoid," Alex butted in. "Everyone in that class has to hand in a paper, not just you."

"What is this, 'obvious day'?" Sidra shot back. "I know that. I'm talking about me, not everyone else."

Alex ignored Sidra's snide remark, just chalking it up to stress. "Look, all I'm saying is that you shouldn't take the assignment personal," she stated calmly, holding her hands up. "Just try to calm down and focus. It's not as hard as you're making it out to be."

"Alex, please for the love of god, back off," Chasity said, sending a searing look Alex's way.

Alex frowned. "What is that supposed to mean?"

Chasity tossed her head back and groaned. "If Sidra wants to be pissed off, let her be. It's not going to kill her to vent," she argued. "Just shut up, stuff a damn peanut butter cup in your mouth, and back off like I said."

Annoyed with Chasity's smart comment, Alex placed her hands on her hips and was thinking of a retort, when she noticed that Malajia was handing her a peanut butter cup while trying desperately to hold in her laughter. Furious, Alex snatched the candy from her hand. "Just give it to me."

Sidra shook her head at the display. "Maybe if I eat something, I'll feel better," she stated. "I have leftovers in the refrigerator down the hall. There wasn't room in our mini-fridge. Chaz, can you walk me?" Sidra asked, slipping her fluffy blue slippers on.

"Yeah," Chasity agreed.

Ignoring the talking girls in the community kitchen, Sidra headed straight for the large refrigerator in search of her food.

"Who the hell ate my food?" she screamed, shoving Tupperware and Chinese takeout containers around.

"You sure that it's not in there?" Chasity asked, leaning up against the doorway.

"I'm not blind," Sidra hissed, spinning around to face her. "I know where I put it, and it's not there."

"*I* didn't steal it," Chasity replied defensively.

"Nothing to get all in an uproar about," an upperclassman named Danielle said, halting her conversation with another girl. "It's not that serious."

"Girl, don't tell me what is serious and what is not," Sidra warned. "*You* probably took it."

"I didn't take your stupid food," Danielle spat. "I don't need it."

"So where did it go? Did it walk out of the damn fridge?" Sidra shot back, throwing her hands up in frustration.

"Sidra, come on," Chasity intervened, stifling a laugh. "I'll treat you to dinner. Stop acting crazy."

Sidra glared at Chasity. "You think this is funny?" she questioned, folding her arms.

"No," Chasity lied, shaking her head.

"You think I'm scared of that thing over there?" Sidra demanded, pointing to Danielle who was glaring at her.

"No Sidra, I don't," Chasity replied. "But, you seem like you're about to snap. And if you fight that one over there, and that friend next to her tries to jump in, *I* will have to jump in, and I just washed and straightened my hair, so I really don't want to sweat it out by fighting."

Danielle sucked her teeth. "Girl, you're not gonna…"

"Oh I *will*," Chasity interrupted Danielle's protest as she pointed at her.

"Yeah, whatever," Danielle huffed, going back to her conversation.

Sidra's face relaxed into a slight smile. She understood Chasity's pain with her hair, for her hair was almost as long as Chasity's. Washing and styling it was a major chore.

"Fine, let's go to dinner." As they walked out of the kitchen, Sidra declared, "you're lucky you told me that you just washed your hair...because I was about to pull everything out that damn fridge."

"Yeah, I figured," Chasity laughed.

Mark pushed his room door open, tossing his book bag on the floor.

"Ugh, I'm starving," he complained to himself as he headed over to his mini fridge.

The flashing light on his answering machine caught his eye. He pushed the button and listened to the message as he popped open a can of soda.

Hearing his father's voice on the machine immediately prompted him to return the phone call.

"Hey Pop, how's it goin'?" Mark said once his father picked up.

"Things are good son. Did you try out for the basketball team yet?"

"Naw. I'm gonna do it next year." Mark sat on his bed as he sipped his drink.

"Good, good." Mark heard his mother in the background.

"Is that Mark on the phone?" she shouted from upstairs.

"Yes, honey!" Mr. Johnson shouted back. "Look Mark, your mother is pissed at you," he informed.

"What? Why? What did I do?" Mark asked, shocked.

"Your midterm grades came to the house a few weeks ago."

"What! They weren't supposed to go there," Mark seethed.

"I'm just warning you," Mr. Johnson responded, right before he handed the phone to his wife.

"Mark," Mrs. Johnson ground out.

"H-hi Mom. How's it goin'?" he stammered.

"Boy don't 'hi Mom' me! What the hell are you doing up at that school?" she snapped.

"Mom…"

"What's with all those C's and D's on your grade card?"

Damn, busted, he thought. "Well, see, what had happened was…um…See, those grades that you had seen was our progress grades. They aren't our actual grades," he sputtered.

"Boy, I don't care! You know better than this. All that money that we are paying to send you to that college, and you're up there screwing around?" Mark sighed before putting his head in his hand. *God, will she ever shut up?* He wondered.

"Mom…Mom, I'll do better," he slid in, interrupting her ranting.

"You just had better…And to think that I was going to let your father talk me into letting him buy you a car."

Mark sat up straight. "Dad's gonna get me a car?" he asked. "When?"

"You're not getting any damn car if you don't straighten up. Get it together boy."

Hearing the dial tone, Mark slammed the phone back into its cradle "Damn it," he huffed.

David and Josh walked into their dorm lounge later that evening and did a double take. Mark was actually sitting at a desk, pouring over a book.

"Mark, are you feeling okay?" David asked with a laugh.

"Huh?" Mark answered as he looked up from his book.

"You're actually studying?" Josh asked.

"What the hell do you think I'm doing?" Mark snarled. "Looking at this dumb ass book for my health?"

"Pissed much?" Josh mocked.

Mark made a face at him.

"I can honestly say that this is the first time since we've been on campus that I have seen your head buried in a book," Josh stated.

"Why the sudden urge to hit the books?" David asked.

"I want my damn car, man," Mark confessed.

"*What* car?" David asked, confused.

"Mom and Dad said that if I don't pull my grades up, then I won't get a car," Mark responded, drawing in his book with a highlighter.

"Since when is Mother Johnson gonna let you have a car?" Josh asked.

Frustrated, Mark tossed his highlighter on the floor. "You're asking me too many goddamn questions," he snapped. "Now, get the hell out of here! I need to study!"

Josh and David just looked at each other and shrugged as Mark put his textbook up to his face.

Chapter 28

"Snow? Well isn't this just great?" Malajia drawled sarcastically. Walking out of her dorm only to be greeted by a snow covered campus was not Malajia's idea of a good start to the day. "I never liked this crap."

"It's so pretty though," Emily smiled, brushing snow off of the railing with her glove-covered hand.

"Yeah, it's pretty, until some of it hits you in the face," Malajia jeered, adjusting her purse on her shoulder.

"What do you mean?" Emily asked.

"She's referring to snowball fights," Alex butt in, carefully stepping down the steps. "Mix fresh snow and wired students, and it's bound to happen."

"Oh. My mom never let me play," Emily shrugged. "She was always afraid that I was going to get hurt."

"Hmm, no shock there," Malajia mocked.

Before Malajia got a chance to make it to the bottom of the dorm steps, she was greeted by a snowball to the neck. "The hell?" she exclaimed as she recognized the two figures running, and then she heard their signature laugh. "Jason, Mark! Ya'll play too damn much," she screamed.

Emily giggled as she tried to help Malajia brush the snow off of her coat.

"They got you good girl," Alex laughed.

Angry, Malajia flung some of the snow from her coat onto Alex, causing her to shriek.

"Shit, shit, shit," Chasity frantically repeated as she ran along the path towards her dorm. Just as she reached the steps, a snowball flew past her head and slammed into the wall.

"You missed, bitch!" she yelled, before ducking inside and shutting the door. She let out a scream as another snowball hit the closed door, startling her. Annoyed, she snatched her scarf from around her neck and headed up to her room.

Sidra turned around as the door opened. "Hey Chaz, how is it outside?" she asked as she shrugged into her dark blue, double-breasted pea coat and wrapped a scarf around her neck.

"It's freakin' snowing," Chasity complained, taking off her boots.

Sidra groaned. "Seriously? I hate the stuff."

"Yeah, well, watch your back when you go outside. Those freaks from Wilson Hall are attacking every girl who lives in this dorm with snowballs," Chasity warned, removing her coat.

"Ugh, that is so middle school," Sidra scoffed. "Finals are in two days. I don't have time for childish games."

"Don't say I didn't warn you," Chasity said.

Sidra thought for a second, before opening the window, and removing some snow from the ledge. "Might as well travel with protection," she said as she formed the snow into a ball.

Chasity shook her head in amusement as Sidra walked out the door.

"I can't wait until these finals are over," Josh declared, adjusting the knit hat on his head.

"*You* can't wait?" David quibbled. "Man, I'm tired of studying. I've never done so much of it in my life. And that says a lot coming from a straight A student such as myself." Just having finished a rigorous study session in their dorm lounge, David and Josh took a much needed excursion to the cafeteria.

Josh shot him a sideway glance. "Just gonna throw that in my face, huh?" he questioned, voice full of disdain.

"Sorry man," David chortled, then stopped suddenly as Jason and Mark, who were hiding behind a tree, jumped out and started pelting him and Josh with snowballs.

"Seriously guys?" Josh shouted, grabbing a handful of snow and tossing it back.

"Hey, watch the glasses guys!" David yelled as a snowball flew past his face.

"Shut up," Mark jeered, throwing one last snowball. "You always complaining about those damn glasses."

Jason laughed as he brushed snow off of his coat with his gloved-covered hands. "Catch you later fellas," he said, walking off.

"Later Jase." Mark was adjusting his baseball cap on his head when he noticed that David was scowling at him. "What?" he exclaimed.

"Instead of throwing snowballs at unsuspecting people, why aren't you studying?" David scolded, brushing snow off of his coat.

"Get off my back," Mark shot back. "It's Saturday."

"Yeah, but finals are *Monday*," David reminded.

Mark sucked his teeth. *David is always so damn serious*, he thought. He was about to fire off a snide remark, but was immediately distracted by a very attractive young lady walking with some of her friends. A smile came across his face as he ambled towards her.

"There goes the wanna-be Casanova," Josh joked, watching his friend coax the girl away from her group so he could talk to her. "How many girls is he kickin' it with on campus now? Two?"

"More like three," David corrected. "One of those girls is gonna cuss him out one of these days."

"Why does this freakin' walk to Chaz and Sid's dorm feel so long today?" Malajia complained, trudging through the snow.

"Maybe because you decided to wear those high-heeled boots," Alex mocked. Malajia grabbed onto Alex's coat for balance just as she was about to fall. "See? I don't understand why you didn't change them when you saw that it snowed. You know this ground is slick."

"I'm sure you would love it if I wore boots as ugly as yours," Malajia sneered, pointing to Alex's brown snow boots. Alex, annoyed by Malajia's snide comment, jerked the arm that Malajia was holding on to, causing her to slip and fall on her butt.

"Damn it, Alex!" Malajia shrieked as she struggled to get up. "That was uncalled for."

"So was your smart ass comment about my boots," Alex shot back. "I already told you to stop talking about my wardrobe."

Emily stifled a giggle as she grabbed Malajia's hand and pulled her up from the ground. As Malajia angrily brushed the lingering snow and salt off of her coat and behind, a figure running up the path towards Torrence hall caught her eye.

"Wait a minute, is that Sidra?" Malajia laughed, watching her friend shield her face from flying snowballs with her expensive satchel.

"Shouldn't we do something? I mean, she's outnumbered," Emily asked as she adjusted her fuzzy pink earmuffs.

"Yeah, we should," Malajia agreed. A sinister smile crossed her face "Get her!" she shouted to the snow throwers.

Alex nudged Malajia, "Some friend *you* are," she chastised.

Malajia nudged her back. "Friend or no friend, we live in the rival dorm. Wilson Hall all day, baby," she joked.

Out of breath, Sidra finally made it to the front door. A snowball hit her in the back as she pushed the door open. Furious, she spun around. "You ugly bastards. I should beat the shit out of you," she screamed, before slamming the door.

Walking up the steps, Alex recognized one of the throwers. *Of course Jackie and her dumb friends would be behind this dorm war,* she thought. "Always the trouble maker," she scoffed. "Don't you people have studying to do?" As soon as she turned her back to head inside, a snowball hit her. "Very mature, Jackie."

"Ouch! What the hell?" Malajia yelled. She was greeted by a pillow to the face once she, Alex, and Emily stepped foot in Sidra and Chasity's room.

"I hope that hurt," Sidra hissed, tossing the fluffy pillow on her bed.

"Yeah, bitch, it kinda did," Malajia seethed, rubbing her eyes. "What the hell was that for?"

"I heard you tell those girls to get me, you heathen," Sidra mentioned.

Malajia relaxed her frown and chuckled. "Oh yeah, I didn't think you heard me," she teased, removing her scarf.

"You know, your mouth is big," Sidra jeered, sitting on her bed.

Emily shivered as she rubbed her shoulders. "Do you girls have any hot chocolate or anything? I'm freezing."

"It *is* cold in here," Alex put in, holding her hand over the vent. "Is the heat on?"

"Yes. *You're* cold because you just came in from outside," Chasity said as she put her coat on.

"Where the hell are you going?" Malajia questioned, sitting on the floor near the heating vent.

"Do I have to explain myself every time I go somewhere?" Chasity asked.

"Yes, 'the evil sister', you *do*," Malajia sneered.

Chasity rolled her eyes. "Bye," she threw over her shoulder as she walked out.

"What do y'all have to eat in here?" Malajia asked, looking inside of Chasity's trunk full of snacks.

Sidra hurried over and quickly closed it, nearly catching Malajia's fingers. "Sid what the hell?" she cried out.

"You get nothing, traitor," Sidra shot back, pointing at her.

Dumbfounded, Malajia sat there with her mouth wide open.

A snowball flew past Chasity's head as she walked outside the dorm, startling her. "Don't start that bullshit again!" she shouted.

"Whatever bitch," Jackie laughed. "I'll get you one of these days." Then her eyes brightened. Jason was coming up the path. "Hey, Jason baby," she yelled, striking her best sexy pose.

He gave her a quick wave and continued walking. He stopped a few feet from Chasity. "I've been looking for you..."

"Jason, when is your next game?" Jackie hollered. Jackie didn't want him talking to Chasity at all.

Jason let out a loud sigh as he looked at her. "Do you mind, Jackie? I'm trying to talk to Chasity."

"Oh, please. You can talk to her ignorant ass later," Jackie pouted, waving her hand in Chasity's direction.

Chasity shot Jackie a venomous look. "Listen, whatever your name is," she snapped, "you don't want to start with me."

"Please," Jackie sneered. "I'll stomp your ass, if you keep on talking that shit."

Chasity frowned as she recalled hearing that very same threat before. She focused on Jackie's face, recognizing her as the same girl who she'd had a confrontation with, in the beginning of the semester. *Well, ain't this some coincidental bullshit?* Chasity began to take a step toward Jackie but was halted by Jason, who lightly grabbed her arm.

"You've been avoiding me," Jason said, completely ignoring Jackie's attempts to attract his attention. "What's the problem?"

"Excuse me?" Chasity asked, fixing him with a blank stare.

"If I made you feel uncomfortable when I almost kissed you, then I'm sorry."

"Jason…"

"You can't blame me for wanting to kiss you. But you don't have to avoid me because of it," he interrupted.

Chasity, unnerved by her response to him, resorted to her default reaction. She lashed out. "I don't have time for this. I have to go," she declared, walking away.

"Chasity!" he shouted after her, but she kept her head down and ignored him.

Chapter 29

"Alex, did you finish your speech paper?" Sidra whispered.

She made an effort to keep her voice down. They were in the library, surrounded by anxious students who, like them, were trying to get their last minute study sessions in before the next day's finals.

"I finished two days ago," Alex replied.

"I didn't ask you *when*, Alex," Sidra snapped.

"Aren't we touchy," Alex commented, leaning back in her chair.

Sidra felt bad for snapping. "Sorry girl."

"It's okay," Alex replied. "Have you finished yours?"

"No, but I'm almost there."

"How much more do you have to do?" Alex asked.

"Umm…I have to write it," Sidra murmured and looked away.

"Sidra!" Alex exclaimed. "You had better go do that paper, girl."

"I know that. But I'm drawing a blank, and I have all this other studying to do," Sidra explained and rubbed her temples. "It's gonna be a long night. It's a good thing that I took that Xtra-N'ergy."

"You took those pills? Why didn't you just drink coffee?" Alex scolded.

"I hate that nasty instant stuff that comes out of those machines. Besides, I only took six."

David looked up from his book, astonished.

"You took six pills? Are you crazy?" Alex frowned.

"Yeah, what's wrong with that?" Sidra questioned, not getting what the fuss was all about. "Two pills are equivalent to one cup of coffee right?"

"No, Sidra, *one* pill is equivalent to *one* cup of coffee," David chimed in. "You just swallowed six cups of coffee in one sitting. And you know how you get."

Sidra's eyes widened. "Oh my god," she said and hurried off.

"She's gonna be sick," Alex predicted, picking up her notebook. David, knowing his childhood friend's reaction to caffeine all too well, shook his head before looking back down at his book.

Mark was sitting at the next table. He had his books open, but he couldn't concentrate. "I need that car. I need that car," he kept whispering to himself. Malajia dropped her books on the table and pulled up a chair.

Mark chuckled. "That's a new look," he commented, taking in the red yoga pants, white T-shirt, and red baseball cap. He couldn't remember ever seeing Malajia in sneakers and without any makeup.

Malajia made a face at him. "My sexy clothes are for me to be seen in. I doubt anybody's gonna pay any attention to me in here," she said, taking a big bag of chocolate candy out of her book bag.

"Can I have some?" he asked, rubbing his stomach with one hand and holding out the other.

"Hell no, I don't like you," she snapped with her nose turned up.

"Why you gotta be stingy?" Mark complained.

"Leave me alone and study. I'm not giving your beggin' ass none of my candy," she said, popping one of the circle chocolates in her mouth.

Watching Malajia with disdain slowly chew, he missed Tatiana's approach.

"What the hell were you doing talking to my roommate?" she demanded.

Startled, Mark and Malajia looked up at her. "What are you talking about?" Mark asked.

"You tried to get my roommate Serena's number after you asked for mine? Are you trying to be a playa? Huh boy?"

"Whoa, it's not like you're my girlfriend or anything," Mark protested, putting his hands up. "You need to chill."

Tatiana looked at Malajia and rolled her eyes. "Who is this? Your new ho?"

"Bitch, please. You don't want none of this, all right?" Malajia sneered. "I'm not one to play with."

Mark looked back at the other students, who were all ears. "Aren't you gonna tell them to shush?"

"Please, nobody wants any of that, you whore," Tatiana retorted.

Furious, Malajia jumped up out of her seat. Mark hopped up and grabbed Malajia before she had a chance to lunge at Tatiana.

"That's enough, take your sloppy ass away from my table," Mark snapped, "and don't let me hear you talk to her like that again."

"You're a joke," Tatiana charged and stomped off.

Mark let go of Malajia, and they sat back down in their seats. "Can you believe her? Why do you continue to talk to these busted ass girls?" Malajia asked, dumbfounded.

"Hey, I defended you, didn't I?" he shot back, pointing to himself.

"Whatever!" she hollered.

"Shhhhh!" a student across the room whistled.

"Oh, *now* you wanna shush?" Mark demanded.

Josh looked around the library and finally located Emily's study group. He walked over and crouched down next to her. "Have you seen Sidra?" he asked.

"No, I haven't. Is everything all right?" Emily responded, putting the top back on her highlighter.

"Not sure," he said, a worried look on his face. "She's high off caffeine pills, and she's starting to act like a fool. We were studying, and then she jumped up and started laughing hysterically, before she took off running."

"Excuse me, this is a study group," a girl named Lisa hissed. "So I would appreciate it if you would leave, John."

"It's *Josh*, actually," he frowned.

"Whatever your name is, you're distracting us."

Josh shot Lisa a glare before nodding to Emily, and walking away. "That wasn't very nice," Emily whispered after she'd gathered her nerves.

"He deserved it. He was the one interrupting our studying."

"If you can call arguing for an hour over an answer to one of the questions studying," Emily put in with more bite than usual. She hated arguments. "If you guys don't quit arguing, I'm going to leave. We're not getting anything accomplished."

"Leave then," Lisa challenged angrily. "We're tired of your whining."

Emily's mouth fell open slightly. She hadn't actually expected to be told to leave the group.

"Okay, if that's the way that you want it," she said as she slowly stood.

"Wait," Lisa relented when she saw Emily picking up her pink notebook. The whole group depended on Emily's detailed notes.

"Oh no. Since I'm leaving, my notebook goes with me." Emily felt a rush of satisfaction as she walked away from the table, leaving the rest of the group dumbfounded. For once, she hadn't backed down.

Jason found Sidra wandering around the third floor of the library, looking dazed and confused.

"Sidra, what's wrong?" he asked.

"I'm lost!" she yelled, startling him.

"Um...okay," he hesitated, not sure how to take her sudden hyper reaction.

"I'm on caffeine overdose right now. Just point me to the restroom, please," she sang, dancing around him.

Looking at her as if she had completely lost her mind, he gave her directions and watched as she skipped off.

Shaking his head, he walked down to the second floor, and found Chasity sitting on the floor in between two book aisles studying. He stared at her for a moment. He thought that even in black tights, a white T-shirt, a ponytail, and nothing but lip gloss on her face, that she was still the most beautiful woman that he had ever seen.

"Chasity," he called softly, approaching her.

Talking to Jason was not on Chasity's list of priorities. She already knew that he was going to bring up their nearly kissing again, and she wasn't ready to handle that. Standing up from the floor, she hurried off without saying a word.

"Chaz, hold on a second." Jason was frustrated. *She is so damn difficult,* he thought.

He was about to follow her down the staircase, when he was stopped by one of his football teammates.

"Do you mind?" he seethed.

"Glad I ran into you Jase, do you have those notes from Calculus?" his teammate asked.

Jason sighed in frustration. *Just move already,* he seethed. "I already gave you the notes yesterday."

The tall linebacker let out a little laugh. "Yeah, funny story—I left my notebook in the weight room."

Jason was clearly not amused. "Why the hell were you working out with your notebook?" he questioned after a few moments of staring at the stupid look on his teammates face. He shook his head as the guy just shrugged. "Just come the hell on," he hissed, directing him to a nearby table.

Chasity, glad that she had lost Jason, took a sip of bottled water and gasped as the water went up her nose. She whipped around to see who had bumped her.

Chasity wiped her face with her shirt. "Sidra, are you crazy?" she asked when she realized her roommate was the culprit.

"No!" Sidra shouted.

"What is wrong with you?" Chasity asked slowly, noticing how Sidra's eyes darted one way, then another.

"Nothing," Sidra exclaimed, "I am perfectly fine. At first I thought this whole final thing was gonna be death, but I am sooooo wired. Those little pills are great. I finished my paper and everything. I'm like a freakin' ball of energy. Hey! I heard this song on my phone a few minutes ago and I just loved it. I listened to it, over, and over and over and..."

Chasity just stared blankly at her rambling roommate. She could barely understand what Sidra was saying. After hearing Sidra say "and over" for the seventh time, she shook her head and walked away.

Sidra skipped around in circles after Chasity left. Then she spied an upperclassman she thought she knew. She couldn't remember. Everything was a little fuzzy.

"Latoya? Is that you, girl?" she hollered. Latoya looked around to see if anybody was watching. Playing nurse to a freshman was the last thing she needed right now, but the kid looked to be in bad shape.

"Sidra, you want help? You look sick."

"Sick? Naw, I feel okay," Sidra said breezily as she hopped from one foot to the other. "But I am so outdone by that stupid Professor Lawrence. She is being completely unreasonable. Not only did I have to do that stupid, pointless paper; I still have to give a speech on the paper and study for the rest of my finals. I mean did you finish your studying?"

"Yeah, most of it. Okay, sweetie," Latoya soothed, cutting off Sidra's monologue. "You need to lie down before you crash."

Josh rushed up, bringing Latoya's nurse duties to an abrupt halt. "All right Sidra, come on," Josh said, taking her hand. "I'm taking you back to your room. You need to sleep it off."

"Hey, it's my good friend Mark," Sidra exclaimed.

"Sidra, honey. I'm Josh."

"You are?"

Josh shook his head. "Yes," he responded, moving some of her disheveled hair out of her face.

"Then who's Mark?" Sidra asked loudly and frowned.

"Time to go," Josh urged, steering her away.

"Isn't he adorable?" Sidra trilled.

"Freshmen," Latoya muttered. "They can't take the pressure."

Jason, having suffered through trying to explain calculus to his teammate for half an hour, wandered around aimlessly. He'd seen enough books to last a year. Rubbing the back of his neck, he was about to walk past Malajia and Mark's table, when he stopped and did a double take. He barely recognized Malajia without her trademark clothing and styled hair.

"Malajia, that's an interesting look for you," he commented, amused.

"I look like crap," she admitted as she fixed her baseball cap on her head.

Mark closed his text book. "Whatchu up to, Jase?" he asked.

"Walking around here looking like a dumbass," Jason joked. "I've had it with this damn library."

"I know what you mean," Mark agreed, leaning back in his seat. "I'm tired of this shit too."

Malajia looked at him. "Tired of *what* exactly?" she sneered. "You barley looked at that damn book the whole time."

Mark glared at her for a second. "Jason, she got candy," he quickly announced,

"Ooh," Jason exclaimed as he quickly snatched the bag off of the table and ran. Laughing loudly, Mark took off after him.

"Why y'all gotta be ignorant?" Malajia hollered, jumping up out of her seat.

"Shhhhh," nearby students whispered. She sucked her teeth and flopped down in her chair. She looked and saw Chasity approaching her table.

"Hey girl," Malajia smiled.

Chasity waved her hand. "Yeah hi, listen…" Malajia snickered at Chasity's callous greeting. "I'm tired of drinking water and the soda machine is busted," Chasity said, leaning down. "I know that you have something to drink in that bag of yours."

"Is that your way of asking me for something to drink?" Malajia asked as she raised her eyebrow.

Chasity rolled her eyes. "Yeah."

"That's what I thought," Malajia replied with a smirk and pulled a bottle out of her bag. "Here evil," she said, handing the bottle to Chasity.

"What's this?" Chasity asked, eying the green contents with suspicion.

"I forgot what it's called, but it's good. One of those expensive fruit drinks." Chasity looked at her skeptically. "Girl, just take it," Malajia insisted.

An hour later, sitting alone at a corner table, waves of nausea hit Chasity. She thought she was going to vomit, she rubbed her cloudy eyes and looked down at her hands. They were now shaking.

"Shit. No, not now," she groaned.

She stumbled over to Malajia's table, slamming her hands down, startling Malajia. "You look crazy," Malajia teased.

"What the fuck was in that drink you gave me?" Chasity asked slowly.

Malajia was shocked at her tone. "It was just juice," she declared. "A mixture of different kinds, I guess."

"You *guess?*" Chasity snapped.

"Why are you shaking like a damn leaf?" Malajia questioned as Chasity sat down in the chair across from her. "You having an allergic reaction or something?"

Chasity put her head down on the table. "No, I'm shaking because I'm so fuckin' excited," she sneered.

"Stop it with the smart ass remarks," Malajia scolded. "I'm actually concerned about your ignorant ass,"

"I'm allergic to kiwis," Chasity informed, voice muffled by her arm being placed over her face.

"Ooooh. Yeah, I think I remember seeing kiwi's in the ingredients," Malajia realized.

"That's just great," Chasity spat out.

"Do you want some water?"

"I'm not taking anything else from you."

"Well, do you need to go to the health center?" Malajia asked, touching Chasity's shoulder. "They might have something to stop that reaction."

"Don't touch me," Chasity hissed. "I'll take something later."

Malajia watched as Chasity closed her eyes. "Don't die," she teased. Chasity, without lifting her head, gave her the finger.

The alarm on David's watch went off. When it beeped a second time, he rolled over and switched it off.

"Get up, you guys," he growled. They'd all been so sleepy, they couldn't face going back to their dorms, and had camped out on the library floor.

"Just five more minutes," Mark mumbled.

"Get up!" David hollered and gave him a poke.

"What time is it?" Alex asked as she stretched.

"Two in the morning. We have to get back to the dorms," David urged.

"I have no love for the library anymore," Alex complained. "If I never see this place again, it will be too soon."

Malajia stirred, then murmured something incomprehensible about quadratic equations.

"Malajia, go back to sleep," Mark ordered with a smirk.

"No, we have to get up," Alex insisted as she shook Chasity.

"Aww, we never finished studying Psychology," Emily realized, bolting up. "We fell asleep."

"Look, since we all have the same class, why don't we go get Josh and Sidra, and finish studying together," Malajia suggested as she rubbed her eyes.

"No. I'm through studying," Chasity put in, rubbing the bridge of her nose. "My damn head hurts."

"If I get a D in that class, I'll be cool," Mark insisted. "I don't care."

"If you go home with anything less than a B, it'll be bye, bye car," David slid in.

Mark thought on that for a second. "All right, let's go get the other two. Daddy needs that car." He started pushing his friends towards the exit as they complained. "Quit your whining. Let's go," he urged.

Mark had dragged Josh out of bed on the way to the girls' dorm. When Malajia came downstairs with Sidra, everyone turned and stared. Her hair was a mess and she looked drained.

"Damn Sid, you look like shit," Mark joked, then quickly gestured an apology when Sidra regarded him with tired, bloodshot eyes.

"Let's finish this so we can grab a couple hours of sleep," Alex suggested.

"We can do this, people," Mark insisted, clapping his hands together enthusiastically.

Five minutes later, they were all asleep.

Malajia looked at her watch and let out a scream.

"Girl, what's your problem?" Alex asked in a groggy voice.

"We have to get ready. Finals start in an hour. I'm not taking them looking like this," Malajia exclaimed, quickly gathering her things. "Alex, Emily, let's go," she hollered, running out the door.

"I can't wait until this damn week is over," Alex groaned, letting out a frustrated sigh as she struggled to her feet.

Jason looked at Chasity, who was laid out on the steps. "You feeling any better?"

"No, I think I'm gonna throw up," she tiredly complained.

"Okay, I'll help you upstairs and get you into the shower," he joked. She popped her head right up.

"Nope, I'm good," she groaned. Jason chuckled as he watched her jump to her feet. "Get out Jason," she demanded, pointing to the exit.

"I swear I am never taking another caffeine pill again," Sidra said as she grabbed her head and followed Chasity upstairs.

Jason and Chasity were waiting for the professor to pass out the exams. Chasity was sitting there trying to keep herself from nodding off. She looked over at Jason who had his head down on his desk.

"Jason," she whispered. He was so tired that he did not budge. "Jason," she repeated, shaking him lightly. When he still didn't answer, she slapped him on the arm, and he popped up.

"I'm up," he declared, rubbing his eyes.

"Let's get this shit over with," Chasity said as she picked up her pencil and Jason sat up straight.

Sidra rushed into the public-speaking lecture hall. She was five minutes late. Everyone had to turn their papers in at the beginning of class. Professor Lawrence was to make sure that they could deliver a polished presentation without notes.

"I'm sorry I'm late," she apologized and handed Professor Lawrence her finished paper. "It's good, I promise."

"Miss Howard, you are too late. I am not supposed to accept this paper."

Sidra stared at her and her mouth began to quiver. "Come on, please don't do this to me," she begged.

"Aww shit. If Professor Lawrence don't take that paper, Sid will flip the hell out," Malajia laughed to Alex and Josh. Once again, the lecture hall's excellent acoustics picked up on Malajia's comment.

"Miss Simmons, do you want to be the first to go?" Professor Lawrence asked, frowning.

Malajia stopped laughing and sat up straight. "No that's okay," she stammered. "You look so pretty today."

Alex shook her head as Josh put his notebook over his face to hide his laugh. Malajia's silly antics never ceased to amaze them.

Professor Lawrence turned her attention back to Sidra, who looked as if she was going to bust out crying any second. "I don't like lateness Miss Howard. You should know that by now," she chastised.

"I know. I'm sorry," Sidra mumbled, looking down at her shoes.

"But in your case, because you are a freshman, I will bend the rules," Professor Lawrence relented, much to Sidra's delight, it showed in the girl's big smile. "Now, take your seat. You're holding up the final."

Sidra gratefully placed her paper on the desk and hurried to her seat.

Mark stumbled out of his math final looking deranged. "Numbers, I—I see numbers, in all different shapes and colors. They're everywhere. I can't escape them. I can't escape them, do you hear me?"

"Mark, why are you looking crazy?" Jason asked, slouched in a chair and feeling drained. He stood up when Mark grabbed Chasity's arm.

"Boy, get off me," she warned, trying to jerk away from him, but he tightened his grip.

"Numbers, make them go away please," Mark rambled, staring in her face.

"I thought I told you never to touch me!" she snapped as she pried his hand off and twisted his arm behind his back.

"Ow, ow, ow," he howled. "That hurts."

"Serves your dumb self right," Jason commented as Chasity removed her hand from Mark's arm. She gave Mark a quick shove when he made a face at her.

As Mark rubbed his sore arm, Alex walked out of her nearby class, feeling relieved. As she approached them, Mark grabbed her arm. "I still see numbers, I tell you, and symbols," he persisted. "Pi, what the hell is pi? And why can't I eat it?"

"Boy," she barked snatching away from him. "Calm your stupid self down."

Completely spent, Mark put his head in his hands and began making whimpering sounds.

"You can stop with the bullshit," Jason advised. "The final is over."

"That's true," Mark said, standing straight up. "Four to go."

After the last exam, the group congregated in Chasity and Sidra's room. Sidra needed to get her wallet, and then they were going out to celebrate.

Sidra slipped her wallet into a bag, took a quick look around, and collapsed on the bed.

"No, Sidra get up," Emily whined.

"You guys go ahead. I'll just stay here on my bed. On my pretty, pretty bed," she murmured and patted the covers.

Jason assumed they would have a bit of a delay, and stretched out on Chasity's bed.

"Get off," she barked, but Jason just buried his head under her pillow. Chasity poked him, but he didn't twitch. He was out cold.

"Give me my damn pillow," she said, giving it a hard yank. With a frustrated sigh, Chasity shrugged out of her coat and curled up at the foot of the bed.

"Since y'all are going to sleep, I might as well get comfortable," Mark concluded. He took off his coat and nudged Sidra. "Move it over, Princess."

Malajia looked over at David, who had sprawled out on the floor. "How come I have to sleep on the floor? I'm a girl," she complained, pointing to herself.

"Malajia, you can go to your own room," Sidra tiredly replied.

"I'm not going a damn step," Malajia retorted. Folding her coat, she tossed it on the floor to use as a pillow.

Josh squeezed between Alex and Emily on the loveseat, but couldn't get comfortable. "Man, forget this," he grumbled and slid off the chair onto the floor.

"Are we still going out?" Emily whispered.

No one answered.

"Okay, just checking."

Chapter 30

"I could sleep for a week straight," Malajia complained as she shoved one of her suitcases aside. "I don't even have the energy to unpack." She shifted a pile of shirts, and sank down on the bed.

"I don't even know why you brought all that crap home," Geri sneered. "Your winter break is only four weeks." She then began to rifle through one of Malajia's bags.

Malajia yawned and then sat up abruptly. "What the hell do you think you're doing?" she barked. "Get your big man hands out of my bags."

"Shut up. I'm looking for your white blouse. I need to borrow it."

"No," Malajia whined, stomping her foot on the floor. "You got plenty of shirts of your own."

Geri pulled the shirt from the bag. "Malajia, I don't give a damn what you say. I'm borrowing it. You're always borrowing my jewelry," Geri charged, pointing at her. Malajia went to open her mouth when Geri interrupted her. "Oh what? You gonna deny it now?"

"Just hurry the hell up and take it," Malajia relented, waving her hand at her grinning sister. "But you better not spill anything on it."

"Calm down. I take better care of your stuff than *you* do," Geri laughed, skipping out the door

"Shut up," Malajia retorted. *A little nap,* she thought, *just a little one and then I'll finish unpacking.* Malajia curled up on her bed and closed her eyes. Her brief moment of quiet was interrupted by the sound of her mother's voice carrying from the other room.

"Malajia! Come watch your sisters while I run to the store."

Sucking her teeth, Malajia darted out of bed. "I hate this house," she huffed, scurrying out of the room.

"Hold on, Alex," Emily whispered and padded across the room to shut the door. "Okay, all clear."

"Girl, I'm so glad to be off that campus," Alex confided, hanging a sweater in her closet.

"Not me. I actually miss school," Emily said wistfully as she played with the hair on her doll's head.

"Already? Are you crazy?" Alex chortled.

"No," Emily laughed, "it's just that now that I'm home, my mom won't leave me alone. She keeps...Well, you know how she is."

"Yeah, I know. Hang in there, girl. Pretty soon she's bound to realize you're not a child anymore. I mean you *are* going to be eighteen in a few months."

"I hope so," Emily said with a sigh.

"You'll be okay. Winter break is only a few weeks."

Emily paused, hearing footsteps outside her door. "I gotta go. My mom's coming."

"All right, girl."

"Bye," Emily whispered and hung up the phone just as her mother came into the room without knocking.

"Hey sweetheart," she said. "I made lunch, would you like some?"

"Um, sure."

"Baby girl, I'm so glad to have you back home," she said, throwing her arms around her daughter. Emily gave a faint smile, and hugged her back.

Sidra scrutinized the items on her dresser, her eyes narrowing. Someone had been going through her things. She knew exactly how she'd left everything in her room. She liked everything arranged just so. Even her forty-two-inch flat-screen television had been moved. She swiveled and flung open the bedroom door.

"Marcus!" she shouted.

"What?" he yelled from downstairs.

"Have you been in my room?"

"No," he shot back.

"Yes, you were," she screamed. "You're the only one who comes in here to watch my TV, because yours is broken."

"So!" he hollered.

"Hey, you two, stop shouting in the house," Mr. Howard hollered from the den.

"Sorry, Dad," Sidra and Marcus simultaneously shouted back. Shaking her head, she grabbed her cell phone off of her nightstand; she sat down on the bed and punched a number on speed-dial.

Chasity tossed aside the magazine she was reading and answered the phone.

"What's up, Sidra," she said. Chasity figured it was only a matter of time before her roommate called.

"Hey roomie," Sidra replied.

"How's it going?"

"Good, getting used to being back home for more than two days," Sidra replied with a laugh.

"Well, what are you gonna do for four weeks?" Chasity asked, picking her magazine back up.

"Girl, I don't know. Relax and spend some time de-boying my room. It reeks of my brothers in here," Sidra replied, straightening a picture frame on her nightstand.

Chasity shook her head and was about to respond to Sidra, when she heard her aunt call her. "Damn it," she groaned.

"What's the matter?" Sidra asked.

"My aunt's calling me. She keeps bugging me to go to the mall with her."

"Christmas shopping?"

"Yeah, I hate shopping around Christmas," Chasity complained. "The mall is always crowded, and you know how much I hate people."

Sidra giggled. "Sweetie, she's trying to make things right with you. Just go," she advised. Chasity had broken down before finals, and told Sidra the whole sorry story of her Thanksgiving.

"Not trying to hear it, Sidra."

Trisha barged in Chasity's room. "Did you hear me calling you?"

Chasity let out a loud sigh. "No," she lied.

Shaking her head, Trisha walked over, and took the phone from Chasity. "Hello?"

"Hi Ms. Trisha," Sidra laughed. "It's Sidra."

"Hi sweetie. Sorry, but I'm cutting you off," Trisha said with a laugh. "We have some shopping to do."

"Good, I'm glad that you're making her go," Sidra remarked, well aware of Trisha's nonstop efforts to regain Chasity's trust. They seemed to be working, Sidra thought. "Make her smile too. Lord knows that she never does that."

"Smile Chaz," Trisha ordered, turning to her niece.

"No," Chasity sneered, frowning.

"She's mad," Trisha said with a laugh.

"She always is. Talk to you later."

"Mark, where are the lights?" Mrs. Johnson asked.

"In that box over there," he replied and pointed to the box on the floor next to the basement door. She walked over and lifted the top.

"Boy, these lights are still tangled," she observed.

"I know that, Mom," he responded, not hiding his exasperation. It was his turn to put up the Christmas decorations outside, and time was running out. As usual, he'd waited to the last minute.

"Mark, you had better get it together," Mrs. Johnson advised.

"Don't worry Mom," he reassured her. "I have everything under control. David, Josh and Sidra are coming over to help."

"Just get it done," Mrs. Johnson ordered, walking into the kitchen.

A few minutes later, the doorbell rang, sending Mark darting to the door. "It's about time," he hissed.

"Oh, hush your face, and let us in," Sidra scolded, stamping her feet on the welcome mat. "My feet are frozen. Do you know how cold it is out here?"

"It's icy out too," Josh said as he stepped into the hall. "Okay, so where're the lights?"

"In that box," Mark ground out, pointing again.

Removing his coat, David headed for the box and inspected the contents. "They're still tangled," David said with a frown.

"I know that," Mark snapped. "Why are you telling me obvious shit?"

"Man, this is a damn mess. It's going to take forever to get them untangled," Sidra complained.

"Why do you think I called y'all?" he retorted. "You can't expect me to do this all by myself."

"Mark, this should've been done weeks ago," Josh scolded.

"If you remember, dumbass," Mark shot back, "weeks ago we were getting ready for finals."

"*Some* of us were getting ready," David corrected, bending down and picking up the box.

"I heard that, nerd," Mark scoffed.

"Mark, you were home for Thanksgiving. Why didn't you do this then?" Josh barked, tossing his knit hat on the couch. "I hate coming over here during the holidays, because you always got us doing extra shit."

Mark frowned at him for several seconds. "Yo, why you gettin' an attitude?" he mocked. Josh gritted his teeth. He hated when Mark turned his frustration around to make it seem like he was the one being unreasonable. "You mad as shit over *Christmas lights* dawg."

David stifled a laugh as he noticed the seething look on Josh's face. "Okay guys, chill out," he put in. "Let's just get started."

"You owe me some cookies or something," Sidra bargained and shot Mark an arch look.

"All right, all right," he shouted.

"You keep that up, and you'll be doing this alone," she warned, pointing a finger at him.

"How can you drag me to this store and then not let me buy anything?" Chasity complained. She despised holiday shopping at the mall, and this was their second trip in two days.

"Girl, we didn't come here for you. I have your presents already," Trisha retorted, running her fingers down the front of a trendy top.

"I didn't ask you to buy anything for me," Chasity mumbled, folding her arms.

"Hey, chill with the attitude, smart ass," Trisha reprimanded, removing the shirt from the shelf.

Chasity rolled her eyes and let out a frustrated sigh. "Can I please go?" she whined.

"No," Trisha replied calmly, then held the shirt out for Chasity to see. "Do you like this? Would it look good on Melina?"

"Nothing looks good on that bitch," Chasity snapped.

Trisha stared at her angrily. "I'm two seconds from shaking you."

"Jason, I'm hungry, can I go buy something to eat?"

Jason eyed his little brother. The kid was always hungry. "Sure man, go ahead," he said with a quick smile, and then frowned as Kyle held out his hand. "What?" he asked.

"Money."

"Kyle, you have money."

"I'm saving that for my new game," Kyle wheedled, smiling.

"Fine, here," he said with a laugh, slapping a ten on Kyle's outstretched palm.

"Cool," he said happily and ran off.

About to walk into the jewelry store, Jason caught sight of a familiar coat on a familiar frame standing by the fountain.

"Chasity?" he called out, excited to see her. He hadn't spoken to her since school let out, and he'd missed her.

She looked around to see who had called her name. Seeing that it was Jason, Chasity walked over. "Hey," she said, surprised to see him.

"How are you?" he asked, giving her a hug.

"Tired, pissed, and cold."

"Forced to go shopping, huh?"

"Yes, I hate it. I have never hated shopping so much. My aunt keeps picking shit up and showing things to me and asking me my opinion, and then she gets mad if my opinion doesn't agree with hers," she responded.

Jason laughed. Chasity had a knack. She could describe any situation to a T.

"What are you doing here?" she asked. "Did you get dragged out here too?"

"Kind of," he said. "My little brother and I are looking for a present for my parents."

"I didn't know that you had a brother."

"Yeah, he's thirteen, his name is Kyle. I thought that I told you that."

"You probably did and I wasn't paying attention," she responded with a shrug.

"Well, at least you're honest," he said.

Kyle ran up carrying a jumbo-sized soda. "Hey Jason, I saw this gift that Mom might want," he declared.

Jason looked at him. "Hey, I thought that you were hungry."

"I was, but once I got into the food court, I realized I was thirsty too."

"Where's my change?" Jason asked.

"What change?" Kyle returned smartly, inciting a frown from Jason.

Chasity watched the easy interchange between the siblings and smiled.

"That's something that I missed," Jason said, returning his attention to her.

"What?" she asked with a frown.

"Your smile...as rare as it is."

"Please," she protested, rolling her eyes.

"Chasity, this is my brother Kyle. Kyle, this is my friend, Chasity," Jason introduced.

"So, do you have a boyfriend?" Kyle asked, going straight for the jugular.

"No," she stammered, stifling a laugh.

"So, what's up with you and my brother then?" he persisted.

"Kyle," Jason exclaimed.

"Huh?" Kyle looked up, eyes wide.

"Do you wanna walk home?"

"I was just asking." Kyle's interrogation stopped abruptly when an older woman trotted up to Chasity. It was a great disappointment. He didn't get many opportunities to roast his older brother.

"Chaz," Trisha asked. "What do you think of this outfit for Melina?"

"I promise I don't give a damn about what you bought for her," Chasity spat out.

"You have way too much attitude, child," Trisha replied and turned to Jason. "Hello again, and who's this young man?"

"My brother, Kyle." Jason said.

"Hey sweetie. You're just as cute as your brother." Embarrassed, Kyle stared at his sneakers.

Trisha was clearly on a roll. Afraid of what her aunt might say next, Chasity prudently interrupted. "Look, we've been here for hours. I'm tired and I'm cold. I want to go home."

"All right, fine, we'll go," Trisha relented. As she adjusted the designer bag on her shoulder she smiled slyly and said, "You know what Chaz? You and Jason would make such a cute couple."

Embarrassed, Chasity's eyes widened. "Are you freakin' kidding me?" she fumed, before storming off.

"Wait, what did I say?" Trisha laughed. With a slight wave to Jason, she hurried after her niece.

"You're right. She's pretty," Kyle said after Chasity and Trisha disappeared into the crowd. "I can't wait to go to college."

"Come on, bro, we still have shopping to do," Jason said as he patted the top of Kyle's curly head.

"How the hell did they get like that?" Josh exclaimed, holding up a string of lights. It had taken the four of them almost two hours to separate the knots and tangles.

"It's my Dad's fault," Mark put in, standing with his hands on his hips. "He just throws everything in the box after the holidays are over."

"I heard that," Mr. Johnson shouted from the basement.

Mark shook his head and looped the strings around his arm. "All right, let's go hang these babies."

"Don't we get a break?" David chimed in.

"No," Mark shouted. "Nobody gets a break until it's done."

"Not so," Mrs. Johnson called from the kitchen. A second later, she appeared, carrying a plate of her freshly-baked chocolate chip cookies.

"Ooh homemade cookies," Sidra exclaimed, clapping her hands. "You're the best, Mrs. Johnson."

"I thought that the three of you could use a break."

"Don't you mean four?" Mark butted in, scratching his head.

"No son, I mean three. You don't get anything until those lights are up." With a huff, she set the plate down on the coffee table.

Josh eyed the cookies on the plate. As much as he wanted to take a break, he'd much rather finish the task first, that way he could relax the rest of the night. "I think we should just finish getting these things up," he suggested.

"Yeah, come on Sid," Mark put in, signaling for Sidra to come with them.

Sidra took a cookie and bit into it. "I am not going out there. It's too cold."

"Fine, be a girl," Mark scoffed.

Sidra shot him a confused glance. "Thank you, I sure will," she slowly put out. She followed the guys to the door and stood with her arms folded as they headed outside.

"Damn, it's cold out here," Josh complained.

"That's already been established," Mark sneered.

"Be careful, guys. Those steps are slippery." Sidra's voice trailed off.

"Shit," Mark shouted. He'd slipped on the thin sheet of ice coating the front steps and careened into Josh and David. They landed in a tangle of limbs on the brick walkway.

"Thanks for the damn warning, Sidra," Mark barked, then jerked his arm from under Josh's leg. "Get off me, Josh!"

"Shut up, I'm trying," Josh shot back. Sidra was laughing so hard that tears were streaming down her cheeks.

"Mommy, Taina keeps putting cookie crumbs in my suitcase," Dana whined.

"Taina, come here," Mrs. Simmons barked. "We're going to be late. You know your grandmother hates for people to be late." Getting the Simmons' clan ready for any trip was a major production, and they were due at her parent's house in New Jersey in two hours.

"It wasn't me, Mommy," the six-year-old pouted. "It was Melissa."

"Taina, stop being stupid. Melissa's in Mom's room," Malajia taunted.

"Geri, get your sisters!" Mrs. Simmons yelled when Taina started crying.

"Mom, I can't. I'm in the bathroom," Geri shouted back.

"Malajia, some help here. Stop sitting there with that sour look on your face and get your sisters," Mrs. Simmons scolded, putting a covered casserole into a canvas carry-all.

"Mom, that's not fair," Malajia complained out of habit.

"Now!" Mrs. Simmons screamed, causing Malajia to jump up.

"Wow, I've never heard that octave before," she mused to herself and took the stairs two at a time to corral her younger sisters.

"I hate Taina," Dana griped as she brushed crumbs out of her suitcase.

"And *I* hate *you*," Malajia retorted. "You're nothing but a troublemaker."

"Mommy, Malajia said she hates me," Dana screamed at the top of her lungs.

Malajia tossed her head back in frustration. "Oh my god, you irk my soul," she groaned.

Geri walked out of the bathroom and grinned at Malajia. "You used to say the same thing to me."

Mr. Simmons hurried out of his bedroom, wearing one shoe and carrying the other. "There are too many women in this house. I'll be waiting in the car."

"I'll keep you company," Maria quickly interjected, happy for an excuse to escape the madhouse.

"Dana, don't say another word, or I'll smack you," Malajia snapped, tossing a purple coat at her little sister. "Put this on."

By the time everybody piled into the Simmons' van, Malajia's sour mood hadn't changed. Dana was having trouble with her seatbelt, and Malajia gave it a good yank.

"Ow," Dana howled. "You pinched me."

"I did not. You're always lying," Malajia shot back.

"Dana, shut up. Malajia, stop provoking her, she's only ten," Mrs. Simmons scolded.

"Well, if you would control your daughter, then I wouldn't have to argue with her," Malajia muttered.

"Malajia Lakeshia, one more word out of you and you're staying home," Mrs. Simmons threatened. "Is that what you want?"

"God yes! Can I?" Malajia begged, brightening at the possibility.

"No," her mother stated flatly.

"Maria, give me back my cell phone, right now," Geri demanded, reaching for it.

"I'm not done yet," Maria snapped, moving her head away from Geri's reach. "You don't say nothing when you use *my* phone."

"Ahhhhhhhh," Taina shrieked.

"Daddy, Melissa's car seat is squishing me," Dana howled.

"You're all loud in my damn ear," Malajia shouted and leaned into Geri.

"Why are you on me? Move," Geri hollered, elbowing Malajia in the ribs.

Mr. Simmons pulled over into the breakdown lane and stopped the car. "That's it!" he thundered, banging his hands on the steering wheel. "Everybody, shut up. Dana, stop yelling, Taina, stop screaming, Malajia, stop whining, Maria, get off the damn phone, Geri, stop shoving Malajia, and Melissa, stop..." He broke off his diatribe. Melissa was sitting in her car seat playing with her toy keys. "Well, never mind about Melissa. Everyone else, just shut up."

"Dad, was all that necessary?" Malajia asked after several seconds of silence, causing snickers from the girls to resonate throughout the van.

"What is wrong with you that you can't push out a boy?" Mr. Simmons asked, glancing at his wife in the passenger seat.

"Don't blame *me*," she returned with a knowing smile. "Don't y'all control that?" He shook his head as he finally put the van in gear and swung back out onto the highway.

"Look, just turn 'em on," Josh pressed. His patience had run out when the ladder fell for the fourth time, and he was bitterly cold.

"Hold on," Mark replied, holding up a hand. "Mom, Dad, come on out. I finally got the lights up." He stammered when he caught Josh and David shooting him ugly looks. "Um, I mean, *we* finally got the lights up."

"This is the last time I'm helping your procrastinating ass," Josh fumed, bundling the coat up to his neck.

Mr. and Mrs. Johnson came scurrying out the front door with Sidra following, and all three carefully negotiated the icy steps.

"Light 'em up, Dad," Mark called. Mr. Johnson grabbed the large plug and plugged it in to the socket.

"Are you kidding me?" Josh shouted. Only five small lights flickered to life.

Mrs. Johnson gasped, and Mr. Johnson let out a hoot of laughter. "All that work for five little lights!"

Josh jerked around and stared at Mark. "Didn't you bother to test the lights to see if they were working?!"

"That would be a no, obviously," David slid in, exasperated. Mark, completely outraged, snatched his knit hat off his head, slammed it on the ground, and started stomping on it while he screamed at the top of his lungs.

"Yeah, *that's* going to get the lights to work," Sidra drawled sarcastically.

"Victoria," Alex cried and threw her arms out wide for a hug. She had not seen her friend since before she left for college. "How's everything, girl?"

"Good, good," Victoria said, "but I can't wait to get to college. Stacey and I are counting on getting into Paradise Valley. Then we can all be together again."

"Well, make sure before you come that you have an understanding with your boyfriend," Alex put in with a laugh. "You know what I went through with Paul."

"Don't even worry about that loser, he wasn't worth your time," Victoria commiserated. "But, I got a bone to pick with you. Why haven't you returned any of my calls the last three weeks? Too busy for your old friends?"

Alex shot Victoria a wary look. She'd learned to censor her conversations. Victoria's attitude peaked any time Alex mentioned her friends from school. "Finals were brutal," she temporized.

Mrs. Chisolm came rushing out of the kitchen, flustered. She was having a bunch of people over for dinner, and had run out of cooking oil, among other things. "Hi, Victoria," she said, "I'm sorry, but I need Alexandra to run to the store for me."

"Ma, you know that I hate that name," Alex protested.

"It was your grandmother's name, learn to love it," her mother scolded, then handed her a list. "Now this is what I need you to pick up."

"Come on Vicki, walk me to the store," Alex said as she grabbed her coat.

Chapter 31

"Hey, why don't you smile? It's New Year's Eve," Trisha chided as she put the finishing touches on her table décor. "You're not excited about the party?"

"Not really in the mood to party," Chasity declared, removing a cookie from a tray. With Christmas now behind them, Trisha decided to throw a New Year's Eve party.

"Well, you need to get in the mood. You're not going to be hiding up in your room all night," Trisha scolded, moving some of her hair from her face. "You have guests to entertain."

"You mean the guests that *you* invited?" Chasity sneered.

Trisha sighed. "So you're mad that I took it upon myself to invite your friends to the party?"

"I'm not mad...I'm *annoyed*," Chasity amended. "You just invited them here without asking me first. I didn't even know about it until Malajia called me screaming in my damn ear about having to buy a new outfit for tonight."

Chasity was used to Trisha making decisions on her behalf, but she never expected her to go so far as to actually go through her cell phone to get her friends phone numbers, and invite them to her party without asking how she felt about it.

"Sweetie, I didn't ask you because I knew what you would say," Trisha began. "You would have told me not to invite them."

"Yeah, exactly," Chasity agreed. "If you knew how I would feel, why would you do it anyway? You completely disregard my feelings when you do shit behind my back like this."

Trisha shook her head. She'd always let Chasity speak freely, and that included the occasional curse word. It didn't mean that she liked to hear it.

"Chaz..." She put her hands together as she searched for the right words to say. "You are a loner and I get the reason why, trust me I do...But you can't stay a loner forever. That is no way to go through life."

"I've been doing just fine being that way," Chasity argued, folding her arms.

"Have you?" Trisha asked. Chasity rolled her eyes. "From what I know about these kids, they are good people and they seem to genuinely care about you...and you need to let them."

Chasity hated being lectured. "I don't need anybody to care about me," she scoffed.

Trisha gave Chasity a long stare. "I don't believe that," she disagreed, tilting her head. "And neither do *you*."

Chasity was caught off guard by Trisha's comment, and it showed on her face in the form of a slight frown. Chasity's silence told Trisha that maybe she had said enough.

"Try to have a good time tonight, okay?" Trisha persisted. She leaned in to kiss her niece on the cheek, but Chasity, not being one to like affection, put her hand on her cheek to block her aunt's kiss. Both annoyed and amused by her niece's defiance, Trisha tapped Chasity on the arm before sauntering off to tend to more party business.

Chasity stood there deep in thought. Sighing, she crushed her uneaten cookie in her hand and tossed the crumbs on a nearby tray.

Music blared through speakers as guests mingled throughout Trisha and Chasity's massive home.

"Ms. Trisha sure knows how to throw a party," Malajia declared, dancing in place as she looked around at the growing crowd.

"Yeah, I know," Chasity bit out. "She's always so over the top."

"She may be over the top, but she seems like she's always fun to be around," Sidra mused, grabbing a glass of champagne off of a tray. "I wish *my* aunts were this much fun."

"I guess," Chasity admitted, looking down at the diamond tennis bracelet that Trisha had given to her for Christmas. Sure, she appreciated the gift, but she still couldn't help but be annoyed with her aunts meddling ways.

"It's a shame that Emily couldn't come," Sidra muttered. "I talked to her today, and she was basically crying to me about how disappointed she was."

"Nobody is surprised that little baby Emily couldn't leave her house," Malajia sneered, adjusting the halter straps on her black cocktail dress. "Her mom is probably sitting on her as we speak."

Alex, grabbing a crab puff off of the hors d'oeuvre tray, shot Chasity a look. "Chaz, I don't mean to be a downer, but I noticed that a lot of your family members from Thanksgiving are here," she declared, changing the subject. She hated for the girls to talk about Emily when she wasn't there.

"Your point?" Chasity questioned, snapping out of her mental trance.

"Your mom isn't going to be here, is she?" Alex asked. "I mean, after everything that happened over Thanksgiving and all."

"No, Brenda won't be here," Chasity replied, pushing some of her curled hair behind her shoulder.

"Wait, what happened over Thanksgiving?" Malajia questioned, realizing she had missed out on some of the juicy details. "Something else happened between you two? Even after the whole coming to school just to put you out of her house incident?"

Sidra looked away, hoping that Chasity wouldn't become angry. After all, it was Sidra who had told the other girls about what was said during her mother's visit behind Chasity's back.

"Yeah, we got into a fight," Chasity answered, surprising Sidra, who'd never thought that Chasity would freely share her business with Malajia.

"A fight?" Malajia exclaimed. "You mean, like, you actually put hands on each other?"

"Yep."

"Who won?" Malajia asked. Alex frowned at her.

Chasity shot Malajia a glance, confirming the other girl's suspicion that Chasity in fact had won the fight.

Malajia smiled. "My girl," she gushed. Ever since hearing about how Brenda had treated Chasity during her impromptu visit on campus, Malajia developed an instant dislike for the woman.

Alex shook her head at Malajia. "Mel, that's nothing to be celebrating," she scolded.

Malajia threw her head back in frustration. "Oh god, Alex! Can you not do this today?" she groaned. "If I want to give Chaz her props for beating that witch's ass, then I'm gonna do that. Don't tell me what to do."

Ignoring Malajia, Alex fixed her eyes on Chasity. "Chaz, I've been meaning to say this to you," she began. "I know that you have bad feelings for Brenda, but she's still your mom."

Chasity narrowed her eyes at her. *Not even ten minutes into the conversation, and she's already offering her unsolicited opinion,* she thought.

"Fighting was completely wrong. I think you two need to sit down, and try to come to some sort of understanding," Alex concluded.

Chasity took a deep breath, clearly getting irritated. "I did not ask for your opinion, Alexandra," she ground out.

Smart ass, Alex thought. Chasity knew how she felt about her full name. "Look, the relationship that you have with your mother is a difficult one, I know. But I just don't want you to look back on this time in your life, and regret the fact that you didn't try to resolve your issues."

Malajia looked at Alex with confusion. "Alex, do you hear yourself?" she questioned. "How can you even fix your mouth to suggest that? After everything that Brenda has done?"

Chasity put her hand up to signal Malajia to stop talking. She didn't need anyone to speak on her behalf. "As usual Alex, you're running your mouth when you have no idea what you're talking about," Chasity hissed.

Alex sighed. "I think I have a pretty good idea based on what I've seen."

"Whatever Alex," Chasity sneered with a wave of her hand. "A reconciliation is never going to happen. We hate each other."

"I'm sure that's not true," Alex protested.

"It is!" Chasity's loud voice radiated off the walls. "I don't give a damn about her. She's not even my real mother. So don't bring that abusive bitch up to me anymore."

"What do you mean she's not your mother?" Alex asked, grimacing.

"I'm adopted," Chasity blurted out.

Malajia's mouth fell open "Wait...adopted?" she exclaimed, unsure if she had heard Chasity correctly.

"That's what I said."

"As in you have a whole different family somewhere?" Malajia persisted. Sidra shook her head at the stupid question.

"Yes, genius," Chasity jeered, rolling her eyes.

Alex was completely astonished. "When did you find this out?" she asked.

"Thanksgiving."

Unbelievable that she would keep something like this from us, Alex thought. "Are you serious? I was with you on Thanksgiving. Why didn't you say anything to me about it?"

"Why? So you could run your mouth about it before I wanted people to know?" Chasity shot back.

"Well, how are you feeling about it?" Alex asked, dismissing the snide question. "Are you okay?"

"I'm dealing with it."

"Damn, sis. I'm sorry to hear that," Malajia sympathized. "I can't even imagine finding out that the family that I grew up with isn't really mine...Well, maybe that wouldn't be so bad, considering that my family never stops working my nerves."

"Malajia, let's not make this about you, okay," Sidra chided, pushing her ponytail over her shoulder.

"Wait a minute. Mel and Sid, how can you just accept the bullshit answer that she gave?" Alex interrupted, not satisfied with Chasity's nonchalant behavior. "Chaz, seriously, how do you *really* feel?"

"I said I'm dealing with it," Chasity repeated slowly, trying to remain calm. "Don't you give me another damn lecture. I'm not in the mood."

Alex threw her hands up in frustration. "What do you mean by you're dealing with it? Your reaction isn't normal, Chaz. This is something major that you found out..."

"Alex," Chasity warned, pinching the bridge of her nose with two fingers.

"You can't just brush your feelings under the rug like that. You really need to talk to someone about this. If not us, then maybe a professional..."

"Alex, will you shut the fuck up?!" Chasity yelled.

"Why are you hollering at me?" Alex exclaimed.

"Didn't I just tell you not to lecture me?" Chasity argued. "I don't want to hear what you have to say. You think you know every damn thing."

"Calm down, Chaz," Sidra softly put in. She felt that she knew Chasity well enough to know when she was at her breaking point.

Frustrated, Chasity turned to leave. "She's fuckin' irritating me." Malajia grabbed her arm, halting her departure.

"No, don't leave," Sidra pleaded. "You don't need to walk away every time you get mad."

"Alex, you need to chill," Malajia slid in. "The girl said she's dealing with it—so let her deal with it."

"So I'm just supposed to stand here and accept her lie, when I know for a fact that she's hurting?"

"Stop talking about me like I'm not standing right the fuck here," Chasity snapped. "You don't know shit for a fact. I don't complain to you. I don't cry to you."

"No, you sure *don't*, and I don't understand why," Alex stated.

Chasity couldn't believe how clueless Alex was. "Really?" she replied, voice dripping with sarcasm.

Alex put her hands on her hips. "You mean to tell me that you were okay with just holding this in?" she asked. She was at the end of her patience with Chasity's stubbornness. "How could you not tell us?"

"I told Sidra," Chasity revealed, relishing the hurt look on Alex's face. Sidra quietly sipped her champagne as she avoided eye contact with Alex.

"Is that so?" Alex seethed.

"Yep," Chasity smirked.

"And you couldn't tell *me*? Even though I was there with you?"

Malajia had planned on just watching the scene play out without butting in any further. But, understanding Chasity's frustration with Alex, because she herself was annoyed with Alex's meddling ways; she felt that she had to speak up. "Alex, nobody tells you anything because all you do is lecture us," she cut in. "You walk around like a big ass nose, just trying to sniff out our problems, so you can tell us what we're doing wrong and how we need to fix them. Don't nobody feel like that all the time."

"I'm just trying to look out for you all," Alex disagreed.

"No, you're being annoying and overbearing," Malajia shot back, folding her arms.

Alex glanced at Sidra, who was still concentrating on her drink while avoiding eye contact. "Well, the devil and her stupid minion expressed their opinions," she ground out.

Alex's insult registered with Malajia after a few seconds. "Did you just call me a minion?" she asked.

Alex rolled her eyes at Malajia and turned her attention back to Sidra. "Sidra, is that how you feel too?"

Sidra looked up, eyes wide. "Huh?"

"You know you heard me," Alex hissed. "Do you feel like them? Do you think I'm nosey and annoying?"

"Um…well…" The last thing that Sidra wanted was to hurt Alex's feelings any further. However, she realized that lying to the girl wasn't going to do her any good either. "Okay, look girl, normally I wouldn't agree with them…but they actually have a point this time."

"Sidra!" Alex exclaimed.

"Maybe not the *way* that they said it," Sidra amended. "But, Alex, you do have a tendency to be very overbearing at times. It's very off-putting."

"Sid, don't sugar coat nothing for her ass. That shit is hella annoying," Malajia spat out with a wave of her manicured hand. "You're trying to mother us Alex, and the last thing we need is another mother. Hell, the ones we have already annoy us."

"Speak for yourself honey, my mama doesn't annoy me at all," Sidra corrected.

Malajia rolled her eyes and let out a loud sigh. "Okay, everybody but Sidra, who has the perfect mom, is already annoyed by our moms."

Alex took a deep breath; she was struggling to keep her tears in. *How dare they gang up on me like this? After all, I only tried to be a good friend to them.*

"I know that I can come on a little too strong sometimes," Alex said, "But I just hate to sit back and watch you all not deal with your issues the right way. As your friend, it's my job to look out for you."

Chasity had had enough. Alex's self-righteous persona was driving her to her wit's end. "Look out for your own damn self, Alex," she snapped.

"I always do."

"Not hardly," Chasity argued. "If you spent half as much time figuring out your own issues as you do sticking your nose in ours, maybe you could figure out why you; miss 'I have it all together all the damn time'; stayed in a dead end relationship for three years with a boy who couldn't even graduate high school."

"Aww shit." Malajia tossed her hands up. *Chasity sure knows how to push the right buttons,* she thought.

Alex's mouth and eyes opened wide. She was in complete shock; Chasity could be so nasty and insensitive with her words. She had never met someone so heartless.

"I cannot believe that you just said that to me, Chasity," Alex seethed, fist clenched.

"Doesn't feel so good when your issues are thrown back in your face, now does it?" Chasity challenged.

"No, that was completely out of line!" Alex yelled, pointing at her. "How can you be so damn insensitive?"

"You mad?" Chasity taunted. "What are you gonna do about it? You gonna lecture me on being a mean girl?"

"Okay, hold it now," Malajia cut in, putting her hands up as she noticed the rage on Alex's face. "Chaz, you wanna go for a walk?" she asked, hoping to stop the impending fight. She for one did not want to see these two girls come to blows. Sure, she enjoyed a good argument, but Malajia was never one for friends fighting each other.

"Yeah, maybe she *should*," Alex fumed, glaring at Chasity.

"My house, bitch," Chasity shot back. "If anybody is walking away, it's gonna be you."

"All right you two," Sidra interjected. "Let's try to bring in the New Year without any bloodshed okay?"

"You're such a bitch Chasity," Alex mumbled, pushing some hair behind her ears.

"A bitch she may be..." Malajia stated, then glanced at Chasity, "and you *are*." Chasity tossed a middle finger up at Malajia. "But she has a point, Alex. You constantly throw our problems in our face when we don't handle them as you feel we should. Nobody likes that, and now you see how it feels."

Alex took a deep breath, trying to calm herself down and gather her thoughts. *Damn, do I really do that?* She asked herself. She looked at the three women standing in front of her, and adjusted the chunky gold bracelet on her wrist before wiping a tear from her cheek. "If that's how I come off to you, then I'm sorry," she stammered. "My intentions are always good, but I guess I need to check my approach. I've been this way since I can remember, but I promise I will try to work on it."

As Alex turned to walk away, Sidra shot her a sympathetic look. "Alex, are you okay?"

"I'm fine." It was the half-truth. "I'm just going to check out that dessert table over there."

Sidra sighed as Alex walked off. "Damn, I hate to see her so upset. I know she means well," she said. "I feel bad."

"Don't," Chasity sneered. "That bitch is lying. She'll have her nose back in our business as soon as we step foot back on that campus."

Sidra successfully concealed a chuckle as Malajia burst out laughing.

"Yes, exactly," Malajia agreed.

"You two are so disrespectful," Sidra mused, shaking her head.

Cheers rang throughout the massive home as the New Year rang in. Sidra held her glass out. "Well ladies, here's to the new year. And a new semester." Chasity and Malajia picked up their glasses of champagne and tapped hers lightly.

"Cheers!"

CPSIA information can be obtained
at www.ICGtesting.com
Printed in the USA
LVHW011626090919
630427LV00012B/958